RYMELLAN 2

SARAH ETTRITCH

SHATTERED LIVES

NORN PUBLISHING
TORONTO, CANADA

Library and Archives Canada Cataloguing in Publication

Ettritch, Sarah, 1963–
Rymellan 2 : shattered lives / Sarah Ettritch.

Short stories.
ISBN 978-0-9813320-5-5

I. Title.

PS8609.T77R96 2011   C813'.6   C2011-900589-1

Editing by Marg Gilks
Cover design by Boulevard Photografica/Patty G. Henderson

First Printing February 2011
Printed in the USA
v1

Published by Norn Publishing
www.NornPublishing.com

For Kim and Helen

ACKNOWLEDGEMENTS

.....

My thanks to the following beta readers for their generous donation of time and their insightful comments: Rephah Berg, Jennifer Brinkman, and Robert Oliver. Thanks also to Marg Gilks, for her consistent and gentle editing, and Patty Henderson, for designing another wonderful cover.

CONTENTS

·····

SHATTERED LIVES

.....

ESLEY STARED AT HER COMM STATION's screen in dismay. She'd managed three paragraphs in two hours. The case wasn't complex; any other day she'd have already finished writing the military's opinion and sent it to the presiding overseer. But today wasn't just any day.

Someone knocked at the door and opened it without waiting for an invitation to enter. Laura strode into the office, shutting the door behind her. "Do you have time to investigate a tip we just received?" she asked as she sank into one of the guest chairs and crossed her legs.

"Yes, I do." Lesley turned away from the comm station. "I don't seem to be getting anywhere with this opinion."

"I'm surprised you agreed to write it. Isn't Mo coming back today?"

"Yes." The *Falcon* had docked with Space Station 72 an hour and five minutes ago, to be exact. Mo would soon be sitting in a conference room at the shuttle base. Would one of the couriers call her name? Lesley swallowed and tried to focus on the conversation.

"If you'd asked me to, I would have told Blair you were busy."

Lesley couldn't blame Laura for doubting her. The first time Mo had returned to Rymel after their separation, Lesley had agreed to write an opinion, wanting to keep herself occupied. What a mistake! She'd almost missed the deadline, and reading the opinion now would probably horrify her.

"You said you'd never try to write an opinion when Mo was on leave again. I remember it clearly. You said Interior supply patrols, yes, Defence supply patrols, yes, investigate tips, yes, opinions, no." Laura ticked off each point on her fingers.

"I have almost a month to write this one, and it's straightforward."

Laura raised an eyebrow. "And you decided to start it today?"

Lesley sighed. "I know, bad idea." By now she should have accepted that her brain stopped functioning when Mo returned and only started working again when she left. At least that had been the case for Mo's past two leaves, and it looked as if her third would have the same effect. Three tours . . . almost two years . . . "I don't know if I want her to get her Papers today or not. Part of me wants to stop living in limbo."

"And the other part?"

Lesley hesitated, but only for a second. "The other part doesn't want it to be over." Two years ago she never would have been that honest with Laura. But somewhere along the way, they'd become friends, despite the almost twenty-year difference between them. Lesley had grown so close to the Finney family that she'd stayed with them the last time Mo was on leave. Mo had bunked at the Military Academy over her first leave and, as far as Lesley knew, would do the same for this one. According to Michael, she couldn't stay on the Middleton estate, not with Lesley so close. Wanting to be fair, Lesley had told Michael that they'd alternate, that she'd stay at the Military Academy the next time. But Laura's invitation had changed her plans. *You can use my son's room—he's at the Indoctrination Academy. And no, I'm not offering so I can keep my eye on you. I know I can trust you.* The sentiment was mutual, hence her honesty. "I do know it's over, but I guess I won't fully accept it until the Chosen Council makes it official."

"You're twenty-seven now. That's the average age for Papers, so you might get them soon, before Mo does."

Ideally she would, and while Mo was on tour. The notification party, the fuss, the "celebration," it would all be over by the time Mo returned. Lesley had decided that she wouldn't live on the Thompson estate, even if she were the Principal. It wouldn't be fair to Mo and their Chosens and would be a disaster in the making.

Laura uncrossed her legs and leaned forward. "I know this doesn't mean much, but you're doing all right, and she's doing all right. Life did go on."

Perhaps, but it had lost its spark. Yes, she could become absorbed in writing an opinion or forget for an hour while she investigated a tip, but the ache was always there. She thought of Mo first thing in the morning, when she closed her eyes at night, and numerous times throughout the day. So many reminders . . . something would catch her eye or ear, and the ache would flare into an unbearable pain. She was trying to keep an open mind about building a life with her Chosen, but that life would be one gigantic lie. Lesley had learned that she could exist without Mo, but couldn't live without her.

But enough with the self-pity; it wouldn't change anything. "Life did go on and I have a tip to investigate," she said to steer the conversation away from Mo, though she knew she wasn't fooling Laura. "What is it, exactly?"

Laura played along. "A counsellor sent us a dispatch. Apparently she's received a fair number of new clients lately, all coming from the same counsellor, who's Joined."

Lesley waited for more, then said, "That's it?"

"Well, we do prefer that everyone err on the side of contacting us," Laura said. "And I doubt anything can top the one I investigated last week."

Lesley chuckled.

"How much time do we spend at the Indoctrination Academy role-playing all sorts of scenarios?" Laura stood. "Months! And people still don't understand what's considered flirting under CT21. I rushed all the way to A3 because someone said, 'I like the colour of your shirt.'"

Lesley chuckled again. The dispatch had made it sound as if two Rymellans had been caught in the act.

"But better that than someone turning a blind eye." Laura blew out some air, then pulled out her comm unit and tapped at its keys. "I've just sent you the dispatch."

Lesley turned back to her comm station and skimmed the missive. Sector B4. She flicked off the monitor and rolled back her chair. "I'm on my way." With luck, investigating the tip would distract her for an hour or two. She'd already arranged to spend the evening with Karen, William, and her new nephew, Richard, and would be busy with supply assignments over the next three weeks. So perhaps she'd already

weathered the toughest day and the rest of Mo's leave would be easier
to bear.

As she reached for her cloak, the ache that dogged her every moment
mocked her.

MO CLAPPED FOR the officer waving an envelope in the air and stared
at the single remaining courier. *Please, please, let him call my name.* He
stepped up to the microphone and peered at the envelope in his hand.
"Lieutenant Steven Hughes." An officer three rows in front of her leaped
to his feet and bounded down the aisle. She clapped again and blinked
back tears.

"Thank you, everyone, and congratulations to all who received their
Papers today," said the lieutenant who'd opened the meeting. "Dismissed."

She remained seated while everyone ripped open envelopes or rose
to leave the room. To whom did she have to beg to receive her Papers?
She'd get down on her knees in front of them, if that was what it took.
She didn't know how she'd bear another six months without Les. Sure,
she could still get her Papers before she left for her next tour, but the
chances of that were slim. Of course, Les could get hers anytime. No,
she couldn't; not if they were Chosens, and they were. So why hadn't
they received their Papers? Les was already twenty-seven, and Mo would
be soon. What was the delay? They could have had a daughter by now,
instead of sitting around waiting for life to resume. Wasn't that the
point, to have children strong in the Way? So where were their flaming
Papers? Where were they?

"Enjoy your leave, Mo," someone shouted from the aisle as he rushed
by.

"Yeah, you too," she said with a wave, though she hadn't the faintest
clue who'd shouted.

Another wonderful flaming leave—three weeks of resisting the urge
to beep Les, of knowing that she was so tantalizingly close, yet out of
reach. Deflated, Mo collected her bag and cloak from the back of the
room and headed to the shuttle base's holding area. Time to rally herself.

The engineer working on the craft parked next to hers gave her a
smile. "Welcome back, Lieutenant Commander. The craft's in tip-top
shape. I ran all the diagnostics myself."

Mo forced a smile and nodded to him. "Thank you, Sub-lieutenant." She hoisted herself into the craft, stowed her bag in a cargo container, and slipped into the pilot's seat.

Half an hour later, she dumped the bag on the floor of her assigned room at the Military Academy's faculty residence. So many memories had stirred as she'd walked from her craft to the residence, but many more would flood her if she were on the estate. Les had thoughtfully stayed elsewhere last time, but where had she stayed? Papa had originally said that Les would stay at the Military Academy, but then Les had stayed with "a friend." What friend? Papa had claimed he didn't know who it was, that Adelaide hadn't been specific. Had he been protecting her?

She sat on the end of the bed with a sigh and picked at her fingernails. Wondering about Les, what she was doing, if she still cared, if she was involved with someone—Mo would only drive herself crazy, thinking that way. They were still together, she reminded herself. Though did Les still believe that, or had she moved on, discovered that life without Mo wasn't so bad after all? Not knowing was the most difficult part, followed closely by the wasted time they'd never get back—birthdays, festivals, family events, just being there for each other. She had no idea how Les had settled into Interior, whether she loved it or hated it. Was she still playing her flute and writing music? Did she look the same?

A couple of months ago, Mo had awakened in the middle of the night in a cold sweat, relieved that it had only been a nightmare. She'd been searching for Les, asking people on the *Falcon*, on the train, everywhere, "Are you Les? Are you Les?" That was her fear—that Les had changed, that she wouldn't recognize her, that they could walk past each other and not realize it.

Her heart pounded. She abandoned the bed for the desk and punched Papa's comm code into the station. "It's me, Papa," she said as soon as he answered.

"Mo! Welcome back. It's so good to hear your voice."

She smiled.

"So?"

Her smile faded. "No."

"No? Oh, I'm sorry. I know how much you wanted them to be ready."

"They'll be ready next time," she said, sounding more optimistic than she felt. "Les hasn't received hers, has she?" They'd promised to tell each other, but did Les still intend to honour that promise?

"No, she hasn't. I would have told you if she had."

"Are you sure?"

"Of course I'm sure," Papa said indignantly. "Not only would the Thompsons tell me, but I do read the weekly announcements, especially the C3 section. You must get those on the *Falcon*."

She didn't read them. She was supposed to, so she'd know who was off limits. The lack of a Chosen ring didn't mean someone was fair game. Chosens were bound to each other the moment they met at their notification meetings, but didn't receive rings until their Joining Ceremonies. But she wasn't interested in dating anyone, and the conversations on the first day of a tour always revolved around who'd received Papers. It wasn't difficult to keep up when someone's status could only change when on leave.

Plus, she dreaded seeing Les's name on the list. She wanted to hear it from Les herself, or, if Les had forgotten about their promise, from someone like Papa. She didn't want to find out about it as a stranger would; she deserved better than that. "I just wanted to double-check," she said to Papa.

"So when am I going to see you?" he asked. "Do you have to stay at the Military Academy? Why don't you come home?"

"Papa, we've been through this. I can't come home, not with Les so close by."

"Even after all this time?"

Her eyes welled. "Even after all this time," she said faintly.

Silence, then, "Okay, so when can I see you? Tell me and I'll clear my schedule."

She brushed away a tear. "Well, I'm having supper with one of my old instructors tonight. And tomorrow I'm spending the day with a friend. I'm free after that."

"Spending the day with a friend, are you?"

She could hear the curiosity in his voice. "Not that type of friend." In fact, friend was pushing it. Argamon, she wished she wasn't so desperate to fill her time! "How about the day after tomorrow?"

"Done! Where should we meet? Oh, Nathan will probably come with me. And Andrew. And Barbara said—"

"I'm here for three weeks, you know," Mo said, brightening.

Papa laughed. "We're all eager to see you."

Her throat tightened. She looked forward to seeing them, too. If not for her family . . .

"Why don't we meet in C4 for lunch and then decide what to do from there?" Papa suggested. "A new eatery opened last week. One of my clients has been raving about it. I'll make a reservation and send you the details."

"Yeah, okay."

"I'm looking forward to seeing you."

"Me too." She paused. "Papa?"

"What?"

No, she'd promised herself she wouldn't ask if he'd seen Les, or about anything related to her. Whatever he said, no matter how mundane, would only remind her that she was no longer a part of Les's life. "Nothing. I'll see you Monday."

"All right. See you then." He terminated the connection.

She sighed and stared at the keyboard. Her fingers twitched. Les was six keystrokes away. Six keystrokes! But not for her. What was Les doing right now? Had Les thought about her today? Did she know how close they were, that the *Falcon* had returned? Or was she too busy running around for Finney?

Mo's hands clenched. How could Les stand working with that woman? Finney better be ready with one big, fat, flaming apology when their Papers arrived. Mo would almost be inclined to move away from C3, so they could get away from her. But why should they let Finney continue to control their lives? Les would probably transfer back to Defence, and someone would eventually replace Finney. They'd be rid of her, and none too soon.

She drew a deep breath and glanced at the time. Still an hour until she met Ross. She'd unpack, keep her hands busy. Those six keystrokes were awfully tempting.

LESLEY ENTERED NOTES into her comm unit as she waited for Janet

Tyson to arrive. Ten minutes ago, the accounting office's receptionist had led her to this meeting room, invited her to sit, and assured her that Tyson would join her shortly. Lesley had grown accustomed to waiting for interviewees. Being summoned for an interview by an Interior officer often had Rymellans running to the bathroom or breathing into a paper bag to calm themselves. She'd learned to take advantage of the time to expand on her notes.

She stopped typing and read over her notes regarding the interviews she'd conducted so far: *Counsellor Abrams became concerned when she noticed that three of her new clients within the past month had switched to her from Counsellor Owen. According to Abrams, it's unusual to receive that many new clients from the same counsellor within that period of time. When Abrams asked the clients why they'd switched, she received typical responses (counsellor wasn't helping, didn't feel comfortable with the counsellor), but decided to report the anomaly regardless. Owen is Joined and all the new clients are female (I checked his file and he's diff-oriented). Abrams doesn't know Owen personally and hasn't heard anything bad about him professionally. She also pointed out that some clients go from counsellor to counsellor until they find one that tells them what they want to hear.*

After interviewing Abrams, I decided that the case warranted further investigation. I interviewed Cynthia Hubert, one of the three clients who switched from Owen to Abrams. Hubert said she transferred because she didn't feel comfortable with Owen. When I pressed her further, she told me that her first few sessions with Owen were fine, but then he started to ask her about her sexual experiences, even though the matter for which she was seeing him (anxiety regarding public speaking) had nothing to do with her sex life. Since Owen quickly backed down on both occasions when Hubert told him she didn't want to answer the questions, and the context was a counselling session, he didn't violate Article CT84. However, since the questions were unrelated to Hubert's problem, I decided to pursue the case further and interview the other two clients.

So here she sat, waiting for Tyson. Although Owen's behaviour disturbed her, it wasn't a Chosen Violation or a violation of the Law. And she'd only heard Hubert's side of the story. Hubert may not have been seeing Owen for a sexual problem, but she may have said something that triggered his questions. Still, when Lesley reported her findings to

Laura, she'd recommend that they refer the case to a military counsellor. He or she could decide whether to report Owen to the organization that licensed and oversaw counsellors.

A woman hovered in the doorway. Lesley rose. "Janet Tyson?" Tyson nodded, her eyes avoiding Lesley's. "Come in and sit down, please."

As Lesley shut the door and returned to her seat, Tyson crossed her legs, then uncrossed them and smoothed her long skirt. She cleared her throat.

"I'm Lieutenant Commander Thompson. I'd like to ask you a few questions about your former counsellor." Tyson's head bobbed. "You were seeing Counsellor Owen, but you recently switched to Counsellor Abrams, correct?"

"Yes."

"Why did you switch?"

Tyson stared at Lesley and clenched her hands in her lap. "Did I do something wrong by switching? Was I supposed to inform someone? I didn't know. Was it a recent amendment?"

"No, you didn't do anything wrong."

"I keep up with all the amendments."

"I'm sure you do. You didn't do anything wrong. I'd like to know why you switched counsellors, that's all."

"Oh." Tyson relaxed slightly. "Well, I don't know. I, um . . . well, it's going to sound silly. I should have handled it better."

"Handled what better?" Lesley asked, keeping her voice even.

Tyson unfolded her hands and started to pick lint off her skirt. "I went to see him because I wasn't feeling that great about myself. My boyfriend had dumped me, I'd auditioned for a part in the festival play but didn't get it, the Animal Commission turned down my request for a dog because of my work hours . . ." She sighed. "Nothing was going my way. I needed to talk to someone. I don't know . . ."

"So you went to see Counsellor Owen," Lesley prompted.

"Yes, and he seemed genuinely interested. He was very kind. He listened to me, helped me see a few things about myself and suggested how to work on them." She met Lesley's eyes. "I really trusted him, felt as if I could tell him anything. But then . . ."

"What happened?"

"I'd become involved with someone new. We had an argument and said things we probably shouldn't have. I was devastated, in tears. I beeped Counsellor Owen to see if he could fit me in and then went to see him." She placed her hand against her chest and shook her head. "I felt as if all the progress I'd made had been wiped out."

"Did Counsellor Owen help?" Lesley didn't want to rush Tyson, but hoped she'd get to the point.

"Well, he could see my self-esteem was crushed." Tyson rolled her eyes. "Again. I felt terrible. He told me he could make me feel better using touch therapy."

"Touch therapy?" Lesley said, masking her shock.

Tyson nodded. "I asked him what it was, and he said that the human touch can have a powerful transformational effect. Touch therapy involves touching certain points on the body, called conductors. Touching them infuses the body with positive energy and raises self-esteem."

Lesley couldn't believe what she was hearing. If Tyson's account was accurate . . . A knot formed in the pit of her stomach. "And did he perform this, uh, touch therapy?"

"No," Tyson said, shaking her head. "He told me to lie down on the couch, but I balked, said I didn't have time and had to leave right away. I rushed out of his office without so much as a good-bye."

"Why didn't you contact us?"

Tyson's brow furrowed. "What do you mean?"

"You weren't alarmed that a Joined Chosen wanted to touch you?"

"Physicians touch me," Tyson replied.

"Physicians are covered under CT48."

"So are counsellors."

"Not for physical contact." And touch therapy definitely wasn't on the list of exemptions listed in the article. CT48 did have a discretionary aspect to it, but Lesley was certain that "touch therapy" wouldn't pass scrutiny. However, she still couldn't accept that Owen may have committed a Chosen Violation. Again, she was only getting one side of the story. Tyson could be exaggerating what had happened, or perhaps she'd misinterpreted; she struck Lesley as being overly sensitive and excitable. "If you weren't alarmed, why did you run out of the office?"

"Because I felt horrible," Tyson said, looking at her as if she were a moron. "The last thing I wanted was someone touching me. And then afterward I felt so stupid about the way I'd reacted. I should have just explained why I ran out, but I was so embarrassed, I couldn't face him. So I decided to see Abrams. A friend recommended her."

"Did Owen contact you after your last session with him?"

"No."

The knot in Lesley's stomach tightened. If Owen's motives had been innocent—if this touch therapy was actually legitimate and she just wasn't aware of it—surely he'd have wanted to know why Tyson had run out and not returned. Any decent counsellor would have followed up.

She'd heard enough. "Thank you," she said, standing to indicate the interview was over. "That's all for now, but we may need to speak to you again." Laura would probably want to bring Tyson in for a chat. Did Tyson realize how close she'd come to an execution site? What a stupid woman! If she hadn't left Owen's office, had agreed to . . . Lesley couldn't bear to think of it. She still clung to the hope that Tyson had spun her an exaggerated yarn.

"So . . . we're done?" Tyson asked.

"Yes, we're done."

Tyson beamed and rose from the chair. "Thank you, er, Lieutenant Commander. Thank you."

Lesley nodded to her. "Good day."

Back in her aviacraft, Lesley sat in the pilot's seat, staring out the window. If Tyson's version of events was accurate, they could be looking at an actual Chosen Violation. She struggled to comprehend it—there hadn't been a Chosen Violation since the Adams Incident thirteen years ago. At least the current situation was nowhere near as bad as that. Her appreciation deepened for how the Interior investigators assigned to the Adams case must have felt. How awful it would have been as they uncovered the horrors the Adamses had committed, discovering yet another violation each time they peeled away a layer of the sordid mess! Both Chosens involved, in addition to two Solitaries—madness. Hearing the name "Adams" always sent a small shock through her. Thinking about them wasn't pleasant, either. Monsters!

She pushed them from her mind and refocused on the investigation. Before she beeped Laura to sound the alarm, she'd better be sure.

Was touch therapy legitimate? A military counsellor would know. She typed Lieutenant Kay Woods' comm code into the craft's comm panel.

"Woods," the counsellor answered. "How are you, Lesley?"

"I'm all right. I have a question for you."

"Sure."

"Have you heard of touch therapy?"

"Touch therapy?"

"Yes. A technique counsellors use. Something to do with touching conductor points on the body to raise self-esteem."

Kay laughed. "Is this a joke?"

"No, it's not."

"Well, I can tell you that nothing we do involves touching the client. Ever. Where did you hear about it?"

"It came up during an investigation."

"Oh." Then, "*Oh*. Argamon."

"Keep this to yourself, okay?"

"I will," Woods assured her.

"Thank you. Thompson out." She terminated the connection, signed into Interior's network, and punched in the code that identified her as a member of the Chosen Tradition investigative group. Now she could access counselling records. Counsellors had to keep detailed client lists that included everyone they'd seen in the past two years. Had other women recently left Owen for another counsellor, or were the three Lesley knew about the only ones?

She entered the appropriate search parameters. The resulting list contained six names; three other women had recently switched from Owen to other counsellors. A quick perusal of their records brought two interesting points to light: all six women were in their twenties and Solitaries. Perhaps Owen had thought that Solitaries would be less likely to resist him. Had any of the women not resisted him? Her skin crawled. She wished Mo was still on tour, safely away from a potential catastrophe.

Mo. She hadn't beeped, but that didn't mean she hadn't received Papers. She could be busy with her family or had forgotten about their promise. Or perhaps she no longer cared . . . Lesley shook herself and again focused on the list.

The remaining four women would have to be interviewed, to see if any had stories similar to Tyson's. It was time to beep Laura—she'd want to involve other members of the group to speed up the investigation. Lesley braced herself as she typed in Laura's code. She was about to give her the worst possible news, though there was still a slim shred of hope that Tyson's story was the work of a depraved imagination.

"Finney."

Lesley drew a deep breath. "Laura, we have a problem."

LESLEY STIFLED A yawn as she pulled a chair out from the conference room table. She nodded to Laura and Woods, both of whom looked as tired as she felt. Why had Admiral Hall invited her to this 07:00 meeting? Laura knew as much about the investigation as she did, probably more. They'd spent half the night searching and wiring Owen's office and then restoring it to how they'd found it, right down to the number of centimetres the door had been ajar. Lesley would have to make it through the day on two hours' sleep, and it could turn out to be quite a day.

An officer she didn't recognize strolled in and dropped a file onto the table. He nodded to everyone as he also sat down. From the meeting's invite list, she deduced that he must be Lieutenant Commander Russell from the liaison office.

Moments later, Admiral Hall entered the room. "Good morning," he said as he shut the door. "Before we start, I want to remind you that everything we say in this meeting is need-to-know. Understood?" Everyone nodded. "Good." He sat at the head of the table. "Based on the interviews Commander Finney's group conducted with Owen's former clients, we know that we probably have a Chosen Violation on our hands."

All but one had told stories similar to Hubert's. One had also said that Owen had raised touch therapy as something they might try in the future. So Tyson had told the truth, and Hubert probably hadn't said anything to prompt Owen's questions about her sex life. A clear pattern of behaviour had emerged, one Laura had taught Lesley to recognize. The search of Owen's office and a careful reading of his recent records hadn't yielded any evidence, which wasn't surprising, or encouraging. If Owen's reasons for asking his former clients about their sex lives had been sound, why hadn't he documented the sexually-related questions or his reasons for asking them in any of his client files? And they hadn't found anything in his office related to touch therapy. No books, no notes, nothing.

"I could justify executing him based on what we have," Hall continued, "but since we're talking about a man's life and destroying a Joining, I'd like to be absolutely sure by witnessing a violation ourselves. Based on what we've discovered, I'm sure we won't have to wait long. It also gives us a bit more time to prepare. I want to avoid the chaos that occurred during the Adams Incident. This time we know what's coming in advance. So let's review the plan for today. Commander Finney?"

Laura leaned forward. "Owen has two appointments with clients who fit the profile. The first is at 11:00 and the second is at 15:30."

Hall pressed a button on the table. The large comm screen on the wall flickered to life. "Channel?"

"Eight."

He switched to eight; Owen's office appeared on the screen. "Good."

"I'll watch from outpost B4-5, two minutes away. My people will be assembled there, ready to move." Lesley would be in that group. They were to bring Owen back here, to headquarters. Again, she wondered why she was at the meeting.

"Unless you need to intervene immediately, wait until the session ends," Hall said. "We don't want to start a panic."

"Understood. I'll also have people out interviewing all of Owen's current clients that fit the profile. We may find a few that brushed off his questions and stuck with him."

"I hope that's all you find," Hall murmured. So far it looked as if Owen was the only one who'd committed a Chosen Violation. Everyone hoped it would stay that way. Hall shifted his gaze away from Laura. "Lieutenant Woods?"

"We're tracking the locations of his Chosen and her parents. As soon as we receive word, we'll break the news to his Chosen's parents. And then we'll go with them to tell his Chosen," she said, grimacing.

Lesley didn't envy Woods. She couldn't imagine how it would feel to find out that one's Chosen had violated the Chosen bond. She certainly wouldn't want to be the bearer of the horrible news.

"Once the home has been vacated, we'll search it," Laura said.

Hall nodded, his eyes still on Woods. "I know it will be an emotional time for the family, but try to keep it quiet. As I said, I don't want a repeat of the Adams Incident. I want to control the flow of information. I want Rymellans to find out about the Chosen Violation from us, not from each other, and only when we're ready to announce it. Which brings me to you, Lieutenant Commander Thompson." She tensed when Hall looked at her. "Someone has to be the military's face during this time. I want that someone to be you. You're experienced at recording announcements, Rymellans know you, and you're involved in the investigation. You'll be able to say that you were present during the planning of the operation and participated in Owen's capture. That will reassure Rymellans. You'll bring credibility to the announcements."

Lesley's heart sank.

"Communications is working on the initial announcement you'll give. When you've returned here, report to the studio and stay there. We'll want to release information in stages."

"Yes, Admiral." *I'm sorry, Mo.*

Hall's attention left her. "Lieutenant Russell?"

Russell straightened. "I've informed the Chosen Council. It will review its data for the lines involved and let us know if we should be concerned about anyone else."

"I doubt it, but knowing that the Chosen Council has checked will reassure Rymellans. At least this time we won't have to deal with children, as we did during the Adams Incident."

"Children?" Laura said, voicing the question in Lesley's mind.

"Yes. The Adamses had children. Two." His brows drew together. "You didn't know?"

"None of the public documents mention children."

"That's not surprising. We didn't change their names, but we did try to protect them. Well, some tried. The debate about them dragged on for weeks, when Rymellans should have been focused on pulling together and reaffirming the Way."

"What debate?" Laura asked.

Hall glanced around the table. "That's true, I doubt any of you would have been aware of what was going on behind the scenes. E8 isn't one of our sectors, and some of you would have been at the Indoctrination

Academy. I'm dating myself," he said ruefully. "I only know about it because I was a commodore at the time and was working out of F8 headquarters." He pursed his lips and drummed his fingers on the table. "I don't see any harm in talking about it now. After the Incident, some Rymellans, including members of the government and military, called for the children's executions. Both parents involved in Chosen Violations? What did that say about the children? What had they learned at home? What had they witnessed? Were they destined to fall? Would there be another Adams Incident in the future if they remained alive?"

"I can understand the concerns," Laura said.

"So can I, but executing children . . . would you have wanted to be the commander at the execution site that day?"

Lesley wished she could see Laura's face, but Laura was sitting next to her. She didn't want to be obvious and turn toward her. "So they were both underage?" Laura asked quietly.

"One was. The other was barely of age. Seventeen, I think. Those wanting the executions petitioned the Law for addition of an article pertaining to children whose parents had both committed Chosen Violations. They also petitioned for a dispensation to Article 62, so the younger one could be executed despite her age."

Lesley's curiosity trumped decorum. "What happened?" Maybe the children were long dead.

"The overseers denied all petitions, saying it would set a dangerous precedent. That didn't sit well with many Rymellans. To be honest, I felt uneasy about it, but I agreed with the overseers. It was an emotional time for Rymellans. Everyone was reacting rather than thinking. If we'd gone ahead and executed the children, would we have regretted it a few weeks or months later, when we'd all calmed down?"

"Not if the children fell, as some predicted," Laura said.

"They haven't. An overseer said to me back then, 'If the children are compromised, they'll eventually find their own way to an execution site. Trust the Way.' He was right."

Lesley shifted in her seat. Maybe he was, but how many Rymellans would they take with them? Four had been executed during the Incident; only two had been Adamses. The knowledge that members of that sick family still walked among them unsettled her. A glance at Woods, seated across from her, told Lesley that she wasn't the only one who felt that way.

"The Chosen Council would have checked all the related bloodlines," Russell said. "And double-checked, I presume. If they'd turned up anything . . ."

Still.

Laura cleared her throat. "Are they living in our sectors now?"

Hall shook his head. "No. They're not our problem." That earned a collective sigh of relief. "So enough about them. We have our own potential crisis brewing. For my part, I'll try to watch the two appointments, but I have a meeting with the government this morning to inform them that we'll soon be invoking Article 553."

Lesley understood why. The curfews and restrictions covered by 553 would help prevent the chaos Hall wanted to avoid.

"If the meeting runs long, I'll miss the 11:00 appointment. I trust your judgment, Finney. Don't wait for me, just move in."

"I will."

"And if nothing happens during the two appointments today, we'll do the same tomorrow."

"Four will fit the profile tomorrow," Laura said. "I'd guess that something will happen in one of those six appointments."

Hall nodded once. "Agreed. I'll be surprised if we have to observe beyond that."

"We have him under surveillance, so he can't do any damage in the meantime."

"Good." Hall paused. "Anything else?" When nobody spoke up, he slapped the table with both hands. "Then let's get to work. Dismissed."

Laura motioned for Lesley to walk with her as everyone rose. "Having you make the announcements wasn't my idea," she murmured after they'd left the conference room.

"I figured that." Lesley shrugged. "Oh well, it can't be helped."

"After this, every Rymellan will know who you are. It will be great exposure for you."

And potentially hurt Mo. At this point, Lesley was sure Mo hadn't received her Papers. She would have heard by now, if not from Mo, then from Michael or one of Mo's siblings. Was Mo upset? Relieved?

Depressed? Would seeing Lesley on a public monitor cheer or darken her day? Perhaps she'd be indifferent and care more about the Chosen Violation than the announcer.

Lesley inwardly sighed. She was losing her focus again. She should care more about doing her duty and playing the role the admiral wanted her to play than about how Mo would react to seeing her image. Her primary concern shouldn't be Mo.

But it was.

LOUNGING ON THE bench in front of the faculty residence, Mo squinted down the path. Nope, couldn't see her, and it was—she swung up her comm unit and checked the time—12:40. They were supposed to meet at 12:30. Maybe the shuttle had been delayed or an aviacraft hadn't been available. She'd wait another five minutes, then beep her.

Her comm unit beeped. Mo snorted; that must be her now. Without bothering to look at the unit's display, she pressed the connect button and barked, "Where are you?"

"At home."

She gasped. "Papa, I'm sorry. I thought you were someone else."

He mumbled something unintelligible, then said, "Listen, I might not be able to see you tomorrow."

Her shoulders slumped. "Why?"

"Uh, government business. I might be called into a meeting. Look, why don't you come home?"

She bit back an angry retort. "I've told you already, I can't be at home right now," she said through clenched teeth.

"Yes, you've said, but I really wish you'd change your mind. I'd feel better if you were on the estate right now."

Something in his voice made her pause. "Why?"

"I just would."

"But why?"

"Can't you do what I ask for once without an argument?" His voice held an edge of irritability.

"I'm not arguing, I'm just asking why," she said, bristling herself.

He took his time answering. "Because I'll worry about you if you're not here. Something's in the air. That's all I can say."

She didn't know what to make of his answer, couldn't decide if he was genuinely concerned for her or trying a new tactic to get her to come home. No, she'd see through that as soon as she arrived on the estate, and be furious with him. Maybe he was being evasive because it was related to the government business he'd mentioned and he couldn't give her specifics. Whatever it was, he was overreacting. She was on Rymel. Everywhere was safe, especially the Military Academy. "Papa, I don't know what you're worried about, but whatever it is, you don't need to worry about me. I'm at the Military Academy, remember?"

"I know, but—"

"I have to go. My friend's here," Mo said, spying the figure striding up the path. "I'll beep you later and we'll talk more about tomorrow, okay?"

He sighed. "I guess it'll have to be."

Mo didn't like cutting him off, but she'd only lose her temper if he kept badgering her to come home. "Bye, Papa." She slipped the comm unit into its holder and stood.

Ann stopped in front of her and eyed her up and down. "It's a good thing you stood up or I probably wouldn't have seen you."

She ignored the barb. "You're late."

"Yeah, well, the stupid aviacraft wasn't ready." She motioned at the knapsack on her back. "Let me drop this off in my room, then let's eat. I'm starved. What are you doing out here, anyway? I would have figured out where you are and knocked on your door."

"I felt like some air," Mo said, following Ann into the residence and up the stairs to the third floor.

Ann opened the door to the second room on the left. "Home!" she announced. "Where's your room?"

"Three doors down on the right." Mo glanced around and noted the bare walls and lack of personal belongings. "Do you always stay in this room, or do you get a different one each time?"

"No, this is mine." Ann shrugged off the knapsack and let it fall onto the bed.

"Oh." Ann was on a three weeks on, five days off rotation. Mo didn't know why Ann was no longer living with her mama; Ann had ignored Mo's questions on the subject. She'd "lived" at the Military Academy for almost a year, but maybe she viewed the room as temporary, regardless. "Have you thought of getting your own place?"

"I don't see the point, given my schedule." Ann walked to the door. "Mess hall or dining room?"

"Dining room. We won't have to shout."

Ann nodded and patted her stomach. "Let's go."

"Don't you get tired of staying here?" Mo asked as they bounded down the stairs to the first floor.

"Don't you?" Ann shot back. "You have a home and a family that wants you there."

So Ann was at odds with her family; Mo had suspected as much.

When they reached the dining room, a server who recognized Ann greeted them, led them to a table, and took their order. Mo lifted the jug from the centre of the table and filled her glass with water, then Ann's. "Why don't you come back to the *Falcon*?" she suggested. "If you're not taking care of your mama anymore . . ."

"No." Ann leaned back in her chair and folded her arms.

"Why not?"

She shrugged. "I've discovered that I like feeling the sun on my face more often."

Mo had a feeling that wasn't the only reason.

"Anything exciting happen on tour?" Ann asked.

"Nope. Oh, David and Angie had their baby, three days before we docked! A boy."

Ann frowned. "Glad I won't have to pretend I care when they start shoving the kid in everyone's face. Why do parents expect everyone to coo over their smelly baby? Dimwits."

"I'll remember that when I have one," Mo said, grinning.

"I'll need a magnifying glass to see yours. And I'll have to watch where I step until the kid is at least five." Ann stamped her foot for emphasis. "You haven't committed suicide, so I guess you didn't get your Papers."

Mo tutted and shook her head.

"You'd better hope they don't do it by height, or you'll get yours the day before you turn thirty."

Why had she agreed to spend the day with Ann? When Ann had returned to domestic duty, Mo hadn't expected to hear from her. But

RYMELLAN 2

several weeks after arriving back on the *Falcon*, she'd received a dispatch from Ann asking how things were going. At the time, she'd still been struggling to cope without Les; corresponding with Ann had been another distraction. They'd stayed in touch. Mo had seen her at least once during every leave. Ann had got the idea of staying at the Military Academy from her. Fortunately they were both at least lieutenant rank; otherwise they'd be sleeping in the barracks.

Each visit followed the same pattern: Ann would get all her short jokes out of her system and then settle down. Mo didn't mind her company, and Ann apparently didn't mind hers. They were both lonely, their lives in a holding pattern. They also loved to fly and to talk about it. Knowing that someone other than a relative was mildly interested in what she was doing had helped Mo get through some dark moments. She'd even talked to Ann about Les, though she was careful about what she said—she still didn't completely trust her. Ann held back details, too. It was an odd . . . friendship.

"Not that I'm giving your height remark any credence, but my Chosen is probably taller than I am," Mo said to her.

Ann barked a laugh. "Probably?" Then her eyes narrowed. "Did Lesley get hers yet?"

"No."

"Since you're staying here again, I guess you're still not over her."

She'd never be over her.

"I wonder if she's over you. Oh, here comes our salad."

Relieved, Mo unfolded her napkin as the server set down their salads and drinks. Ann inched her chair closer to the table. "How is the new batch of pilots?" Mo asked, jabbing her fork into a piece of lettuce.

Ann grimaced. "They're okay, I guess. Maybe I'm biased, but our class was one of the best."

Finally, something Mo could agree with wholeheartedly. As she and Ann nibbled their way through a leisurely lunch, they discussed Mo's last tour on the *Falcon* and Ann's work on 72 in more detail. Over tziva, they threw around a few ideas about how to spend the afternoon. Mo chuckled to herself when they settled on flying speed sims against each other, if they could book simulators on such short notice. They were pilots, through and through.

"Let's just head over there." Ann stood. "If simulators are available, great. If not, I guess I wouldn't mind going for a swim."

Ann had suggested a public lake in C7, but Mo had quickly shot down the idea. She'd managed to avoid lakes for almost two years. The Recreation Centre had several pools. "I'd rather race."

"You might not feel that way after I've beaten you," Ann said as they neared the residence's exit.

Mo snorted. "Still clinging to that fantasy?" Ann had never beaten her. Not in the simulators, anyway; she'd beaten her to the door. Mo shielded her eyes as they stepped out into the sun. "You domestic pilots—"

Her comm unit chimed. Not beeped—chimed. So did Ann's. Chimes seemed to be sounding all around Mo. Her mouth dropped open at the same time Ann's did. The government or military would make a mandatory announcement in five minutes. Everyone nearby was converging on a public monitor just up the path. Mo and Ann joined those assembled in front of it. Someone had already turned it on.

"Wonder what's going on?" Ann said.

"It can't be that the Preeminent Ruler has died," said an officer near them, referring to the reason for the last global announcement, years ago. "She's young—relatively young."

Mo swallowed. The Preeminent Ruler was around the same age Mama had been when she died. Wait a minute—could this announcement have anything to do with Papa's government business? He'd sounded worried. She waited impatiently for the announcement to begin, listening to the speculations of those around her.

When the chimes were sounding every two seconds, the insignia of the Interior Division appeared on the large monitor mounted above the unit. Interior. Not good. The chimes stopped. The insignia faded. Mo covered her mouth.

"It's Lesley," Ann breathed.

Yes, she could see that, thank you. And she wasn't hallucinating. The strip under Les's image read *Lt. Cmdr. L. Thompson*.

"My fellow Rymellans," Les intoned. "I have grave news. I ask you to remain calm and to remember that we are all Rymellan and that, together, we are strong."

Mo registered the words, despite focusing more on Les than on what she was saying. That nightmare had been just that—a bad dream. She would have recognized Les anywhere, even if Les had aged or changed her hair, though she hadn't. Les looked tired, but otherwise the same as when Mo had last seen her.

"Earlier today, Interior witnessed a Chosen Violation."

Many around Mo gasped; several couples reached for each other.

"This is not another Adams Incident. One person has fallen. I belong to the team that investigated and apprehended the criminal, and I assure you that we have contained the situation. At this time, we have no reason to suspect that others are involved in the crime, but our investigation is ongoing. If others are involved, we will find you." Les looked directly through the screen, as if meeting the eye of every viewer. "And we will punish you. Death to those who commit a Chosen Violation."

The crowd rumbled its agreement.

"The military has invoked Article 553, effective immediately. I will remind you of what that means. There is now a curfew of 8:00 p.m. for all Rymellans, with the exception of Interior personnel and those whose professions require them to be outside their homes after that time. To be outside your home between the hours of 8:00 p.m. and 6:00 a.m. is now a violation unless you are accompanied by a member of the Interior Division or you are working at a profession that requires you to be away from your home during that time."

Now Mo could see why Papa wanted her home. They'd have to cut their days together short until 553 was lifted. Well, tough, because she couldn't go home. Her insides were quaking at the sight of Les. She wanted to elbow her way to the front, reach up, and press her hand against the monitor. What a terrible time to be on leave.

"We have increased the military presence in all sectors," Les continued. "Curfew violations will not go unnoticed or unpunished." She paused. "We understand that news of a Chosen Violation is shocking and upsetting and that you will look to each other for support and comfort. Do so privately, with your families, not publicly. Public discussion of the Chosen Violation will not be tolerated. We will disperse groups of more than four Rymellans, unless the group is within an area immediately surrounding a public monitor. Be prepared to answer any questions the military poses to you quickly and honestly. Your cooperation with the military is always important, never more so than now.

"When Article 553 is in effect, the punishment for several articles is upgraded to execution. I'll read those article numbers now—pay close attention: Article 73, Article 74, Article 101, Article 122, Article 167, and Article 168. All these articles relate to cooperation with the military."

"Maybe I should have stayed on 72," Ann murmured.

"Article 553 will remain in effect until we have completed our investigation. I will announce the name of the criminal later today."

Please, no more announcements. Why had Les agreed to do them? Surely someone else had been available. Anyone would have leaped at the chance to become so widely known; it would do wonders for anyone's career. Oh. Mo felt sick.

"I know this announcement has upset you and I encourage you to discuss it with your families. However, I remind you that emotional distress is not an excuse for violations against the Way, and that we will not tolerate public speculation about the nature of the violation or those involved. Above all, fellow Rymellans, remember that disobedience means death. Death to those who commit a Chosen Violation. Death to those who disobey. Death to those who violate the Way. Thank you for your attention."

The insignia of the Rymellan government replaced Les's face. It quickly faded. The Preeminent Ruler appeared on the display. "Greetings to all Rymellans. We are all shocked by the horrible news Lieutenant Commander Thompson has just delivered, but we must remain calm. The military has the situation under control. The criminal is in custody, and we all want to see the criminal punished. Commander Finney of the Interior Division will execute the criminal tomorrow morning at ten o'clock."

Mo's jaw tightened.

"At two o'clock in the afternoon, those of you who reside in D2 and nearby sectors are invited to view the criminal's body as it is carried from the execution site in D2 to the Wall's crematorium, where it will burn, as all criminals burn. The criminal's ashes will be added to the communal urn for offenders, and the name of this heinous individual—I will not refer to this person as a Rymellan—will be added to the Wall of Offenders as a reminder to all of us of what happens to those who fall from the Way. We will broadcast the procession. All non-essential businesses will close for the day, to allow as many of you to attend or view the procession as possible."

Ann jabbed Mo in the ribs and whispered, "We should go." Mo ignored her.

"All Level Four and Five classes from the Indoctrination Academies in Sector D2 will attend the procession. Several members from each class will march at its rear." She paused. "I would like to extend the gratitude of all Rymellans to Interior for capturing the criminal and protecting the Way. Our military works tirelessly to preserve our way of life. We might comfort ourselves by saying that this is the first Chosen Violation we've had in thirteen years, but that would be folly. The Adams Incident taught us that serious threats to the Way can arise at any time, as happened today. We must always be on guard. Only our continued diligence and the protection of our military will keep us safe.

"Before I close, I would remind you that Article 553 is in effect and that you are to give the military your full cooperation at all times. Because of what has happened, what I am about to say has never been more meaningful to me and to all of us. Disobedience means death. Death to those who commit a Chosen Violation. Death to those who disobey. Death to those who violate the Way. Thank you." Her image faded. The text of Article 553 started to scroll slowly up the display.

"Flaming Argamon, can you believe it?" Ann said. "Who would do something like that?"

Mo knew Ann didn't expect an answer. She couldn't imagine why anyone would fall from the Way and didn't want to try to understand such a warped mind.

"All right, everyone, move along," an officer in an Interior cloak shouted.

"Looks like they're cracking down even here," Ann murmured. "Let's start walking."

Mo fell into step with her. Rymellans strode quickly past, their heads down, but she managed to glimpse the occasional shocked or disbelieving face. She probably looked shattered too, but for a different reason. Les had looked okay. She looked okay! Mo felt dejected and stupid. She'd imagined Les pining for her, especially now, while Mo was on Rymel. But Les probably hadn't given her a second thought. Argamon, she probably wasn't even aware that the *Falcon* had docked; she was too busy capturing criminals and furthering her career.

Okay, now she was being immature. Did she honestly expect Les to address Rymellans with tears streaming down her face? And how she looked wasn't necessarily an indication of how she felt. Mo looked fine, even though her life often felt like an endurance test. She wasn't shut away in her quarters, depressed. She took pride in her duties, hence her promotion. She regularly socialized and belonged to a quartet that gave concerts on the *Falcon*. Granted, the main reason she'd forced herself out of her quarters was so Les would be proud of her when they reunited, but only she knew that. Outwardly, she'd moved on. Inwardly, her life was on hold. Les may or may not feel the same. Mo didn't know; that was the problem.

"So should we go tomorrow?" Ann said.

"No."

"Why not? You know Lesley will definitely be there. You can see her!"

Which was why Mo wouldn't be going—she visualized herself breaking from the sidelines and rushing to Les. "I can't, Ann. I might do something I'll regret."

Ann stopped and peered at her. "Mo, you have to get over her. You're going to get yourself killed."

No, she wouldn't. She'd never get over Les, but she'd also never fall from the Way. She wouldn't disappoint Les and disgrace her family. *Believe!* she reminded herself. They were Chosens. She just had to hang on until they received their Papers. So she'd stay away from the procession. Constantly seeing Les on the monitors over the next few days would be difficult enough. Each time would be salt in an open wound. Seeing her in the flesh, within reach . . .

"We can watch it here," Mo said. "They'll probably set up monitors in several of the auditoriums." The prospect of seeing Les in the procession didn't thrill her, but she couldn't skip watching it; it would be the main topic of conversation for a while. Plus, she was curious—she'd never seen an execution procession. "Anyway, let's get to those simulators."

Mo suspected they'd become her refuge, something to soothe her every time an announcement ripped her apart.

LESLEY WEARILY CLIMBED the stairs and crept along the hallway so she wouldn't wake her parents. She slipped into her bedroom and quietly shut the door. What a long day, with no relief in sight. Tomorrow, the execution, followed several hours later by the procession.

Hall had ordered an autopsy, to determine if a medical problem was behind Owen's fall. They'd performed the usual tests and turned up nothing, but perhaps slicing his brain or another organ would provide a clue—too late for Owen, but not too late for the Chosen Council to understand the implications for the Owen line.

She changed into her pyjamas but didn't get into bed, despite her fatigue. Instead she gazed out the window in the direction of the Middleton estate. She often did so at night, even though Mo wasn't there. How was Mo feeling? How had she reacted to the news, to the announcements? Lesley knew she should hope that the sight of her on the monitors hadn't affected Mo at all beyond curiosity, but that would mean Mo didn't love her anymore. If she truly loved Mo, shouldn't she be pleased if Mo had moved on? Shouldn't Mo's happiness be the most important thing to her?

Mo had been at the back of her mind, and sometimes at the forefront, all day. Today Lesley had not only witnessed a Chosen Violation with her own eyes, but had seen the turmoil, distress, and pain one caused—two families devastated, numerous lives shattered. Officers rarely shed tears during an investigation, but many eyes had been moist today. But not Lesley's. She hadn't cried since she'd left Mo standing outside her aviacraft. She'd become so used to repressing her feelings, pushing everything down so she could get through her days, that she sometimes wondered if she could still cry, if her smile would ever be genuine.

Lesley wanted to be with Mo more than anything, but they'd had to part, not just for their sakes, but for the two women they hadn't yet met. She might pine for Mo and struggle to give her life meaning, but she wouldn't put her Chosen through what Owen's Chosen was going through. Mo wouldn't either. Mo might believe that she'd have trouble accepting her Chosen, but she never gave herself enough credit. She'd do it. She'd serve the Way. Lesley wouldn't have loved her all these years otherwise.

Laura had been right to insist that they split up. They never would have committed a Chosen Violation, but remaining together until their Papers arrived would have been weak in the Way. The Way must come first, no matter what. She and Mo weren't criminals, weren't depraved like the Adamses and Owen. They hadn't allowed their personal desires to dictate their behaviour. They were strong in the Way and would be remembered for their devotion to it, in both their personal and professional lives. They were born Rymellan. They'd live the Rymellan Way. And they'd die Rymellan.

ALBERT WATKINS STROLLED into his office in Sector C3's Chosen House, opened the blinds, and set a mug of steaming tziva on his desk. Mornings were his favourite time of day; he always prepared Chosen Papers before lunch. Nothing beat the excitement of requesting the list of Principals in the sector whose time had come and seeing a name or two appear on the screen. Most days, the list was empty. Many of Rymel's wealthiest and oldest families resided in C3; their estates occupied large tracts of land. As a result, the sector population was much lower than average, but a number of Rymellans of Joinable age called it home. If any were Principals, he'd be one of the first to know, beaten only by the scientists who'd determined their matches years ago.

But this morning he was in a foul mood. He shouldn't take a Chosen Violation personally, especially since he'd had nothing to do with the Owen Joining, but he couldn't help it. Every Chosen Violation reflected badly on the Council, and the Owen Joining had lasted a mere eight months. What a disaster! The Council's scientists had been up half the night poring over the data related to the Owen line. They hadn't found any errors, of course, but they'd had to check. At least this violation hadn't been on the level of the Adams Incident, when military had demanded that the Council review every Joining even remotely related to the Adamses.

Oh well, the day could only improve. Owen would be executed in a couple of hours, and you could bet that many from the Council would be at the execution procession, including him—D2 wasn't that far away. But first he had work to do. He switched on his station screen and requested the list of Principals whose Papers should be prepared that day. A single name appeared on the screen: Lesley Thompson. Now wasn't that interesting . . . on the same day she'd walk in an execution procession in triumph, she would receive her Chosen Papers. It was almost poetic.

Watkins rubbed his hands together in glee. What better way to take everyone's mind off a Chosen Violation than to announce that Thompson would Join? Everyone knew her—they'd all been in front of their comm stations since her first announcement of the Chosen Violation, and she'd also appeared on the monitors several years ago. Just last night, his mama had said she slept better, knowing that Interior had officers like Thompson moving up its ranks, and he'd overheard others expressing similar sentiments this morning on the train. Several of his colleagues had even wondered aloud when she'd Join. Rymellans trusted and respected her. Yes, very good timing, indeed.

He'd talk to Thompson about spotlighting her Joining. If she agreed, and he was sure she would, he'd contact communications and set the plan in motion. They'd arrange to show images of the happy couple on the monitors and periodically interview them, so Rymellans could see how delighted they were with each other. Interest in the Joining would run high; Rymellans would crowd the courtyard on the couple's Joining Day. Owen's Chosen Violation would soon be forgotten, mentioned only in the Indoctrination Academies. The Adams Incident would continue to remind Rymellans of the depravity of Chosen Violations, as it should.

That Thompson was a Principal didn't surprise him. Some lucky man or woman was about to gain the Thompson name and one of the most eligible Chosens on the planet. Thompson was personable, attractive, strong in the Way, and clearly headed for admiral. Her Chosen's family would be ecstatic, and he was about to find out which family it was—not that he could tell anyone outside the Council. He'd earn a swift execution if he revealed any details before Thompson and her Chosen had been notified.

To ensure the integrity of the Chosen Tradition, the files of the two Chosens involved in a Joining weren't associated with each other, and made no reference to each other, until a Council member with the appropriate authorization level asked to link the files. The data system contained a master list accessible to only a handful of the Council's members. Scientists who determined matches could add to it but couldn't read it. Linking files, as he was authorized to do, would be through indirect access. The system notified the military every time someone accessed the list, either directly or indirectly, and the military regularly audited all accesses. Anyone who accessed the file inappropriately or without the proper authorization would find military on his or her doorstep and have a considerably shorter life than he or she had expected!

Hardly able to contain himself, Watkins asked to link Thompson's file with her Chosen's and waited for the name of her Chosen to appear on his screen. Seconds later, he frowned and squinted at the display. Something was wrong. Two names had appeared; he gasped when he read the second. At about the same time, his eyes widened when he understood what he was seeing.

He immediately beeped his superior. An unusual day was turning into an extraordinary one, and it was only 8:10!

LESLEY HELD HER breath as Laura carefully lifted a small vial of green fluid from the silver case that lay open on the ledge in front of her. Laura looked calm, even though she'd confided to Lesley that she hated this part of an execution the most. Apparently a commander had accidentally killed herself when loading her stick and Laura worried that she'd do the same. But her gloved hand was steady as she inserted the vial into her stick and snapped the receptacle lid shut. The stick wouldn't be armed until she lifted it to Owens' neck and pressed the green button on its handle. After that, she'd only have to press the trigger to deliver the deadly chemicals into the bloodstream. Owen would die within seconds.

The officer next to Lesley coughed. Only a handful of officers were observing Laura's preparations. Hall had surprised Lesley when he ordered her into the hut at the execution site's entrance without offering an explanation for why her presence was required. *When we leave the hut, take up the rear and follow the lead of the officers in front of you,* was all he'd said.

Laura holstered her stick. After closing and sealing the silver case and returning it to its secure storage container, she peeled off the gloves and inserted them into a plastic bag. "Is he ready?" she asked the military physician waiting nearby.

The physician nodded. "Yes, Commander."

"Then let's proceed," Hall said. "Observers first."

Following Hall's earlier instructions, Lesley waited for the other observers to leave the hut and then joined them outside. They'd formed a double column. She stood in the remaining open position at the rear, surprised to find herself on Hall's right.

"Forward!" one of the lead officers barked. The group marched up a path lined with military and entered a dirt clearing ringed by more military, though they'd left a gap at its southernmost edge. The two lead officers peeled away in opposite directions and joined the end of the lines near the gap. The officers in front of Lesley did the same. *Follow the lead of the officers in front of you.* She pivoted to her right, to stand to the left of the officer she'd just marched behind, and found herself with a front row seat to the execution. Not six feet away, Owen waited, secured to a metal pole. He'd been sedated by the physician, and his head had fallen forward; the metal chains held him upright.

Lesley looked past him and noticed the Rymellans gathered on the other side of the fence, straining for a glimpse of the criminal. Executions weren't open to the public, but they did take place outside. If Rymellans happened to be passing by during an execution, they were always welcome to watch. Apparently many Rymellans were "passing by" that morning. Considering that Owen had committed a Chosen Violation, she couldn't blame them.

"Let's join hands," Hall said.

She reached for her neighbour's hand and resisted the urge to walk forward and take Hall's. No circle this time. "Disobedience means death. Death to those who commit a Chosen Violation. Death to those who disobey. Death to those who violate the Way. Death to those who violate the Way. Death to those who violate the Way!"

Everyone dropped their hands but remained silent. The incomplete circle and the absence of applause made the gesture feel strange, almost warped. But that was the point—the Way had been tainted. Owen's execution would cleanse it.

Footsteps thudded up the path. Laura and the physician marched into the clearing and stopped in front of Owen. With her left hand, Laura grabbed Owen's hair and lifted his head. "Anthony Burke Owen, you committed a Chosen Violation and must give your life for the Way." Owen didn't respond; his eyes were closed. She pulled the stick from its holster and raised it to Owen's neck, pressed the green button, and moved her thumb to the trigger. "Disobedience means death. Death to those who commit a Chosen Violation. Death to those who disobey. Death to those who violate the Way." She pressed the trigger and let go of Owen's hair. His head fell forward again; he looked as he had when Lesley entered the clearing.

The physician examined him, then nodded. "He's dead."

Laura holstered her stick and offered her right hand to the physician and her left to Lesley. Once the circle was complete, everyone chanted the *Words Every Rymellan Knows* and burst into applause. When Laura moved to the centre of the clearing and thrust her right fist into the air, they clapped wildly again. There was no better service to the Way than to eliminate a threat to it, no greater satisfaction.

Hall stepped to Laura's side as two undertakers rolled a stretcher into the clearing. "Take the body to the D2-4 morgue immediately," he said to them, then he turned to Laura. "Thank you, Commander Finney."

She nodded to him. Lesley remained focused on Hall and Laura, though out of the corner of her eye, she could see the undertakers working near the pole.

"Every Chosen Violation is an abomination, and so are those who commit them," Hall said. "Commander Finney and her group will march directly behind those carrying the body, to honour them for dealing with this latest fall swiftly and efficiently. Today we should all be proud to be Interior officers. Dismissed."

Lesley hesitated, unaware of the protocol for leaving the execution site. The observers she'd entered with started to form up in the middle of the clearing, behind Laura and the physician. Relief flooded through her when Hall joined the end of the line and motioned for her to do the same.

The military lining the path saluted the group marching past. Later, the procession route would be lined with Rymellans. Would Mo be there? Lesley's pride turned to shame. She'd just witnessed a man die because he'd committed a Chosen Violation, and here she was, hoping to bump into Mo. If her peers knew what she was thinking, they wouldn't salute her.

Lesley would never commit a Chosen Violation, but she'd forgive them if they all wondered how long it would be until she found herself secured to a metal pole.

"SO WE'VE GOT a triad," Jean Simpson, a senior Council scientist, said. The small group clustered around Watkins' screen moved in for a closer look. Simpson pointed to the display. "This is the superimposed data from the three Chosens' files. It's almost beautiful, isn't it?"

"What are the odds?" Watkins asked.

"Extremely low, and only possible with a same-oriented Joining."

"Which is why we haven't had one for 232 years," Mary Stone said as she bustled into the room. The House's archivist plunked into a chair a short distance from the group and started to tap away on her comm unit.

Watkins swung around to face the others. "So let me get this straight. All three of them are Chosen to each other."

Simpson nodded. "Correct. In layman's terms, it's a tie—well, a bit more than a tie, actually. Three ties. When we evaluated the data from their psychological and genetic tests, these three had results that were the best match for each other. Exactly the best match. So Chosens one and two are tied as the best match for Chosen three, Chosens one and three are tied as the best match for Chosen two, and—well, you get the idea. Given the number of parameters measured for both types of evaluations, the probability of this happening is . . . it's . . ." She shook her head in frustration, unable to express how rare it was. "Let's just say I never expected to see a triad in my lifetime. Did you say the last one was 232 years ago, Mary?"

"Uh-huh," Stone said absently, still focused on her comm unit.

"There's usually a larger gap between triads."

"Is it because Thompson is so strong in the Way?" asked Richard Howard, Watkins' supervisor. He pointed to the screen. "Look at these projections. Look at how strong in the Way her children will be with either one of these Chosens."

"Any pair among the triad will produce children who are projected to be equally strong in the Way, so it's not Thompson per se," Simpson said.

"Here." Stone waved her comm unit at everyone. "A treatise on triads." She muttered the words to herself as she scanned the information on the unit's display. "Oh, that doesn't sound very good."

"What?" Howard asked.

Stone looked up. "When the first triad surfaced, we declared them unnatural and a threat to the Way. So we turned one member of the triad into a Solitary, over the protests of those who said that not Joining Chosens was even more unnatural and asking for trouble. It turns out they were right."

"What do you mean?" Watkins asked.

"It worked for the first two triads, but not for the third. Apparently the one who'd been turned into a Solitary crossed paths with one of the Joined Chosens." Stone grimaced. "You can guess what happened."

"What bad luck!" Watkins said.

"I'd call it stupid," Simpson said. "Not Joining Chosens together? That's a Chosen Violation waiting to happen. Not only that, triads aren't unnatural or a threat to the Way. They're rare, but natural."

"But technically it wasn't a Chosen Violation," Stone said. "They *were* Chosens."

Simpson shook her head. "Not if we turned one into a Solitary, but I understand what you're saying. Yet another reason it was a regrettable course of action. Anyone who grumbles about the frequent audits of our data and assigned matches should read that treatise to understand why it's critical that the integrity of our matches is protected. A Chosen should never be arbitrarily changed to a Solitary."

"And that's why we decided to Join the three Chosens together," Howard declared.

"Um, no, we didn't," Stone said. "Not then, anyway. And Jean, I'd practice saying that triads are natural and not against the Way. According to this, the view that triads are unnatural and a threat to the Way comes up every time a triad does. It happened with the last one."

"And it'll definitely happen with this one, considering who's in the triad," Watkins murmured.

Stone's brow furrowed. "Why, who's in it?"

Watkins read the names.

She paled. "Oh dear."

"Yes," Watkins said. "If anyone does consider the triad unnatural and against the Way, you know who they'll blame. And everyone will expect the triad to fail because she's in it."

"Which would be completely unfounded," Simpson snapped. "None of the data indicates that she's more likely to commit a Chosen Violation than anyone else. We wouldn't Join her if it did."

"That won't stop the talk," Stone said.

Simpson nodded wearily. "No, I suppose it won't."

"Let's not get sidetracked," Howard said. "Please go on, Mary."

Stone continued to read, then barked a laugh. "Oh, you won't believe this. You'll love this, Jean. After the Chosen Violation related to the third triad, we decided to avoid Joining the three Chosens together by executing one member of the triad. We always executed the oldest member."

"You can't be serious," Simpson said.

"It's right here," Stone said. "Can you imagine, showing up for your notification meeting and being told, 'Sorry, you're in a triad and you're the oldest member, so if you'll just follow me to the execution site, thank you.'"

"I guess that was one way of solving the problem of having a Chosen walking around who wasn't Joined to his or her Chosen," Howard said sardonically.

Watkins rolled his eyes.

"How long was this enlightened solution to the problem in effect?" Simpson asked dryly.

"Until an Advocate Samuels successfully argued that the practice of executing the oldest member was barbaric and that, in the case of female triads, it reduced the number of children strong in the Way that could come of the Joining." Stone looked up. "So the practice was discontinued and we finally decided to Join the three Chosens together. Unfortunately, most triads were still touched by execution, regardless."

Watkins frowned. "Why?"

Stone looked back at her screen, brushing aside a stray lock of hair that slipped over her eyes. "Hmm . . . in one case, one of the triad members committed a Chosen Violation with a Solitary. But more commonly, jealousy within the triad was an issue. One member of the triad frequently assaulted another, treated another rudely in public, or publicly expressed the sentiment that the Joining was flawed. Despite repeated warnings and strikes, the behaviour continued until execution was deemed appropriate. That's why we now have Article CT134 in the Tradition."

"Article CT134?" Simpson said.

"Yes. Triads have two years to schedule the Joining Ceremony, not one. If the Principal and one of the other triad members think the third member will have a destabilizing effect on the triad, therefore threatening the viability of the triad and the Way, they may petition for the execution of that triad member. However, the case must be made and the execution performed before the triad Joins. And . . ." She read some more. "That's exactly what's happened for most of the triads since then. The Principal and another member successfully petitioned for the execution of the third."

"So the Principal is always safe?" Watkins asked.

"Yes."

"Is CT134 still in effect?" Howard asked.

Stone nodded. "I presume so."

Watkins spun around to his station, quickly verified that it was, and spun back again.

Howard frowned. "So the Thompson triad could be reduced to two Chosens." Watkins shifted nervously and looked at Howard, who said, "I know, I know, but a case has to be made and Thompson is the Principal. If she lives up to her reputation, she'll ensure that the article is only exercised if she's absolutely convinced that the triad won't be viable."

Watkins remained silent but looked uncertain.

"Did the last triad end with CT134?" Howard asked.

Stone skimmed to the end of the treatise. "No. The three Chosens Joined." She smiled. "And remained Joined until death. Their natural deaths."

"Female?"

"Yes."

"How many daughters?"

Stone's brows shot up. "Fourteen."

"Fourteen!" Howard breathed. "If this triad is as successful, think of the children."

"And every one of them projected to be very strong in the Way," Simpson added.

"I'm still not sure how it works in practice, though," Watkins said. "How do the articles apply to them?"

"Exactly the same way they apply to a Joining of two," Stone said. "In fact, there's a set of articles that applies specifically to them, many of which state that the usual articles apply to all three Chosens and that the word 'Chosen' refers to both Chosens."

"So they can mix and match however they want within the triad, is that what you're saying?"

"Yes. As long as all sexual activity remains within the triad, nobody cares about the details."

"It sounds to me like we need to brush up on everything concerning triads," Watkins said. "The Joining Ceremony must be slightly different. And what's the protocol for notification?" His hands flew to his head. "The Chosen rings? The names?"

"I'll find and dispatch the relevant documents to everyone," Stone said.

"Thank you." Howard tapped his upper lip. "My son knows Thompson, we were just talking about her last night. Thompson and Middleton are already involved. Well, at least they *were* involved. They split up when they turned twenty-five."

"That's happened before," Simpson said. "They're Chosens. The time apart won't have made a difference."

"But what about CT134?" Watkins said. "If they're already involved . . ."

Howard's face darkened. "Albert, Thompson's the Principal. She won't do anything rash!"

"You *hope* she won't do anything rash. Considering that she's already involved with Middleton and that the third Chosen is—"

"Yes, that's going to be interesting. We knew it would happen at some point and cause a stir, but obviously we didn't anticipate a triad, and with two of our oldest families." Howard tapped his lip again. "Do you think we should notify the military before announcing it?"

"The military? Why would we notify the military?" boomed a voice from behind them.

Everyone turned. Humphrey Stevens, one of the Chosen Council heads, stood in the doorway. "I got here as soon as I could. So we've got a triad," he continued briskly as he strode into the room. "What's all the fuss about? It's happened before, there are records available, and how the articles apply to them is explicit. What we need to do is prepare for their notifications, because I'm sure they'll be filled with questions, especially about how to conduct themselves. Did I hear you say the Thompson and Middleton families are involved?"

Howard nodded.

"Those are two of our best lines. I don't want any mistakes or omissions on our part, especially any that result in a Thompson or Middleton at an execution site. Who's the Principal?"

"Lesley Thompson."

"Good. If anyone can guide them through this, she can, but hold their Papers until tomorrow. Thompson already has a busy day, and we need extra time to prepare. If any of you were thinking about going to the execution procession, forget it. We have too much work to do. You can catch the replay on the monitors." Stevens paused. "I'll schedule a meeting for 4:00. We can review exactly how the notifications will go, including what information we need to provide to them. So come on, we have a busy day ahead of us. Let's get to work."

Nobody moved. He stared at them. "Are you deaf? I said, let's get to work. Why are you all standing there looking like you're about to wet yourselves?"

"It's the third Chosen," Howard said.

"The what?"

"The third Chosen in the triad."

Stevens folded his arms. "What about her?"

Howard glanced at the others and bit his lip. "It's the Adams girl."

JAYNE ADAMS GLANCED around the clearing, prepared to dart back down the path if necessary. But nobody was around. Everyone was at home, glued to their comm stations, as she would have been if she hadn't lost track of the time. She felt uneasy being outside while Article 553 was in effect, but the prospect of spending another agonizing minute cooped up in her apartment had outweighed her reservations. Only a couple of hours, she'd told herself, intending to be back in the safety of her home well before 2:00, when the execution procession would start. But it was already 1:55. Even if she ran home, she'd miss the beginning of the procession, so she'd risk a public monitor this once.

She leaned her sketchbook against the left side of the monitor's podium and tapped the *On* button to bring the monitor to life. It displayed the huge, cheering crowd assembled near D2's execution site. Jayne listened intently to the commentator's droning voice as the camera panned over the area.

One of the Indoctrination Academy's classes came into view. She flinched, reminded of her time at the Academy. Her experience of Levels One to Three hadn't been worse than anyone else's, but after the Incident, everything had changed. Not only had none of the children wanted to commit social suicide by associating with her, but angry parents had deluged the Academy with letters and visits, demanding that their children be protected from the Adams taint. In response, the Academy had isolated her from the others outside of classes. That had left her plenty of time to sketch in peace, but she'd been terribly lonely and sometimes subjected to pain. The indoctrinators had brought out their rods at the slightest perceived provocation. If she'd even looked at them—

Jayne jumped when a loud roar erupted from the crowd. The image on the monitor shifted to one of the elevated platforms holding representatives from the military and government, and then to an approaching aviacraft. Excitement shot through her. It was about to begin. She moved closer to the screen, wanting to see and hear every detail of what happened next. Like all Rymellans, she wanted to be sure that the criminal had been executed for falling from the Way. After all, *Disobedience means death. Death to those who commit a Chosen Violation. Death to those who disobey. Death to those who violate the Way.*

LESLEY'S JAW DROPPED when she peered out the aviacraft window. So many Rymellans were assembled that, apart from a circular landing area that would receive the craft and a narrow strip that marked the procession's route, she couldn't see the ground. When the craft touched down, she left her seat and followed Laura to the front. The six military selected for the honour of carrying the corpse and the rest of the Chosen

Tradition group joined them. They waited while military outside hastily erected a tent that would initially shield the head of the procession
from the gathered crowd. When it was ready, Laura slid open the door.
The deafening roar of the crowd assaulted the ears of everyone inside.

The six military arranged themselves around the body bag that had
rested on the floor of the craft for the entire journey; the rest of the
group stepped outside. Two drummers were waiting for them, their
drums hanging from straps around their necks, ready to set the pace.
While those who would carry the corpse removed it from the body bag
and bound its hands and feet, Lesley and the others formed up and
prepared to march. Once everyone was in position, one of the drummers spoke into her comm unit. Seconds later, the din of the crowd
slowly faded to silence.

"My fellow Rymellans," the Preeminent Ruler said. "The execution of
a criminal is always unfortunate, but the Way must be observed. When
it is not, punishment is swift, as it was for the criminal executed this
morning. It doesn't matter what position you hold in our society. It
doesn't matter where you live. It doesn't matter who you are. All that
matters is obedience to the Law and the Chosen Tradition. Disobedience
means death. Death to those who commit a Chosen Violation. Death to
those who disobey. Death to those who violate the Way.

"Today I am announcing that Admiral Derek Lacey will lead a review
of all procedures and curriculums at our Indoctrination and Learning
Academies. In addition, Admiral Michael Hall will lead a review of all
procedures pertaining to our counsellors' obligations to the Way. I am
also announcing that all Rymellans will undergo a refresher examination within two months. The examination will focus on key areas of
the Law and Chosen Tradition. The Indoctrination Academies in each
sector will dispatch details to you.

"And now, if you will all join with me in singing the Song of Rymel."

The Rymellans gathered along the route sang the song a cappella,
their voices ringing out with pride. Lesley and those assembled with
her enthusiastically joined in.

Rymellan we are and always shall be,
We are one, Chosen and Solitary.

The Law and Chosen Tradition are the Way,
Protect it we must, and be sure to obey.
Rymellan we are and always shall be,
We are one, Chosen and Solitary.
The Way is the foundation of our society,
With no Law and Chosen Tradition, we would not be.
Rymellan we are and always shall be,
We are one, Chosen and Solitary.
Disobedience is not tolerated, punishment is quick,
Chosen Violations will lead to an executioner's stick.
Rymellan we are and always shall be,
We are one, Chosen and Solitary.

As the final refrain ended, those assembled clapped and whistled loudly. The military responsible for the body hoisted it onto their shoulders. At Laura's barked command, the drummers started their beat. Everyone started to chant the *Words Every Rymellan Knows* and the procession moved forward.

As soon as those with the body left the tent, the crowd erupted. When Laura and her group became visible, the crowd went wild. It felt to Lesley as if the ground were shaking, though she knew it wasn't.

A flower bounced off her shoulder. Another followed, then two more. Every type of flower rained down on the procession, their scent filling the air as the marchers crushed them underfoot. The beat of the drums slowed as the footing became more hazardous with each step. Lesley strained to see more than a few feet in front of her.

The military carrying the body occasionally pleased the crowd by thrusting the cadaver into the air or veering off to the side so those lining the route could see for themselves that the criminal was indeed dead. The body bounced as its bearers walked and weaved, performing their macabre dance.

When the procession was about halfway to its destination, groups of teens ran from the sidelines to join its rear. Level Four and Five classes from nearby Indoctrination Academies were in attendance, and the indoctrinators were taking full advantage of the display. "This man committed a Chosen Violation," they screamed into their megaphones.

"Death to those who disobey. Death to those who violate the Chosen Tradition. Look, look at the corpse! That's what will happen to you if you commit a Chosen Violation. Look at the executioner. She will come for you if you commit a Chosen Violation. Know the articles. Know the articles. Know the articles. Death to those who disobey!"

JAYNE FELT SICK and averted her eyes from the monitor. Was that what it had been like for her parents? What had she hoped to accomplish by watching? Did she think it would help her to understand? If she didn't understand after thirteen years, she wouldn't understand by watching the procession for a criminal who'd had nothing to do with the Incident—which, curiously, the Preeminent Ruler hadn't mentioned. Jayne could have taken the omission as a sign that this recent crime would displace the Incident from the notorious position it held in the minds of Rymellans, but she knew better. What this man had done, while terrible, didn't compare to what they'd done. This one would eventually blow over.

She'd seen enough, and was about to turn off the monitor when she heard the crunch of a footfall on gravel. Orange flashed in the corner of her eye.

Oh no.

"Well, what have we here?" a female voice said off to Jayne's right. "An Adams watching the execution procession for a criminal who committed a Chosen Violation. I guess it brings back fond family memories for you, right Jayne?"

Jayne remained silent and kept her eyes on the monitor. Of all the military who could have walked through the clearing, why did it have to be this lieutenant? Everyone who patrolled E6 treated her like dirt, but this one was the worst. Not long ago, this lieutenant had struck her with a level three violation for speaking up, not back, when the lieutenant had insulted her. That had cost her almost a full month's living allowance. If Carol hadn't bailed her out, she would have starved.

"I've heard they don't die right away when they're executed," the lieutenant said.

"What happens to them?" a male voice asked. Great, there were two of them.

"They jerk around, like this."

A burst of laughter followed the lieutenant's words. Now that they'd had their laugh, maybe they'd leave her alone. She turned off the monitor and turned toward her sketchbook.

"Whoa, whoa, whoa!" the lieutenant said.

Jayne froze.

"Where do you think you're going? Article 553 is in effect. You do *not* walk away from military right now, Jayne. And I think you, especially, should watch the rest of the procession. Don't you agree, Tim?"

"Definitely."

"Keep an eye out." Jayne winced when the lieutenant grabbed her arm and twisted it behind her back. "Turn the monitor back on," the lieutenant barked.

Jayne managed to tap the button with her free hand.

"Now watch!" the lieutenant shouted into Jayne's ear, making it ring.

"You're violating Article 822," Jayne managed to gasp.

"What did you say?" The lieutenant jerked Jayne's arm up. Pain shot through her back; she cried out and sank to her knees.

"Cheryl, be careful," Tim said. "Don't break her arm. We don't need the hassle."

Cheryl snorted. "What hassle? Obviously I would have been acting in self-defence when she attacked me."

"Hey, wait a minute," Tim said slowly. "We're just having a bit of fun here, not trying to have her executed."

"Why not?" Cheryl said. "We'd get medals for bringing her in. Though I'd miss not having her around to play with." She grabbed Jayne's hair and pulled her head back. "If I transferred to another sector, would you miss me?" she asked, pouting. "I bet you would." Her pout turned into a sneer. "Now get up!"

Jayne struggled to her feet. When her head neared the top of the podium, Cheryl pushed it forward, smashing Jayne's chin against the podium's edge. Her teeth snapped together. Cheryl giggled. "Oops. You'll get a nasty bruise there. And here I thought you couldn't get any uglier. Oh look, it's the executioner." She pointed at the screen. "See, that's a true Rymellan, right there. And there's Thompson, right next to her.

Another true Rymellan. I bet they'd love to get their hands on a freak like you, Jayne. See, they protect Rymellans. They don't protect freaks."

"Maybe we should beep them, see what they're doing after the procession," Tim said.

Jayne couldn't breathe. The thought of being in the presence of Finney and Thompson terrified her. She turned away from the monitor. Cheryl slapped the side of her head. "Keep watching!"

Gulping back the bile that rose in her throat, Jayne watched.

THROUGH THE FLOWERS that still showered the procession, Lesley glimpsed the entrance to the crematorium. The drummers had almost reached it. They beat on their drums five times in rapid succession, then the drums fell silent.

The procession stopped. Everyone stood quietly while the military carried the body through the gates. Once they'd disappeared from view, Laura turned to face the procession and thrust her right fist into the air. The crowd roared its approval and, as the floral storm resumed, it spontaneously broke into the Song of Rymel.

Lesley started to sing along but faltered. Was Mo here? She quickly recovered and resumed singing, but her mind remained on Mo. Was Mo all right? Was she proud of her? All the feelings Lesley had locked away suddenly started to surface. She desperately fought for control; she couldn't break down here, in front of a crowd and live on the monitors. *Focus on the words. Sing. Smile and sing.* She did, and wept inside.

SURPRISED, JAYNE WATCHED Thompson's face. For a moment it had almost looked as if she was going to cry, something Jayne would not expect of an Interior officer. They were all cold, calculating, and single-minded. Then again, if they were going to get emotional, an execution procession would be just the place, wouldn't it?

Another stab of pain. Her arm throbbed and her neck felt stiff. Suddenly the lieutenant released her arm and shoved her roughly to one side. Unprepared for the move, Jayne stumbled and fell. Everything burned. She gripped the podium, slowly hefted herself to her feet, and faced her tormentors.

"I certainly enjoyed that, did you?" Cheryl said cheerfully. "It's important that we spend time getting to know those who live in our sector, so I'm so glad we were able to spend the last little while together." Tim laughed; Jayne gritted her teeth. "Now get your ugly face out of here and stay home. If I run into you again, I might not treat you as nicely."

Relieved, Jayne turned off the monitor and bent to retrieve her sketchbook. She started to walk away, her eyes downcast.

"Wait a minute," Cheryl said.

Jayne held her breath.

"What's that you're carrying? Your sketchbook? I should take a look at it, make sure nothing's in it that violates any articles."

No, please, not her drawings! Jayne held the book against her chest. She'd get over the rest of the abuse, but handing over her sketchbook would be giving them a part of herself.

Cheryl beckoned for the sketchbook. "Give me the book, now! Unless you'd rather receive a level four strike?"

Jayne reluctantly held it out, mortified to see it trembling in her fingers.

"I think she's going to cry," Cheryl said to Tim, watching Jayne.

Tim glanced at Jayne. "Let's just go, we've had our fun. Give her the book back." He reached for the sketchbook.

Cheryl pulled it away from him. "No, I want to look." She flipped through the pages. "Oh look, a leaf," she said in a high-pitched voice. "And here's another leaf. And isn't that cute—another leaf." *Flip.* "And another." *Flip.* "And yet another." She snorted and shook her head. "Just think, we've had a true genius living in the sector all this time and we didn't even know it. A leaf artist. Imagine." She grinned. "I don't know why you waste your time doing this, Jayne. You really stink at it."

Hot tears stung Jayne's eyes. She bit her lip—hard.

Cheryl smiled smugly and threw the sketchbook on the ground. "Pick that up or I'll strike you for littering. And then get out of my sight. I've had enough of you for one day."

Jayne swallowed and picked up the sketchbook. She turned and slowly walked away, expecting them to call her back again. When they didn't, she quickened her pace and eventually risked a look over her shoulder. They were nowhere in sight. She broke into a run and raced toward her sanctuary.

MO FOLLOWED THE flow as everyone left the auditorium, but unlike those around her, she wasn't pumping her fist in the air, cheering, or babbling on about the procession. If she heard one more person excitedly say that Finney and Thompson had attended this Military Academy, she'd scream. Cool air washed over her as she passed through the auditorium's front doors.

"Woo!" Ann shouted, making her jump. "Chalk one up for the Way!" She ruffled Mo's hair.

"Don't do that," Mo snapped, covering her head with her hands.

"Come on, Mo, you haven't cracked a smile all—oh!" She grabbed Mo's arm, pulled her off to the side of the path, and waved at someone in the crowd. An officer waved back and maneuvered his way over to them. He smiled at Ann.

"Hey there," Ann simpered, her voice suddenly an octave higher. She turned to Mo. "This is Ensign Paul Bennett. And this is Lieutenant Commander Mo Middleton."

"Pleased to meet you, Lieutenant Commander," he said, still staring at Ann.

Mo mumbled a hello.

"I met Paul at the track this morning," Ann said. "We, uh, bumped into each other when we were jogging." They grinned at each other like idiots. "What did you think of the procession?" she asked him.

"Thought it was great! And guess what? Thompson and Finney went to this Military Academy!"

Mo dug her fingernails into her palms.

"I know Thompson," Ann said breathlessly, placing her hand on her chest.

Bennett's eyes widened. "Really?"

"Yeah, she used to be a pilot. Well, she still is, but only supply. We were in the same year and flew together for a while on the *Falcon* and 72."

"Wow!"

"But that's nothing compared to Mo, here. She—"

"Ann!" Mo barked.

"Uh, she knows her, too."

"Oh," Bennett said, barely glancing at Mo. "So you want to do something?"

"Sure! Uh . . ." Ann's eyes slid to Mo.

"I'll talk to you later." Mo forced a smile. "Have fun."

"Yeah," Ann said, already walking away with Bennett.

As she wandered away, Mo wondered why she'd bothered saying anything; they wouldn't have noticed if she'd left at the beginning of their conversation. What to do now? There was no point beeping Papa or Neil or anyone else in her family. With 553 still in effect, by the time they arranged to meet somewhere away from the estate and everyone managed to make it there, it would practically be time for them to leave. She wouldn't be good company anyway. Might as well go back to her room.

When she reached the faculty residence, she slumped on the bench outside and thought about the procession. She'd been okay until the end. Up to that point, Les's appearances on the screen had been frequent but brief—mainly shots of her marching next to Finney, and with all the flowers, sometimes all Mo had made out were their cloaks. But then the close-up of Les's face as everyone sang the Song of Rymel, when Les had almost cried . . . She'd almost cried—cried!—in front of everyone. Yesterday Mo had been upset that Les had looked fine; now she was upset that Les obviously wasn't fine.

Les's struggle to maintain her composure had endeared her to those in the auditorium, who'd all moaned in sympathy, interpreting Les's emotional display as evidence of her devotion to the Way and pride in a job well done. But Mo knew better. Les was devoted to the Way and would be pleased at how efficiently Interior had handled the Chosen Violation, but she would never cry or even come close to crying in front of a crowd. Yet she had!

Mo curled her hand around her comm unit. She wanted to beep Les so badly. Les's distress may have had nothing to do with their separation—in a way, Mo hoped it didn't. She'd hoped Les hadn't moved on, but now she realized how selfish that was. She loved Les and wanted her to be happy. And she wanted to talk to her, and be with her, and have daughters with her. Argamon!

"Mo!" Ross called, coming up the path. Mo stood and started to salute, but Ross waved the gesture away. "I told you not to do that. I know I'm a commander now, but you don't report to me and I hate ceremony unless it's absolutely necessary. I'm not Commander Dunlop," she said, referring to an uptight commander on the *Falcon*.

Mo dropped her hand. "Sorry."

"Did you watch the procession?"

"Yeah, in one of the auditoriums."

"I'm all keyed up after seeing it," Ross said.

"Me too," Mo said, knowing she sounded as keyed up as a sleeping baby. The Way had triumphed, a cause for celebration. Everyone would be out partying, as Ann and Bennett probably were. If Les hadn't been at the centre of it all, Mo might not feel so deflated. She wouldn't be as jubilant as everyone else, but maybe she would have beeped Papa or Neil. Maybe she would have tried.

Ross studied her. "With everything cancelled, I'm at a loose end. We added a new combat sim last week that's rather challenging on the highest level. Want to give it a whirl?"

"You want to fly a sim with me?" Mo asked, surprised.

"We haven't flown together for years. And I'll admit that I do have an ulterior motive. I want to pick your brain about some new additions we're considering to the curriculum. Though we might not be able to talk much while we're flying. I wasn't exaggerating when I said it's a challenging sim. We can talk over supper afterward." Ross started to stroll away and motioned for Mo to accompany her. "Come on."

Mo followed her without argument. Ross had an ulterior motive all right, one that had nothing to do with the curriculum. It wasn't what she'd said; it was what she hadn't said about the procession, especially those in it. Mo was fortunate—she had people around her who cared. Did Les?

JAYNE STUMBLED INTO her apartment and made a beeline for the bathroom, tossing her sketchbook onto the sofa as she passed. She reached to open the medicine cabinet, then stopped and stared in dismay at her reflection in the mirror. Her chin, already throbbing, had turned an angry red. Good thing she wouldn't be going out for a few days, not after what had just happened. Her hand shook as she drew a bottle of painkillers from the medicine cabinet, struggled to remove the cap, and tipped several pills into her hand.

After gulping down a couple with a glass of water, she returned to the living room and eyed the sketchbook. She'd been making real progress on capturing the detail in leaves, but the sketchbook would only remind her of an encounter she'd rather forget. Blinking back tears, she ripped it to shreds. The recycling chute in the apartment's small kitchen sucked the pieces from her hands. Now she was down to one empty sketchbook. That new pair of shoes she was saving for would probably have to wait.

She sank onto the sofa in the living room with a sigh. How stupid to go outside, today of all days. She should have listened to her gut and stayed indoors. The Incident had created a different set of rules for her; pushing them was as risky as pushing the Law. Flaming military, swaggering around in their orange cloaks doing whatever they pleased.

No, she couldn't blame them. Running into her during an execution procession for a Chosen Violation had been too appealing an opportunity for her tormentors to resist. Since she'd created the situation by leaving her apartment, she had only herself to blame. It had been her fault. It always was.

MO GRABBED HER comm unit from the night table and squinted at the time—09:27. She set it back down, rolled onto her side, and pulled the blanket over her head. The creaking floors and hurried footsteps in the corridor were getting to her. She should get up, but for what? When she'd beeped Papa last night, he'd said he'd be tied up in meetings all day, so their plans were still on hold. She could beep Kary, see if she wanted to meet for lunch or an early supper. But truth be told, Mo wasn't in the mood to socialize.

Spending time with Ross had distracted her for a bit, but then she'd had plenty of time to brood on her own. And, oh yeah, to hear Les's name dropped in every flaming conversation she happened to overhear. Yesterday had been one long reminder that she no longer shared Les's special moments. What a day to remember for Les, but Mo hadn't been a part of it; she hadn't been there to cheer her on and to embrace her afterward and tell her how proud she was. No, she'd sat in an auditorium, like a stranger whose only connection to Les was a familiarity with her image on a screen. At least this time another woman hadn't screeched Les's name from the sidelines, but that would change. She and Les weren't Chosens. They'd never be together again. This drudgery known as her life wasn't a temporary state of being. She had years of this to look forward to, while pretending she cared about some woman she'd rather not meet in the first place.

Les was clearly on the way up. Her appearances on the monitors would only increase, especially since she apparently hadn't given two thoughts about how Mo would feel about it. Mo pulled the blanket off her face and balled it in her hands. She'd hear about every one of Les's career milestones and imagine the celebrations afterward, while her own milestones took place in obscurity. It wasn't fair!

Not only that, she'd overestimated her importance to Les. Had she honestly believed that Les would pine for the rest of her life, instead of striving to honour the Tradition by embracing her Chosen and her family? This was Les, right? Les had almost cried at the procession because she was proud of her role in capturing the criminal. Argamon, next time they printed a new edition of *What It Means to be Rymellan* for the Indoctrination Academies, they should put Les's image on the front cover! Yeah, Mo had been kidding herself all this time. Les would eventually view her as nothing more than a footnote, someone she'd bided her time with before Joining.

Mo sighed and rolled over again. Okay, why was she suddenly mad at Les? What else was Les supposed to do? Lie around in bed all day, like her? Disobey orders? Finney had probably shoved her in front of the monitors and made sure she was front and centre at the procession. That was who Mo should be mad at—Commander flaming Finney. From the moment she'd got her claws into—

Someone rapped at the door. Mo lay still. Whoever it was could just move along and leave her alone. Her jaw clenched when they rapped again, louder. Would they give up, already? She was on leave . . . if she wanted to take a day off from her life to indulge in a little self-pity, that was her business. After almost two years of dragging herself out of bed and making a great show of enjoying her life, she deserved one. Tomorrow she'd get back to acting as if she cared.

"Lieutenant Commander Middleton!" shouted whoever was on the other side of the door. "If you're in there, please come to the door, or I'll be forced to activate your beacon."

That got her attention. She kicked off the blanket. "Just a minute," she called as she scrambled into her housecoat. Wait a second . . . it better not be Andrew or Nathan disguising his voice. Andrew, in particular, would pull a prank like this. But she couldn't risk not opening the door. Ignoring someone with the authority to activate a comm unit beacon would likely offend someone very powerful.

She tied the housecoat's belt, swung the door open, and—a gold-cloaked courier stood in the corridor. "You are Lieutenant Commander Ramona Middleton?" he said.

Mo gaped at him. *Nod, you imbecile, nod!* She nodded.

The courier handed her an envelope, then bowed. "Congratulations."

"Thank you," she said, more out of habit than because she was coherent.

He smiled and strode down the corridor. Somehow Mo had the presence of mind to shut the door. In her hand, her fate. She turned the envelope over several times. Opening it would either shatter her dream forever or give her a reason to keep hoping. If she was the Principal, it would be a matter of waiting to see if Les also received her Papers today. If not, and her meeting wouldn't take place in C3 . . . She tossed the envelope onto the desk, sat on the bed, and stared at it.

Only a few days ago, she'd wondered who to beg to receive her Papers, positive that their arrival would bring her and Les back together. Since then, she'd doubted. To open that envelope, she needed to believe again, needed to reach inside and find that part of herself that never wavered. Les was her Chosen. She had to be. If she wasn't—no, Mo had to believe. She had to believe!

She took a deep breath, then went to the desk. Her hands shook as she carefully ripped open the envelope and slid out the sheets inside. Another deep breath, then she started to read. *Lieutenant Commander Ramona Middleton . . . pleased to inform you that I will introduce you to your Principal . . .*

Mo stopped. She wasn't the Principal. If her meeting wouldn't take place at the Chosen House in C3, it was over. Really over. She swallowed and forced her eyes back to the page. Okay . . . *introduce you to your Principal on July 10th, at 11:00 a.m., at the Chosen House in your Principal's sector of residence, C3.*

She blinked and read it again . . . *at the Chosen House in your Principal's sector of residence, C3.*

Okay, that said C3, right? Her brain wasn't translating it to what she wanted to see, was it? She traced the letter and number with her hand. C . . . 3 . . . it really did say C3! And she was certain she wasn't dreaming. But she wouldn't celebrate, not until she knew for sure. A shot of adrenaline had just resuscitated her flagging hope, but it was still only hope. It wasn't outside the realm of possibility that her Principal was another woman in C3, though that would be too awful to bear. It must be Les, and if it was, she could see Les *today*. And she could beep her right now, as she'd promised.

But what would she say? Flaming Argamon, just talk! She was beeping Les, not someone she didn't know. At least she hoped she wasn't beeping someone she no longer knew. She punched in Les's comm code and tried to slow her breathing. Les's message played. "Les, it's me. Mo. We promised to tell each other—" *Calm down!* She was talking so fast, she sounded as if she'd inhaled helium. "We promised we'd tell each other when we received Papers," she said, trying to enunciate her words. "Well, mine came. Um, today, they weren't waiting for me when the *Falcon* docked. I'm not the Principal. The funny thing is, my Principal lives in C3!"

A quaver had crept into her voice. She gulped and forged ahead. "It has to be you, right? So if—when you get your Papers today, beep me. Here are the details of my meeting, in case you want to compare them to yours." Mo read them, making sure to mention that someone named Albert Watkins was handling her case. "So beep me, okay?" she said again. "Even if you don't get them. Remember, I want to say a proper good-bye."

Her chin trembled. She disconnected, not wanting to end the message by sobbing into her comm unit. A hundred things she could have said flooded her mind. She'd say them later, in person. Until then, she'd have to keep herself busy; she didn't want to sit alone in her room, biting her fingernails and tormenting herself with the worst possible scenario: not hearing from Les at all. If Les didn't beep . . . if she wasn't Mo's Chosen and didn't honour her promise . . . Or what if Les listened to the message and desperately hoped that her Papers wouldn't arrive today? What if she—okay, enough. See? She couldn't wait alone, or she'd become an incoherent wreck.

Mo punched another code into the comm unit. "Good, I caught you before you went into a meeting," she said when Papa answered.

"I'm about to go into one."

"I have to talk to you. Just for a minute."

"Are you all right? You sound funny."

"Papa, my Papers came." He gasped. "Ten minutes ago."

"Are you the Principal?"

"No." Her eyes filled. Hope mingled with fear. "My Principal lives in C3. C3!" No reaction. "Papa?" Apparently she'd rendered him speechless. "It has to be her, right? I mean, the Way . . . it wouldn't be that cruel, would it?"

"I want you to go home," he said firmly. "I'll excuse myself from the meeting."

She was hoping he'd say that. "But what if—"

"Everyone will understand when I tell them your Papers just arrived."

"But—"

"We have plans to make. And I'll feel better if you're at home."

So would she. If Les didn't beep . . . if she wasn't her Chosen . . . Mo would need her family more than she'd ever needed them before. "But what if Les is home and it's not her?"

"She won't be home. She'll still be dealing with the Chosen Violation, probably stuck in meetings all day like I would have been." He paused. "I'll beep Adelaide, let her know what's happened and that Lesley might have to stay somewhere else for a while."

"No! Please don't do that, Papa! Don't tell anyone, okay?" If he ruined her chances of speaking to Les one last time, she'd never forgive him. "Keep this between us for now."

"Nathan might be home."

"If he is, I'll tell him when I get there. I want to make sure he keeps it to himself."

He tutted. "All right, all right, but we can't wait too long."

Hopefully they wouldn't have to. As soon as Les beeped to say she'd received her Papers, they could shout it from the rooftops. But if Les hadn't beeped by the time the sun set, Mo didn't want her entire family staring at her as the realization sank in that she'd never speak to Les again and would be forced into a relationship with a stranger—in three days!

"I'm leaving now," Papa said. "When I get home, I want to see your aviacraft there."

"I haven't even showered."

"Then get going!" His voice softened. "I'm looking forward to seeing you."

"Me too." She terminated the connection and checked her messages. None. Well, a whole five minutes had passed, and if Les was in a meeting, she'd probably turned off her comm unit.

After a quick shower, Mo checked her messages again and beeped the residence coordinator to surrender her room. She was in the middle of stuffing the few things she'd unpacked into her bag when someone knocked at the door. Mo's heart leaped into her mouth. It couldn't be—no, she'd beep first, surely. Her heart stopped racing when she opened the door to Ann.

"I'm on my way to the dining room for a late breakfast," Ann said. "You eaten yet?"

"Uh . . ."

Ann looked past her into the room. "You unpacking the rest of your stuff?"

"Um, not exactly." Mo walked over to the bed and motioned for Ann to follow her. "My Papers just came."

Ann's jaw dropped. "Your Chosen Papers?"

What else? "Yeah, my Chosen Papers. You didn't hear the courier?"

"I was probably in the shower."

"Oh." And yet her hair looked as if she'd just dragged herself out of bed. Maybe she'd spent the night with Ensign Bennett and didn't want to say. "They came about half an hour ago. So I'm going home."

Ann's face fell, then she quickly masked her disappointment with a smile. "Good. I thought I'd have to spend my entire downtime babysitting you. I have things I want to do."

Mo rolled her eyes and returned to her packing.

"I thought you'd be a wreck when your Papers came."

The wreck part would come later, if Les wasn't her Chosen.

"You the Principal?" Ann asked.

Mo shook her head.

Ann looked away, thoughtful. "Wonder what your name will be."

"There's a good chance it'll be Thompson."

Ann snorted. "Time to give it up, Mo. Seriously."

She might as well tell her. "My Principal lives in C3."

Silence, then, "No way."

Mo zipped up the bag and gestured toward the desk. "See for yourself. My Papers are right there."

Ann picked them up and read the top page. Underneath were a map to the Chosen House and a notification meeting rules refresher. "Argamon," Ann breathed. She threw the sheets back onto the desk. "I guess you won't be needing me anymore. Enjoy your life." She marched from the room.

For a split second, Mo considered not doing anything. Then she sighed and ran after her. "Ann! Wait a minute."

Ann spun around. "What?"

"Just because Les is probably my Chosen doesn't mean we can't hang out."

"You say that now."

"I mean it! Look, I know you never show up for stuff when you're on a break, but I'll send you an invitation to the notification party, okay?" She must be insane. "You can catch up with everyone."

"Well, I'll have to check my schedule, see if I'm available," Ann said, shrugging.

"Yeah, do that. Anyway, I have to go. Check your dispatches!" Without waiting for a reply, she returned to her room and tried to quell her growing excitement at the thought of celebrating with everyone at her and Les's notification party. They'd hold a joint one—it would be silly not to. She couldn't wait to dance with Les—she'd told her they'd dance again! No, she shouldn't imagine what they'd do. She knew it was irrational, but she'd always been afraid that visualizing and planning what would happen when they received Papers would jinx their chances. Though Les's Papers must be in a courier's bag by now, right?

Mo lifted her bag from the bed and grabbed her Papers from the desk. Time to go home . . . and wait.

"IN CONCLUSION, WE recommend that information be distributed to all Rymellans about the acceptable therapies and techniques employed by counsellors, along with a list of suspect behaviours to watch for. We have also included the list of articles we would like covered during the refresher examination." Hall glanced around the table. "Agreed?"

Affirmative sounds filled the room. Lesley stifled a yawn and stretched her legs under the table. Apart from a couple of quick breaks, during which she'd barely had time to dash to the bathroom, they'd been in the room since 09:00. They'd ordered in lunch.

"I'll dispatch this to the government immediately," Hall said. "Before we adjourn, I'd like to say two things. First, I'm pleased with how you've all handled the past couple of days. This morning I reviewed yesterday's sector report. Only six strikes related to Article 553. Impressive. If other regions report the same, we'll likely lift 553 tomorrow. Until then, keep up the good work." He stood. "And now the type of announcement I always enjoy making. I invited Lieutenant Commander Thompson because I thought she'd have valuable input to offer regarding our report to the government."

Lesley had been wondering. Over half the room outranked Laura.

"But that's not the only reason." He turned to Lesley and smiled. "Finney and Thompson, stand up."

She rose to her feet, resisting the urge to look at Laura.

"Commander Finney, Lieutenant Commander Thompson, I'm pleased to announce that you will both be awarded the Medal of the Protector for protecting the Chosen Tradition. Congratulations."

Everyone rose to their feet and clapped. Cries of "Good work!" and "For the Way!" filled the room. Lesley was taken aback—she hadn't done much—but she smiled and said, "Thank you."

"The Preeminent Ruler will present you with the medal at an awards ceremony to be announced soon."

The Preeminent Ruler! Mo would—Lesley continued to smile.

"At the same ceremony, Counsellor Abrams will be presented with the Commendation of the Way for her diligence. I have sent her our congratulations." Hall paused. "And that brings us to the end of the meeting. Finney and Thompson, if you would remain behind, please. The rest of you, dismissed."

After everyone else had left, Hall rounded the table to join Lesley and Laura. "Again, congratulations." He exchanged glances with Laura; Lesley had the feeling Laura knew what he was going to say next. "I continue to be impressed with your work and dedication, Lieutenant Commander," Hall said. "Commander Finney's days as a commander are running out. Next month, she'll be promoted to commodore."

Laura had mentioned her promotion when they'd lunched together last week, but in her usual self-effacing manner, had quickly moved on to another topic after confirming that she'd still head the Chosen Tradition group.

"Commander Myers will retire next year. That will leave me two commanders down." Hall assumed a more relaxed stance. "Commanders have a tremendous amount of power. Anyone who may be promoted to that rank must undergo a six-month training program. You're exactly what we look for in commanders. I'd like you to enter the training program next month, but the choice is yours. It's perfectly acceptable to not want to advance to commander. About a third of those we approach decline to advance."

"And we don't approach many," Laura added. "Only the best."

"We've had our eye on you for years, as you know. Perhaps you've already given some thought to this decision."

Lesley had. Her work would always be her sanctuary; she didn't have to pretend that it interested her. And as she'd said to Mo, having career goals, something to strive for, would give her a reason to get up in the morning. "Yes, I have. I'd be honoured to enter the training program."

Hall and Laura smiled. "Excellent," Hall said. "I'll make the arrangements. Dismissed."

"I'm having a 'the mentoree catches up with the mentor' moment," Laura said as they left the room. Lesley hoped that meant Laura was proud, and a glance at Laura's face confirmed that she was. "We'll have to remove you from the Defence and Interior supply lists. You should still have time to investigate the odd tip, and I want you to continue writing opinions. Hall wanted to keep you on the monitors, but I told him you'll be too busy."

"Thank you," Lesley said with relief.

"Don't thank me. I've only bought you some time. He'll probably bring it up again once you've completed the training program."

Then in the meantime, she'd keep her eye out for other opportunities, perhaps request that Blair assign her more cases. Unfortunately the medal news would be all over the monitors, and perhaps the presentation, too.

"Congratulations on the medal," Laura said, as if she'd read Lesley's mind.

"Congratulations to you, too. You deserve it. I don't feel I do."

Laura's brows rose. "Why?"

"I understand why you're receiving it—you head the group and you executed him. But why am I receiving it? Why aren't the other members of the group?"

"They weren't involved in the investigation to the extent that you were. You decided to move forward with the case. You were involved in every step of the investigation. They conducted a few routine interviews, that's all." Laura stopped in front of her office. "What time do you start your patrol tomorrow?"

"11:00."

"Then let's meet here at 09:00. I want to talk to you about the training program."

Lesley nodded and murmured a good-bye, then continued on to her own office. Her comm unit had been off all day; the first thing she did when she sat at her desk was check her messages. She had twenty-two! She decided to scan the list before listening to them, to see if any required her immediate attention. Most of her recent messages had been congratulatory in nature and could wait. Higgins—probably congratulatory. Thompson—Lesley would be home in a couple of hours; Mama could wait. Middleton. Middleton? She couldn't breathe. Middleton! *Lt. Cmdr. R. Middleton!* That could only mean one thing. Or was she beeping because she was sick of seeing Lesley's face all over the monitors? With trembling fingers, Lesley selected the message and played it.

Les, it's me. Mo.

Lesley started to weep.

We promised to tell each other . . . We promised we'd tell each other when we received Papers. Well, mine came. Um, today, they weren't waiting for me when the Falcon docked. I'm not the Principal. The funny thing is—

Lesley paused the message, stood, and walked to the window. *Les.* She hadn't heard that for almost two years. Two years of pushing down and locking away her feelings, struggling to keep them at bay, only to have one word instantly disarm her. *Les.* She drew a shuddering breath and wiped away her tears. So Mo hadn't been the only one clinging to the possibility that they could be Chosens. Had Lesley fooled everyone, or just herself? And now what? All she could do was try to make sense of it, try to understand how she was supposed to live the rest of her life without the only woman she'd ever loved and ever been interested in loving. Try to assure herself that the crushing sense of loss threatening to drive her to her knees would eventually subside.

She hadn't taken much leave since joining Interior. If she asked, would Laura grant her leave, effective immediately? She wanted to be as far away from C3 as she could get, didn't want even a glimpse of Mo and her Chosen. But she couldn't stay away forever. How would she make sense of this? She and Mo were only five months apart in age; they'd met before they understood they existed. Never to see her again . . . The last two years had been difficult, but she'd had hope—buried, but there. Without it . . .

Her comm station beeped. Lesley stepped toward it and peered through her tears at the screen. Hall. She cleared her throat and pressed the connect button. "Yes, Admiral."

"Can you come back to the conference room? There's one more point about the investigation I'd like to clear up."

"Of course. I'm on my way." Afterward, she'd tell Laura about Mo and request permission to go home. She wanted to pack a bag and be away from the estate as soon as possible. Later, when she'd pulled herself together, she'd listen to the rest of Mo's message and figure out what to say to her. Now she wished she hadn't promised to reply. It was over. Talking to Mo would only hurt.

But first, Hall. Lesley headed to the bathroom to splash water on her face. She studied herself in the mirror, straightened her collar, and squared her shoulders. Presentable—barely.

She could hear chatter and laughter emanating from the conference room as she approached. Hall must be in the middle of another meeting and someone had raised a question that required her input. All she had to do was get through the next couple of minutes and then go see Laura.

Hall, on his feet, motioned for her to enter. She walked in—and stopped dead. Applause and cheers filled the room. Hall walked over to the Chosen Council courier standing at the front. "I ran into a very patient courier in the lobby," Hall said, to laughter. "She's looking for you."

Blood rushed to Lesley's face.

"Lieutenant Commander Lesley Thompson?" the courier said.

She stepped forward. "Yes."

The courier handed her an envelope and bowed. "Congratulations."

The room burst into applause again. Lesley could hardly breathe. Mo . . . her Papers . . .

"Open it!" someone shouted, then another. She glanced at those gathered—Blair, Laura, the Chosen Tradition group, Woods, other colleagues with whom she worked, in the past or in the present. "Open it!" more shouted. But not Laura, who looked mortified, her hand covering her mouth.

Lesley ripped open the envelope and drew out her Papers. "I'm the Principal," she said after skimming the first paragraph. She forced a smile. It wasn't genuine. Not yet.

Congratulations and applause rang out again. "This is turning out to be quite a day for you, Lieutenant Commander," Hall said, beaming.

If what she suspected turned out to be true, he didn't know the half of it.

He turned to Laura. "I think it would be appropriate for the lieutenant commander to take a two-week leave, don't you, Commander?"

"I completely agree," Laura said, her eyes on Lesley's face. "We shouldn't have a problem finding others to fill her supply assignments. And I'm sure the lieutenant commander would like to inform her family. Let's not keep her any longer."

Hall clapped his hands together. "Dismissed."

Lesley graciously accepted murmured congratulations on her way out of the room. Forget her family, she wanted to listen to the rest of Mo's message!

Laura caught up to her in the corridor. "I tried to tell him that it might be better if you received your Papers in your office, but he wouldn't hear of it. Are you all right?"

"I might be. I want to get back to my office, have a few minutes alone."

"Sure. You beep me if you need me, okay?"

Lesley nodded absently and quickened her pace. After shutting her office door, she started Mo's message again, from the beginning. Still standing, she listened.

Les, it's me. Mo. We promised to tell each other . . . We promised we'd tell each other when we received Papers. Well, mine came. Um, today, they weren't waiting for me when the Falcon docked. I'm not the Principal. The funny thing is, my Principal lives in C3! Mo's voice started to shake. *It has to be you, right? So if—when you get your Papers today, beep me. Here are the details of my meeting, in case you want to compare them to yours.*

Lesley paused the message and drew out the top sheet from the envelope she still held, then hit *Resume*. Her excitement mounted as she listened to Mo's meeting details. The same Council member was handling their cases and her meeting would take place one hour before Mo's. Not only would Watkins not have time to meet with another Principal before Mo's meeting, but the two meetings were always held an hour apart. Karen, David, Neil, other Principals she knew—they'd met their Chosens an hour later.

So beep me, okay? Even if you don't get them. Remember, I want to say a proper good-bye.

Lesley sank into her chair, her vision blurring. There wouldn't be any good-byes today. Mo had been right all along. She'd been flaming right all along. *Mo Middleton, I love you. I flaming love you!* She wouldn't have to imagine Mo with someone else, nor would she have to try to care for someone else. Lesley lowered her head onto the desk and cried, filled with joy and shame. Yes, shame! She never should have doubted the Way. Mo hadn't.

A knock at the door had her reaching for a handkerchief. "Just a minute," she shouted.

"It's Laura," came the muffled reply.

Lesley dabbed at her eyes and blew her nose. "Come in."

Laura took one look at her and shut the door. "I was starting to worry." Her forehead creased. "You should go home. I'll go with you, if you like."

"It's okay. I'm not upset, I'm happy."

Laura raised a brow. "You don't look happy."

"Mo's Papers came today."

"*What?*"

"Her Principal lives in C3. The same member is handling our meetings and they're one hour apart. She's my Chosen." Saying it almost had her in tears again, but she managed to fight them back.

Laura swallowed. "Lesley, I—"

"Don't." Lesley rose and lifted her cloak from its hook. "I would have done exactly what you did under the same circumstances. I hope you'll come to our notification party, all of you."

"We will."

"Good." Lesley slipped into her cloak. "I'm going to the Military Academy. I'll beep her on the way."

"Um, I wouldn't go to the Military Academy," Laura said sheepishly.

"Why not?"

"She's at home."

"Oh." Lesley gave Laura a long look. "I guess I'll head that way, then. Thanks for letting me know." Without another word, she turned and left.

JAYNE READ HER Papers for what must have been the twentieth time, then sighed and let the sheets drop to the table. This was the moment she'd dreaded since the day she turned eighteen and learned that she wasn't a Solitary. When she'd turned twenty-five last month, the thought that she was old enough to receive Papers had flitted across her mind, but she'd ignored it, since it was rare to be notified so early. Yet here was her notification, in black and white, right before her eyes.

And somewhere, some poor woman had received her Papers and was probably celebrating the news with her family and looking forward to the future, not knowing what was about to hit her. What a shocking disappointment it would be when this Albert Watkins told her who her Chosen was! The poor woman would be saddled not only with the Adams name, which was bad enough on its own, but with Jayne.

Although Jayne wasn't naive enough to believe everything others said about her, she sometimes wondered if there must be some truth to the whispers. They couldn't all be wrong, could they? What if there was substance to what they said? What if she *had* inherited her parents' taint? What if she *was* ugly, and stupid, and everything else they claimed in their taunts? She'd always told herself that she had no friends because it would be social suicide to associate with her, but what if that wasn't the only reason nobody had ever taken an interest?

Now someone would at least pretend to, but Jayne wished it would be by choice, not because she was forced on the woman. She'd always been forced on people, making the rounds with reluctant yet dutiful relatives until she was old enough to live on her own. For once, it would be nice if someone other than Carol chose to spend time with her, but why would anyone want to? Even her own parents hadn't cared enough to want to see her grow up. That said a lot about her, none of it good.

If her Chosen couldn't see past her name and family history, Jayne would have to accept whatever her Chosen was willing to give. It would be nice to have some company every once in a while, someone to talk to, to walk with, to share the occasional meal. If that was all her Chosen could manage, it would have to be enough. It was certainly more than she had now, especially since Carol had Joined.

Jayne read her Papers again. C3. Home to many old families. Respectable families. Her mouth felt dry. She sipped tziva from the mug that sat at her elbow.

Someone tapped a familiar pattern on her apartment door, then Jayne heard the door swing open. Moments later, Carol bustled into the kitchen. "What's the panic?" she barked, shrugging off her cloak and throwing it over the back of a chair. "Don't tell me you've been docked your allotment again. I helped you out last time, but I can't keep doing that. Ronald won't be pleased if I hand you another bunch of credits." She frowned. "What happened to your chin?"

"Oh, I was stupid, banged it on a cupboard door," Jayne said, avoiding Carol's eyes. Hopefully her chin would look better by Friday. "Anyway, I haven't been docked my allowance." She waited while Carol plunked into a chair and poured herself some tziva, then pushed her Papers across the table.

Carol instantly recognized them. "Already? But you only just turned twenty-five." She scanned the top sheet. "When did they arrive?"

"About two this afternoon." The courier had practically thrown the envelope at her.

"Three is an odd time for a notification meeting. Notifications usually take place in the morning. I've never heard of one taking place this late."

"What do you think it means?" Jayne asked, holding her voice steady despite her fear.

Carol shrugged. "I don't know. There's probably some Chosen Council function that day and so the notifications are later." She pointed at the sheet. "Your Chosen lives in C3. That's one of the oldest sectors."

"Filled with respectable families, none of which will want me," Jayne said quietly.

Carol looked at her. "Your Chosen belongs to one of those families. That means you belong to one of them, too."

"I doubt it'll be that easy." Especially with a Chosen Violation fresh on everyone's mind.

"Maybe not in the beginning, but once they get to know you, I'm sure everything will be fine," Carol said as she returned her gaze to the sheet in front of her.

"I'll be a good Chosen to her."

Carol lifted her head again. "I know you will. And she'll eventually realize that, too. Look at me and Ronald."

"You don't have the name."

"I have the blood."

"Only on your mama's side." And Jayne's aunt never missed an opportunity to remind everyone that she was the good sister who'd had no idea there was a monster in her midst. That was the name of the game for Jayne's relatives—distancing themselves from the Incident and expressing nothing but disgust for those involved. Unfortunately their contempt extended to her. Apart from Carol, none of her relatives had bothered with her much since she'd turned seventeen. She was a walking reminder of what had happened; her mere existence sullied their reputations and names. "Carol, I'm their *child*." She couldn't distance herself. *Freak!*

Carol was honest enough not to argue. She glanced at the sheet again. "So, you'll be introduced to your Chosen in three days. Do you have anything to wear?"

"I . . . yeah, I'm sure I have something in the closet."

"And I'm sure you don't. We'll have to go to the Trading Centre."

"Carol, I—"

"Don't worry, I've been putting aside credits for this. I wasn't expecting it to happen so soon, but it doesn't matter. I have enough for a new outfit and a bit to spare. I was saving for caterers in case you were the Principal."

A lump formed in Jayne's throat. "Why? I know you said you were going to, but you were nineteen. I didn't think—I mean . . ."

"You didn't think I'd actually do it?" Carol eyed her over the rim of her mug. "Why wouldn't I? It didn't look like anybody else was going to. Anyway, it was nothing, just a few credits here and there."

"Does Ronald know?"

"Yes, he knows. He's okay with it. I told you, it's not a big deal."

"It is to me." Jayne went to Carol and embraced her, forcing Carol to set her mug on the table. "Thank you so much." A new outfit wouldn't make a difference, but Carol's gesture mattered more than Jayne could express.

"It's nothing, really," Carol said gruffly. She gave Jayne a squeeze. "I can't believe you're being Joined. You're so young." Suddenly she pushed Jayne back. "No sketchbook."

"But—"

"No. Absolutely not. You can't possibly take a sketchbook to your notification."

Jayne felt a frisson of anxiety. She never went outside without a sketchbook. What would she do with her hands?

"You'll be focused on the meeting and your new family," Carol assured her. "You won't even miss it."

She could sit on them, perhaps.

"Jayne," Carol said urgently.

"Okay. I won't take one with me."

"Good." Carol drained her mug and studied Jayne's face. "What about Robert?"

Jayne immediately forgot the sketchbook. "What about him?" she asked, sitting down next to Carol.

"Have you told him?"

When she didn't answer, Carol said, "You haven't told him, have you? Are you going to?"

"I don't see why I should."

"Come on. You have to tell him. How do you think he'll feel if he finds out by reading a public announcement?"

"I doubt he'll care."

"Of course he'll care," Carol said sharply. "He's your brother! He should hear it from you. Why don't you beep him, let him know? I'm sure he'll want to be involved. He'll want to support you."

Jayne snorted. "Robert, supportive?" That would mean he'd be thinking of someone other than himself. "And what does he know about being Joined? He's a Solitary."

"That may be, but he's older than you and he's been with Kelly for years. And he's the only person who can stand with you on the steps of the Chosen House on your Joining Day. Do you want to stand all by yourself?"

Hmm, stand with Robert or alone? Not a difficult question to answer. "I don't need him to stand with me."

"You're so stubborn, you know that?" Carol said, shaking her head. "Why don't you give him a chance? He wants to be involved in your life, Jayne. He misses you. He's sorry about what happened, he really is."

"Is he, now?"

"He knows he handled it badly."

Jayne's eyes almost fell out of her head. "Handled it badly? Is that what he said? *Handled it badly?*"

Carol placed her hand on Jayne's arm. "Calm down."

Jayne drew a deep breath and slowly exhaled.

"Why won't you agree to see him? Even once a month?"

"I saw him on his birthday," she mumbled.

"Only because Kelly practically begged you on her knees to have supper with them. And when you were there, you hardly said two words."

Jayne shot to her feet. "Well, I'm sorry my visit didn't meet everyone's expectations. I was there, okay? I didn't even want to go. And yes, Kelly begged me, not Robert. I don't know why you two won't get it through your heads that we want nothing to do with each other."

Carol opened her mouth, then clamped it shut when Jayne raised her hand. "And don't tell me again how sorry you think he is. I've heard it all before—how young he was, how he'd do it all differently if he had the chance, how he'll make it up to me. And you know what? I don't care, because I know that's you talking, not him. We both know he's not sorry. So stop trying to push us together. It's not happening, Carol. It's not." She sank back into the chair, trembling.

Carol lifted her hands in a gesture of surrender. "All right, all right. I just thought you might want him around right now."

"I have you." She looked at Carol. "I hope," she added hesitantly, mortified at her outburst.

"Of course you do."

Jayne sighed. "I don't know why you take his side."

"I'm not taking his side. I'd like to see the two of you talking to each other, that's all. You're each other's closest family."

As of her notification meeting, that would no longer be true. And yes, she'd complained about being lonely, but she'd never be so desperate that she'd let Robert back into her life.

"Okay, so you don't want to tell him," Carol said. "Do you mind if I do, just to let him know?"

"Do whatever you want. Just don't talk about him anymore."

"Fine." Carol leaned forward. "Oh, guess what Ronald heard on the train the other day."

"What?" Jayne asked, settling back to listen to Carol recount a story about Rymellans she didn't know. Anything was better than talking about Robert. If she never heard his name again, it would be too soon.

MO BIT HER thumbnail and stared out the living room window. "What time is it?"

Papa sighed. "Two minutes later than the last time you asked."

About 16:30, then. She groaned when she tasted blood and shoved her hand into her pocket. She needed that thumb to fly. "Les should have had them by now."

"She could still be in a meeting."

Or hadn't been in a meeting all day and wasn't her Chosen.

"Come sit down."

"I can't. Why hasn't she beeped?" Mo turned away from the window when Papa didn't respond.

He shrugged. "I don't know. Why don't you have a bite to eat? You barely touched lunch."

"I can't." She couldn't do anything, not until she knew one way or the other. "Who else do we know in C3 that's female, same-oriented, and the right age?"

"We've already done this," Papa said with a pained expression.

"Maybe we forgot someone. Oh, what about Julie Slater?"

Nathan, lounging on the sofa, lowered his biology textbook. "She's twenty-three."

"Oh. And you're sure Tina Lane was already notified?"

"Positive."

"Okay. What about—" Her comm unit beeped. She yanked it from its holder. *Lt. Cmdr. L. Thompson.* "It's her!"

Papa and Nathan stood. She took a deep breath and pressed the connect button. "Hi."

"I got my Papers. Our details match," Les blurted.

Her knees buckled. "Where are you?" she managed to say as Papa gripped her arm.

"Approaching the estate. I'll land next to your craft."

Mo had to ask. She'd rather work at rekindling their love than live a lie while Les despaired. "Les . . . is this still what you want?" She'd sounded tentative. "Be honest. I'd rather know the truth."

"Mo, I want this more than anything."

"Are you sure?"

"Yes! I can't wait to see you. Why don't you come meet me?"

Mo didn't need to be asked twice. "I'm on my way!" As soon as she disconnected, she started to cry. "Papa, it's true, it's actually happening," she wailed.

He embraced her. "It's about time we had a Middleton-Thompson match."

Nathan patted her back. "Congratulations."

She pulled away from Papa. "I'm going."

"Here," Nathan said, holding out a handkerchief.

Mo hastily wiped her eyes. She'd cry when she saw Les, so there wasn't much point in worrying about how she looked.

Papa followed her into the hallway. "Mo, you have to come right back. The Thompsons have to be told, we have to plan the party, they'll want to arrange the notification lunch . . ."

"I know." If it were up to Mo, they'd go right to the lake and catch up. But she could be patient; after all, they had the rest of their lives. The rest of their flaming lives! She punched her fist into the air and grabbed her cloak. "See you in a bit."

She went to hop on her bike, but decided against it. What would she do with it when she met Les? A military patrol wouldn't be too impressed with a bike left out in the middle of nowhere and would strike her, so she'd have to walk it back. Strolling arm-in-arm with Les was much more appealing. She started walking as fast as she could without running, chewing her other thumbnail while keeping her eyes peeled for Les.

Her breath caught in her throat. Was that Les, walking toward her? Argamon, it was her! "Les!" Mo broke into a run, almost tripping in her haste to reach her. She wanted to touch her, squeeze her, make sure she was real. And then she was in Les's arms, her lips on Les's neck, her cheek, pressed against her mouth; she ran her hand through Les's hair and then collapsed against her and sobbed.

Les held her and stroked her hair; Mo could feel her trembling. She raised her head and brushed away Les's tears. "We did it, Les. We survived." And nobody would ever have the power to come between them again.

Les took Mo's face in her hands. "We never should have doubted the Chosen Council. No, *I* never should have doubted the Chosen Council."

"I had my moments," Mo admitted. "But inside, I always knew. We've always loved each other like Chosens."

"And we'll always be together," Les said, touching her forehead to Mo's.

Mo nodded, dazed. It would be nice to have something pleasant sink in for a change.

Les ran her fingers through Mo's hair. "It's long."

"I'm overdue for a cut. I'll get Neil to cut it before the party." And what a party it would be! "How did you know I'd be here and not at the Military Academy?"

"Laura told me."

Laura? "Who's Laura?"

Les's brow furrowed for a moment, then she said, "Oh. Finney. Laura Finney."

Mo felt her mouth tighten. So it was Laura now, was it? They'd talk about that later. She wouldn't let Finney, or whatever the flaming Argamon she was called, put a damper on their reunion.

"I want to hear how you've been, what you've been doing," Les gripped Mo's shoulders, "everything."

"I want that, too. I mean, I've wondered how you're doing in Interior, if you like it." And about the friend Les had stayed with during last leave . . . They'd also have to discuss their careers, with her being in Defence and Les being in Interior. But again, that could wait. "And the last few days must have been insane."

"It wasn't my idea to go on the monitors," Les told her.

"I figured."

"I just hoped you were proud of me." Les swallowed.

Mo compressed her lips until she was sure she could hold herself together. "Oh, Les, of course—" Her comm unit beeped. Papa. "I know, I know, we're coming back," she muttered.

Les motioned for the comm unit and took it from Mo. "I have to tell my parents," she said to Papa. "Why don't you come over to us and tell everyone else to meet us there? We should all have supper together, start celebrating."

"That's a splendid idea!"

Les handed the comm unit back to Mo. "Do you have your Papers with you?" she asked.

Mo shook her head. "Bring my Papers with you," she said to Papa. "I'll see you there." She disconnected to forestall any argument. "Do you have yours?"

"In my inner pocket." Les sighed. "We'd better go. I do have to tell my parents. But let's walk. I'll come back for the craft later."

Mo smiled when Les stretched out her arm and snuggled into her as they strolled toward the Thompsons'. She slipped her arm around Les's waist. "Mo Middleton Thompson," she murmured, looking up at her. "It has a nice ring to it."

Les briefly closed her eyes. "It certainly does."

MO SIPPED HER juice and surveyed the dance floor, relieved that she had a minute to herself while Les danced with a cousin. A joint notification party with Les was a dream come true; she still half-expected to wake up in her bed on the *Falcon*. Fortunately Interior had lifted 553 the previous day. An afternoon party wouldn't have been the same.

Someone tapped her on the shoulder and asked her to dance. Oh well, it had been nice while it lasted. She turned around and gaped. "Are you serious?"

"It's the only way we can talk. You've been on the dance floor all night," Ann snapped.

Mo couldn't deny that. "Okay." She set her glass on a nearby table and walked onto the dance floor, muttering, "I can't believe I'm doing this."

"I'll lead," Ann said.

"Fine." She felt Ann's hand on her back. "So what do you want to talk about?"

"I was just wondering what you'll be doing. Will you be going on tour? Is Lesley transferring back to Defence?"

Mo waited until they'd completed the next dance step before replying. "No, I'm not going on tour. As for Les, I don't know. I'm not sure what's going to happen there."

"You mean you might never go on tour again?" Ann exclaimed.

"They want her to be a commander," Mo said, leaning toward Ann even though nobody else could hear her over the music. "And she seems to enjoy what she's doing. But she doesn't want to stop me from doing what I enjoy, either. So we're not sure what we'll do. All we've decided so far is that I'll sit out the next tour." She let go of Ann's left hand so Ann could spin her around, then grasped it again. "You just might see me on 72 every once in a while."

"Maybe we'll fly together."

"Maybe. I won't be flying a regular rotation—not right away, any-way." No more separations, even short ones, unless she had no choice. Les would no longer have time to fly supply for Defence, not with her six-month commander training, so Mo had replaced her on the supply list. Les had said there was always work, that she'd had to turn down supply opportunities. But would Defence want Mo to do more? And how would she and Les resolve their careers long-term? What would she do if Les remained in Interior? Mo wanted to build a home with her, not relegate her to off days.

She caught a glimpse of Les and felt herself smile. Worrying about their military careers could wait. Tonight she felt optimistic about the future; somehow they'd work it out. She'd rather have this problem than others she could have faced—such as how to accept someone other than Les as her Chosen. "I don't want to leave Les right now," she said, refocusing on Ann.

Ann snorted. "Mo, she's your Chosen. You won't have to worry about her fooling around on you while you're flying a rotation."

"I wouldn't!" Why did Ann always have to reduce relationships to sex? "I meant that I don't want to buzz off and fly rotations after we've just been separated for almost two years."

"Oh." Ann paused. "I guess it'll be a while before we hang out when I'm off."

"The Military Academy is less than ten minutes away. If . . . you think you'll still be there." Mo interpreted Ann's lack of response as confirmation that her room at the faculty residence would be her home for the foreseeable future. "You're on a three-week rotation, right?"

Ann nodded.

"Beep me next time you're off. I'll see what I'm doing." She was in a generous mood. Plus, Les's impromptu two-week leave would be over by then.

"Yeah, okay," Ann said, though she didn't sound very enthusiastic about the idea.

"If you'd rather spend your time with Ensign Bennett, I'll understand. Where is he, anyway?"

Ann frowned at her. "What do you mean? Why would I bring him here?"

"I don't know, I thought maybe—"

"He was a bit of fun, that's all. I'd forgotten about him until you brought him up."

"Sorry," Mo mumbled, not knowing what else to say. They finished the dance in silence, then parted and clapped for the band. Ann wasn't a bad dancer; Mo's toes had survived unscathed.

The band segued into its next piece. Oh no, a slower tempo. Everyone around them started to waltz. Mo stared at Ann in horror. Ann shrugged. "We might as well."

Suddenly Les was there. "Do you mind if I have this dance with Mo?" she said to Ann.

"No, go ahead," Ann said, to Mo's relief. "Thanks for rescuing me."

Rescuing *her*? "Thank you," Mo murmured to Les. "You have impeccable timing."

Les smiled. They positioned themselves and were about to fall into step with the music when Mo saw Ann standing at the edge of the dance floor on her own. She felt smug; at least *she* had a dance partner. But Ann looked lost and a bit uncomfortable, and had kept to herself most of the evening. She'd skulked around the ballroom and observed, rather than participated. Ann not having anyone to waltz with shouldn't bother Mo, but it did.

She pulled away from Les and scanned those around her. "Andrew!" she shrieked, waving her arms about. Les quickly moved to the left to avoid a punch in the nose.

On his way off the dance floor, Andrew turned and backtracked. "What?"

"Remember I introduced you to Ann earlier? The lieutenant over there." Mo nodded toward Ann.

He followed her gaze. "Yeah."

"Ask her to dance."

"What? She's old," he said, pulling a face.

"Excuse me? She's the same age as me."

"Well, yeah. Old," Andrew said. Les smothered a grin with her hand.

Mo knew he was teasing but still wanted to slap him. "Just do it, okay?"

He sighed and slumped his shoulders. "Okay. But only because it's your party." He shuffled toward Ann.

Mo rolled her eyes, but instantly forgot about him when Les pulled her into an embrace. "It's your notification party, too," she said into Les's shoulder as they swayed to the music. Despite the part of her that had always believed they were Chosens, she'd never expected to be at Les's notification party, giddy with joy. If Mama were here, tonight would have been perfect. A couple coming onto the dance floor caught her eye—Finney and her Chosen. Make that almost perfect.

Mo had silently fumed when Finney had offered congratulations but no apology. Maybe expecting an "I'm sorry" had been unreasonable, but an "If I'd known, I wouldn't have separated you" would have been nice. And regardless of whether Les remained in Interior, Finney would be part of their lives. To Les, she was Laura. They were friends, though Mo wondered how genuine the friendship was on Finney's side.

What better way to watch someone than to be her friend? Every time Finney—or rather, Laura—came up, Mo had to bite her tongue. Curious, how Finney had stayed on as Les's mentor when she could have backed out, and then had ended up as Les's commanding officer. And Les had stayed with her while Mo was on leave—again, the perfect setup for Finney. Frankly, Mo wouldn't care if she never saw Finney again, but Les would be hurt if the friendship wasn't real. At least Finney couldn't touch them now. Mo could afford to sit back and see if Finney still had time to mentor Les, to see her when off-duty, or if she was suddenly too busy.

She closed her eyes. Forget Finney; she was in Les's arms the night before the Chosen Council would give them to each other. "Should we ask tomorrow if we can hold the Joining Ceremony right there and then?" she asked dreamily, then felt the vibration of Les's chuckle.

"The Chosen Council might agree, but my mama won't. She'll want a grand ceremony, with half the sector in attendance."

"Can we at least commission the house so we can move into it the moment we're Joined?" She didn't mind staying overnight at the Thompsons' or having Les stay with her, but couldn't wait for them to have their own home.

"We'll see what land I get."

It had to be almost 01:00; Alan and Adelaide would present Les with a deed soon. Mo remembered when Mama and Papa had surprised her with land on her eighteenth birthday. She opened her eyes and raised her head. "I wish my mama were here. She would have been so pleased." She swallowed. "Do you think we can visit her soon? I haven't gone yet this leave." She'd paid her respects every leave, slipping onto the estate when Papa had assured her that Les would be on duty.

Les stroked Mo's cheek. "Of course. We'll go as soon as we can."

"I guess you haven't visited since we separated." She'd felt compelled to search for Les's name on recently slotted articles near Mama's resting place, but had never spotted it.

Les looked away for a moment, then met Mo's eyes. "I've visited. I go every few months. But I didn't want to ruin your visits, so I never slotted anything. I've felt bad about it, but I can't hurt your mama. I can hurt you."

Mo melted inside, but then guilt snaked through her. She hadn't thought of Les when she'd slotted articles. "Did you see my articles?" she asked faintly.

"I didn't look. I couldn't."

"I should have thought—"

"No, no," Les said, shaking her head. "She's your mama. It's only right that you were thinking of her. If I'd been in your boots, I would have done the same."

Mo's eyes welled; she squeezed them shut so she wouldn't blubber and rested her head on Les's shoulder. Every time she thought she couldn't possibly love Les any more than she already did, Les said or did something that proved her wrong.

Too soon, the dance ended. As Mo clapped, Alan and Adelaide strode onto the stage. The musicians put down their instruments and filed off for a well-earned break; one handed Alan a microphone as she passed him. Alan raised his hand to quiet everyone. Mo patted Les's arm. "I'll wait here for you," she said, then looked at Les in surprise when Alan called both her and Les to the stage.

Hand in hand, they made their way through the crowd, drowned in applause, and stood next to Les's parents. Mo surveyed the faces peering up at her—her family, friends, and fellow pilots. When they teased her about the big, goofy grin on her face, she'd laugh along with them. Yeah, she was deliriously happy. What a change from just a few days ago.

Alan began to speak. "On behalf of the Thompson and Middleton families, I want to thank you all for coming tonight. We're celebrating not one notification, but two. How often does that happen?" Another round of applause answered his question. "Lesley and Mo have important appointments tomorrow morning," he said, to much laughter, "so we'll be leaving you shortly. But we have the ballroom until three, so the party isn't over. I hope you stay and continue to enjoy yourselves."

Cheers and whistles greeted his words.

"As you know, Lesley is the Principal of her Joining, and so my Chosen and I have a presentation to make to her tonight." He faced Les. "Before I hand the microphone to your mama, I just want to say that I hope you and Mo live a long and happy life together and that you have . . ." He faltered, clearly fighting tears. A smattering of applause grew to a supportive crescendo. Alan drew a deep breath. "I wish you many daughters," he said hoarsely, then quickly handed the microphone to Adelaide, who looked as if she were about to grab it from his hand.

"Thank you, Alan," Adelaide said as Les hugged him. She swept her arm toward Les and Mo. "I'd say the Chosen Council has outdone itself this time."

"Yes!" the crowd shouted as one.

"The Thompsons and Middletons have been neighbours for many generations. Our children have played together, grown together, and now will Join together. Two strong, respectable families will now become one. I can't tell you how pleased I am that Lesley and Mo will Join. Mo, we watched you grow along with our daughter. Welcoming you into our family as our Chosen daughter will be effortless because we already love you and consider you part of our family."

A chorus of "Aw" rose from the crowd. Mo shot Les a sidelong glance. Maybe she *was* dreaming, because Adelaide had almost sounded sentimental.

"And now, the presentation." Adelaide turned to Les and accepted a folded piece of paper Alan had pulled from his inner jacket pocket. "Lesley, this is a deed to land on the Thompson estate, land you now own. I'll echo what your papa said—may you and Mo lead long and happy lives and have many daughters."

She handed the deed to Les, who unfolded the paper and read it. Les's face flooded with blood; she looked sharply at her parents. Mo tensed. Had they given her only a small plot of land, or a piece located in a far corner of the estate? Karen had received the land owned by Adelaide's late uncle, a prime location with a stately house and enough real estate to hand down to her children. Only one of the uncle's children had been a Principal, and he'd decided to live elsewhere. Les embraced Adelaide and murmured into her ear. Ever polite, Les would hug Adelaide no matter what land she'd received. Mo couldn't wait to look at the deed.

When Les wordlessly handed it to her after hugging Alan, Mo skimmed it and understood. They'd not only given her more than enough land to build a house and pass down to children, but also part of the lake. Maybe this signaled a change in Adelaide's attitude toward Les. Nah, that *would* be dreaming; Adelaide never let honesty get in the way of appearances. Still, she and Alan had been incredibly generous. Mo stepped toward Adelaide to thank her, but then Les turned to address everyone.

"I also want to thank you for coming tonight," Les said. "After the events of the past week, I'm sure you can all appreciate how wonderful it is to stand here and celebrate the Chosen Tradition." More shouts, cheers, and applause. "This is a joint notification party." She smiled at Mo. "I won't embarrass Mo by telling you how I feel about her."

"No, it's okay—go right ahead," Mo shouted.

Les grinned and shook her head as she waited for the resulting merriment to die down. "Like I said, I won't embarrass her by telling you how I feel, but I will say that when I'm introduced to my Chosen tomorrow, it will be the happiest moment of my life." Uh-oh, now Les looked like Alan had minutes ago. Mo wasn't surprised when she cut her comments short. "Good night, everyone." Les waved and handed the microphone to Adelaide.

"The band will resume playing in ten minutes," Adelaide announced before turning the microphone off and setting it on one of the musician's chairs.

"I can't believe they gave us part of the lake," Mo said when Les slipped her arm around her shoulders and steered her toward the steps, apparently eager to get off the stage. Les motioned for Mo to give her the deed and read it again, maybe to convince herself that it was indeed true.

Papa met them at the bottom of the steps. "Time to go," he said briskly. "We have to be up tomorrow. I'll meet you outside."

Mo turned to face Les. "I'll thank your parents properly tomorrow, at our notification lunch." She squeaked out the last part in excitement. Les seemed at a loss for words. "I better go. Next time I see you . . ."

Les bit her lip and nodded. They studied each other, then shared a kiss, a sweet, gentle kiss. Anything more would embarrass Les. "I'll see you tomorrow, at the Chosen House," Mo squealed.

She ducked through a side door to avoid being delayed by well-wishers, but couldn't resist a glance over her shoulder. Les stood watching her. Mo smiled and wiggled her fingers, then tore herself away.

She'd desperately miss Les, but not for long. Tomorrow they'd stand in the Chosen House, where Albert Watkins would inform them that the Chosen Council had selected them for each other. They would Join, build a home together, and have daughters—daughters they'd love and cherish and bring up true to the Way. No more uncertainty; no more separations. She was Les's and Les was hers. Nothing would ever come between them now. Nothing could.

JAYNE THREW THE blanket aside in frustration, sat up, and turned on the lamp. By now it must be almost three in the morning, and she still hadn't slept a wink. Good thing her appointment was in the afternoon, though she planned to take an early train to ensure she arrived on time.

Giving up on sleep for the time being, she padded into the kitchen and poured a glass of water. Several mugs sat on the counter, waiting to be washed. After Carol and Ronald had left around eleven, she'd returned to sorting through her drawings, looking for two or three to show her Chosen, ones of which she was proud. Then she'd realized the futility of it and gone to bed.

She could be the most beautiful Rymellan alive, the most intelligent woman to ever grace the planet, and her Chosen would still see only her name. What difference would a few drawings make? Did she seriously think her Chosen would care, that her Chosen would think, *Oh, Jayne isn't worthless after all?* Tomorrow her Chosen would see the daughter of two depraved criminals. She'd see actors in those hideous masks, the "Adamses" stumbling around the stage during the Festival of the Way. She'd hear every announcement and speech made over the past few days in which "Adams," "Chosen Violation," "weak in the Way," and "worst crime in history" had been mentioned in the same breath. All while hoping her notification meeting was only a bad dream.

Her drawings weren't any good anyway. Carol said she liked them, but then, she would. Jayne's final report from the Learning Academy had stated that she spent far too much time sketching, considering how little talent she had. The report had contained other criticisms, such as "too quiet" and "never interacts with her peers or participates in group activities." Carol had laughed over that last part and had told her to ignore the entire report, but the sketching remark had stung. Jayne had never forgotten it.

She gulped down the water and set the glass next to the mugs. Getting herself keyed up wouldn't help her sleep. She climbed back into bed and reached for the sketchbook that was never far away, flipped to an empty page, and . . . nothing. Sleep wasn't the only thing eluding her tonight. Sighing, she tossed the sketchbook onto the floor and switched off the lamp. Hopefully her lack of inspiration would be temporary, but who knew what tomorrow would bring? Sketching had always soothed her; she could lose herself in it and forget for a while. But would it still offer that solace after tomorrow? If her Chosen hated her . . .

Why couldn't she have been a Solitary? How would she live with someone else? Her apartment was small, but it was her own little haven. Nobody called her names in here or glared at her disdainfully. No matter what she faced when she ventured outside, she could return home and feel safe, as she had after her latest run-in with the lieutenant. But soon she'd have nowhere to hide, nowhere to be alone until she'd gathered enough strength to weather the next bombardment. She'd share space with a Chosen who resented her presence and wished she'd die, thereby releasing her from a commitment she despised. And then there was her Chosen's family. Would they accept her, or would they stick her in a corner during family occasions and pretend she didn't exist?

Jayne was lonely now, but she was also alone. She'd learned that she felt worse in a room full of people than she did when she was by herself. When she was alone, she didn't have to watch as others smiled and joked with each other, touched each other fondly, and shared their concerns and triumphs. Her loneliest times had been at the Indoctrination and Learning Academies, surrounded by others her age. Here, in her apartment, she could fool herself into thinking she wasn't missing anything, that she was content to spend most of her time amusing herself. That it didn't matter to her that she could die and nobody would notice.

Well, Carol eventually would. And now her Chosen would too, and would likely rejoice, having honoured the Tradition even though she'd hated and resented Jayne from the moment she'd met her. No article could force love, compassion, and kindness. As long as they remained together to the bitter end and— Jayne swallowed. Her parents hadn't . . . what if she *was* like them? Maybe her Chosen had good reason to be afraid, to distrust, to expect the worst from her. Maybe she wouldn't disappoint her Chosen in the long run, after all.

Fighting panic, she turned over and balled the pillow in her hand. At this rate, she'd never sleep, and tonight might be the last night she could truly dream.

LESLEY LANDED HER aviacraft in the holding area for C3's Chosen House, then tugged at her collar; her dress uniform always felt tight around her throat. She smiled at her parents. "Ready?"

"Are you?" Mama asked.

"Of course I am. After all this time . . ." A lump formed in her throat. She swallowed; it wouldn't do to lose her composure before they were even inside.

"Ah, yes," the young Rymellan at the reception desk said when they presented themselves after hanging their cloaks. "I'll let Albert Watkins know you're here." He swivelled in his chair and spoke a few words into his comm station.

A slightly balding man on the plump side bustled into the reception area. "I'm Albert Watkins," he said, beaming. "I recognized you immediately, Lieutenant Commander. Welcome to C3's Chosen House. It's an honour to meet you."

"Thank you," Lesley said, a little overwhelmed by his effusive manner. He belonged to the Chosen Council; she was a lowly lieutenant commander. "But the honour is mine."

He inclined his head.

She turned to her parents. "These are my parents, Adelaide and Alan." Her siblings were waiting at the Thompson home; Mo's siblings would soon join them there. Only parents were allowed to accompany Chosens to notification meetings.

Watkins nodded to them. "If you'll follow me, please."

To Lesley's surprise, he led them to a room that was already occupied. The woman sitting near the desk at the front smiled up at them. "This is Counsellor Morris," Watkins said. "I asked her to be present with us today, as Article CT54 permits me to do. Please sit down."

A counsellor? Lesley lowered herself stiffly into a chair. Perhaps Watkins routinely involved a counsellor. Any family would be pleased to have their daughter Join with Mo. Nothing about her background would shock or disappoint—quite the opposite. And in this case, he must have guessed that the two families already knew each other, given the proximity of their estates. He might even know about her and Mo. The counsellor wouldn't have to do anything at this meeting besides offer congratulations—unless Mo wasn't her Chosen! Lesley tensed, then forced herself to relax. Watkins would meet with Mo next. Mo was her Chosen.

She felt foolish. She knew her Chosen's identity and already loved her, yet she was ready to jump out of her seat. Imagine how Rymellans meeting their Chosens for the first time must feel!

Watkins opened a file and arranged several papers in front of him. After what felt like hours, he lifted his head. "I suppose we should begin. Counsellor Morris, feel free to jump in at any time."

He appeared hesitant, almost apprehensive. Though Lesley expected good news, her stomach churned. Mama shifted in her chair.

"Lieutenant Commander, when you were at the Indoctrination Academy, do you remember any mention of triads?" Watkins asked.

What an odd question. Perhaps he thought a mini-lecture on some aspect of the Chosen Tradition would help everyone relax. "A brief mention," she said. "And since then, I've become more aware of the articles in the Tradition that pertain to them." Well, she remembered a conversation with Laura a few years ago, during which they'd briefly touched on triads.

"Of course you'd know of the articles," Watkins quickly said. "You're an Interior officer."

Lesley crossed her legs. "I don't know the details. Since we currently don't have a triad, there's no—" She suddenly understood the reason for the counsellor's presence. No, it wasn't possible. Not her. Not Mo. "You're not saying . . ."

Watkins nodded. "Yes."

She sat speechless, blindly reaching for Papa's hand. When his hand gripped hers, she clung to it.

"Lieutenant Commander Thompson, are you all right?" Morris asked.

She wasn't but nodded numbly.

"I'm not," Mama said. "What's going on? I don't remember anything about triads at the Indoctrination Academy."

"You wouldn't," Watkins said. "Triads are only discussed as part of the Level Five same-oriented curriculum, since they're only possible with same-oriented Joinings. Of course, now that we have one, that will change."

"A triad suggests three," Mama said, frustration evident in her tone. "What does that mean here?"

"I have two Chosens," Lesley murmured, finding her voice.

Now Mama had apparently lost hers.

"Two Chosens?" Papa echoed faintly.

"Yes, that's what a triad is," Watkins said. "A Joining of three Chosens." His explanation met stunned silence. After glancing at Morris, Watkins held up an image of an inverted triangle and touched each tip of the triangle with a pencil. "Each point is a Chosen. The lines of the triangle represent the best match for each Chosen. As you can see, a triad is formed when each Chosen is equally the best match for the two other Chosens in the triad." He lowered the diagram. "They're rare. Having two equal matches for a Chosen is unusual. It's almost impossible for those two best matches to also be the best match for each other."

"Not impossible enough!" Mama snapped. "Why haven't I heard of three Chosens being Joined before?"

"As I said, it's rare. We Joined the last triad 232 years ago."

"So Lesley will Join with two Chosens?"

"Yes."

Papa sucked in his breath. "I'm finding this very hard to understand. A Joining is between two Chosens. It seems unnatural to Join three. If my daughter wasn't involved, I'd wonder if it was against the Way."

Watkins leaned forward. "I assure you that triads are natural and not against the Way. The Chosen Tradition has included articles about them for many years."

"Though how the Tradition treats them has evolved over time," Morris said. "In the past, some Rymellans viewed them with suspicion. When we announce this triad, history may repeat itself. Some may initially react the way you did."

"Except they won't know my daughter, like I do," Papa said, frowning. "They won't be so quick to change their minds."

"Your daughter has an excellent reputation. The Council is pleased that she's the Principal." Watkins looked at Lesley. "Lieutenant Commander, you have our full support. We'll do whatever we can to help you."

"We'll remember that when the Thompson name is being dragged through the mud," Mama muttered, too low for Watkins to hear, but Lesley caught it.

"The best you can do is support your daughter and her Chosens," Watkins said to Papa. Lesley felt Papa squeeze her hand.

"You haven't said much, Lieutenant Commander Thompson," Morris said. "What do you think about being in a triad?"

She didn't know what to think. Two Chosens? How would a triad work in practice? The rings, living arrangements, children, sex—dear Argamon, the three of them wouldn't have to do it together, would they? She wouldn't *have* to sleep with her other Chosen, would she? And would Mo? No, any articles to that effect would be unenforceable. Anyway, there was no way she would share Mo with someone else. Ever. Just the thought made her want to break something. They belonged to each other, period. Her other Chosen would have to accept that. *Other Chosen* . . . And Mo had another Chosen . . .

Her mind froze. She was assuming Mo belonged to the triad. But what if notifications for triads were handled differently and she wouldn't meet the other triad members today? Nothing else was turning out the way she'd expected; perhaps the Chosen Council had summoned Mo to meet someone else. Before she tried to make sense of anything, Lesley wanted to know for sure that Mo was her Chosen. "I have questions about how the triad is supposed to work," she said. "But right now, I'd like to know who my two Chosens are."

"Of course." Watkins moved the triad diagram aside and lifted a sheet of paper. "Your first Chosen is twenty-six years old and resides in Sector C3. She belongs to the military."

Lesley's heart skipped a beat. It had to be Mo. It had better be.

"Her papa is a member of the government and runs his own tailoring business. Her mama is deceased. She has five siblings. Two are Chosens, three are Solitaries. I believe you know her." Watkins lowered the paper and smiled. "Her name is Ramona Middleton."

"Thank goodness," Papa said as Lesley let out the breath she'd been holding.

So it wasn't a complete disaster; she and Mo were Chosens. As for . . . the other one . . . she could almost feel sorry for her. The woman would have been better off a Solitary. Lesley couldn't think of any other circumstance in which she'd consider that true.

Watkins set Mo's information sheet on top of the diagram. He heaved a sigh, then lifted another sheet and squared his shoulders. Morris's chair creaked as she straightened. It almost looked as if they were bracing themselves. "Before I reveal the name of your second Chosen, I want to remind you that the Chosen Council selected this Chosen because we determined that she's the best match for you, equal to Ramona," Watkins said. "Please try to bear that in mind."

Lesley glanced at Papa in alarm. His smile might have reassured her if it hadn't looked so forced. Nor did she find solace in Mama's grim expression. The triad was unwelcome news to all of them, but while she and Papa were trying to put on brave faces, Mama's displeasure was plain.

Watkins cleared his throat. "Your second Chosen is twenty-five years old and resides in Sector E6. Both her parents are deceased."

"What a shame," Papa murmured. "Was it an accident?"

"We'll get to that in a moment," Watkins said. "She has one sibling. He's a Solitary." He hesitated, then looked at Lesley. "Her name is Jayne Adams."

Lesley felt a shimmer of shock, as she always did when she heard the name "Adams." But she usually heard it as part of the phrase "Adams Incident." Her mind needed extra time to understand what it meant in this context. "Are you telling me that one of the Adams children is my Chosen?" she asked, every bone in her body resisting the notion.

Watkins licked his lips. "Yes."

"No," Mama breathed.

The blood drained from Papa's face. Lesley pulled her hand from his and leaped to her feet. "That's impossible! I'm strong in the Way. We're a respectable family. And I'm supposed to believe that an Adams is my best match? Equal to Mo?"

"Sit down, Lieutenant Commander," Watkins said quietly.

"You haven't explained to me how this is possible. I'm not sitting down until I understand. Explain!"

"Sit. Down. Remember where you are. Do I have to beep Commander Finney?"

Papa pulled on her sleeve. "Sit down, Lesley." He sounded tired, defeated.

"We don't need Commander Finney," Morris said as Lesley sat and glared at Watkins. "Everyone is understandably shocked. Lieutenant Commander Thompson is merely trying to digest the news."

Digest the news? Lesley would have laughed if she wasn't so horrified.

"The Council determined that Jayne Adams is your Chosen using the same methodology it used to determine that Ramona Middleton is your Chosen," Watkins said, setting the sheet down. "You can't accept one as your Chosen and not the other."

"And it's not a reflection upon you or your family," Morris added. "We all know you're strong in the Way. And no one would dispute the respectability of the Thompson family."

"Until now," Mama muttered. Then louder, "First you tell us that Lesley belongs to a triad. Then you tell us that one of her Chosens is an Adams. Is that it, or do you have any other surprises up your sleeve?"

Watkins' eyes bulged. "I beg your pardon. You are speaking to a member of the Chosen Council and everything we're discussing is in accordance with the Chosen Tradition. I—"

"Again, this is a huge shock to everyone," Morris said, cutting across him. "I'm sure the same things would be running through your mind, if you were in her position."

Watkins still sat stiffly. "That may be, but it doesn't hurt to remind everyone of what we're doing here."

"That's just it, though," Mama said. "We came here expecting to hear the name of our daughter's Chosen. Just the one, mind. We expected a Chosen who, on the surface at least, seems to be a good match for her. I have a hard time believing that the daughter of two sick criminals is a match for *my* daughter. And what we've heard goes against everything I've been taught."

Watkins' face reddened. "But it doesn't. Triads have been a part of the Tradition for ages. And I assure you that Jayne Adams is your daughter's Chosen. Surely you don't doubt the Chosen Council? *That* would go against everything you've been taught."

"He's right, Mama," Lesley said, wanting to defuse the situation. Arguing with him would get them nowhere, except perhaps to an execution site. "If we—I—don't accept . . . her as my Chosen, it would bring every Joining on Rymel into question, and it would bring Mo as my Chosen into question, and I know without a doubt that Mo's my Chosen."

Watkins bowed his head toward Lesley. "Thank you."

She nodded in return, but inwardly seethed. Despite knowing he was only the messenger, she hated him. *Hated* him.

"The Council understands that belonging to a triad may be a challenge. As I said earlier, we're pleased that you're the Principal. It gives us hope that this triad will be as successful as the last one."

"And it will ensure that the Adamses don't threaten the Way any further by reproducing," Lesley said, a hard edge to her voice.

"What do you mean?" Watkins asked, his brow furrowing.

"It's obvious, isn't it? There's something wrong with the Adams line. First two Chosen Violations, now a triad. Its taint is spreading. Well, it ends here. The brother's a Solitary and she won't be reproducing."

"You won't have children with her?"

Lesley folded her arms. "Is there an article that says I have to?"

"Well, no," Watkins admitted. "But the triad isn't her fault."

"Perhaps not. But even though someone can't be blamed for being ill, if they knowingly pass on their illness to others, they're no longer blameless. It's too much of a coincidence that an Adams is involved in a triad. As I said, there's obviously something wrong with the Adams line. To protect the Way, it would be best that she not have children, and I'm in a position to see that she doesn't. She won't be having *my* children, and I'm confident that she won't be having Mo's, either."

"To refuse her children would not be within the spirit of the Tradition."

"It would be within the spirit of protecting the Way," Lesley countered.

Mama smirked. "That's the first sensible thing I've heard since we entered the room. Apart from hearing that Mo is your Chosen," she added softly, patting Lesley's knee.

Watkins frowned. "But not the best attitude for the Principal of the triad to have. As the Principal—"

"I will accept her as my Chosen! At the same time, I'll protect the Way. Don't you dare suggest that I should have a different priority." Lesley stared at him, challenging him to contradict her.

Morris interjected. "We're getting off track. Talk of children is premature." She turned to Watkins. "You brought up the lieutenant commander being the Principal. Let's continue along that vein and discuss the rest of the day."

Watkins tore his gaze away from Lesley and looked past the Thompsons. "You'll be introduced to Ramona—Mo," he amended, glancing at Lesley, "at eleven."

"Will I be present when she's told about the triad and the identity of her other Chosen?" Lesley asked.

"I believe we can be flexible here," Morris said to Watkins. "I don't see why you can't introduce Mo to her Principal and then tell her the rest. Having the lieutenant commander present may help."

Watkins pursed his lips. "You're right, nothing says we can't introduce one Chosen and then proceed from there. So yes, you'll be there."

Lesley silently thanked Morris. "Good." And afterward, she and Mo would be left to deal with everything. What a mess it had all turned out to be. Today was supposed to be their perfect day, the start of their life as Chosens. Now it was ruined, their lives were ruined, everything—ruined.

"At 3:00, I'll introduce you all to Jayne. We thought it would be best to give you and the Middleton family some time to absorb everything before you meet her. But keep the triad and the identity of its members to yourselves until Jayne has been informed."

"What about the rest of the family?" Mama asked. "We'll all be having lunch together, since we thought we'd arrive home with two Chosens and that would be it."

"You can tell your family, but nobody else," Watkins said, scowling.

"We're not exactly dying to tell anyone," Mama said under her breath.

Watkins didn't hear her. "You should return here by 2:45 and enter through door C."

"What about Mo?" Lesley asked.

"She should come with you, of course. You'll both be introduced to Jayne." He paused. "I think we'll conduct Jayne's meeting in the same way we'll conduct Mo's—introduce you to Jayne and then tell her about the triad."

She could hardly wait. "So I will be present when you introduce Mo to her?"

"Yes." Watkins' face softened. "Look, I know this is a huge shock—two huge shocks. But if anybody can deal with this, you can. You have to believe in the triad for it to work. Your two Chosens will need you to believe."

Too many conflicting thoughts and emotions jammed Lesley's mind for her to formulate a coherent response. She'd try to sort everything out later, with Mo.

"I'm now officially advising you that, since you know the names of your two Chosens, you are bound to them from this point forward in accordance with all the articles in the Chosen Tradition. You are now in a position to commit a Chosen Violation if you violate any article in the Chosen Tradition that applies to a Joined Chosen. Do you understand and accept what I've just told you?"

"I understand and accept it," Lesley said numbly.

"Then if you would please read this over and provide your confirmation . . ." Watkins spun the comm station monitor at the left edge of the desk toward her. Lesley read the single paragraph it contained, which included the names of her Chosens, then pressed her thumb against the display in the designated spot until the station beeped.

"Thank you," Watkins said, spinning the monitor back to its original position. He surveyed the Thompsons and smiled weakly. "Well, this is certainly an exciting and historic day. I have this information packet for you about triads." He handed Lesley an envelope. "I want to bring two points to your attention. First, as a triad, you have two years to schedule your Joining Ceremony."

That quick ceremony she and Mo wanted would have to wait.

"Second, Article CT134 is an important one for triads. I've included detailed information about this article. Please read it over, and if you have any questions, any at all, don't hesitate to beep me or Commander Finney. I'll be meeting with her after we've announced the triad to make sure she understands it."

Lesley almost laughed out loud. Laura would love being called in to have an article of the Chosen Tradition explained to her. She'd probably end up explaining the article and describing its history to *him*. Suddenly it wasn't funny. What would Laura think of the triad, of one of Lesley's Chosens being an Adams? Her opinion mattered to Lesley, on both a personal and professional level. And how would Lesley's peers react? Would she still start the commander training program, or would she suddenly be unsuitable?

Watkins checked his notes one last time. "I think that's it for now. Do you have any more questions before we close the meeting?"

Lesley glanced at her parents and wondered if she looked as pale and bewildered as they did.

"Very well. Let's stand," Watkins said when no one responded.

Lesley stood and dropped the envelope onto her chair. Everyone moved together so they could join hands. "Disobedience means death. Death to those who commit a Chosen Violation. Death to those who disobey. Death to those who violate the Way. Death to those who violate the Way. Death to those who violate the Way!" They clapped half-heartedly. Lesley didn't bother to muster a smile.

"I'll see you again in about half an hour. Once I've told Mo that you're the Principal, I'll beep you and let you know what room we're in. All the rooms are located along this hallway." Watkins gathered his papers and left the room. Morris trailed after him, closing the door behind her.

Lesley swung to pace the room. "We have to accept her. We have to," she said, more to convince herself than anyone else. Her mind turned to Mo, who at that moment would be on her way to the Chosen House, filled with hope for the future. Lesley wanted to sit and weep, but fought it by stopping in front of Papa and focusing on him, willing him to say that it would be all right, that the situation wasn't hopeless.

But his face told her that he couldn't give her what she sought. "You still have Mo. Mo is your Chosen. Don't forget that," he said with a sigh.

His words deepened her despair. "But there's someone else, for both of us. Who expects to hear that at their notification meeting? Who expects their Chosen to have another Chosen?"

"I know."

"Today was supposed to be the start of our life together as Chosens."

"It is."

"Not the way we envisioned it," Lesley said bitterly.

"No."

"So what are we supposed to do, Papa? What are we supposed to do?"

He shook his head. "I don't know. But I know you, and I know Mo. I have to believe you'll make it work, and you'll have to believe that too. Somehow you'll have to come to some arrangement with Adams that you can all live with."

"Or you could have Adams executed," Mama said.

Lesley and Papa turned to her. The envelope Lesley had left on her chair lay open on Mama's lap. In her hand were several sheets of paper. "Remember he mentioned Article CT134? Listen to this." She read from the top sheet. "Article CT134. If the Principal and one of the other triad members believe that the third member will have a destabilizing effect on the triad, therefore threatening the viability of the triad and the Way, they may petition for the execution of the third member. However, the case must be made and the execution performed before the triad Joins." Mama lifted her head. "So if you and Mo can make a case that the triad won't be successful if Adams remains alive—and let me tell you, any advocate could scribble a case on a scrap piece of paper in five seconds—your problems are solved. You won't have to Join with her. You and Mo can live the life you've always wanted."

"We can't do that," Papa snapped.

Mama looked at him. "Why not?"

"Adelaide, we're advocates. We're supposed to preserve the spirit of the Way, not trample all over it when it doesn't suit us."

Mama tapped the paper with her finger. "This article exists for a reason."

Papa nodded. "Yes. From what you've read, it should be exercised if the triad is in trouble. This one isn't."

"It has an Adams in it!"

"And? We don't execute children for the crimes of their parents, with good reason. This woman hasn't done anything to threaten the triad. We haven't even met her yet and you want to send her to an execution site." They glared at each other.

"Executing her would be harsh, don't you think?" Lesley said, hoping to break the tension by shifting their attention to her.

"Would it?" Mama's eyes remained on Papa. "What sort of life will she have with you and Mo? You two love each other. She'll be in the way and she'll know it. And do you really want to be Joined to an Adams?"

"It's not a matter of want, Mama. If it was a matter of want, I would have Joined with Mo the moment she turned twenty-five. And if Adams was my only Chosen, I would have no choice but to accept her."

Papa nodded. "She has a point. Since when can Rymellans reject their Chosens?"

"Since when do Rymellans have two Chosens?" Mama shot back.

"If she wasn't an Adams, we wouldn't be having this conversation, at least not yet," Papa said.

"So you're not ruling it out, you just think it's too early to discuss it." Mama slid the sheets back into the envelope. "I can agree with that. So fine, we'll go along with this," she waved her hand around, "triad, for now. But I'll be watching her, and the moment she steps out of line, we'll have this conversation again. I won't let her destroy our family."

A chill ran up Lesley's spine. "Don't worry, Mama, I know what my priorities are." One she'd made clear to Watkins, and the other was protecting Mo. Her hands clenched. If Adams threatened Mo in any way . . .

She reclaimed the envelope, sat down, and began to read how the articles of the Tradition applied to triads, aware of her parents reading over her shoulder. Later she'd go over everything she could find on triads with a fine-toothed comb, learn exactly what her obligations were to Adams.

As she read the information on Article CT134, an ugly thought formed in her mind, one she initially rejected, but that kept coming back. What if Adams wasn't really her and Mo's Chosen? What if the

Chosen Council had thrown them together in the hope that she and Mo would exercise CT134?

MO GRINNED IN anticipation when Watkins pulled a sheet from the pile in front of him. "Your Principal is twenty-seven years old and obviously resides in Sector C3," Watkins read. "She's a member of the military. Both her parents are advocates. She has two siblings. Both are Chosens. I believe you know her." He smiled. "Her name is Lesley Thompson."

Tears stung Mo's eyes as she bowed her head. Papa squeezed her shoulder. "That's wonderful," he said. "The Middleton family is pleased."

"I thought you might be," Watkins said.

Mo looked up. "When can I see her?"

"Whenever you're ready."

She stifled a snort. She'd been ready for this moment for years. The counsellor Watkins had insisted be present wouldn't be needed. "I'm ready."

Watkins pressed a button on his comm station. "We're ready for you, Lieutenant Commander. Room Four."

"We're on our way," Les said, to Mo's delight. Morris opened the door. When Les walked into the room a minute later, Mo stood and broke into a smile. Her Chosen. And so dashing in her crisp white uniform.

Her smile faded. Les's answering smile was strained and her eyes were a little too bright. Behind her, Adelaide and Alan stood grimly. Mo didn't understand. Last night at the party, everyone had looked forward to this moment. What could have happened in the meantime? Had Les argued with her parents? Suddenly the counsellor's presence worried her.

She relaxed slightly when Les embraced her and whispered "I love you" into her ear, but her uneasiness returned when Les continued to cling to her. Something was tearing Les apart, and whatever it was, Alan and Adelaide knew about it. Finally Les let her go.

"Welcome to the family, Mo," Adelaide said. She tucked an envelope she'd been holding under her arm, grasped Mo's shoulders, and kissed her cheek, but she looked unhappy. Alan's face told the same story. Confused, Mo sat down. Les sat next to her; Papa and Les's parents sat behind them.

"Normally I'd ask you to say hello to each other, but I can see that's not necessary in this case," Watkins said with a small smile.

Nobody responded to his comment. Mo could feel the tension in the air. She'd expected this meeting to be a joyous one. Instead, an undercurrent of negative emotion ran through the room, as if the Thompsons were going through the motions, pretending they were pleased when they weren't. Actually, they weren't doing all that good a job of pretending. Mo wanted the meeting to be over so she could find out what was going on. "I guess you need my confirmation and then we can be off," she said to Watkins.

"Not quite. I have more news for you today."

More news?

"Can I tell her?" Les said.

Watkins glanced at Morris, who nodded. "All right. But not the name."

Mo grew more confused when Les said, "Before I tell you, I want you to know that nothing will change between us. Nothing at all."

She swallowed and braced herself, though for what, she had no idea. Watkins had said they were Chosens.

"Do you remember learning about triads when we were at the Indoctrination Academy?" Les asked. "Well, not learning, exactly, because they were only mentioned in passing." She sounded bitter. "But do you remember hearing about them?"

Vaguely. "You mean when there are three Chosens? I think Indoctrinator—" Her breath caught. "No. Not us."

Les closed her eyes and nodded.

This was a sick joke, right? "No. Not us. This can't be happening to us."

"I don't understand it either," Les murmured.

"No, we can't have another Chosen. We love each other too much. No, no." Please, if she said no enough times, would it go away?

"What's all this talk about another Chosen?" Papa asked, leaning forward.

Mo wouldn't answer him. She wouldn't say it—that would make it real. She looked at Les. Her Chosen. Nobody else's. Hers!

"A triad is a Joining of three Chosens," Watkins said. "It can only happen with same-oriented Joinings."

"I've never heard of this before," Papa said, sounding indignant.

"Neither had we," Adelaide said. "We just found out."

"Triads are natural, though rare. There are articles addressing them in the Chosen Tradition," Watkins said. "I have a diagram I can show you."

"We don't need the diagram," Papa said firmly. "The Middleton family fully supports the Chosen Tradition and the Chosen Council. If you say they're natural, then they are."

Mo turned to gape at him.

"So you don't have any problem at all with the notion that your daughter has two Chosens?" Morris asked as Adelaide and Alan exchanged a sidelong glance.

"I would never question the Chosen Council."

Oh, now she understood. Mo faced forward in disgust. She couldn't wait to hear what he really thought once they got out of this flaming room. More importantly, what did Les think? Les always tried to honour the Way. Would she expect them to have a relationship with this other Chosen? Children? She'd said nothing would change between them, but . . .

"I'm sure you'd like to find out who your other Chosen is," Watkins said to Mo.

She bit her tongue and slipped her hand into Les's.

Watkins pulled another sheet toward him. Mo waited, aware of Les's eyes upon her. "Your second Chosen is twenty-five years old and lives in Sector E6. Both her parents are deceased. She has one sibling. He's a Solitary." He took a deep breath and looked at Mo. "Her name is Jayne Adams."

Mo tightened her grip on Les's hand. "Adams? As in Adams Incident? Is that why her parents are dead? Because they were executed?"

"Yes."

"Now just a minute," Papa sputtered.

Watkins shifted his gaze to Papa. "Yes?"

After a long silence, Papa mumbled, "Nothing."

"Mo, are you okay?" Les asked.

"No. I don't know. We need to talk about it." She stood. "Can I provide my confirmation now, please?"

"Don't you have any questions, Lieutenant Commander Middleton?" Morris asked.

Oh yeah, she had a bunch of questions, starting with how in the flaming Argamon this could have happened. But why ruin this wonderful meeting by being dragged to an execution site? Her questions would wait until she could scream them. She smiled at the counsellor. "Not at the moment."

Watkins nodded. "Then I'm now officially advising you that, since you know the names of your two Chosens, you are bound to them from this point forward in accordance with all the articles in the Chosen Tradition. You are now in a position to commit a Chosen Violation if you violate any article in the Chosen Tradition that applies to a Joined Chosen. Do you understand and accept what I've just told you?"

"I understand and accept it." Watkins spun the screen toward her and Mo pressed her thumb against it until the station beeped.

"Thank you. Here's an information packet about triads." Watkins handed Mo an envelope. "I'd like to highlight two points. As I explained to Lieutenant Commander Thompson . . ." He trailed off when Mo raised her hand.

"Would it be all right if my Principal explained it to me later?" she asked. "I'm not sure I can handle explanations right now."

"I don't see why not. Oh, but I do have to tell you that you'll meet Jayne at 3:00."

"We'll all come back together," Les said.

"Good. Let's close, then." He stood and motioned for everyone to do the same. As they joined hands and said the *Words Every Rymellan Knows*, Mo felt as if she were at a farewell ceremony, not a notification meeting. "See you all at 2:45!" Watkins said cheerfully.

They all followed Watkins and Morris from the room. After they'd left the Chosen House, Mo spun to face everyone. "I hate to ask this, but would you mind taking the train so Les and I can talk about what just happened?" she said to Papa, Adelaide, and Alan. She and Papa had taken the train to the meeting; they'd all intended to return to the Thompsons' together in Les's aviacraft, looking forward to a lavish lunch to celebrate the Joining of their families. "We might not get another chance before we have to come back, and we really need to talk." And Les better not contradict her.

"We don't mind," Adelaide said. "In fact, maybe we'll take a little stroll before we get on the train, figure out how to deal with this."

"Yes, let's," Papa agreed.

Adelaide handed Les her envelope. "You take this. We can't look at it on the train."

"We'll wait for you near the estate's main entrance," Les said. "I want to be there when everyone else hears the news." She grabbed Mo's hand. "Let's go."

They strode to the aviacraft in silence. As soon as they were safely inside and Les had slid the craft's door shut, they tossed their envelopes onto a seat and embraced.

"I don't understand it," Mo murmured. "Today was supposed to be it. We were supposed to belong to each other."

"We do." She felt Les shake her head. "I can't believe we're in a triad with an Adams."

Mo pushed her away and stepped back. "That's all you care about? That she's an Adams? You don't care that we're in a flaming triad?"

"No, that's not what I—"

"I wouldn't care if we were in a triad with someone in a family so respectable, they regularly broke into the Song of Rymel," Mo shouted, shaking with anger. "I don't care who the third Chosen is, I care that she flaming exists!"

"Okay, okay," Les said, holding up her hands. "I feel the same way. I wish we weren't in a triad. But you have to admit, being in one with an Adams doubled the shock."

Maybe, but the Adams part bothered Mo a lot less than the triad part. "Why did this have to happen to us? I can't believe it. First the separation, then nothing but joy that we're Chosens, and now this? And we're talking the rest of our lives, here. It's not like we'll go to the notification meeting this afternoon and then it's over." Mo slapped her hands against her thighs. "What are we going to do with her?"

"Nothing. Between our meetings, I read the information Watkins gave us. We don't have to have a relationship with her."

"Are you sure?"

"I'll read more about the articles and I'll talk to Laura, but I'm pretty sure."

     RYMELLAN 2

"Then what's the point of this flaming triad if we can act like we're not in one?"

"We can't act like we're not in one," Les said, closing the gap between them and taking Mo's hands. "We *will* be Joined to her. I guess the expectation is that we'll eventually . . . love her."

"Well, we won't. I'll never love anyone else, especially her. So what's the point?"

Les bit her lip.

"What?"

"Article CT134."

Mo scrunched her face up in concentration. "It must be an obscure article, because it's not coming to me."

"It is. It's specific to triads, sort of a safeguard, I think. According to the historical information, triads have been volatile. Most have ended at execution sites."

"Oh, great!"

"So they added something of a loophole to the Tradition. CT134. Here." Les picked up one of the envelopes, rummaged inside it, and pulled out a sheet. "Read this."

Mo read the information about Article CT134 and handed it back to Les. "So if you and I were to make a case, she'd be executed?"

Les nodded.

"Les, I'd like the woman to disappear, but not like that."

"What if that's what they want us to do?" Les said carefully.

"Who? Our parents?"

"No, the Chosen Council. Don't you think it's odd that out of all the women we could have ended up with in a triad, we ended up with her? I didn't tell you about this, but Admiral Hall was talking about the Adams children just the other day. He said that after the Incident, some Rymellans petitioned to execute the children, but the overseers denied the requests. Maybe they're hoping we'll manage one execution for them."

She couldn't believe Les, of all people, would suggest such a thing. "That's hard to believe, Les."

Les's face tightened. "So you think she's really our Chosen, then. Yours and mine. An Adams."

When she put it like that . . . "I don't know. But if they want us to exercise the article, don't you think Watkins would have steered us that way? I mean, he didn't even discuss the article."

"You didn't give him a chance," Les said. "He told me about it. And he may not be in on it. I'd imagine anyone who knows would be high up. We're talking about fiddling with a Joining, here."

Mo swallowed and glanced around. Nobody could hear them, but she still felt uncomfortable. "Or she could be our Chosen and this triad is legitimate." That felt uncomfortable, too.

"I don't know what to believe, to be honest." Les sighed. "If she is our Chosen, well, that's unbelievable. If she isn't . . ."

"I hate to say this, but let's assume she is."

Les's brow furrowed. "Why?"

"Because despite what's happened, I'd like to see my twenty-seventh birthday. So let's forget we had this conversation." Mo drew a shaky breath. "And as far as CT134 goes, not unless we're absolutely sure. I already hate her. I hate this triad, hate what they've done to us. But I won't execute her unless she somehow forces us to that. I can't." Her chin trembled. "I want our daughters to be proud of us, Les. They won't be proud if we kill her because we love each other. We wouldn't be proud of ourselves, either. We'd see her every time we looked at each other. Executing her would rip us apart."

And the triad might do the same. They wouldn't lead the charmed lives she'd imagined, supporting each other's careers and raising daughters. To have everything she'd hoped for given to her and then snatched away . . . the last few happy days had been nothing but a cruel illusion, a puff of smoke that had dissipated the moment Les said the word triad.

Bewildered, Mo sank into one of the passenger seats and rested her head against the seat in front, but her eyes remained dry. The enormity of the day's events hadn't sunk in. She couldn't cry when everything felt so surreal. She could be angry, though. Oh yeah, angry about how unfair it was. For almost two flaming years they'd suffered alone, honoured the Way, desperately tried to find meaning in lives without each other. If they'd ended up with other women, they would have honoured their Chosens to the bitter end, done all they could to limit the pain and emptiness to themselves. They didn't deserve to be in a triad. This time, the Way was asking too much. Too much.

The seat in front of her squeaked. She felt Les's fingers in her hair. "We'll do whatever's best for us," Les said softly. "We might be pressured to execute her."

Mo lifted her head. "Les—"

"I know. I don't want to do it without good reason either. It would go against everything I believe. So we'll have to stick together." She touched Mo's cheek. "That's the only thing that makes sense today. That we're together."

Les's comm unit beeped. "We're heading to the train station," Adelaide said. "Are you on your way?"

"We will be in a minute."

"Make sure you are. We have to tell everyone the news and have lunch." The connection went dead.

Les shook her head and slid the comm unit into its holder. "Let's just try to get through today," she said with a sigh. "Perhaps after we've met her, we'll have a better idea of how things will go, have a sense of whether she'll be difficult or respect our relationship."

Now Mo felt like crying. It didn't matter. Execute her or Join with her—either could, and probably would, destroy her relationship with Les. Today was supposed to bring an end to any possibility of losing Les. But there was no end. She could never relax. Not anymore.

LESLEY OPENED THE door to the Thompson home with trepidation. As she stepped over the threshold, Jason popped into the hallway, then darted back into the living room, calling, "They're back!" Those inside chattered excitedly.

"I'll make sure all the caterers are in the kitchen or dining room and shut the doors." Mama strode down the hallway.

Lesley tightened her hold on Mo's hand and walked into the living room. Concern erased the smiles on the faces of those waiting. "What happened, did you fight on the way home?" Mary asked.

The few chuckles quickly died when a scowling Michael walked in, a sombre Papa on his heels. Lesley threw her information packet onto an end table—Mo had left hers on the craft—and scanned the room. Only the children weren't here. Barbara's parents had taken Jacob and

Lynn for the day and had kindly offered to take Karen and William's son as well.

Neil rose from the sofa, his eyes wide. "What's going on?"

"Wait for Adelaide," Michael said. Several fidgeted impatiently or cleared their throats.

Finally Mama strode in and nodded. "They can't hear us."

"So what's going on?" Neil said again.

"The notification meeting was horrible," Michael said.

"What do you mean?" Jason asked. "Obviously Lesley and Mo are Chosens."

"Yes," Michael said, moving farther into the room so everyone could see him. "But they have another Chosen."

"I don't understand," Barbara said as the others exchanged puzzled glances.

"They're part of a triad." Papa said. "Three Chosens, equally matched. I'd never heard of them before this morning. It can only happen with same-oriented Joinings. Apparently the last one was 232 years ago."

"It's a triangle," Mama added, tracing the shape in the air with her hands.

"Triads were mentioned during my training," Karen said. "I think it came up when I was doing a course on reproductive technology. If I remember correctly, the last triad had quite a few daughters."

"You mean all of them will be Joined?" Nathan asked.

"That's the idea." Mama grimaced, whispered to Papa, and squeezed herself onto the sofa next to Karen.

"Is this a joke?" Jason asked, dropping with a thud into a chair.

Michael sighed. "I wish it were. And you haven't heard the best part yet."

Jason frowned. "I'd think this triad is bad enough."

Mo squeezed Lesley's hand; she squeezed back.

"It's got to be the other Chosen," Neil said. "Who is it, Papa?" He looked at Lesley and Mo. "Who is it?"

"Ever heard of the Adams Incident?" Michael said before Lesley had a chance to speak. "Well, their daughter is Chosen sister to all of you. Congratulations to us."

Everyone gaped, then started talking at once. Jason leaped to his feet. "No! This is outrageous!" he bellowed; the others grew silent and stared. "You'll have the Adams name." His mouth moved; he looked as if he were struggling for air. "The Thompson and Adams names will be linked," he whispered hoarsely.

Lesley sucked in her breath. She hadn't given any thought to the names. Chosens normally had two last names, though they only used the Principal's socially. Perhaps they could choose which two names to retain, but somehow she doubted it.

"And you can bet this whole triad is her doing," Matthew said, his mouth twisting. "There's something wrong with that family. Every time an Adams is involved in a Joining, something goes wrong."

"And it's not just your family affected, Jason," Mary said. "Ours is, too."

"It's not fair!" Jason shouted, his voice regaining its vigour. "Why our family?"

"Why not our family?" Karen asked.

Jason's hands clenched. "Because we're a respectable family that doesn't consort with criminals, that's why!"

"Any family's daughter could have been a match."

"But *we* ended up with her. Her parents were sick criminals. She's their flesh and blood and they brought her up, so she's probably sick too. We don't deserve her."

"No family does," Matthew said.

"Oh, come on. You haven't even met her," Karen said.

Mary grimaced. "I wish we didn't have to. I wonder if she looks like them."

Jason shuddered. "A walking reminder." He looked at Lesley and Mo. "If I were you two, I'd keep an eye on her day and night. Or maybe you shouldn't. She'll do us all a favour if she commits a Chosen Violation."

"Jason!" Papa hissed.

"I'm only saying what every Rymellan will think when they hear about this."

"That's not what I think," Karen said. "Does that mean I'm not Rymellan?"

"Karen, maybe you should stand by your family instead of someone you've never met," Matthew said.

Karen frowned. "Why do I have to take sides? And that's my point. We haven't met her."

"My Chosen is doing what the Tradition expects of her," William said, placing a protective arm around Karen's shoulders. "Accepting her sister's Chosen into the family."

Jason snorted. "That's easy for you to say. After all, you're not a Thompson by blood. You won't care when everyone starts to whisper."

William recoiled as if he'd been struck. Karen shot up, her face red. "And that's what it's all about, isn't it, Jason? What everyone else will think."

"When they find out my sister is in some type of unnatural arrangement with an Adams? Yes, Karen, I'm a little worried about what everyone will think," Jason shouted.

"Worried about Lesley, or about you?" Karen shouted back.

"Enough!" Mama roared. "This isn't helping."

Jason threw up his arms and stepped away, muttering. Karen folded her arms and sat back down. "What's her name?" she asked.

It took Lesley a few seconds to understand the question. "Jayne."

"How old is she?"

"Twenty-five."

"Yeah, I guess that's why it took so long for us to get our Papers. We were waiting for her to turn twenty-five," Mo said bitterly.

"He didn't tell us what she does," Papa said.

Lesley turned to him. "You're right, he didn't." If she hadn't felt so overwhelmed during the meeting, she might have noticed and asked.

"So what happened during the meeting?" Andrew asked. "What did he say? I mean, how did you find out? Did he tell you about Adams first, or the triad?"

"I hope he told you about Mo first, Lesley," Nathan said.

Lesley nodded. "He did. Well, first he told us about the triad." She recounted her meeting up to the point when Watkins had confirmed that Mo was her Chosen. "Then he moved on to the other Chosen. He didn't seem eager to—"

"Yes!" Jason suddenly shouted. Everyone's attention shifted to him. Lesley's heart sank. He hadn't been listening to her; he'd opened the information packet from Watkins. From the triumphant look on his face, she could guess what he'd just read. "It's okay, everyone," he said excitedly. "We can execute her. That will solve everything. No triad. No Adams. Only Lesley and Mo."

Lesley snatched the sheet from his hand. "I know about the article."

Shock crossed his face. "If you already knew, why didn't you say something? Why did you just stand there and let us all think we'd be related to an Adams?"

"What article? What are you talking about?" Neil asked.

Mama jumped in when Lesley hesitated. "An article that allows Lesley and Mo to execute her."

"Only if they can make a case that a triad with her won't survive," Papa quickly added.

"There you go." Jason smiled and held out his hands, palms up. "Problem solved."

Some smiled back at him; others mumbled their disagreement. "You can't execute someone because they're inconvenient," Karen said.

Jason tutted and frowned at her. "We won't be. The fact that she's an Adams means the triad won't survive."

"I completely agree," Mary said. "A triad would cause a stir on its own. Who knows how Rymellans will react to a triad with an Adams in it?" She pointed at Lesley and Mo. "If you exercise your right under this article, the whole unsavoury situation can be resolved before anyone even knows about it."

Papa vigorously shook his head. "A case has to be made that she *is* a threat. Not that everyone *thinks* she is a threat."

"You're splitting hairs," Jason said.

"You're a decent advocate. You know I'm not splitting hairs."

Jason shrugged. "I could make a case either way."

"You can't do it. You're too close."

"No, but I know plenty of advocates who would be willing to prepare a case, especially one that will dispose of a threat of this magnitude to the Way."

"Dispose of a threat to the Way?" Karen said incredulously. "Jason, you're talking about executing someone, not throwing something into a recycling chute."

Jason rolled his eyes. "Don't be so soft. Lesley, just give me the word and I'll contact an advocate who specializes in the Tradition."

"You can't tell anyone about the triad until all Chosens have been notified," Lesley reminded him.

"I can set up an appointment."

"Lesley, don't do it," Karen said. "At least get to know her first."

"I can probably get you an appointment for tomorrow," Jason pressed. "Any advocate will clear his schedule for this. After you've met her today, you can talk, make up your minds, then see the advocate. It won't take long to prepare a case. As Mary said, it'll all be over before anyone knows about it. Perhaps the Chosen Council won't have to announce the triad at all, since it won't be a triad by the time it announces this week's notifications."

"You're talking about a capital case, Jason, which advocates rarely handle," Papa said. "It will take longer than a day to prepare," he held up his hand to forestall Jason's protest, "no matter how foregone you think the conclusion is."

"At least we'll be able to say we're preparing a case when everyone asks what we're doing about it." He turned to his sister. "Lesley?"

"Excuse me, I believe the article states that Les and one of the other Chosens have to present the case," Mo said. "So don't I get a say in this?"

"Of course you do," Matthew said quickly.

"Good. We, Les and I, just talked about it. We're not making a decision right now. We've just been told we're in a triad and we'd like some time to understand what that means before we talk about executing anyone."

"Don't be such a baby!" Mary spat. "You don't have to waste time understanding what it means. There's a solution staring you in the face, if you'd only have the guts to take it."

Mo's face tightened. "It involves executing someone. If you don't mind, I'd like more than thirty seconds to make up my mind."

"I would have thought you'd want to be rid of her."

"Not like that."

"Two military officers and you're both flaming stupid!" Jason snarled, tapping his temples.

"We're not saying we'll never consider the article, we're saying it's premature," Lesley said through clenched teeth.

"Try to keep in mind that this Adams woman is as much Lesley and Mo's Chosen as they are each other's," Papa said. "You shouldn't doubt the Chosen Council."

"That's a bit strong, Alan," Michael said; Lesley had almost forgotten he was there. "What I see is the Chosen Council in a difficult situation. Every once in a while these triads occur and the Council has to spout that they're natural. But three Chosens? Please! The Council, in its wisdom, added CT134 to the Tradition for a reason. It allows families like ours—respectable families—to deal with an undesirable situation in a manner that doesn't violate the Way."

"It's as if they wrote it for this very situation," Mary said. "And let's face it, how much of a case would the advocate need to prepare, given who it is?"

"Exactly," Jason agreed. He turned to Mama. "What do you think?"

Mama caught Lesley's eye before answering. "I agree with Lesley. Am I happy she's in a triad? No. Do I want an Adams as my Chosen daughter? Definitely not. But do I think she should be executed? I'm not sure yet. Let's see how it goes."

Jason sighed and shook his head. "Should I set up an appointment?" he asked Lesley again.

"I agree with my Chosen," she said, managing to smile at Mo. "No appointment."

Some groaned; others nodded. "You're doing the right thing," Neil said.

"No, you're not!" Jason said, his hands clenching again. "Don't you understand why this article exists? Even the Chosen Council recognizes that triads are undesirable. And you're in one with an Adams. Open your eyes, Lesley!"

"It's too early to make a decision," Lesley said slowly.

"Well, I don't know what it'll take for you to come to your senses, but I'll tell you one thing. I'll eventually Join and have children, and no child of mine is going anywhere near an Adams. I'm positive I won't be the only one who'll feel that way. So who would you rather turn your back on? An Adams, or everyone else?"

"You can only speak for yourself, Jason," Barbara said softly.

Lesley wasn't so sure. News of the triad and the identity of the third

Chosen had split both families down the middle. If Rymellans who loved her and Mo wouldn't accept the triad and Adams, how would Rymellans in general react?

"I'm disappointed with you, Mo," Mary said. "Doesn't our name mean anything to you?"

"How can you ask that?" Mo exclaimed as Lesley squeezed her hand and moved closer to her.

"You don't seem very interested in maintaining its respectability."

"Adams will use the Thompson name socially, not the Middleton name," Papa said.

Mama sighed.

"That might be, but how will I explain to the sector that my daughter is involved with an Adams?" Michael asked.

Mo spun toward him. "Is that all you care about? Your next run for the government?"

"Don't act as if my concerns are trivial. I'm the one who'll be here dealing with the consequences while you're off flying a patrol somewhere."

"And what about Mama?" Matthew said.

Mo shrank against Lesley. "What about her?"

"Have you thought about what she would want?"

"Don't start with that, Matthew," Michael said.

"Papa—"

"Don't." Michael held Matthew's gaze until Matthew looked away.

"Look, we're not making a decision right now," Lesley said, wanting to bring the discussion to a close before Mo got hurt. "Let's drop it and have lunch. We have to be back at the Chosen House for 14—um, 2:45. Mama, what will we do about supper? I assume she'll be coming back here."

Jason's eyes bulged. "Are you serious? You're bringing her here, to the estate?"

She didn't have much choice. "We're not hosting her for lunch, so you'll have to meet her over supper."

"I won't. If you think I'll eat with that woman, you can forget it."

"You won't meet her?" Lesley asked him.

"No," Jason said, his face grim.

His answer stunned her. "If you can't do it for her, do it for me and Mo."

"I am doing it for you and Mo. I won't help you endanger yourselves. You're in shock and operating on automatic. Once you've had time to think, really think, you'll thank me for not being there. You'll see."

"I won't be there either," Mary said.

"Anyone else?" Lesley asked quietly.

Matthew raised his hand. "Count me out."

"I'll be there," Nathan piped up.

Lesley wanted to hug him.

"You'll be there, right Papa?" Mo asked.

"Yes, yes," Michael said, his mouth pinched.

"So will we," Karen said. Andrew, Neil, and Barbara nodded in agreement, though Andrew looked unsure.

"It's good to know where everyone stands," Lesley said in disbelief.

"I don't think we should have her here for supper tonight," Papa said.

"What?" Lesley gasped. From the corner of her eye she saw Jason gloating, while Mama gaped.

"Hear me out. I propose that we have her for supper tomorrow, instead. Just the, uh, triad, me and your mama, and Michael."

"William and I would like to meet her," Karen said.

"I know, but it'll be embarrassing to bring her tonight," Papa said. "We'd have to explain why half of you don't want to meet her. And it will be intimidating for her. She'll be by herself."

"You could always have a picnic at the Wall of Offenders," Matthew said.

Papa's voice cut through the snickers. "And now I'm even more convinced that a quiet supper without all of us would be better, after we've all had a chance to sleep on what's happened. And she can bring someone with her tomorrow, so she won't be alone."

"Her brother," Lesley murmured.

"Oh, so now there will be two Adamses here. Why don't we just open up the estate to every criminal out there?" Jason said.

Lesley closed her eyes. The entire day had turned into one unending nightmare and she'd only been in a triad with Adams for a couple of hours. If it was always going to be like this, CT134 might not be such a bad idea. "I like your idea, Papa, let's invite her for supper tomorrow. And now let's go through to the dining room. I'm sure lunch is ready to be served." Without giving anyone a chance to reply, she steered Mo into the hallway.

"What are we going to do, Les?" Mo moaned. "What are we going to do?"

Lesley rubbed Mo's back. "I don't know," she whispered. "Let's just get through today."

JASON STOOD NEAR an open second-floor window and watched as the group returning to the Chosen House started out for Lesley's aviacraft. "Good luck!" someone—it sounded like Neil—yelled. Lesley looked over her shoulder and waved, then said something to Mo. Scowling, Jason pulled out his comm unit, typed a quick dispatch, and sent it. Moments later, he read the replies and grunted in satisfaction.

When he could no longer see Lesley and those with her, he headed downstairs and slipped out the back door. Mary and Matthew soon joined him. They strolled farther across the grounds, away from any curious eyes peering out a back window. "So how will we stop this insult?" Matthew asked. "We've got to do something. They're both too soft."

"Maybe they're just overwhelmed," Mary said. "It's a lot to take in."

"That may be, but they're military officers who should be capable of making a decision under pressure, especially one that's in the best interests of themselves, their families, and the Way."

Mary kicked a stone off the path in disgust. "I can't believe Papa. I thought he'd stand up for Mama's name."

"Give him a chance," Matthew said. "He has to play along today. The Chosen Council wouldn't appreciate it if he didn't show up with Mo. They might consider that a sign of disrespect they couldn't ignore. The same goes for Adelaide and Alan. Anyway, he's not the one we need to convince. Lesley and Mo are."

"I'm positive they'll exercise the article," Jason said. "They just need time to think."

Mary raised her brows. "Or perhaps a little push?"

Jason's eyes narrowed. "Meaning?"

"Meaning that if they were presented with a compelling case for execution, I'm sure they'd act. Especially Lesley. If she can be convinced that the Way is threatened if Adams remains alive . . ."

Matthew nodded. "You're right. She'll do whatever it takes to protect the Way, including persuading Mo."

"Once the shock wears off, she'll talk to Mo about executing. I'm sure of it," Jason said.

"And we should be ready with a case so that no time is wasted when she does come to her senses," Mary said. "Then again, why wait? Let's give her a case to help her along."

"But she and Mo have to request that a case be prepared first," Matthew said, his brow furrowing.

Jason shook his head. "No, they don't. I read the full text of the article. They have to authorize its presentation, but anyone can prepare a case."

"And the longer they delay preparing a case, the longer they have to form an attachment to the woman." Mary's face hardened. "The Adams woman is not only a threat to the Way, she's a threat to them. We need to do whatever we can to help them make a decision and make it quickly, before her influence contaminates them. Or do you want to see *them* at an execution site?"

Jason blanched and pulled out his comm unit. He searched the code directory for the name he wanted. Moments later, a strong voice emanated from the unit. "Phillips here."

"Advocate Phillips? This is Jason Thompson. We met at a lecture a few months ago."

"Yes, I remember. How are you?"

Jason forced a chuckle. "I'm not sure. I was wondering if I could set up an appointment with you for sometime tomorrow. I'd like you to prepare a case on behalf of my sister, Lesley."

"Uh . . . I'm quite booked."

"It's urgent. I can't give you any details right now, but you'll understand when we meet."

"I'm intrigued. And since it's for the lieutenant commander, I'll squeeze you in." Phillips paused. "How does half past four sound?"

Jason glanced at Mary and Matthew. "I'll go," Mary mouthed, pointing to herself.

"That's fine. Um, I'll have someone else with me. Two names will go on the case, and the other person will represent the second party."

"The lieutenant commander and the other party won't be with you?"

"No. I'll explain everything tomorrow."

"All right. Half past four tomorrow, then."

"Thank you. Good-bye." Jason terminated the connection. "If we're lucky, this'll all be over in a few days," he said to Mary and Matthew.

They smiled.

JAYNE STOOD IN front of C3's Chosen House and gazed up the steps that led to the entrance. She'd arrived in C3 two hours ago. That had left plenty of time to worry about the notification meeting, now only minutes away. Part of her wanted to wheel around and make a run for it, but she willed herself forward. Despite what Rymellans thought they knew about her, she wasn't weak in the Way. She believed in the Way and would prove it.

As she ascended the steps toward the double doors, she couldn't avoid thinking about her parents. They'd probably arrived at the Chosen House filled with optimism and curiosity and left it expecting to live out their lives together. Well, they had. They'd died together too, and so she'd face this meeting alone. No great loss; they hadn't cared anyway. She pushed them from her mind, swung open the doors, and hung her cloak on an empty hook.

Before she could open her mouth, the Rymellan at reception looked down his nose at her. "I know who you are. Wait there and I'll let Albert Watkins know you're here."

"Thank you," she mumbled. She didn't have to wait long; a man soon approached her from across the foyer. "Welcome to Sector C3's Chosen House," he said with a smile. "I'm Albert Watkins."

"Thank you," she said, this time meaning it. As she'd wandered around outside, several people had smiled and nodded to her, but they hadn't known her identity. He did. Given where they were and why, she wouldn't have been surprised if he'd been less than cordial.

"Follow me." Watkins led her into a room where another woman waited. "This is Counsellor Morris." Morris slightly inclined her head.

The counsellor's presence didn't surprise Jayne. Her Chosen must be taking the news that she'd Join to an Adams badly.

"Please have a seat, Jayne," Watkins said.

She tried to sit still while Watkins shuffled through the papers in a file in front of him. What she wouldn't give for a sketchbook. She looked at the counsellor, then quickly focused on Watkins' desk. Another rejection, and in front of an audience. She should be used to it by now, but she wasn't. And this would be the worst, the ultimate rejection, the one she'd dreaded since her eighteenth birthday. She played with the buttons on her shirt. The room felt unbearably hot.

"Let's begin," Watkins said. "The Principal of your Joining is twenty-seven years old. She obviously resides in Sector C3 and is a member of the military."

Jayne squeezed her eyes shut. Not the military! Oh no, don't let it be the lieutenant from E6! No, it couldn't be. She doubted very much the lieutenant lived in C3. But it didn't matter. No military member would ever be pleased with her. While fretting outside, she'd convinced herself that if her Chosen were mild-mannered and thoughtful, maybe they'd eventually manage a friendship. A military member? Forget it.

"Both her parents are advocates," Watkins droned on. "She has two siblings. Both are Chosens." He looked up. "Her name is Lesley Thompson."

Jayne registered and rejected the notion simultaneously. "Do you mean Lieutenant Commander Lesley Thompson, the one on the monitors?" The one who'd just taken part in capturing a criminal who'd committed a Chosen Violation? The one who'd walked in the execution procession?

"Yes, Lieutenant Commander Lesley Thompson," Watkins said, his brows drawing together.

He must think she was an idiot. Who else would it be? Lesley Thompson. Strong in the Way, rigid, cold, single-minded—in addition to being educated, accomplished, and respected, none of which applied to Jayne. Compared to the lieutenant commander, she was nothing, and felt certain Thompson would see it that way. Everything she feared would happen. Everything.

Her chest heaved rapidly and her head started to float. The room spun. She grabbed the arm of the chair to steady herself.

"Are you all right?" Watkins asked, sounding far away.

"I'm fine," she managed to mumble. "Just surprised."

"Would you like some water?"

Jayne shook her head. Watkins looked to Morris for help. "Jayne,

I can understand why you find the prospect of Joining with Lesley Thompson daunting, but try to keep an open mind," Morris said. "She is your Chosen."

"Over time, I'm confident the match will be pleasing to you," Watkins added.

Their words brought Jayne back to her senses. She mustn't give the impression that she doubted the Chosen Council. "I'm—I'm sorry. I meant no disrespect to the Council."

Watkins waved away her apology. "It's not the first time I've had someone almost faint on me at a notification meeting. Are you sure you don't want a glass of water?"

"I'm sure. Thank you."

"Are you ready to meet the lieutenant commander?"

No. She would never be ready. The thought of meeting Lesley Thompson terrified her, but she had no choice. "Yes," she said, still hardly believing that Thompson was her Chosen. And Thompson was here, waiting. She must be devastated, disappointed, maybe angry.

"Jayne, I'd like to offer you a bit of advice before the Thompsons are brought in," Morris said. "The Thompsons are a respected family. I can see that you're already familiar with the lieutenant commander and her reputation. If I were you, I'd follow the lead of your Principal. And honour the Tradition. Don't follow in your parents' footsteps."

Blood rushed to Jayne's face. "I won't!" she blurted. She wasn't a criminal, like them.

"I'm sure your parents would have said the same thing at their notification meetings."

She shivered, sure Morris was right. But then, every Rymellan would say it, and 99.99 percent of them would never commit a Chosen Violation. But most Rymellans didn't have— She gulped several times. What if she was like them? No, stop it. How many times had she gone over this in her head? She wasn't like them. She would never be like them.

"I'll bring the lieutenant commander in now," Watkins said.

Jayne nodded. Might as well get the public humiliation over with, at least. The private humiliation could last the rest of her life.

Watkins pressed a button on his comm station as Morris opened the door. "We're ready for you, Lieutenant Commander. Room Six."

"We'll be right there," came the reply.

Jayne recognized Thompson's voice; she'd heard it enough times recently, never imagining that she was listening to her Chosen. Would that voice eventually elicit a smile, or evoke hatred? She sat on her hands, and almost jumped when she heard a tap at the open door.

Watkins motioned for the Thompsons to enter. Jayne stood, hoping she didn't look as terrified as she felt. Thompson walked in, followed by two people who must be her parents. Jayne's heart beat faster as the tall, slender, blond woman approached. The Interior insignia on Thompson's dress uniform drew her eye. Never in a million years would she have expected to be in the same room with this woman, especially this room.

She glanced at Thompson's face. Expecting to see anger, resentment, and disappointment, she saw . . . nothing. Thompson's eyes contained no hint of how she felt or what she thought. They looked impassive and detached. Jayne knew Interior officers were cold, but the complete lack of emotion disturbed her.

Thompson's voice broke into her thoughts. "I'm Lieutenant Commander Lesley Thompson." She extended her hand.

The move surprised Jayne. Thompson was being courteous. "Jayne Adams," she mumbled in response as she shook Thompson's hand. She couldn't help snatching another look at her, but jerked her eyes away when Thompson nodded.

"These are my parents, Adelaide and Alan." Thompson moved aside. Alan looked Jayne in the eye and grasped her hand. Adelaide looked past her, her fingers barely brushing Jayne's before she pulled her hand away. After an awkward moment, everyone moved to their chairs and sat.

"Thank you." Watkins cleared his throat. "Normally I'd ask if you have any questions and then you'd provide your confirmation," he said to Jayne. "But I have more news for you."

Jayne blinked. More news? Did it have anything to do with who she was? She struggled to remain calm and waited for Watkins to continue.

"Do you remember the Indoctrinators mentioning triads when you were at the Indoctrination Academy?" Watkins asked.

She'd rather not think about the Indoctrination Academy and didn't have to—she could recite every article in the Tradition from memory, including the obscure ones. Nobody could ever accuse her of not knowing the Chosen Tradition! Triads? Yes, the Tradition contained numerous articles about them. A Joining of three Chosens, only possible when dealing with a same-oriented Joining. Each Chosen was the best match for—oh dear Argamon, no. Not two. One would be difficult enough, especially with an Interior officer, but two? She became aware that everyone was waiting for her to speak and sensed Thompson looking at her. "I'm part of a triad?" she asked, hoping she'd jumped to the wrong conclusion.

Watkins nodded. "Do you know what it means?"

"Yes."

"I have a chart I can use to explain it to you if you like."

"No, it's okay," she said quietly. "I understand what a triad is." The brief discussion at the Indoctrination Academy came back to her. Rymellans had viewed previous triads with suspicion, and with her in this one . . . everyone would blame her. She always told herself that life had already dealt her its cruellest blow and that she'd lived through it and survived. Now she wondered if the worst was yet to come.

As if life were mocking her thoughts, Article CT134 rocketed into her mind; she almost cried out. The Principal and her other Chosen could execute her! She snuck a sidelong glance at Thompson, the woman who now held her life in her hands. As much as she hated to admit it, Morris was right. The best thing she could do was keep her head down and go along with whatever Thompson and the other triad member wanted. One step out of line, one perceived insurmountable inconvenience, and her life would be over. She'd be the one executed, regardless of whether it was her fault.

She hadn't expected her Chosen to love her; she'd hoped to be treated as a human being and left alone to sketch. But her Chosens didn't have to tolerate her existence in their lives at all. Unlike one Chosen, who'd have had no choice but to accept her, two Chosens could reject her without violating the Way. Was that why Thompson didn't seem upset—because she knew the triad would be short-lived?

"If you don't have any questions, I'll tell you about your second Chosen," Watkins said, then took her silence as an indication to proceed. "Your second Chosen was notified earlier today because she also resides in Sector C3. She's twenty-six years old and is a member of the military."

Jayne's shoulders sagged. One military member was bad enough, but two? And they both lived in C3? She couldn't bear to think of the implications.

"Her papa is a member of the government and runs his own tailoring business. Her mama is deceased. She has five siblings. Two are Chosens, three are Solitaries. Her name is Ramona Middleton."

The name meant nothing to Jayne.

"I'll bring her in now." Watkins spoke a few words into his comm station.

Soon thereafter, a short woman with thick black hair, also in full military dress, strode into the room with her papa. The new arrival breezed toward Jayne and extended her hand. "I'm Ramona Middleton," she announced. "But call me Mo. Nobody calls me Ramona." She shook Jayne's hand.

When Mo pulled her hand away, Jayne realized she hadn't introduced herself, but Mo was already taking her seat on the other side of Thompson. "Les," Mo said with a nod as she sat. Thompson nodded in return.

Les? They definitely knew each other.

"Michael Middleton," Mo's papa murmured as he shook her hand. Jayne sank into her chair and sat on her hands again.

"And now you're all together," Watkins said with a satisfied smile. "Do any of you have questions?"

"I do," Mo said immediately. "When do we all have to be together?"

"What do you mean?"

"There are three of us, right? And there are activities that Chosens normally do together. The Dance Hall, parties, concerts, that sort of thing. Do we all have to be in attendance, or is it only necessary that two of us be present?"

Watkins clasped his hands on top of the file in front of him. "If the Chosens in a Joining would normally attend together, then you should all attend together. Now, nothing in the Tradition dictates that you must attend social events with your Chosen, but it would be rather odd for a Joined Chosen to attend such events alone."

"Odd? Interior would investigate a Chosen who regularly attends social events alone," Thompson said.

"And in your case, attending social events with only one Chosen would likely elicit the same response, especially if it's always the same

Chosen," Watkins said. "So use this as your guideline—if both Chosens would normally be expected to be present, then it's something the three of you should do together. Does that answer your question?"

Mo sighed. "Yeah."

Watkins' face clouded. "When you read the material I've given you, you'll see that what you do in private is your own affair. But when you're in public, you would do well to treat each other as equally as you can."

Thompson shifted in her seat. "We'll need time to adjust to our new circumstances."

"Of course," Watkins said, brightening. "That's true of all Chosens, not only those in triads."

"What will our names be?" Thompson asked.

"Like all Joinings, your name will be used socially. Legally, you'll take all three names. We decided that the names of the two non-Principal Chosens would appear in alphabetical order. So your full names will be your first names followed by Adams Middleton Thompson."

"That's a mouthful," Mo said.

Nobody laughed.

"Do you have any questions, Jayne?" Watkins asked her.

Jayne shook her head. He wouldn't be able to answer the only question she cared about: how long did she have to live?

"Any more questions?" Watkins looked past them—to the parents, Jayne presumed.

"I'm sure questions will come up over the coming weeks. Can we contact you when they do?" Thompson asked.

Watkins nodded. "Feel free to beep me or to set up a meeting. And this would be a good time to mention that we'd like you all to see a counsellor for the next little while. Lieutenant Commander Thompson, I'll contact you in a few days to set up a time. Please coordinate with your Chosens."

"You mean we'll see the counsellor together?" Mo asked.

Watkins nodded.

Out of the corner of her eye, Jayne caught Mo rolling her eyes at Thompson.

"If there are no further questions, I'll need Jayne's confirmation." Watkins paused, then forged ahead. "Jayne, I'm now officially advising you that, since you know the names of your two Chosens, you are bound to them from this point forward in accordance with all the articles in the Chosen Tradition. You are now in a position to commit a Chosen Violation if you violate any article in the Chosen Tradition that applies to a Joined Chosen. Do you understand and accept what I've just told you?"

"I understand and accept it," Jayne said, certain that she'd just disappointed her Chosens. If she'd said no, she would have been at an execution site within the hour.

He swung the comm station screen toward her. She carefully read the paragraphs it displayed, then pressed her thumb in the designated spot and made a vow to herself: no matter what happened, she would remain loyal to her Chosens until the day she died. Unfortunately that day might not be far off.

"Counsellor, do you have anything to add before we close the meeting?"

"Just that you're all welcome to beep me at any time," Morris said.

Watkins stood up, beaming. "Well then, congratulations. I look forward to seeing you all at your Joining Ceremony."

Jayne hadn't thought much about her Joining Day, but given the alternative, she now fervently hoped to be there.

"Shall we?" Watkins said.

Everyone rose from their seats. Thompson quickly grabbed Mo and Adelaide's hands. Jayne ended up holding Watkins' and Alan's. "Disobedience means death. Death to those who commit a Chosen Violation. Death to those who disobey. Death to those who violate the Way. Death to those who violate the Way. Death to those who violate the Way!"

Their applause was tepid. Everyone avoided each other's eyes. Watkins gathered his papers. "Oh, I almost forgot." He handed Jayne an envelope. "Information about triads. Pay particular attention to the sheet about Article CT134. If you have any questions, beep me."

Her skin crawled; she just knew everyone was looking at her. "Thank you," she murmured. Watkins and Morris left the room. Jayne swallowed and clutched the envelope to her chest.

"Uh, we were wondering if you'd like to come to supper tomorrow night," Thompson said. Jayne turned to face her. "We obviously didn't know about the triad, so we didn't plan a notification supper for tonight."

The thought of having supper with them filled Jayne with dread. Her mind went blank. She stared stupidly at Thompson.

"And please bring a guest or two with you," Thompson continued as if she'd replied. "Perhaps your brother?"

Jayne snapped out of it. "I'd like to bring my cousin and her Chosen, if that's all right." Please, let Carol and Ronald be free.

Thompson looked as if she were about to speak, then nodded. Alan touched Thompson's arm. "Why don't you and Mo take Jayne home? It will give you a chance to talk. We can take the train."

Alan's question told Jayne more than he'd perhaps intended. He hadn't said, "Why don't you take Mo and Jayne home?" Now she was certain that not only did her two Chosens know each other, but their families were close, and it apparently wasn't unusual for her Chosens to do things together. And wouldn't they all be taking the train, but to different destinations?

"Yes, we should take her home," Thompson said. Neither her face nor her voice offered any clue that she might prefer to throw herself off a cliff. The woman had shown more emotion on the monitors; here, she was unreadable. Mo, at least, wasn't a blank slate; her politeness didn't fully mask her dismay.

Jayne didn't relish a three-hour train ride with them. She could talk to them at tomorrow's supper, with Carol and Ronald there to support her. "No, it's okay. It's a long train ride."

"You live in E6, right?" Mo said.

She nodded.

"It'll only take about half an hour."

"We're both pilots," Thompson said. "I'll fly you home."

"Oh." Both pilots, both in the military, and both from C3. If they hadn't looked so different and their last names weren't Thompson and Middleton, Jayne would have wondered if they were twins.

"Let's go." Thompson whirled and walked away. Mo followed her. Jayne had no choice but to trail after them.

"LOOKS LIKE THE nearest landing area is here." Mo stabbed her index finger onto one of the craft's panels, which currently displayed a map of the area around Jayne's apartment. "Do you know where that is?" she asked Jayne.

Jayne leaned forward in her passenger seat to peer over Mo's shoulder. "Yes. It's not far from where I live."

Thompson tapped a panel a few times. "Do up your seatbelt," she said.

Mo twisted around in her seat. "Have you flown before?" she asked as the craft lifted off.

Once, years ago, when— Her hand tightened around the information packet on her lap. She felt ill.

Amusement—or was it contempt?—flickered across Mo's face. "Are you okay? Aviacrafts aren't like passenger shuttles. They do fly a little faster."

"I'm fine," Jayne said, her cheeks burning. She wasn't about to tell them that the military had flown her and Robert to their uncle's right after they'd dragged off her parents. Now here she was again, sitting in a craft with military personnel. How could these two women in orange cloaks be her Chosens?

She glanced at Thompson's back and shrank into her seat. If Thompson knew what Jayne had just thought, she'd land the craft at an execution site. Jayne must never question the Chosen Council in front of them. True, conversations between Chosens were supposed to be privileged, but with CT134 hanging over her head, she couldn't be too careful. Any excuse, any reason, no matter how flimsy . . . It wouldn't take much of a case for a stick to be at her neck. One word from her Chosens would be enough.

"Let's talk about tomorrow," Thompson said, her tone making it sound like a command. "Supper will be served at 19—7:00. We'll come fetch you and your guests."

Jayne swallowed. "No, that's okay. I don't mind taking the train." Yet another long stretch without her sketchbook, because they couldn't know about her sketching. Not ever. They'd make fun of her, just like the lieutenant had. They were all the same.

"Are you sure?" Thompson said.

"Yes."

"If you *insist* on taking the train, then we better have a look at the schedule." Mo whipped out her comm unit.

"We'll definitely fly you all home, though," Thompson said. "Otherwise you won't get home until two or three in the morning."

"Thank you, um . . ." What should she call her? "Lieutenant Commander."

Mo looked at Thompson. "Lesley," Thompson said.

Jayne wasn't sure if she should apologize. Fortunately, Mo spoke. "There's a train from the station closest to you that will get you into C3 just after six. That will leave plenty of time to walk to the estate."

The estate?

"We'll meet you at the station. Beep one of us if you're running late," Lesley said.

Beep Lesley Thompson? She couldn't imagine it.

Mo turned to Lesley and murmured something, then smiled and touched Lesley's arm. Her fingers lingered for a moment, then she ran them along Lesley's forearm and lifted her hand. Jayne quickly looked at the envelope on her lap. Argamon, these two didn't just know each other, they were *together*! She knew a caress when she saw one.

Jayne's hand went to her neck; her situation was more precarious than she'd thought. Did the Chosen Council expect her to believe that she'd just happened to end up in a triad with two military women who were already a couple? What had they offered Lesley and Mo to agree to a triad with her? Medals? Promotions? Credits? Each other? Had they sat around a table with members of the Chosen Council and discussed how long they'd put up with the charade before they presented a case for her execution? What had they decided would be palatable to Rymellans? A day, week, month? How long until Lesley smiled on the monitors and informed everyone that she'd removed a threat to the Way by executing another Adams? Talk about a direct route to admiral. Would they eventually figure out a way to get rid of Robert, too? She may hate him, but she didn't want him to die at an execution site for a violation he hadn't committed.

Jayne couldn't believe it. Thirteen years ago, her parents had died at an execution site. That was supposed to end it—they'd paid for their violations. The circle had reformed, but it had excluded her. She remained on the outside and continued to pay for their crimes. First the petitions to have her executed, then the last thirteen years of social isolation, taunts, whispers, constantly looking over her shoulder for a patrol, strikes on her record because some Interior idiot was having a bad day or felt like a little entertainment. They'd taken everything from her—everything! And now this. Despite believing in the Way, following it, struggling not to be bitter or to blame others for judging her, they'd kill her in the end anyway. She'd never stood a chance. How naive of her to think that one day—one day!—it would be over and they'd leave her in peace.

She lifted her head. Her two Chosens—no, her two executioners—were staring ahead. They'd probably forgotten she was there, which suited her fine, though tomorrow she'd sit and eat with them. She'd managed to square her shoulders and hold her head high in the face of abuse that would have destroyed those weaker than her, so somehow she'd carry on polite conversation with the two military who would kill her. She wouldn't hand them their precious case on a silver platter. If they wanted her chained to that pole, they'd have to present a case they knew wouldn't be accepted if her last name wasn't Adams. But would they care? Would anyone care that the case didn't hold water?

When Lesley landed the craft, Mo rose and slid open the door. They seemed as eager to be rid of her as she was of them. "We'll see you tomorrow," Mo said.

Jayne mumbled a good-bye and hopped out of the craft. Almost immediately it lifted off. She watched it rotate and burst away, then trudged to her apartment, deflated and tired. Why fight it? Those who wanted her dead had already won. She wasn't weak in the Way, but she'd meet her end at an execution site regardless, and everyone would say she'd deserved her fate. Her destiny had been decided at birth. Now all she could do was wait for them to come for her.

"NOW YOU KNOW why they added CT134 to the Tradition," Lesley said when Mo finished reading the brief history of triads Watkins had given them. The aviacraft, on auto-navigation, banked toward the Thompson estate.

"Three triads were successful, not counting the earlier ones when they turned one into a Solitary," Mo said.

"Wow, three triads out of all the ones on record. I don't like those odds.

And we're in a triad with an Adams. If all those other triads couldn't survive, how will this one? It includes the daughter of two criminals. Two criminals executed for Chosen Violations."

"And us. Why us?"

Lesley didn't respond. The answer she'd suggested earlier had made Mo nervous.

Mo sighed. "I keep hoping I'll wake up tomorrow and find out it's all a bad dream. Just the triad part, though. Not the you part."

Lesley chuckled.

"And can you believe how everyone reacted? We're the ones in the triad, not them." Mo shook her head at the memory.

"They're worried."

"So? That doesn't mean they should breathe down our necks to make a snap decision. We're the ones who'll have to live with the consequences, not them." Mo shoved the history back into the envelope. "We have to tell her about us. Soon."

"We'll tell her tomorrow."

"What did you think of her?" Mo asked.

Lesley shrugged and checked the navigational panel. "I don't know." The thought of laying eyes on an Adams had set her heart racing as she'd approached the meeting room. Then she'd stepped over the threshold, had seen her . . . Adams was just a woman, and a rather shy one at that. The only remarkable feature had been the bruise on her chin. But what had Lesley expected? Someone who looked like the actors staggering around the stage during the Festival of the Way? A flashing sign on Jayne's forehead that read *I'm a threat to the Way*? Someone twitching to rush from the Chosen House and commit a Chosen Violation? Lesley felt silly, but at the same time, she would not let her guard down. Jayne may look normal, but that didn't mean she wouldn't take after her parents and threaten the triad. The Adams line was tainted. *Tainted!*

"She's almost as tall as you."

Lesley didn't need to look at Mo to know that Jayne's height bothered her; the lift in Mo's voice said it all. "So are a lot of other Rymellans. Who cares?"

After a moment, Mo said, "Do you think she . . . you know, looks like either of her parents?"

Lesley grimaced. "I have no idea. I've never seen images of them, nor do I care to."

Mo grunted.

"What about you? What did you think of her?"

"Not much. I mean, not much in the sense that she didn't say much, so I don't know what to think."

"Tomorrow will be interesting."

"Yeah."

"Don't you find it odd that she's bringing her cousin and not her brother?" Lesley asked.

"Maybe he's busy."

Or perhaps he had no respect for the Chosen Tradition and had told Jayne he would never acknowledge her Chosen. Several of the Thompsons and Middletons were struggling with the news, but they had good reason. He didn't. Any family would have been a step-up for him and his sister. Landing two families in C3—well, they couldn't have done better. So already, a red flag. Lesley would keep her eyes open for others.

"I keep reminding myself that we're Chosens," Mo said. "That's the only way I can cope with this right now."

Lesley put her arm around Mo and tried to convince herself that everything would be all right, that their lives, careers, and relationship would weather the storm. But she couldn't. That morning she'd been so sure of her future; now the only certainty was that her life would be nothing like she'd imagined.

The worst part was not knowing what to do. She agreed with Papa that it was too soon to exercise CT134. She understood Mo's position that executing Jayne for the wrong reasons would probably destroy them. But how would they know if and when to execute? How could they predict the future? Unless Jayne blatantly threatened the Way, how could they be sure? Criminals went to execution sites because they'd clearly violated the Way. At what point could she and Mo be confident that Jayne would cross the line or threaten to push them over it, making it impossible for the triad to survive? How would they *know*? Hall's words came back to her: *If we'd gone ahead and executed the children, would we have regretted it a few weeks or months later, when we'd all calmed down?*

But if they didn't execute this Adams because they were unsure, would they live to regret it? Would their lives become a cautionary tale for future Rymellans? Would historians refer to her and Mo as fallen Rymellans who'd failed to protect the Way?

Usually the Way provided the answers, but in this case, it posed questions. Perhaps it would still offer her guidance, and she'd seek advice from those she trusted, like Laura. But with so many conflicting opinions already evident among her and Mo's families, and with her own feelings ranging from disbelief to resentment to anger to grief, how would she know who to listen to? Could she even trust herself, be certain that her relationship with Mo and their now-perilous dream of a life together wouldn't cloud her judgement?

She silently recited the *Words Every Rymellan Knows*, words that always strengthened her, reminded her of who she was and what was important. *Disobedience means death. Death to those who commit a Chosen Violation. Death to those who disobey. Death to those who violate the Way.*

They rang hollow.

BESIEGED

.....

ESLEY MOVED AWAY FROM THE LIVING room window and lifted her mug from an end table. Sleeping on yesterday's events hadn't helped at all, especially since she'd tossed and turned all night. What had Mo said? *It's not like we'll go to the notification meeting this afternoon and then it's over.* No, they were stuck with her—forever. Unless they decided to execute her.

She sipped her tziva and grimaced. Cold. She'd spent too much time gazing out the window, wondering if her life would ever make sense again.

Mo padded into the room, yawning into her hand. "It's almost 10:00. Why didn't you wake me?"

Lesley shrugged. "I figured you needed your sleep."

"How long have you been up?"

"About an hour and a half. What time did you finally drop off?"

"I don't know. Around 03:30, maybe? But then I woke up at 05:45, and 06:30, and 07:40."

Lesley could relate; she'd managed about three hours of broken sleep. "Did you have the same nightmare I had, about ending up in a triad with an Adams, or did that actually happen?" Not expecting an answer, she raised her mug. "Do you want some?"

"No, I think I'll get dressed and head home, see how Papa's feeling." Mo paused. "I'm not answering beeps today. I won't know what to say."

Yes, what would they say when their friends beeped to congratulate them? Everyone would assume that she and Mo were giddy with happiness and entering a new phase of their lives as Chosens. They were entering a new phase, all right, but not one to celebrate. At least their friends would be sympathetic and supportive. They'd know that she and Mo weren't weak in the Way, that they'd ended up in a horrible situation through no fault of their own. What would happen tomorrow, when the Chosen Council announced the weekly notifications and their military peers found out? What would Rymellans who didn't know them think?

Lesley slipped her arm around Mo and kissed the top of her head. "We'll get through this," she murmured, more to reassure herself than Mo.

Mo looked up at her. "How? And when will we be through it, exactly? I'm not seeing an end, here. Not one we can live with, anyway."

"Depending on how things go, that could change."

"Maybe," Mo said, frowning. "But we can't let anyone rush us into a decision. I know she's an Adams, and if I could, I'd make her disappear, but that doesn't mean I want us to present a sham case."

"I don't want that, either." Lesley steered Mo toward the hallway, wanting to get to the kitchen so she could dump the cold tziva and prepare a fresh jug. She could at least have hot tziva; she hadn't completely lost control of her life.

"Where are your parents?" Mo asked at the bottom of the stairs.

"Mama's in the study, working out the details of tonight's supper with the caterers." Mo snorted, making Lesley smile. Even though Mama had just received the shock of her life and considered Jayne and her family to be beneath the Thompsons, she'd arrange a supper that would impress the Preeminent Ruler. "Papa had a case this morning. I doubt he would have scheduled it if he'd known what was going to happen."

"What about Jason?"

"He's out too, assisting on a case. Mama said he's staying with a friend tonight."

"Good. Tonight will be difficult enough without him coming home while they're still here."

She silently agreed.

"Anyway, I'll go get dressed." Mo patted Lesley's arm and thumped up the stairs, sounding like an elephant despite her size.

Lesley stared after her for a moment, then headed for the kitchen. Her comm unit beeped; her fingers tightened around the mug's handle when she read the name: Laura. She reluctantly pulled the unit from its holder and pressed the connect button.

"Good morning," Laura said cheerfully. "I didn't wake you, did I?"

"No, I've been up for a while," Lesley said as she entered the kitchen, "though I did get up a little later than usual."

"I figured you'd be up late celebrating, that's why I waited until now to beep you."

She'd been up half the night, but not celebrating.

"Anyway, congratulations again. I know you and Mo—"

"Laura, I—"

"—will have a wonderful life together. I'm beeping to invite the two of you to supper. You'll be flooded with invitations, so I thought I'd ask before everyone else does."

Lesley poured the cold tziva into the recycling chute's liquid collector, set the mug on the counter, and desperately searched for the right words to tell Laura about the triad.

"I'd like to get to know Mo better," Laura continued, after waiting for Lesley to respond. "I only really know her through you. Now that I can treat you like a couple, I'm hoping that will change. So would you like to come for supper sometime next week?"

If not for the triad and its third member, Lesley would have immediately said yes. Mo's face tightened every time Laura's name came up in conversation. Lesley wanted her to get to know Laura, in the hope that Mo would eventually stop blaming her for their separation. They were to blame; they'd forced Laura to abruptly split them up.

"Lesley?" Laura prompted, puzzled by Lesley's silence.

"Um . . ." Laura knew about triads, but Lesley had no idea how she viewed them. Did she think they were unnatural and against the Way? "Laura, what do you think about triads?"

"What?"

"Triads. Three Chosens Joining. What do you think about them?"

Silence. Then, "Why are you suddenly asking me about triads?"

Laura's voice was quiet, but hard. It set Lesley's heart pounding. She already regretted asking the question. If Laura ranted about how awful triads were, telling her would be even more awkward and embarrassing.

"What have you heard?" Laura barked.

"Nothing," Lesley said, confused by Laura's reaction. "Just forget the question." She hesitated, then forged ahead. "I have to tell you something. My notification meeting didn't go as I'd expected."

"What do you mean? Don't tell me Mo isn't your Chosen."

"No, she is. But . . . I have another Chosen. I'm in a triad. We're in a triad."

"*What?*"

"Mo and I, we're in a triad." Silence. "We're really shocked," Lesley said, compelled to fill the void. "The Chosen Council gave us a historical treatise to read. Triads have been volatile and Rymellans have treated them with suspicion, so we don't understand it. We're strong in the Way. I just hope everyone remembers that." Including Laura. "We're just—honestly, it doesn't feel real." Still no response. "Laura?"

"Will you be home later?"

"Yes. But we're hosting our, um, other Chosen for supper."

"What time?"

"She's arriving around 18:00."

"I'll drop by this afternoon. Finney out."

"Laura, wait!"

But she'd disconnected. Lesley lowered her comm unit in dismay. Laura hadn't ended a conversation with *Finney out* for ages. She was already distancing herself, and she hadn't heard about the Adams part yet.

MO SWALLOWED THE last bit of oatmeal raisin cookie and grabbed another from the cookie jar. Okay, this really would be the last one, but she'd take the cookie jar with her in case she felt like another one later—or in five minutes. Cradling it in her arm as she nibbled on the cookie, she strode from the kitchen and stopped short, almost bumping into Mary. "I didn't hear the front door," she said, surprised to see her. "No appointments today?"

Mary ignored the question. "I want to talk to Papa. Where is he?"

"He's not here." She'd hoped to talk to him too, but according to Nathan, Papa had left that morning, saying only that he'd be back by four.

Mary frowned and eyed the cookie jar.

"You want one?"

"No." She wandered into the living room.

Mo followed her. "He won't be back until four," she said when Mary sank onto the sofa.

Mary groaned. "I have to leave before then. Tell him I'll beep him later."

Mo expected her to leave, but Mary stayed put. "Why don't you sit down for a minute?" Mary said with a tight smile.

Great. She didn't feel like talking, especially about the triad. Nevertheless, Mo lowered herself into a chair. She took the time to open the cookie jar and pull out three more cookies before setting it on the end table.

"So how are you feeling?" Mary asked.

She chewed a piece of cookie while pondering what to say. "Still in shock, I guess."

"Have you and Lesley talked any more about CT134?"

Oh, so Mary didn't care about her after all. She should have known. "Since yesterday? We told you, it's too early to make a decision."

Mary leaned forward. "You hadn't met her at that point. Now you have."

"And it's still too early to make a decision. We don't know enough yet."

"Lesley will be a commander. She'll have to make decisions like this quickly."

"Les will deal with criminals. We're not talking about a criminal here."

"Oh, don't be so naïve," Mary said with a snicker. "Adams is the daughter of two criminals, two criminals who committed Chosen Violations. It's only a matter of time."

"If it was only a matter of time, they would already have executed her!" Mo snapped, then shoved another cookie into her mouth. She shouldn't defend the woman who could take Les away from her, but Mary's lack of concern for anyone but herself irritated her. And no way would she tell Mary what Les had told her, that some Rymellans had wanted to execute Jayne after the Incident. She'd never hear the end of it. "She's still alive. That says something."

"We'll see what happens when she's Joined," Mary responded ominously. "Her parents took two other Rymellans down with them. How many will she take down? What if it's Lesley?"

"It won't be! Les is strong in the Way. And don't you dare say it could be me." Mo stood, already tired of the conversation. "I'm going to the Trading Centre." She wanted to stock up on a few things before the triad went public.

"I'm sorry," Mary called as Mo reached the hallway. "I know how much of a blow it must be to find out that Lesley doesn't belong only to you."

Mo froze. "Nothing will change between us."

"You say that now, but who knows what the future will hold?"

"Nothing will change, Mary," Mo said, whirling to face her. "We don't have to have a relationship with her."

"She's your Chosen. You'll fall for her whether you want to or not."

"No, I won't. The way I feel about Les . . . I could never feel that way about someone else."

Mary nodded. "I can see why. Lesley's a beautiful woman."

"Yes, she is." Though that wasn't why Mo loved her.

"It's easy to see why women would be attracted to her. Your other Chosen, for example."

Did Mary think she was stupid? "I know what you're trying to do and you can stop it right now."

Mary placed her hand on her chest. "I'm only speculating about what it'll be like to have three Chosens Joined together. I'm sure Lesley will rebuff any advances your other Chosen makes."

"Of course she will. If she wanted to be with someone else, she had plenty of opportunity during our separation."

"You're right, of course," Mary said soothingly. "But this Adams woman, she's not just anybody. She's Lesley's Chosen. The Chosen Council says they're meant for each other."

"She's my Chosen too, and I wouldn't be interested," Mo said harshly. "I'm off to the Trading Centre."

She stomped down the hallway, grabbed her cloak, and stormed out the front door, mad at herself for letting Mary get to her. It would be nice if Mary supported her instead of playing on her insecurities, but all she cared about was herself. When Les had said they wanted more time, she'd meant more than a few hours. Not even a day had passed since their notification meetings and Mary was already applying pressure. What next? Would Matthew show up later and lay a load of guilt on her? Would Papa duck out of supper?

And now Finney was getting in on the act, too. According to Les, Finney didn't know about Jayne but was already upset enough to want to discuss the triad in person. When she heard the rest of the story, she'd probably urge Les to execute, not wanting an Adams in her sector. Mo didn't want Jayne in their lives either, and if there was a way to get rid of her without executing her, she'd be all for it. If they were lucky, Jayne would say or do something that would make it easy for them; make it clear that she was a threat to the Way and that not exercising CT134 would be against the Way. If they were lucky . . .

She chewed her thumbnail. She hated thinking that way, but she hated being in a triad. She felt guilty for hoping that Jayne would give them a reason, but would be relieved if Jayne did. Les having another Chosen terrified her, but that other Chosen was also hers. So how in the flaming Argamon was she supposed to deal with this without losing her mind? No matter what she thought or felt, it was wrong. And right. Argh! She hopped on her bike and pedalled toward her aviacraft.

A cloud of dust up ahead caught her attention. Papa seemed to be doing some stomping of his own. She slammed on her brakes and skidded to a stop in front of him. "I thought you were only coming back at four."

He squinted at her. "I can't focus. Usually I can shut everything out at the workshop, but not today. Two shirts, ruined! Andrew shooed me out before I could do any more damage. Where are you going?"

"The Trading Centre. I want to go before—"

"Before everyone's whispering about you? How are we supposed to make sense of this mess?" He shook his head and stared at his feet. "I've been thinking a lot about your mama today. Wondering how she'd feel, what she'd do."

"What do you think she'd want me to do?" Mo asked, not sure she wanted to know.

He blew out some air, then lifted his head. "She'd probably want to give her—Adams—a chance. She *was* an indoctrinator, she'd want the letter of the article followed. But she'd also want to protect her name. I wish she were here. She was always the stronger one."

"You're saying that Mama would want what Les and I have decided? To wait and see?"

"Yes, but not everyone in the family agrees, and I'm the one they'll complain to."

"Just tell them you're supporting me. I'm the one with the power to exercise the article." Others could call for Jayne's execution without considering the consequences, but not her and Les.

He skirted around the bike and gave her a clumsy hug. "Here I am worried about me when you're the one . . . well, you're the one whose life will never be the same." He stepped back and gripped her arms. "You seem so calm."

Numb, more like. "Only because I don't quite believe it. It's still not real." Right now, she couldn't think past tonight's supper. One day—no, one hour at a time was all she could handle. Maybe part of her hoped the triad would somehow disappear and she'd never have to believe it.

"It'll be real tonight," Papa warned.

"Yeah." Could he say awkward? She was determined to remain objective, to view supper as an opportunity to observe Jayne and learn more about her, but looking for what? A reason to exercise the article that she and Les could live with? "Tonight we're going to tell her about us. Our relationship."

"Maybe that will help you decide what to do."

"Les said that she'll probably say what she thinks we want her to say. She knows about the article." And unless she was an idiot, she had to know that she was the prime candidate for execution.

"That's true. The real test will be time."

But they only had two years to decide about CT134. Could Jayne keep up an act that long and only reveal her true self when it was too late?

"I should let you get on," Papa said gruffly. "I think I'll visit the crypt. Your mama can't hear me, but I feel like talking to her anyway."

If there was a chance Mama would answer, Mo would be there in a shot. "Mary's at the house, looking for you."

Papa grimaced. "I'll go around." He pressed his lips together.

"What?"

"I know I said your mama would want to give her a chance, but if we open the door to this woman, will we be letting in a wolf in sheep's clothing?"

If they were, Mo fervently hoped they'd recognize the wolf for what it was before it tore her, Les, and their families apart.

LESLEY SNAPPED OFF her station's monitor when Mama tapped at her half-open bedroom door. For the last hour, half of her mind had read background material on articles related to triads, while the other half had worried about Laura's reaction. She'd heard the knock at the front door; she knew why Mama was here. "Yes?"

Mama leaned around the door to peer into the room. "Commander Finney is here to see you."

"I'll be right down."

"She's waiting outside. She didn't want to come in."

"Why not?"

"She said she doesn't feel like sitting down, she feels like walking."

"Oh." Lesley didn't know what to make of that.

She followed Mama downstairs with a heavy heart. Losing Laura's friendship and respect would not only hurt, it would put her on the wrong side of her commanding officer and a soon-to-be commodore. And this would be the worst time to lose a valued advisor she desperately needed.

As she buttoned her cloak, she wandered into the living room and surreptitiously glanced out the window. Laura stood rocking on her heels, her back to the house and her hands clasped behind her. Her rigid posture wasn't a good sign. Despite telling herself that Laura's view of the triad could change with time, Lesley still felt apprehensive.

When she swung open the front door, Laura looked over her shoulder. Her expression gave Lesley pause. She looked almost fearful. Did she think Lesley was a threat to the Way?

"Let's walk," Laura said.

Lesley fell into step with her, and after considering and rejecting several conversation openers, decided to wait for Laura to speak.

"I'm sorry about my reaction earlier," Laura said. "The triad came as a bit of a shock."

"I should have prepared you, not just blurted it out like that," Lesley said, feeling herself relax. "I didn't know how to tell you."

"I'm not sure you could have prepared me."

"I could have led up to it better, but I just wanted to get it out. It was difficult for me to say."

Laura cleared her throat. "And now it's my turn to tell you something . . . difficult. Difficult for me, anyway."

Lesley kept her eyes focused on the path ahead. Perhaps she'd read too much into Laura's apology.

"You said that you've read a historical treatise about triads?" Laura asked.

"Yes, the Chosen Council gave it to us. A condensed version, but enough to get across that triads have been volatile and that not everyone is comfortable with them. Some Rymellans say they're against the Way, but the Chosen Council obviously doesn't think they are."

"Did it say much about the last triad?"

Lesley played along, suspecting that Laura had fallen back to a comfortable subject—history and the Chosen Tradition—until she was ready to say whatever was on her mind. "It was successful. Fourteen daughters." The Thompson triad certainly wouldn't have fourteen daughters. But she was getting ahead of herself. The Thompson triad might not Join.

"Did it say what their names were?"

"No, it wasn't that detailed. We want to find out more about them, though. After all, they succeeded." She and Mo had wondered how old the Chosens were when they Joined, among other things.

"I can tell you a bit about them."

Lesley wasn't surprised.

"Their names were Eleanor, Miranda, and Charlotte." Laura paused. "Finney."

"Finney?" Lesley blurted, stopping in her tracks. "You're a descendant of the last triad?"

Two steps ahead, Laura turned to look at her. "One of many. They did have fourteen daughters over two hundred years ago, though I'm sure there have been a number of Solitary descendants."

"Is this the difficult thing you wanted to tell me?" Lesley asked slowly, not understanding why Laura would find it difficult to tell *her*, of all people.

"It's reared its ugly head twice in my life, so I'm a little sensitive about it," Laura said sheepishly. "Once at the Learning Academy when a classmate found out, and then at the Military Academy." She shook her head. "When I was having problems at the Learning Academy and wished I'd never heard the word triad, my mama suggested that I learn about them—Eleanor and company. The more I did, the more proud I was—am—to have them as ancestors."

"That's how you became interested in the history of the Chosen Tradition," Lesley stated.

Laura nodded.

Lesley wondered if she would have reacted as matter-of-factly to Laura's revelation if Laura had told her last week. She hoped so. A thought struck her. "Did Morton have anything to do with it rearing its head at the Military Academy?"

"He found out when he dug into my background after my run-in with him, the one I told you about. Maybe I should have mentioned it, but . . . You asked why he has a bad attitude toward me." Laura bit her lip.

"And you told me. You didn't lie or hide anything. You weren't under any obligation to tell me about your family history." Perhaps she'd ask more about the consequences of Morton's discovery later. Right now, she had her own triad to worry about.

"When you told me you're in a triad, all that ran through my mind was how triads would be all over the monitors and on everyone's lips, and you know at least half of it will be negative and ignorant, maybe more."

"I'm expecting most of it to be negative, if not all of it," Lesley said.

"Why?" Laura asked. "Rymellans are familiar with you. You have a great reputation. Perhaps I'm being too pessimistic and this triad will be the one that finally puts all the nay-saying to rest."

Lesley doubted it. If anything, it would provide the naysayers with more ammunition. "You didn't give me a chance earlier to tell you about the third triad member."

Laura's brow furrowed. "Why would the third triad member make a difference?"

Now it was Lesley's turn to say something difficult. She swallowed. "Remember when we were at the early morning meeting on the day we captured Owen, and Hall told us about the Adams children?"

"Yes," Laura said, looking even more confused.

"Well, I met one of them yesterday. At the Chosen House."

Laura's face froze. She stared at Lesley and opened her mouth, but nothing came out.

"So now you see how bad this is. An Adams and a triad." And she and Mo, caught up in it.

"Bad?" Laura exclaimed, finally finding her voice. One hand went to her head. She stepped to the left, then to the right, then faced Lesley again and dropped her arm to her side. "Lesley, you will be under *so* much pressure."

"You mean about Article CT134?" Lesley asked.

"Yes."

So Laura had jumped right to that. Lesley wanted to share her suspicions about the triad, but held back. Telling Laura she thought the triad might not be authentic would be crossing over the line. Mo, yes. They were Chosens; communication between them was privileged. Not so with Laura. Lesley trusted her, but Laura's primary concern would be the Way. She wouldn't put Laura into a situation that could force her to make an agonizing choice; friends didn't do that to each other. Laura couldn't report what she didn't know. "We're already under pressure from our families," she said. "Not everyone, but a few."

"You do understand the article?" Laura said. "She has to threaten the triad to the point that her continued existence pretty much guarantees that the triad will fail. You can't execute her on a whim."

"I know, and we don't intend to."

"Good, because I'm the one who'd have to do it, since you're the Principal," Laura said, patting her chest with both hands.

"You won't be C3's commander for much longer."

"I will be in charge of this sector until Hall finds a replacement, which could take a while. So you listen! I don't hesitate to stick criminals who violate the Way. I'd do anything to protect the Way, that's why I'm in the military. I didn't join Interior and rise to commander to stick Rymellans who haven't committed a violation. So I do not want to be called to an execution site because the three of you couldn't work something out." Her face was red and her breathing rapid.

"You won't be," Lesley said, lifting placating hands. "The article says the Chosen has to threaten the viability of the triad."

Laura grimaced. "That's too open to interpretation for my taste, especially in this case. What does 'threaten the triad' mean? If she disagrees with you, is that threatening the triad? How about if you have an argument or she gets along better with one of you and the other one doesn't like it? Will I be beeped then?"

"No!"

"It's a stupid article!" Laura said, surprising Lesley with her honesty. "I'm not saying I wouldn't uphold it," she quickly added, "but it doesn't belong in the Tradition. I know the history. I know that triads have been . . . problematic at times. That shouldn't mean we give Chosens permission to kill each other."

"In this case, I'm sure some Rymellans will be glad the article exists and will hope that Mo and I do exercise it," Lesley said carefully. "Including some in our own families."

"Sometimes the most courageous thing you can do is nothing." Laura met Lesley's eyes. "This could be one of those times. And it could get rough."

It already was.

"So, an Adams is your Chosen," Laura said, sounding as if she couldn't quite believe it. "I'll be honest, when Hall told us about the children, I—" Her comm unit beeped; she glanced at it. "Hall," she mumbled, pulling the unit from its holder. She walked out of Lesley's earshot. Lesley waited, relieved that Laura would still be a strong ally, especially given her ancestry.

Laura strolled back to her. "I have to go. Listen, can I tell Hall about this, give him some warning?"

"Go ahead." She'd rather Hall learn about the triad from Laura than from the Chosen Council's weekly announcement.

"I'll tell him to keep it to himself, though I guess it'll be public soon enough. I'll beep you tomorrow. I want to hear more about her—um, Adams. And I guess I'll have three supper guests. We'll have to arrange a time. And remember, I'm living proof that triads can work," she called over her shoulder as she walked away and waved.

"I'll talk to you tomorrow," Lesley called back. Concern now tempered her relief over Laura's reaction. Pressure to not exercise CT134 could be just as bad as pressure to exercise it. Everyone seemed to have a personal stake in what happened—or at least felt they did—but only she and Mo would suffer the consequences. And Jayne. As much as Lesley would like to, she couldn't forget about Jayne.

CAROL INSERTED THE top end of her comm unit into the trade station and punched in her intended destination. Seconds later the station beeped. She withdrew her unit and moved away. "I don't know why we're taking such an early train," she said as Ronald paid for his passage. "We're rushing there to sit in a waiting area for half an hour."

"I don't want them to have to wait for us," Jayne said. The less she aggravated them, the better.

"And we'll be sitting twiddling our thumbs after a three-hour train ride," Carol muttered. "A three-hour train ride with you and no sketchbook. How long do you think you can keep that up?"

Jayne stepped toward the trade station and inserted her comm unit.

"The longer you leave it, the harder it'll be to tell them," Ronald said.

"I don't feel comfortable telling them right now," she mumbled as she entered the code for Station C3-8.

"Look, I know you're sensitive about it, but they're your Chosens. You can't hide it from them forever," Carol said. "It'll be a strain you don't need."

Jayne was only half listening. Why hadn't the station beeped and the *Thank you. Please remove your comm unit* message appeared on the display? She sensed someone looking over her shoulder.

"What's wrong?" Ronald asked.

"I don't know, it's not—" The station beeped, but her relief turned to dismay when she read the display: *Your request could not be completed. Please remove your comm unit and see the station attendant.* Why did this have to happen now? They'd be late!

"Are you sure you have enough credits?" Carol asked as they walked to the station's information counter.

"Positive." She'd checked earlier to make sure.

The station's attendant frowned when they approached. "Yes?"

Jayne swallowed. "I, uh, tried to trade for passage, and the trade station told me to see you."

"Give me your comm unit," he demanded, holding out his hand.

Carol shifted her weight. Jayne hoped she wouldn't choose today to get snotty, as Carol sometimes did when others treated Jayne rudely. She gave the attendant her comm unit.

He scowled and gingerly held it, as if he could catch something. "Where are you going?"

"C3-8."

"Just a moment." He whirled, pushed open the swinging door behind him, and disappeared, presumably into another room.

Great, there went her comm unit. "We'll be late."

"We'll have plenty of time, even if we miss the next train," Ronald said.

"You sure you have enough credits?" Carol asked again.

"Yes," Jayne hissed, then rubbed her temples. She watched others stride up to the trade stations, pay for their passage, and carry on their way. The station she'd used wasn't rejecting anybody else's request, so it couldn't be out of order. She tried to wait patiently, but grew more agitated with every passing minute. What if he never came back? He had her comm unit. "Where is he?" she said to nobody in particular.

"This is getting ridiculous." Ronald leaned over the counter. "Excuse me," he called. "We have a train to catch."

Jayne stared at the door, willing the attendant to reappear, but he didn't.

"Excuse me!" Ronald called again.

"Jayne," Carol said urgently.

Jayne spun toward her. "What?"

Carol jerked her chin at something over Jayne's shoulder. She turned to look. A lieutenant and sub-lieutenant were making a beeline for them.

"I told you!" the attendant said, suddenly back at the counter. He pointed to Jayne and looked at the lieutenant. "You said if she bought passage to C3 again, to let you know. Well, I went one better. I put a watch on it, so she'd have to come see me if she tried."

The lieutenant nodded to him. "You did well. Thank you." He shifted his attention to Jayne and motioned for her and her companions to move away from the counter with him, out of the attendant's earshot. "Why are you going to C3?" the lieutenant asked.

Jayne hesitated, not wanting to tell him about the triad. Carol jumped in. "Do you monitor everyone's travel this closely? Travelling to C3 isn't a violation."

"No, but we can't be too careful." The lieutenant looked down his nose at Carol. "Some Rymellans require more monitoring than others."

"Did you hear that, Jayne? You're a Rymellan today!" Carol exclaimed.

The lieutenant's face tightened.

"Carol, please!" Jayne placed a restraining hand on Carol's arm, then quickly answered the lieutenant, hoping to divert his attention away from Carol. "We're going to visit someone."

"In C3?" the lieutenant said incredulously.

"Yes, we're going for supper."

"Is this mystery person Joined?" the sub-lieutenant asked, his eyes narrowing. "Four were executed during the Incident and there are three here," he murmured to his partner.

"I beg your pardon!" Ronald said. "I resent the implication."

"Then perhaps you should be more careful about the company you keep," the lieutenant said, his eyes still on Jayne. "Who are you visiting?"

Why did she have the feeling that her answer would only make things worse? She hesitated again.

"Lesley Thompson," Ronald said. "Lieutenant Commander Lesley Thompson. She invited us for supper."

The lieutenant stared at them. "And what about yesterday? You were alone," he said to Jayne. "Were you visiting her then, too?"

"I saw her, yes."

Disbelief was written all over his face. "And let me guess, tomorrow you'll be heading to D5 to have tziva with the Preeminent Ruler." He turned to the sub-lieutenant. "We'll have a good story to tell at the outpost tonight." The sub-lieutenant shook his head as the lieutenant stepped toward Jayne. "You're apparently determined to get yourselves into trouble, and I'm happy to oblige." He grabbed Jayne's arm. "Let's take them in."

"I'm telling the truth!" Jayne cried as the sub-lieutenant moved toward Ronald.

"Do you think we're that stupid, that we'd tell you something you can easily refute?" Carol said when the lieutenant reached for her arm.

"I think you're all having a laugh at the military's expense," the lieutenant replied.

"And what if we're not? Do you want to be the one to explain to the lieutenant commander why you hauled off her supper guests?"

"Don't you think you should at least beep her?" Ronald added. "I assume you'll end up doing that at some point. You can't strike us without verifying that we're lying."

Ronald was right, but Jayne wasn't sure which she'd prefer: being struck, or having Lesley dragged into this mess. Article CT134 loomed. Then again, if they didn't show up for supper . . . She inwardly sighed. They might as well just take her to an execution site and get it over with.

"Maybe we *should* beep her," the sub-lieutenant said uncertainly, letting go of Ronald's arm. "What if they're telling the truth?"

Jayne winced when the lieutenant tightened his grip on her arm. "Oh sure, that's exactly what they want us to do," he said, "bother her with this nonsense so they can laugh at us."

"This one's right, though." The sub-lieutenant jerked his thumb at Ronald. "She'll be beeped anyway."

"Not by us." The lieutenant's grip relaxed. "I know, I'll beep Ramsey, see what he thinks."

Oh great, now they were involving E6's commander. The lieutenant let go of Jayne and Carol. "Stay with them," he said to his subordinate, then pulled out his comm unit and walked away.

Jayne rubbed her arm and refused to look at the sub-lieutenant hovering in her peripheral vision. Carol sighed.

The lieutenant rejoined them. "He's beeping her." His eyes bored into Jayne. "And he said it will give him great pleasure to throw the three of you back into the Indoctrination Academy for a refresher stay."

Jayne exchanged a sidelong glance with Carol, but kept her mouth shut. Would Lesley tell Ramsey the truth? If she denied it, Ramsey would know that she'd lied the moment the triad became public knowledge. But since he didn't care when his people struck Jayne for breathing, why would he care if Lesley had her thrown into the Indoctrination Academy? And what would stop Lesley from turning around and using the situation to show that Jayne was weak in the Way? They could be plotting that very scenario right now.

She started to fidget. When the lieutenant leaned to his left to shoo away a couple of gawkers, she glimpsed the clock over the platform entrance behind him. If they didn't board the next train, they'd definitely be late. What was taking so long?

Jayne tensed when the lieutenant's comm unit beeped. He moved away again, gesturing with his free hand as he talked. A minute later, he returned. She searched his face.

"So?" the sub-lieutenant said.

The lieutenant's upper lip curled. "He said to let them board the train."

Surprise flickered across the sub-lieutenant's face. "So she's actually visiting Thompson?"

"I don't know. All he said was to let them go to C3."

"The attendant still has her comm unit," Carol said.

Jayne silently thanked her. Too focused on making the next train, she'd forgotten about her comm unit and would have boarded the train without it.

Without a word, the lieutenant led them back to the counter. The attendant straightened and eyed Jayne smugly. "Deduct passage to C3 and then give her comm unit back to her," the lieutenant said.

The attendant's eyes widened. He opened his mouth, then clamped it shut and did what he was told.

"And remove the watch on C3," the lieutenant said as Jayne accepted her comm unit. "If she wants to go to C3 again, let her."

"If that's what you want me to do," the attendant said stiffly.

"It is." The lieutenant whirled and walked away, motioning for the sub-lieutenant to follow.

"What, no sorry?" Carol said sarcastically.

Jayne was already heading toward their train's platform. "Come on," she said over her shoulder. As she bounded down the stairs, the absurdity hit her: she was rushing for the train so she wouldn't be late for supper with two military who were supposedly her Chosens.

The train was pulling into the station when they reached the platform. They found two pairs of seats facing each other. Jayne sat on her hands. "You should have brought your sketchbook," Carol said, frowning at her. "You can't keep it a secret forever."

"I might not have to," Jayne said. "Especially after what just happened."

"You really think they'll exercise CT134?"

"Carol," she sighed, "they're a couple."

"You don't know that for sure."

Yes, she did. Either that, or they'd really hit it off during their notification lunch. "Trust me, they are. Even if I wasn't . . . me, they wouldn't want me around. And remember what we talked about?" She'd told Carol and Ronald about her suspicion that the triad had been deliberately arranged, something she wouldn't dare repeat on the train, even though nobody was sitting near them.

"I don't know, if they—" Carol waved her hands around to suggest unknown schemers "—wanted to get rid of you, they'd just get rid of you. They wouldn't have to dream up some elaborate scheme to do it."

Ronald snorted. "In other words, no need to worry, Jayne. If they really wanted to, they could kill you anytime."

Carol burst into laughter and squeezed his arm. "Now you know why I'm not a counsellor," she gasped before turning her attention back to Jayne. "But seriously, you have to let your Chosens get to know you."

She'd rather take Counsellor Morris's advice—keep her head down and go along with whatever Lesley and Mo wanted. The fewer excuses she gave them to kill her, the harder it would be for them. Maybe.

Jayne jumped when her comm unit beeped, then stared at it in surprise. The only person who ever beeped was sitting across from her. She pulled the unit from its holder, read *Lt. Cmdr. L. Thompson*. "It's her! Lesley!" she shrieked, resisting the urge to hurl the comm unit away as if it were a poisonous snake.

"Answer it!" Carol snapped.

She pressed the connect button, her heart pounding. "Um, hello?"

"It's Lesley. Did you make it to the train all right?"

"Yes, we did. We're on the train now." She paused. "I'm sorry they had to beep you."

"I told Commander Ramsey about the triad," Lesley said, her voice even. "I figured that would allay any concerns they have about you travelling to C3."

Jayne stifled a groan. What had Ramsey said?

"I guess Mo and I will see you at the train station in a few hours, then."

"Yes. Thank you," Jayne said, then wanted to kick herself for sounding dumb.

"Good-bye." Lesley terminated the connection.

"See? That's a good sign," Carol said as Jayne slid the comm unit into its holder. "Two good signs. She not only set Ramsey straight, she beeped to see if you were all right."

"She's just being polite," Jayne said, sitting on her hands again.

"That's better than being rude. Anyway, we've already had our run-in with the military, so the day can only improve," Carol said cheerfully, settling back into her seat.

Jayne stared out the window, watching the tunnel lights whip by. She'd like to believe Carol, but considering that one wrong word could lead to an execution site, she couldn't. With Article CT134 hanging over her head, the day could get worse. Much, much worse.

JASON TENSED. SOMEONE was coming, the hallway carpet muffling their footsteps as they approached Advocate Phillips's waiting room. He forced himself to look at the doorway. A man strode past and the footsteps faded away. Jason slowly exhaled.

Ever since he'd arrived, he'd had the irrational fear that Lesley would suddenly appear. He knew she wouldn't; she was nowhere near Phillips's office. He gripped the arms of the wooden chair. No, she was at home, preparing for supper. The thought of an Adams on the estate made him sick. Lesley must be in shock, or she'd be here, not planning to give Adams a flaming guided tour of the house. She'd better not show Adams his room. He'd shut the door, hoping to send a message, but Lesley might be too out of it to understand.

More footsteps. He tensed again, then felt dizzy with relief when Mary walked in. "Where have you been? Our appointment's in a couple of minutes."

Mary sat in the chair next to his and crossed her legs. "I'm on time," she said, unperturbed.

"Barely." He stared at Phillips's office door and almost jumped when it opened.

Phillips and another Rymellan strolled into the waiting room. "The amendment should be posted within two weeks," Phillips was saying.

The woman with him smiled. "Thank you."

"Always a pleasure to serve the Way." He nodded to her and turned to Jason. "Jason! Nice to see you again."

Jason stood and swept his arm toward Mary. "This is Mary Middleton."

Phillips nodded to her. "A pleasure. Please, come in." They filed into his office. "I have to admit, our conversation yesterday left me very curious." He gestured to the two chairs in front of his desk and sat in his own chair. "What can I do for you?"

After glancing at Mary to see if she wanted to start, Jason cleared his throat. "As I said yesterday, I'm here for my sister, Lesley. She received her Chosen Papers a few days ago and had her notification meeting yesterday. I couldn't tell you everything when we spoke because not all the Chosens had been notified."

"Not notified? But you contacted me in the afternoon."

"I know, but we have an unusual situation on our hands."

"Hold on." Phillips pulled a pad toward him and poised a pen over the paper. "Start from the beginning."

"Lesley and Mo—um, Ramona Middleton—"

"My sister," Mary said.

"—are Chosens, and both families are pleased with the match. Our sisters have been involved for a long time, though they split up when they turned twenty-five, of course."

"It sounds like congratulations are in order," Phillips said, confusion plain on his face as he scribbled on the pad.

"That would be true if they weren't in a triad."

Phillips stopped writing. "A triad?"

"Do you know what that is?" Mary asked.

"I do. I specialized in the Chosen Tradition in my final year and have advocated or consulted on the few cases related to it since I graduated."

Jason nodded. "That's why I contacted you."

"There hasn't been a triad in over two hundred years."

"Until yesterday," Mary said.

Phillips cocked his head. "The only reason I can think of for you being here is Article CT134. I can't think of any other reason why you'd want or need to involve an advocate."

"You're right." Jason paused, wanting to choose his words carefully. "Lesley and Mo don't know we're here. They're understandably in shock."

"We all are," Mary said.

"We want to prepare a case for the execution of the third Chosen, so they can move quickly once they've decided to execute."

"Don't you think it's a little soon for that?" Phillips asked. "Why are you so sure they'll want to execute?"

Jason gulped. "The third Chosen is an Adams."

The blood drained from Phillips's face. "Are you telling me that your sisters are in a triad with one of the Adams children?" he asked, his voice husky.

"I am."

"Unfortunately," Mary murmured.

Phillips dropped his pen and leaned back in his chair. "That's unbelievable! Not that I'm questioning the Chosen Council. It included Article CT134 in the Tradition for cases like this."

"That's what we said!" Mary exclaimed, pointing to herself and then to Jason.

"You can imagine how horrified the families are," Jason said. "Our sisters are devastated. They're just going through the motions right now."

"Understandable," Phillips said. "You know, we tried to execute the children after the Incident. I helped prepare one of the cases. The Adamses spat on everything we hold dear, and who knows what they taught their children. It seemed clear to me and to many others that we'd all be safer if we rid Rymel of their existence. But the overseers didn't see it that way. I wonder if any of them will regret turning down our petitions when they hear about the triad." He shook his head. "Your poor sisters."

"Now you understand why the first thing we did was book an appointment with you," Jason said.

"Yes. They must be going through a terrible time. I'm sure your support means a lot to them."

Jason shifted in his seat.

"Makes you wonder, doesn't it?" Phillips continued. "We said the Adams line was horribly tainted, and it turns out we were right."

"Exactly!" Jason said, nodding vigorously. "I just said yesterday that whenever an Adams is involved in a Joining, something goes wrong."

"So can you make a case?" Mary asked.

Phillips snorted and picked up his pen. "In my sleep, and I'll be happy to do so. The Way has just handed me the opportunity to reverse a bad decision made by short-sighted overseers, and to eliminate a dire threat to the Way in the process. I won't squander it."

Jason shot Mary a smug look.

"Now, I can see why expediency is critical, but we'll be proposing that someone who hasn't violated any articles be executed, so we can't rush this case."

Mary slapped the arm of her chair. "Would you want your family spending time with an Adams?"

"The article's in the Tradition," Jason said. "And we're talking about an Adams. How much of a case will we need?"

"Their reputations are on the line and both family names will be sullied. We have to move quickly, to minimize the damage," Mary said, her voice rising.

"That woman will be in my home tonight," Jason added. "In my home!" he repeated hoarsely.

Mary opened her mouth, but closed it when Phillips held up his hand. "I understand your concerns. Believe me, if I were in your position, I'd share them. I *do* share them, and so will all Rymellans. But we'll only get the one chance with the overseers, as you well know, Jason. And given that we've already been turned down once, we don't want to blow our chances this time because we're impatient." He bowed his head to write notes. "The children had their ages on their side last time. Her age won't protect her this time."

"Until yesterday, I didn't even know there were any Adams children," Jason said. "It came as a complete shock."

"I can imagine. Rymellans will share your shock when this goes public tomorrow."

"We were hoping the triad wouldn't be a triad by then," Mary said.

"Unfortunately I can't move that quickly," Phillips said with a small smile. "But I'll clear my calendar, make this my top priority."

"Thank you," Jason said.

"Who's the Principal?"

"Lesley."

Phillips made a note. "If my memory serves correctly, I met her once. I gave a talk to the Chosen Tradition group at the Military Academy. I believe she was there. Ironic that she'd end up in a triad with an Adams."

Jason chuckled. "I don't think she quite appreciates the irony right now. Perhaps when it's all over."

"Quite."

Mary leaned forward. "This case. I assume it will describe why Adams is a threat to the Way?"

"Of course," Phillips said. "In accordance with the article, the case has to show that the triad won't be viable if the Chosen in question remains a member. An unstable triad is a threat to the Way. So if I can show that a triad with Adams won't be viable, and I believe I can easily do that, then I've shown that Adams is a threat to the Way, a key point if we want her executed. It's not a difficult case. But as I said, we'll only get the one chance, so I want to be thorough, make sure I've covered everything. I'll also consult with several of my colleagues. I'm sure they'll all be eager to help."

He swivelled toward his comm station. "Give me a second," he murmured, tapping away at the station's keys. "Ah, yes, here's the case I worked on just after the Incident." He made a note on the pad, then pressed a button on his comm station. A familiar click indicated that a connection had been established. "Herbert? I want you to contact the archives. I want everything they've got on Article CT134. Every case, opinion, dramatization, amendment, and anything else you can think of. And send me everything they have on the Adams Incident, too."

"The Adams Incident!" Herbert sputtered.

"Yes. Most of the records are sealed, but get what you can. I also want all the information you can find on Jayne Adams. J-a-y-n-e. Find out her sector of residence and send Julie over there to see what she can dig up. I have a feeling that, as of tomorrow, many Rymellans will be anxious to talk to us. Have her drop by a military outpost, see if anyone is willing to share any information about Adams' record."

"I will."

"And Herbert, this is your top priority. Drop everything else." Phillips terminated the connection and swung back to Jason and Mary. "It may take a day or so to retrieve the material related to CT134, but I'll start working on the case right away. I should have something for you within a few weeks' time. When will you tell your sisters about the case?"

Jason and Mary exchanged a glance. "As soon as it's ready," Mary said.

"Or as soon as they say they want to prepare a case," Jason said. "Whichever comes first."

"Do you want me to present it to them, or would you rather I provide it to you in writing first?" Phillips asked.

"In writing," Jason said. Lesley might ignore his pleas to see Phillips, but she couldn't ignore a case he placed in her hand. He was sure that once she read it and knew that Adams threatened the Way, she'd persuade Mo to execute. Then it would just be a matter of authorizing Phillips to present the case to the overseers. "Once the case is presented and accepted, how long would it be until she's executed?"

"Things would move very quickly," Phillips said. "Adams would be seized immediately and dead within the hour."

JAYNE CLIMBED THE steps to Station C3-8's waiting area and immediately spotted Lesley and Mo, their orange cloaks drawing her eye in the almost empty room. They were supposedly her Chosens, but two military usually meant trouble, and these two could do more than strike her or harass her for a laugh; they had the power to decide whether she lived or died.

Her stomach fluttered when Mo's eyes locked with hers. Mo spoke to Lesley, then they both looked in Jayne's direction. "There they are," Jayne murmured absently to Carol and Ronald. She drew a deep breath and forced herself to walk over to them.

"Welcome to C3-8," Lesley said, her smile not reaching her eyes.

"This is my cousin, Carol White, and her Chosen, Ronald," Jayne said, noting as she did that Mo's cloak had a Defence insignia on it, a detail she hadn't noticed yesterday. She'd assumed that since Lesley was in Interior, Mo must be too.

"Jayne doesn't need to tell us who's who," Carol said with a smile. She gazed at Lesley. "I recognize you from the monitors."

"Yes, I'm Lesley." Lesley shook Carol's hand, then Ronald's. "And this is Mo," she said, turning toward Mo.

"Pleased to meet you," Mo said with a nod, though she also shook their hands.

"It's about a twenty minute walk to the estate. This way." Lesley took a couple of tentative steps toward the exit, then glanced over her shoulder and lengthened her stride, apparently satisfied they were following. Several paths led in different directions; she chose the one that veered into a wooded area.

"How was the train ride?" Mo asked, falling into step with Lesley.

"It passed quickly," Jayne said when Carol nudged her. It would have flown by if she'd had her sketchbook.

"Good," Mo said absently.

They walked in silence, Lesley and Mo leading the way. Jayne preferred the silence to forced polite conversation; she suspected there would be plenty of that over supper. They eventually turned off at a sign that read *Thompson Estate*. When the house came into view, Carol turned to Jayne and raised her brows appraisingly. Jayne withered. Not only did the Thompson family apparently own a large block of land, but her entire apartment could probably fit into one of their closets. Did everyone in C3 live like this? Was there a Middleton estate too?

Lesley swung open the front door, stepped across the threshold, and moved aside. "Please, come in." Mo was already stepping into the hallway; Jayne and the Whites followed. "I'll take your cloaks," Lesley said. Her parents and Mo's papa entered the hallway from a room off to the left as Lesley wordlessly accepted Jayne's cloak and hung it over Carol's. When Lesley removed her own cloak, Jayne noticed that she wasn't in uniform. Neither was Mo.

"This is Carol White, Jayne's cousin," Mo said. "And her Chosen, Ronald."

"Welcome to our home," Alan said, shaking their hands. Adelaide and Michael nodded and also shook their hands, but remained silent. "Why don't we show you through to the sitting room," Alan said to Carol and Ronald, "and give the, um, triad a few minutes to themselves."

Jayne's heart sank as she watched Carol and Ronald disappear down the hallway. Apprehensive, she turned to Lesley and Mo, convinced that the Thompsons and Middletons had planned in advance to separate her from the others.

"Why don't we go into the living room? Mo and I want to talk to you for a minute," Lesley said, motioning to the doorway from which her parents and Michael had emerged.

"Sure," Jayne said, her mind racing. They wouldn't tell her they planned to execute and then expect her to have supper with them, would they? *We've concluded that the triad won't be viable with you in it, so we'll be exercising CT134. Tziva?* No, she was letting her imagination run away with her. If they decided to exercise the article, they wouldn't bother to tell her. They'd present their case and then forget about her, not giving her a second's thought as she was dragged away.

Jayne was so preoccupied with what they wanted to discuss that she hardly registered the living room's furnishings and decor. At Lesley's invitation, she sank into a chair. They sat on the sofa across from her. As she stared at them, waiting for them to speak, the full gravity of her situation sank in. If the triad Joined, she'd live with these two women, be trapped with them behind closed doors and always at their mercy. Could she trust them? Dare she try?

Lesley looked at Mo, then crossed her legs. "Um, Mo and I have known each other for a while."

"The Middleton estate is next door," Mo said, "so we grew up together."

So there was a Middleton estate. And they were neighbours. And their families were close. But she'd hear them out before she deemed her situation completely hopeless.

"We've also been in a relationship for a long time," Lesley said slowly.

So Jayne had been right. She wouldn't tell them she'd already guessed, in case they reacted badly.

"Obviously we didn't know we were Chosens," Lesley said. She smiled at Mo, the first time she'd shown any emotion since Jayne had met her.

Since they seemed to genuinely believe they were Chosens, Jayne scratched "each other" off the list of what the Chosen Council may have promised them to temporarily be in a triad with her. She doubted credits would have enticed them, so that left career advancement—and the satisfaction of protecting the Way, of course.

"We were very happy when we figured out from our Chosen Papers that we are," Mo added.

Happiness that must have turned to crushing disappointment

when they learned about the triad. Execution loomed again. Somehow she had to convey that she had absolutely no intention of elbowing her way into their relationship, and do so without insulting them. "How long have you been together?" she asked, to give herself time to think.

They looked at each other. "Well, we got together when we were fourteen," Mo said.

Fourteen. Argamon.

"But we put our relationship on hold when we turned twenty-five."

Jayne almost said, "That must have been difficult," but stopped herself, not wanting to suggest they were weak in the Way. No matter how strong they were in the Way, it must have been heart-wrenching—they obviously cared very much for each other and could actually be Chosens. But they might be eager to take her words the wrong way.

"We wanted to tell you before supper, in case our parents said something," Lesley said. "We didn't want you to find out that way."

"Oh. Thank you," Jayne said. When they continued to stare at her, she realized they were hoping for more. Time to make it clear that she'd stay out of their way. "I'll respect your relationship. I'll never interfere with it in any way."

She couldn't blame them for the scepticism in their eyes, considering she'd just agreed to never have a romantic relationship for the rest of her life. If she were anyone else, she would have thanked them for telling her and left it at that, but then, anyone else's neck wouldn't have been on the line the moment Watkins said her name at Lesley's notification meeting. Anyone else would expect children, at the very least. Nobody else would agree to sit on the sidelines while the other two triad members carried on as if she didn't exist, only acknowledging her in public.

But she wasn't anyone else. She was an Adams. Lesley and Mo couldn't possibly appreciate how the Incident had warped everyone's perception of her, but surely the last twenty-four hours had given them an inkling. Somehow she had to build on it, help them understand why she'd accepted years ago that there would never be a special someone.

Unfortunately the coming days could do it for her. She hoped their reputations wouldn't come under fire when the Chosen Council announced the triad, but realistically, they'd probably get a small taste of what she'd experienced since the Incident—and would probably execute

RYMELLAN 2

her, as a result. So rather than trying to come up with a sanitized way of explaining why she'd never expected a relationship with her Chosen, she might as well be candid with them. Trying to protect herself by softening the truth and avoiding uncomfortable conversations would only backfire. They'd see the truth for themselves soon enough, and she was starting to realize that how she came across to them would likely bear little on whether they decided to exercise CT134.

Jayne sat on her hands. "When I turned eighteen and didn't receive a Solitary Notification, I knew I wouldn't be a desirable match for anyone. I'm aware of what everyone thinks of me. So my only hope was that I'd end up with a Chosen who would eventually see past all that and become a friend. That's all I've ever hoped for. And that's still all I'm hoping for. So I mean it when I say that I'll respect your relationship, not only because I never expected a relationship with my Chosen, but because the triad depends on your relationship remaining strong." She said that last part at the same moment her brain worked it out, and fervently believed it. If their relationship ever wavered, the triad could fall apart. To be associated with another failed Joining was the last thing she wanted. For that reason alone, she'd never come between them. Of course, she probably wouldn't get the chance.

They both peered at her; Jayne could almost hear the wheels turning. "When we found out about the triad, we hoped that we could come to some arrangement with you that we can all live with," Lesley finally said.

"For us, our relationship is the most important thing," Mo said, grabbing Lesley's hand. "I mean, if you're okay with being a friend, then that is an arrangement we can try to live with."

"I'm okay with it," Jayne said, trying not to let her mouth hang open, even though Mo's "try to" wasn't lost on her. Were they saying they'd let her live if she left them alone? Done! She'd intended to do that anyway. But did that mean they hadn't agreed to be in the triad? They seemed sincere. If they weren't, they should have joined the theatre, not the military. Jayne still couldn't accept that she'd just happened to end up in a triad with them, but maybe they weren't in on the scheme.

She suddenly saw them in a new light. They weren't just going through the motions until it was time to get rid of her; they honestly believed they had a decision to make. Maybe those behind the plan had chosen

Lesley and Mo because of their blind dedication to the Way. She felt a pang of something she'd never expected to feel toward them: sympathy. Still, she wasn't safe yet. Those who wanted her dead had two years to wear them down. And if her mere presence in their lives started to grate, they could change their minds.

"Then we'll see how it goes," Lesley said, unknowingly reiterating Jayne's last thought. "Let's join the others."

When Jayne entered the sitting room, Carol raised her eyebrows at her. Jayne responded with a small smile, to let her know that nothing dire had passed. She'd tell her later about the polite conversation they'd just managed to have without anyone explicitly mentioning CT134.

"Would you like something to drink?" Alan asked.

She agreed to a glass of grape juice. After accepting it from him, she sat in the empty chair nearest to Carol and listened to the others engage in small talk. Nobody seemed interested in involving her in the conversation, though she caught all the parents eyeing her when they thought her attention was elsewhere. Let them get the gawking out of their systems; she didn't mind. She was most interested in Lesley and Mo, who were mainly conversing with each other— out of her earshot, unfortunately.

A woman hovered in the doorway. Adelaide exchanged a few words with her and then announced that supper was ready to be served. Jayne followed everyone to the dining room, where ten chairs were aligned at a long table.

"We've never seated a triad before," Adelaide said. "We've put Lesley in the middle, since she's the Principal. Mo, you're at her right."

Jayne gathered that she must be at Lesley's left and took that seat. Since they'd placed Lesley at one end of the table, Jayne found herself across from Mo. Carol and Ronald took the two seats next to her, and the parents occupied the three chairs closest to Mo.

"If all our siblings were here, we'd have to sit in the other dining room," Mo said as two caterers rolled in the first dish.

Other dining room? Jayne hoped she wouldn't have to go to the bathroom. She'd probably get lost.

"You have five brothers and sisters, right?" Carol asked, picking up her fork and starting in on her salad.

Mo nodded. "Four brothers and a sister. Only one of my brothers is Joined, though. My sister and two of my brothers are Solitaries. My youngest brother is a Chosen, but he's only nineteen. "

"We thought we'd welcome three Chosens into the family, but we were wrong," Michael said.

Lesley's fork stopped on the way to her mouth. "Look at us. There will be more Chosens Joined into the family than there are children. How many families can say that?"

"How many would want to?" Adelaide muttered.

"You have a brother, don't you?" Lesley said to Jayne.

On paper, maybe. "Robert. He's a Solitary." And that was all she wanted to say about him.

"Do you live with your brother?" Alan asked.

They all looked at her. Uncomfortable in the spotlight, she lowered her fork. "No, I don't."

"What do you do?" Adelaide asked.

Jayne had dreaded this question. How would she explain to them why she'd never pursued a vocation? Nobody would hire her for positions that required contact with Rymellans, and nobody would want to work next to a reminder of the Incident in those that didn't. Truth be told, she hadn't tried to find a position. After graduating from the Learning Academy with a lousy final report that essentially said she was worthless, she hadn't felt up to facing one potential rejection after another. She'd lost herself in her sketching, and it had been easier to stay there. Art College had flitted across her mind, but that would have meant providing a portfolio of drawings that everyone except Carol mocked. When they'd rejected her application, she wouldn't have known if they'd refused her because she lacked talent, or because her last name was Adams.

Adelaide interpreted her silence as confusion. She gestured toward Lesley and Mo. "These two are in the military. We're advocates," she said, pointing to herself and Alan. "Michael's a tailor. What do you do?"

Two caterers chose that moment to bustle into the room and collect empty salad bowls. Unfortunately the interruption didn't deter Adelaide. "So what do you do?" she asked again after the caterers had left.

Jayne swallowed. "I'm not doing anything right now."

"Why not? What do you do with your time, then? And you said you live alone. How do you manage if you're not earning credits?"

Again, she felt everyone's attention on her. When Carol drew breath, Jayne placed a restraining hand on Carol's arm. She appreciated that Carol wanted to support her, but she had to be the one to answer Adelaide's questions. "I draw an allotment," she said, feeling smaller by the minute.

Adelaide's brow furrowed. "Usually Rymellans draw an allotment when they're ill. Do you have an illness we should know about?"

Was Adelaide asking a trick question? "No," she said quietly, then leaned back to allow a caterer to place the main dish in front of her. She picked up her knife and fork. The food no longer appealed and her mouth felt dry, but she wouldn't insult them. She'd clear her plate if she had to choke down every mouthful.

"You can't draw an allotment when you're Joined, you know," Adelaide said, ignoring her meal. "You can only draw an allotment if your Chosen doesn't have the means to support you. So are you planning to depend on these two?"

Blood rushed to her face. She hadn't thought that far ahead. Being dependent on them mortified her. If they Joined with her, they'd have to feed and clothe her as well. They'd rightly consider her a burden. Despite her earlier conversation with them, CT134 loomed again.

She wanted a sip of water, but her glass was empty and she didn't trust herself to reach for the water jug. Adelaide glared at her, waiting for an answer.

"I think Mo and I should discuss these sorts of details with Jayne," Lesley said. "Privately."

Jayne turned to her in surprise, then quickly turned away. Fortunately Lesley was focused on her mama.

Adelaide's eyes narrowed. "Do you?"

"Yes," Lesley said firmly.

Others murmured their agreement, their heads bent over their plates, but Adelaide wouldn't let it drop. "She'll become a Thompson. Thompsons don't sit around. Thompsons don't depend on—"

"I said we'll discuss it privately," Lesley repeated as Mo rolled her eyes.

"Oh, well, fine then." Adelaide picked up her fork. "Another thing

Thompsons do is go to college. All Thompsons have gone to college. Well, almost all."

Lesley's face tightened. She looked as if she were about to speak, but then grabbed a piece of bread from the bread basket and buttered it.

A heavy silence settled over the table. Jayne focused on her plate. What was she doing here, in this house, on this estate, with these strangers? She should be at home curled up on the sofa, reading a book, planning her next drawing, or sewing a button on her cloak. But could she ever relax at home again, when the apartment door could burst open at any time?

Adelaide had crushed the seed of hope that her conversation with Lesley and Mo had planted. Maybe her two "Chosens" would give her a chance, but not those around them, who had two years to persuade them to execute. Well, when the door burst open, she wouldn't beg for her life. She wasn't a criminal and wouldn't act like one. As they led her to the execution site, she'd hold her head high.

Jayne silently laughed. No, she wouldn't. She'd be a wreck. Her name would end up on the Wall of Offenders, with her parents'. The military would destroy all her artwork, as they had her papa's. And the name Adams would become even more synonymous with "criminal."

LESLEY HUNG HER cloak and then peered into the living room, surprised to see a light on; she hadn't noticed it as she'd approached the house. Mama and Papa looked up at her, mugs in their hands. "I didn't think you'd still be up," Lesley said.

"Well, we are." Mama sipped her tziva. "Mo not with you?"

"No." Given how much they'd tossed and turned the previous night, they'd decided to spend tonight apart. Perhaps one of them would manage to sleep through the night without waking.

"It's good to have her around again," Papa said. "We couldn't see her when, uh . . ."

"We were separated?"

He nodded. "We didn't want to make things more difficult for her. And we didn't want to keep anything from you."

If she'd ever found out that her parents had seen Mo, it would have taken all her willpower to not pester them for details.

"So what do you think now?" Mama asked.

"About what?" Lesley asked, confused.

"CT134. It's becoming clearer that she doesn't suit you and Mo, which means a triad with her will be difficult."

"How is it clearer?" Lesley said, irritated that Mama was raising the article again so soon.

Mama gave her a withering look. "The woman doesn't have a vocation and doesn't care!"

Lesley folded her arms. "I don't know, Mama, she didn't look as if she didn't care to me."

"And she hardly said a word during supper."

"After the way you jumped down her throat, I'm not surprised."

"I didn't jump down her throat!" Mama said indignantly. "I just asked her questions, questions that needed to be asked."

"There's a difference between questioning and badgering."

"While your mama's questions may have been a little strong, we do need to get to know her," Papa said.

"I agree. But perhaps a gentler approach would be more effective."

"You don't care that she doesn't have a vocation?" Mama asked.

"I'm curious to know how she spends her days." And perhaps they would have found out, if Mama hadn't intimidated the woman into silence.

"You didn't find out anything more when you took her home?" Papa asked.

"No." She and Mo had expected a few minutes alone with Jayne on the way to her apartment, after taking Carol and Ronald home. But Carol had invited Jayne to stay the night, so they'd dropped the three of them off near the White home.

Mama drained her mug and rested it on her knee. "How did she react when you told her about you and Mo?"

More honestly than I expected. She would have predicted that Jayne would quickly agree to respect their relationship. Who wouldn't, with CT134 hanging over her head? But Jayne's explanation had convinced Lesley that she was telling them the truth, not just what they wanted to hear. Either that, or Jayne was a skilled manipulator. She didn't strike Lesley that way. "She said she'd respect our relationship. I believe her."

"You believe her, just like that?" Mama asked, shaking her head.

"At the moment, I have no reason to suspect she's lying. We have to see how things go, Mama. To be honest, I don't know how we're supposed to figure out whether the triad will be viable with her in it. Unless she does something blatant . . ." And if Jayne were anyone else, CT134 wouldn't be under discussion until there were clear signs that the triad was struggling, and this one was too young to struggle. Everyone was assuming it was bound to fail because of Jayne's family history. *I'm aware of what everyone thinks of me.*

"Perhaps we should take a look at the cases that have been presented in relation to Article CT134," Mama said.

"You know, that's not a bad idea," Papa said. "I'm curious."

Lesley had to admit that she was, too. What reasons had those who'd exercised the article provided? How had they known that the triad wouldn't be viable with the executed member?

"I'll contact the archives tomorrow, see if they can dig them up." Papa pulled his comm unit from its holder, presumably to make a note of his intention.

"That commander beeping could be a sign that she's not as meek as she appears," Mama said.

"It sounded to me as if he just wanted to double-check that she was coming here," Lesley retorted, wishing she'd been alone when Ramsey had beeped.

"I can understand why they track her movements. It's good to know the military in E6 are so diligent." Mama paused. "I wonder how Commander Finney will handle having an Adams in this sector, if it comes to that. And how will everyone else? As of nine a.m. tomorrow, this isn't our secret anymore. Everyone will know."

They'd find out if Rymellans still regarded triads with suspicion, and Lesley's friends and peers would learn that not only was she in a triad, but in one with an Adams. Lesley nodded wearily. "I'm going to bed. Tomorrow could be a long day."

She climbed the stairs, glad that she'd spend the night alone. Not because Mo would have kept her up, but because she'd be lucky if she slept a wink.

MO GROANED AND cracked open an eye when her comm unit beeped. What flaming time was it? She rubbed her eyes and blinked at the display—09:45—then read the name: *Cmdr. T. Baker.* "Middleton," she croaked, sitting up.

"Good morning, Mo."

"Morning, Commander," she mumbled.

"Admiral Jensen has requested a meeting with you this afternoon at 13:00. She's also asked me to attend."

Okay, she hadn't slept well, but she felt coherent. "Admiral Jensen wants to see me?" So far, her exposure to Jensen had consisted of seeing the admiral's name at the bottom of Defence certificates and in the occasional article in Defence bulletins.

"Yes." He cleared his throat. "Maybe she's read this morning's announcements."

Flaming Argamon! The Chosen Council's announcements had gone out at 09:00. And Admiral Jensen was already asking to see her? Usually Rymellans didn't read the announcements as soon as they were released; after all, they had an entire week before the next batch. But if just one person connected to the admiral had read them early . . . news of a triad would spread like wildfire. "Where's the meeting?"

"B5 headquarters. Why don't you meet me in the lobby at 12:45?"

"Okay."

"It's a rather interesting, uh, announcement," Baker said.

"Which part, the triad part or the Adams part?" Mo asked, deciding on the spur of the moment that pretending she didn't understand why the announcement was a shocker would be stupid. If she was honest about it, maybe others would be too. They could clear the air and move on.

Silence, then Baker chuckled. "All of it."

"We were shocked too." *Still are.*

"I can imagine. Congratulations are certainly in order in regards to Lesley. As for the rest . . ."

"Yeah, I know."

"Whatever Jensen wants, we'll deal with it together, okay?"

"Yep," she said, trying not to worry.

"See you at 12:45. Baker out."

As soon as he disconnected, Mo punched in Les's code. "I've just been told I have to see a flaming admiral this afternoon," she blurted before Les could say a word.

"The triad went public at 09:00."

"Yeah, I've already connected the dots," Mo snapped, then took a deep breath. "Sorry."

"Do you know what he wants?"

"She. Jensen. No, I don't. Baker beeped me and told me to meet him at 12:45. At least he'll be there too."

"Do you want me to go with you? I can read in the craft while you're in the meeting."

"Would you fly us there? It's at B5 headquarters." She hated flying over B5.

"Sure. Too bad it isn't at B2 headquarters. I could show you my office." Les paused. "And get a feel for how people are reacting without having to stay long. I haven't heard from anyone. I'm not sure if that's a good or bad sign."

Mo quickly checked her messages. "Neither have I, apart from Baker."

"Well, for me, Laura was the big one, and she'll definitely be there for us."

Yeah, Flaming Finney had turned out to be a descendant of a triad. And now she wanted to have supper with all of them. How wonderful! Though it couldn't be any tenser than last night's supper. And though it grated, Mo had to admit that Finney's support was important.

"Part of me is glad I'm on leave," Les said. "The other part wishes I wasn't. I'm in the dark."

"At least Hall hasn't asked to see you."

"True. Look, why don't you come over? We can have an early lunch and then go."

"I just got up," Mo protested.

"Did you sleep okay?"

"Not really. You?"

"Same."

"Let me shower, then I'll head over."

"See you in a bit, then."

They said good-bye and disconnected. Mo sat on the end of her bed with a sigh. She had no idea what Jensen wanted, but her gut told her that whatever it was, it wasn't good.

JAYNE SPREAD RASPBERRY jam on a piece of bread and covered it with another piece, completing her sandwich. She took a bite as she walked to the kitchen table, then swallowed quickly and set the plate on the table when her comm unit beeped. "Hi," she said, sitting down.

"You still at our place?" Carol asked.

"Uh-huh. I'm just having lunch, then I'm heading home."

"Why don't you stay another few days? Let the initial shock blow over."

"Carol, I won't face anything I haven't faced before."

"I don't know, Jayne," Carol said quietly. "The triad is *the* topic of conversation today. Everyone's talking about it—about you. And I'm only getting the polite version. Who knows what they're saying when I'm not around?"

"So everyone's talking, what else is new?"

"This feels different. I'd feel better if you stayed with us a little longer."

"They won't be saying anything I haven't heard before."

"Will you at least stay until I get home? Please?" Carol sounded worried.

"Okay," Jayne said, despite knowing that Carol would come home and try to persuade her to stay another night. She didn't want Carol fretting all afternoon.

"Good," Carol said with a sigh of relief. "I'll see you later."

"Bye."

Jayne lifted her sandwich and took another bite. So everyone was talking. She could guess what they were saying—the triad was her fault; the triad was doomed to failure; poor Thompson and Middleton. Those who'd petitioned for her execution after the Incident would be crowing that the overseers had made a mistake, and those who knew about Article CT134 would be discussing the odds that Thompson and Middleton would prepare a case.

Let them talk; they couldn't make her feel any worse than she had last night, when Adelaide had swiftly cut her down to size. Jayne knew who to watch out for in that family—in addition to Lesley. Rymellans could talk all they wanted; only what Lesley and Mo thought would count in the end.

So Carol needn't be concerned about her. How the talk would affect Jayne was irrelevant. How it would affect Lesley and Mo was the important question, and Jayne's life depended on the answer. What were they hearing today? Unlike Jayne, they'd be unprepared for the onslaught, unaccustomed to having whispers and suspicions swirl around them and their dedication to the Way questioned.

Once again, Jayne felt a pang of sympathy and wondered how she could support them. For a split second, she considered beeping one of them—probably Mo—to ask how they were, but then she decided against the idea. She doubted they'd want to hear from her today, and they might interpret her concern as an attempt to save her own skin. In time, if the triad survived, perhaps they'd trust her enough to accept that any support she offered was genuine, not a ploy. For now, they'd have to rely on their own strength, and she'd have to hope they were strong enough to resist the temptation to exercise CT134. Would they honour the spirit of the article when their reputations were under fire and everyone was urging them to execute, or would they buckle under the pressure and throw a sham case together?

Jayne savoured the next bite of her sandwich. From this point forward, any meal could be her last.

MO PUSHED OPEN one of the double doors at the entrance to B5 headquarters, hoping she appeared calmer and more confident than she felt. Nobody stared and pointed at her, but she was just one of the many anonymous Defence members striding through the crowded lobby. She'd probably face gawkers if she were at the Military Academy, on 72, or anywhere else pilots hung out, but not here.

Baker stood chatting with one of the officers behind the reception counter. "Commander," Mo said with a nod when she reached him.

He nodded in return. "Let's go to Admiral Jensen's reception area. This way."

Mo walked next to him, fighting the urge to ask if he'd gleaned any information concerning the reason for the meeting. "Almost there," he said as they turned a corner and approached a glass door at the corridor's end. The gold lettering on the door read *Admiral S. Jensen, Reception*.

The woman behind the desk smiled warmly. "Yes?"

"Commander Baker and Lieutenant Commander Middleton. We have an appointment at 13:00," Baker said.

The woman, one Lieutenant Boyd, according to the nameplate sitting on the desk, peered at her comm station. "Oh, yes. The admiral will be with you shortly. Please, hang your cloaks and have a seat."

As they settled in two of the chairs waiting against one paneled wall, Mo glanced around and caught Boyd staring at her. Boyd coloured slightly and looked away. Apparently she'd read the Chosen Council's announcements too, or heard about one in particular.

"Let me do the talking," Baker murmured.

"Okay," Mo said, relieved.

"We'll miss you, this tour. I suppose it's too early to know when you'll be back on the *Falcon*, especially with . . . with what's happened."

The triad wasn't the only factor that could delay her next tour on a ship. Mo still didn't know how she and Les would resolve their diverging career paths. "Yeah, everything's sort of on hold right now."

"I can imagine."

No, he couldn't.

"When you do return, I hope we gain Lesley as well."

If she returned. Mo hoped she would, but she wasn't sure how she could without Les having to sacrifice her career goals. "She'd definitely be with me, so yeah, she'd be flying full-time again."

"If she comes with you as a pilot. She could come aboard as part of Interior."

Mo hadn't thought of that. Every ship had a handful of Interior officers on board, but commanders were rarely among them, if ever. If they promoted Les to commander, Mo couldn't see them assigning her to a Defence ship, though how many commanders had pilots as Chosens?

The mahogany door near Boyd's desk swung open. A commodore emerged from Jensen's office, nodded to Boyd, and left the reception area. Mo's heart pounded; she clenched her hands in her lap and thought about Les, who was probably lounging comfortably in the aviacraft with her nose in a book.

Boyd's station beeped. She glanced at its display, then looked in Baker's direction. "You and the lieutenant commander can go in now, Commander."

"Thank you," Baker said, rising. Mo followed him into Jensen's office. She and Baker stood at attention behind the two empty chairs in front of Jensen's desk.

Jensen leaned back in her chair and touched her fingertips together. "If you would close the door, Lieutenant Commander," she said.

Mo did so, then resumed her stance at Baker's side. She stared at a point on the wall behind Jensen's left shoulder as Jensen studied them in silence. "At ease," Jensen finally said. Mo expected an invitation to sit, but none came.

Jensen straightened and rolled her chair closer to the desk. She rested her elbows on the desktop and touched her fingertips together again. "Like many Rymellans, I started my day by reading the Chosen Council's weekly announcements. And like many Rymellans, I was shocked when I read about the triad, and not just a triad, a triad with an Adams." She grimaced. "Not something people want to read with their morning tziva."

Mo kept her eyes focused on that point on the wall.

"I already know who Thompson is," Jensen said, her gaze taking in both Mo and Baker. "When I read that another lieutenant commander is involved, I naturally requested that lieutenant commander's file. I was quite dismayed when I discovered that not only is a Defence member involved, but a Defence member under my purview."

She leaned forward. "We have a problem. Your Chosen—or in this case, Chosens—must accompany you on tours. I'm concerned about how a crew will react to having an Adams on board. Morale is important for any military operation, whether it be a routine patrol or a key operation that has the potential to turn a campaign. Everyone has to work together on tour. There can be no dissension, no whispers." She focused her attention on Mo. "Given that, I have no choice but to remove you from the *Falcon*'s roster. Permanently."

Mo stifled a shocked retort. Beside her, Baker shifted his weight. "With respect, Admiral, Adams isn't military," he said.

"Of course she isn't," Jensen said with a snort. "We'd never let her in."

"No, we wouldn't. So while I understand your point, I'm not sure everyone has to like everyone else's Chosen in order for morale to be healthy and for our military members to work as a team."

Mo silently agreed. There were certainly a few non-military Chosens on the *Falcon* that she'd happily see sucked out of an airlock.

"Under other circumstances, I'd agree with you, but these are extraordinary circumstances." Jensen leaned back in her chair again. "This goes beyond not liking someone. Having an Adams on board a ship could be disruptive. Most see her as a threat to the Way. Does it make sense to have a Defence ship carrying a threat to the Way?"

"Of course not," Baker said, "but—"

"There are no buts, Commander."

Baker fell silent.

"And it's not only Adams, is it? I read your file, Lieutenant Commander." Jensen spun toward her station screen. "And what did I come across? You had problems on your very first tour of duty. What was it again?" She scanned whatever was on her screen. "Oh, yes. Not mentally fit for duty." Jensen swivelled to face Mo. "Not . . . mentally fit . . . for duty."

Mo's cheeks burned. She met Jensen's eyes and refused to look away.

"Admiral, did you read the entire file, especially the circumstances surrounding Lieutenant Commander Middleton's medical leave?" Baker asked. "She received the Medal of Service to the Way for saving the entire B5-1 Learning Academy."

"And had a breakdown!"

"She was willing to sacrifice herself to save others. As it was, she lost her mama in the crash."

"A terrible tragedy, but does everyone have a breakdown when they lose a parent? And what will happen if she sees real action and we experience casualties? Another breakdown?" Jensen shook her head. "I'll grant you that, viewed in isolation, the lieutenant commander's medical leave wouldn't raise any alarm bells. But now we have new information, information suggesting that the lieutenant commander's state of mind after the crash could have been indicative of a weakness in character and perhaps a weakness in the Way."

"Lieutenant Commander Middleton is one of our best pilots!" Baker said, clearly exasperated. "And her dedication to the Way has never been in question!"

Jensen glared at Baker. "Yet she has an Adams for a Chosen, and a second Chosen, too. So until further notice, she's grounded. No tours."

Mo resisted the urge to wave at them. Had they forgotten she was there? She was short, not invisible. "Admiral, does this mean I'll never fly again?" she asked, her voice sounding even because her legs were doing all the shaking.

"No, I said no tours," Jensen said, still looking at Baker. "I think the supply list is the right place for you at the moment. When the triad has some time behind it and Rymellans see that it's stable and that Adams is observing the Tradition, I might be willing to let you back onto one of my ships." Jensen's gaze settled on Mo. "Of course, if for some reason the triad ceases to exist, you'd be welcome on any tour immediately. In fact, I may have an open spot on the *Hawk* for a senior pilot, one that will lead to commander rank. If not for the triad, I'd have no problem recommending you for the position. But given your current circumstances, I can't put your name forward. You do understand."

Yes, she flaming-well understood! Maybe Les was right and the triad wasn't real. "Yes, Admiral." Despite the rage coursing through her, she sounded calm.

"Good. You're still a pilot in the Defence Division. I want you ready to fly a tour at any time, and I'll be monitoring your simulator scores and your performance while flying domestic. Commander Baker, consider yourself informed that the lieutenant commander will not be returning to the *Falcon* in six months. Dismissed."

As they collected their cloaks, Mo could tell from the set of Baker's shoulders that he wasn't pleased, nor in the mood to talk. He didn't turn to her until they'd almost reached the lobby. "I'm sorry, Mo, especially about her dragging up your medical leave." He scowled. "You're not the first pilot to require intensive counselling, and you certainly won't be the last, especially if we go to war. Experienced counsellors like Willis are on board for a reason, and she knows it."

"It's all right," Mo said. Actually, it wasn't, but Jensen should be the one to apologize, not Baker. "It's not your fault. You did the right thing back then."

Her assurances didn't mollify him. "We'll sort this out, I promise. I can't believe she's grounded you!"

"At least I'd already removed myself from the next tour," Mo said, trying not to get caught up in his indignation. If she gave in to her anger, she'd likely say a few things she'd later regret. "Maybe in six months, she'll have changed her mind." Yeah, and maybe Mo would be admiral by then, too. "And to be honest, given the triad and Les's career, I'm not sure when I'll be in a position to go on tour again."

"Mo, you're a born pilot. You'll be wasted on domestic. Maybe you will have to miss a few tours because of the triad, but once everything's settled, you'll want to be out there again."

Maybe, but wanting and having were two different things. The longer Les was tied to Rymel, the more she'd become entrenched in her Interior career. Mo had already considered the possibility that she'd never go back on tour, but she'd thought it would be by choice, not because an airhead admiral was trying to manipulate her. "I guess we'll see what happens."

Baker grunted.

"I was planning to pick up my things just before the *Falcon* undocked, so I could say good-bye to everyone. But if it's all right with you, I think I'll pick them up in a few days."

His forehead creased. "I haven't assigned anyone your quarters. I hoped you'd only be off for one tour."

"I think you better go ahead and assign them," Mo said quietly, then looked down at her feet to hide her face.

"I'm sorry," Baker said again. "I'll do whatever I can to change Jensen's mind."

"Thank you," Mo said. "I'll send you a dispatch if my status changes." Though he could find out before she did. "Permission to leave."

Baker pressed his lips together, then said, "Permission granted. It's been a privilege to serve with you, Lieutenant Commander." He nodded to her.

Mo saluted him. "And with you." Her vision blurred. She whirled and walked away. He already felt bad; he didn't need to see her cry.

She fought tears all the way to the aviacraft and bit her lip as she slid open the door, determined not to sob her heart out when she was safely inside. She had to be stoic for Les, not add yet another burden to those Les already shouldered.

Les's nose wasn't in a book; she was reading something on her comm unit, and looked up when Mo entered the craft. The curiosity on her face quickly turned to concern. "What happened?" she asked, shoving the comm unit into its holder.

Mo plunked down in the passenger seat and shrugged. "You know how we were eventually going to have to figure out what to do about our careers, with you in Interior and me in Defence? Well, we don't have to worry about that anymore, because my career just went down the drain." She forced herself to meet Les's eyes, then reached for her and squeezed her eyes shut. Feeling Les's arms tighten around her only made it more difficult to maintain her composure, but somehow she managed not to sniffle.

"What happened?" Les asked again, softly.

"I'm no longer welcome on tours. Not as long as I'm in a triad and would have a threat to the Way tagging along, anyway. Domestic only, unless the triad disappears."

"She said that? That if the triad goes away, you can go on tours?"

"Yeah, she did. Of course, she didn't elaborate on how the triad could suddenly go away. I'm starting to think you're right about the reason we're stuck in this triad."

Les drew back. "What did Baker have to say?"

"He didn't like it. He said he'll try to change her mind." She decided not to tell Les that Jensen had brought up her extended medical leave, not wanting Les to regret her decision back then to sound the alarm. "I doubt she will, though. Not unless we exercise CT134. And we're not going to, not because of this."

"She won't be the only one with authority who'll want us to exercise it."

Mo was starting to appreciate that. "Have you heard from anyone yet?"

"A few dispatches, all carefully worded to basically acknowledge that they've seen the announcement." Les chuckled. "But what else can they say? Congratulations would be insincere and honesty would probably be rude." She grasped Mo's hand. "We have to stick together on this. Will you be all right flying domestic for now?"

"I was going to be doing it for the next six months anyway." And she'd always believed that as long as she was with Les and in a cockpit, she'd be content. Flying was flying, right? It wasn't as if she was seeing real action on tour. But domestic service didn't have the same air of excitement about it. Plus, pilots on tour always ribbed those left behind to watch over the planet. Most, like her, meant it good-naturedly, but some seriously believed they were better than their domestic peers. Well, she'd never cared for snobs. "It's a good thing it's not your wings being clipped. I can imagine what your mama would say." Mo adopted Adelaide's tone and diction. "If you'd listened to me, Lesley, you wouldn't be flying in circles around the planet, pretending to be a fighter pilot."

Les laughed, then grew serious. "I'm sure Jensen will change her mind—perhaps not for a year or two, but she will. So we'll have that conversation about our careers. I was hoping that once I had a few years of service as a commander under my belt, I could transfer back to Defence and we could think about going on a tour, perhaps with a daughter or two along."

"And our other Chosen," Mo added dryly.

"Yes. Her too," Les said, bemused.

"I wonder how she's doing today." Not that Mo cared. She should, but Jayne didn't appear to have much to lose, and nobody would pressure her about CT134, even if she did. Mo knew she was being surly, but right now, after just being told she'd probably still be flying domestic when she was fifty and all her friends outranked her, she didn't flaming care.

"Actually, I was thinking that perhaps we should go see her tonight," Les said hesitantly.

Mo looked at her. "Why?"

"Because I think we need to show everyone that we're a triad, not a couple and an odd one out. When I said we need to stick together, I meant with her, as well."

"She has nothing to lose!" Mo snapped. She'd just been relegated to domestic duty for the rest of her life and had her mental state after Mama's death thrown in her face, but Les was concerned about poor old Jayne. "She doesn't have a career or a reputation to protect. And CT134 isn't an issue for her—I mean, not in the same way it is for us."

"True, but what if everyone's reacting the same way Jason and Mary did? They immediately pointed the finger at Jayne. What if those around her do the same? She's more vulnerable than we are."

"But she has nothing to lose," Mo said again, her irritation with Les's concern rising.

Les's grip on Mo's hand tightened. "Mo, I'm thinking about us. If we signal where we stand on the triad, at least right now, perhaps Rymellans won't pressure us to exercise the article right away. They might take their cue from us and give us some time." She paused. "I could be wrong, but I think we need to behave as if the triad's legitimate and we genuinely want to give it a chance. We need to show what we think following the Way means right now."

Mo didn't believe for an instant that being seen with Jayne would delay any pressure concerning CT134, but she could see Les's point about showing where they stood. With any luck, the triad's togetherness would get back to Jensen. Ideally she'd read a dispatch about it while having her flaming morning tziva.

"We'll have to see her again at some point anyway, and soon. We can't ignore her," Les said.

"Yeah, okay, let's go see her," Mo mumbled. The day couldn't get any worse.

Les pulled out her comm unit. "What's her comm code again?" she murmured, then punched in a code, apparently having memorized it after beeping Jayne the previous day.

"Yes, um, hello," Jayne said, after her comm unit must have beeped for at least thirty seconds.

"Hello," Les replied. "Mo and I were wondering if we could visit you tonight. Perhaps around 7:30?"

"Oh." A pause. "My apartment isn't very big."

"If there isn't enough room for us to sit down, we can stand," Les said, her tone light.

Silence, then, "You'll be able to sit."

Les's brow furrowed. Mo stifled a laugh. Jayne had sounded serious.

"Can we make it eight?" Jayne asked. "I'm still at Carol's."

"Sure, that's fine. Can you dispatch your apartment identifier to me?"

"Yes. Sure. I'll do that right away."

"Thanks. We'll see you later. Good-bye."

"Bye."

Les terminated the connection.

"Don't tell her about my problem with Jensen," Mo said.

"Why not?"

"Because she doesn't need to know those sorts of details. All she needs to know is that I'm on the supply list right now because I dropped from the next tour. Things could change in six months." Mo doubted they would, but she and Les would deal with the problem. They didn't need Jayne poking her nose into it.

"We haven't discussed what we do in any detail," Les said. "She doesn't even know you've been on tour and that you're a fighter pilot. Perhaps she thinks you fly aviacrafts."

Mo snorted.

"Then again, she probably has no idea what you do in Defence. All she knows is that we both have aviacraft licences. Without my mama around, perhaps we can actually have a civil conversation and not only tell her what we do, but find out how she spends her time."

"So you're going to tell her you belong to a group that investigates Chosen Violations?" Mo asked. Last night's supper had been awkward. Discussing Chosen Violations with Jayne would be awkward squared.

"She probably saw me in the procession."

"Even if she did, she still wouldn't know you're in a special group. And will you mention that you'll be undergoing the commander training course?"

"After what Jensen just did, I think I'll tell her about the commander course when I know for sure I'll be taking it. Anyway, let's go." Les turned to the navigation panel.

Mo fastened her seatbelt. As the aviacraft lifted off, she suddenly wanted to tell Les to change the coordinates to those for the Military Academy. The simulator always soothed her, and she hadn't flown a sim with Les since they'd separated. But that would mean facing her peers at the pilot training complex. She wasn't ready for that, not after Jensen. She'd naively assumed that her military record and family name would speak for themselves and trump any misgivings Rymellans had about Jayne and the triad. But it hadn't with Jensen, and now she had to face the possibility that those she considered friends could turn their backs on her.

KEVIN STEWART SURVEYED the group gathered in his living room with satisfaction. Word had rapidly spread; around thirty people had managed to squeeze themselves into the room, many representing their families. Any newcomers would have to listen in from the hallway. Gwen and the children weren't among those assembled. They'd gone to her parents, so the children wouldn't inadvertently hear something they shouldn't.

He raised his hand. "Let's begin." Those chatting quieted; others settled back in their seats. "We were right," Kevin said when he was sure he had everyone's attention. The front door thumped shut; two new faces peered over the shoulders of those leaning against the living room doorway. "You've all seen the announcement," he continued. "What we said would happen has happened. But they ignored our warnings. They let her live."

Tom Morgan snorted. "I still remember that pompous fool sitting there all smug, telling me I didn't understand the Way. That a dispensation to execute a twelve-year-old would set a dangerous precedent, especially since she hadn't violated any articles."

"But she was—is—the product of two criminals," Ellen Finch said. "Both committed Chosen Violations. Both lines are obviously flawed. And this girl is a combination of both lines."

"Which is why we have this!" Kevin thrust his finger toward the names of the three triad members displayed on the comm station screen he'd swivelled to face the group. "Not only is she involved in an unnatural formation, but with two military members, one on the rise. The Adams taint is spreading, growing stronger. If we don't stop it, we could be witnessing what history will show as the event that triggered the downfall of the Way."

Alarmed gasps filled the room.

"We have to do something!" someone cried.

"But what?" said another.

"Whatever we do can't violate the Way. We're not criminals," a third said nervously.

Kevin signaled for silence. "We have an opportunity to rid ourselves

of this threat once and for all without violating any articles," he told
them. "Article CT134. The Principal and one of the other members of
that abomination can execute the third Chosen. In this case, they'll
have to show that Adams will be a threat to the Joining and to the Way
if she remains alive." Laughter rippled through the assembly. He smiled.
"Exactly. So, my friends, Article CT134 gives Thompson and Middleton
the power to execute Adams."

Everyone spoke at once. Kevin waited for the din to die naturally,
pleased to be in the company of like-minded Rymellans. "I have no
doubt that Thompson and Middleton will execute Adams. I'm sure
they've already engaged an advocate. What worries me is the influence
Adams has over them. We've seen how the Adamses work their charms,
how they whisper into the ears of innocent Rymellans." Kevin's mouth
twisted. "I'm sure Adams is already spreading her poison. We must help
and support Thompson and Middleton, let them know that Rymellans
are behind them and will applaud their decision to exercise CT134."

"But how, Kevin?" Cynthia Stewart asked.

"If we're not careful, we'll be the ones executed," Ellen said. "We don't
want to be seen as criticizing the Chosen Council."

Kevin shook his head, ignoring the front door as it announced more
arrivals. "The Chosen Council added the article to the Tradition, so suggesting that it be exercised and supporting those who exercise it can
hardly be seen as criticizing the Council. Trust me, we won't be the only
ones calling for her execution. She's fair game now."

"So what do we do?" Tom asked.

"I propose that we send a dispatch to Thompson, since she's the
Principal. This will serve two purposes. First of all, it'll let her know
that they're not alone, that Rymellans will support her and Middleton's
decision to execute Adams, as we would have supported the decision
thirteen years ago. If," Kevin finished derisively, "those idiots had found
the courage to do what should have been done, instead of hiding behind
misguided concerns about offending the sensibilities of Rymellans who
all wanted it done anyway." His chest felt tight. He paused to catch his
breath. "Second, it will allow us to put forward our case for why we
think they should execute Adams. I'm sure Thompson is well aware of

the reasons, but we need to drive them home, counter whatever Adams
is whispering in her ear."

"Each write a dispatch, you mean?" Tom asked, frowning.

Kevin nodded. "And we'll write them now. Together."

Several in the room coughed or whispered to their neighbours. "I'm
not sending a dispatch to Thompson," Cynthia said.

"If we bombard her with dispatches, she'll see it as harassment,"
another said.

"I don't want the military on my doorstep," a third chipped in. Everyone murmured agreement.

"Let's write one well-crafted dispatch, instead," Ellen said. "We can
tell her we've written it on behalf of a group of concerned Rymellans.
Personally, I'd be more impressed that a group is behind the appeal.
She'll have no idea how many of us there are. She might imagine hundreds, thousands."

"And who volunteers to send it?" someone asked indignantly. "I won't.
You know who they'll come after first. It's not fair to expect one person
to take that risk for everyone."

"It's not a violation to send someone a dispatch!" Kevin snapped.
"And are you telling me that nobody here is willing to stand up for the
Way? An Adams could Join with two Rymellans, one of whom is on
her way to admiral."

"If Thompson survives long enough," someone murmured. "We don't
know when Adams plans to involve her in a Chosen Violation."

"Yes, if she lives," Kevin said, meeting the eyes of those nearest him
one by one. "And maybe that's what Adams wants. Imagine the power
she'll have if she's Joined to an admiral. Think of the possibilities! We
could be the only ones standing between her and the destruction of the
Way. And nobody is willing to send a dispatch?"

"Adams has to be executed," someone said firmly.

"Exactly."

"Why don't you send the dispatch?" someone else asked.

Kevin shook his head. "If I do it, Thompson will likely dismiss it. The
same applies to Cynthia and Tom. It has to be someone else, someone
she'll consider impartial."

"What about the Adams son?" Ellen asked. "Even if the daughter is executed, he'll still be around."

"I wish we could do something about him, but we can't. Fortunately he's a Solitary, so at least he won't be reproducing."

Several looked at Kevin in horror. "If Adams has children . . ." one woman said, her voice strained.

"Yes. This is our final chance to end this."

The enormity of the crisis silenced everyone.

"Maybe there's another way to contact Thompson," a man said from the doorway. "I believe the military has an internal system for sending actual documents, just like most organizations do. If we write the dispatch on paper, somehow send it through that system . . ."

"We'd need a military member to send it for us," Kevin pointed out.

"Surely most, if not all, will be sympathetic," Tom said.

"Who wants to start asking military if they'll help us?" someone asked wryly. Nervous laughter met the comment.

Kevin looked at everyone in disgust. Cowards, all of them! He'd send a dispatch; he'd ask military, even if it meant his life. Shouldn't all Rymellans be willing to die for the Way? But he couldn't do it, because Thompson wouldn't take him seriously. She should! His knowledge of the Adams' depravity was based on firsthand experience.

"Why don't we start composing a letter? We can figure out how to get it to Thompson once we're done," someone said.

Grateful for the suggestion, Kevin smiled. "Yes, let's do that." Maybe discussing the danger and seeing in black and white the reasons Adams had to die would reacquaint some in the room with their backbones. "Let's split into groups. Tom, take those in the hallway. Ellen, grab everyone to your left. Everyone else gather around me."

Chattering, those assembled moved into groups.

The front door thumped shut again. "Grab whoever just came in," Kevin shouted to Tom.

"Um, Kevin," someone near the doorway called, his face pale. Those in the hallway suddenly grew quiet. A moment later, Kevin understood why. Two Interior officers squeezed themselves into the living room. Everyone stared at them, fear in their eyes.

"I assume you're in charge here, Kevin," Lieutenant Brock stated.

Several around Kevin nodded; one pointed at him. Kevin licked his lips. "This is a peaceful meeting," he said, finding his voice. "We're not doing anything wrong."

Brock approached Kevin while his partner hung back. "We heard a rumour that you're all here because of the triad."

"We're not doing anything wrong," he said again. "The Chosen Council added CT134 to the Tradition. We're allowed to offer an opinion to those in a position to exercise it."

"Oh, so your plan is to pressure Thompson and Middleton to exercise CT134?"

A bead of sweat tickled Kevin's brow. He swallowed. "Like I said, the Chosen Council added CT134 to the Tradition. We simply want to tell them why we think they should exercise it. We will, of course, accept whatever decision they make." He hid his trembling hands behind his back.

"Relax, Kevin," Brock said, unbuttoning his cloak. "We're not here to strike you, we're here to join you."

JAYNE BOUNDED UP the steps to Station E6-4's waiting area and hurried outside. She'd intended to leave the Whites' the moment Carol arrived home, but Carol had persuaded her to stay for supper and then had spent ages trying to convince her to change her plans with Lesley and Mo. What was Carol so afraid of? So people were talking. So people were blaming an Adams for the triad. What else was new? What had Carol intended to do, have Jayne stay with her until the talk died down? The talk would never die down, and Carol couldn't be with her twenty-four hours a day. Jayne had to go home at some point, and she couldn't keep Lesley and Mo away from her apartment forever.

But she wasn't ready to show them her drawings, not yet. She'd left her sketchbook at Carol's and hoped to reach her apartment in time to remove the few drawings that hung on its walls. They didn't need to see her bedroom, so she'd throw her drawings, sketchbooks, pencils—anything that might give away her secret—into it and shut the door. Though, given the time, she might run into Lesley and Mo before she reached her apartment. If she did and they ridiculed her drawings, they could go ahead and execute her. She'd rather die than have them laugh at her art for the rest of her life.

Minutes later, almost at her apartment, she relaxed. There was no sign of Lesley and Mo. It should only take her five—

Two people were running toward her. She veered to the left, but still they came right at her. Suddenly she was sprawled on the path, her breath knocked from her. The world went white; pain exploded behind her left eye. She tried to struggle to a sitting position, but a weight held her down. Someone was on top of her, straddling her. "Thought you'd stay away and hide?" he shouted.

She glimpsed his face just as he drew back his arm. His fist slammed into her mouth. Something sharp scraped down the back of her throat. She lifted her hands to protect herself, but the next blow came from her left. Her ears rang; she closed her eyes in agony. Another explosion of pain; fluid trickled into her right eye, blinding her.

The weight on her chest lifted. She rolled to her right, started to push herself up, desperate to get away. "We should have killed you years ago," another man yelled. Pressure on her back; a searing pain; she collapsed onto the path. "For the Way!" Fire radiated through her back; she cried out.

"Hey!"

Something thudded next to her. Receding footsteps, approaching footsteps. *No, no more. I can't take anymore . . .* She tried to crawl away. The stones on the path dug into her arms, but she couldn't move. *Too much pain. Too . . . weak.*

"Les, she's been stabbed!" someone exclaimed—a woman. "Don't move, Jayne. Don't move." Jayne knew . . . the voice. But . . . who . . .

"This is Lieutenant Commander Thompson. Medical emergency at my coordinates. I repeat, medical emergency at my coordinates. Send immediate assistance. Reporting a Level 5 assault. Repeat, a Level 5 assault. Lock down the sector."

"Medical aviacraft dispatched. I'm connecting you to a physician."

"Physician Ackers, Lieutenant Commander. What's the nature of the injury?"

"She's been stabbed. She's bleeding."

"Where . . ." The voice faded.

"... keep the pressure on."

"I'm pushing as hard as I can, Les. The bleeding ..."

"... with me, Jayne. Come on, Jayne, stay with me."

Jayne opened her eyes. She couldn't see Lesley. She couldn't see anything. Why couldn't she see anything?

"I see the medical aviacraft, Jayne. I see the craft! Come on, Jayne, stay with me. They're almost here. Just one more minute, Jayne. Hold on for one more minute."

No, no, she needed to sleep. So tired. So fed up. So cold. So tired. She let the darkness take her.

LESLEY WATCHED THE medical personnel work on Jayne, still struggling to digest what had happened. A group of Interior officers rushed by, in the direction she'd told an earlier group the assailants had fled.

"It looks like they're getting ready to put her on the craft," Mo said, so softly that Lesley barely heard her.

"Why don't you go with her and I'll follow in my craft?"

"Yeah, okay." Mo frowned. "But they won't expect me to make decisions for her, will they? I mean, I don't even know her."

"I'll beep Carol, ask her to meet us there. We can defer to her." Lesley paused. "I dread telling her what—"

One of the emergency physicians approached them, the same one who'd told a dazed Mo to go into the medical aviacraft and wash her hands. Physician Shaw. "How is she?" Lesley asked.

"She's stable enough to transport, but we have to get her to the infirmary right away," Shaw replied.

"Will she survive?" Mo asked, her face pale and a slight tremor in her voice.

"It's touch and go. We really do need to get her to the infirmary. Are you both coming?"

"No, just me." Mo squeezed Lesley's hand. "I'll beep you, let you know where I'm waiting."

"I'll be following in my aviacraft," Lesley said, not wanting Shaw to think that she wasn't planning to show up at the infirmary at all.

"Then let's go," Shaw said to Mo. She turned away, then turned back. "Oh, Jayne did briefly regain consciousness. She wanted me to tell you something, both of you. It seemed pretty important to her. She struggled to form the words, even though I told her to stop."

"What did she say?" Lesley asked.

"She said to tell you she's sorry."

CLOSING RANKS

.....

JAYNE GINGERLY FELT THE GAP IN her top teeth with her tongue, careful not to move her mouth or open her eyes. Someone was sitting next to the bed, and she didn't want them to know she was awake. She ran her tongue along her lower teeth. Intact. Next she wiggled her fingers and toes—they seemed to work. She wasn't feeling any pain, thanks to whatever they were pumping into her. Best of all, she could see light through her eyelids. For one panicked moment, as she'd lain on the path after the attack, she'd thought she was blind.

Hearing her mystery guest shift position, Jayne cracked open her left eye, hoping to see Carol and not Lesley or Mo. Not blind, but her field of vision was impaired. It took a moment for the room's other occupant to swim into focus. "Carol," she croaked.

Carol leaned forward, her forehead creased. She bit her lip, then released it to say, "Well, good afternoon."

Afternoon? "What time is it?"

"It's just gone one. How do you feel?"

"Pleasantly numb."

"You gave us such a scare." Carol held her hand to her chest, blinking rapidly. "But you're going to be all right."

"How do I look?" She could tell the areas around her eyes were swollen.

Carol grimaced. "You've looked better, but who cares? You're alive. That's all that counts."

But for how long? Ironic that the physicians had saved her, considering most Rymellans wanted her dead.

"Do you remember what happened?" Carol asked.

"Yes. And don't say I told you so."

Carol opened her mouth, closed it, then opened it again. "They caught them, the two who attacked you."

Did she know them? It had happened so fast. "What are their names?"

"Cameron Gibbs and Nicholas Peck."

Nicholas Peck? He lived in the building next to hers, just a few minutes away. She'd never had a problem with him beyond the usual glares.

"They were executed a few hours ago."

Jayne closed her eyes and groaned.

"They violated Article 235! The military couldn't look the other way this time."

Maybe not, but she doubted many would have objected if it had. "I agree, but now everyone will resent my existence even more." If that was possible. "They probably think my attackers should have been awarded medals, not executed."

"That's why your apartment isn't the best place for you right now," Carol said slowly. "You should stay with Ronald and me for a while."

No! She wouldn't be driven from her home. Words spoken by one of her attackers rang in her memory: *Thought you'd stay away and hide?* "I won't hide, Carol. I won't let them keep me away from my apartment."

"Jayne, it would only be for a couple of weeks, until things settle. Please don't be stubborn about this."

Jayne clenched her hands. "You wouldn't like it, if you couldn't go home."

Carol nodded. "You're right, I wouldn't. But I hope I'd have the sense to realize that my life is worth more than making a point. We talked about it, and we all agreed that—"

"You didn't talk about it with Lesley and Mo, did you?" Jayne asked, mortified.

"Of course I did! We were here half the night, until the physicians told us to go home. I only just got back about an hour ago. I'll have to beep them, let them know you're awake." She paused. "You were lucky they came along when they did. I think you can stop worrying about CT134, at least for now."

After she'd been assaulted, creating more trouble for them than she'd already caused? They were probably sitting in an advocate's office right now. "Why?"

Carol scratched her nose. "If they wanted you dead, they could have stood by and let you bleed."

She swallowed. "That would have been cold-blooded."

"No more cold-blooded than exercising CT134 for no good reason."

If they exercised CT134, they wouldn't have to watch her die. But Carol was right, they'd helped her, probably saved her life. She was starting to feel torn between keeping her guard up and letting herself trust them. But two years was a long time. If she relaxed, started to believe the triad would Join, and then they turned around and executed . . . No, she had to remain wary, but at the same time, try not to cast everything they said and did in an ominous light.

Someone tapped at the door. A physician strode into the room and looked at Jayne. "Good, you're awake," she said briskly, then turned to Carol. "Would you give us a minute while I examine her?"

Carol rose. "I'll be outside."

"Okay," Jayne said.

The physician held up three fingers. "How many do you see?"

LESLEY ABSENTLY RETURNED the nod of a physician's assistant she passed in the corridor on the E6 infirmary's third floor. Her head felt fuzzy; she couldn't remember the last time she'd risen past 10:00. On the *Falcon*, obviously, but that didn't count.

Next to her, Mo yawned. "I'm starting to wonder if we'll ever get any sleep again," she mumbled. "I read somewhere that if you don't get enough sleep, you'll eventually go insane."

"I think that's if you don't dream," Lesley said. "And you were sleeping okay until our notification meetings, so it hasn't been that long."

"I didn't get much sleep the night before, with the party and the excitement and everything."

"For me, it started with the Chosen Violation. It wasn't that I couldn't sleep, it was early morning meetings and late nights spent investigating."

"Don't worry, I'll let you know if you start showing signs of going crazy." Mo grinned. Lesley couldn't help but smile.

They took a moment to compose themselves before entering Jayne's room.

"Look who's here," Carol said from the guest chair. She stood.

"We're not staying long," Lesley said, motioning for Carol to sit back down. On the aviacraft, they'd decided to do what would be most comfortable for them and probably for Jayne, rather than hang around all afternoon for appearance's sake. Everyone knew the triad was less than a week old, so a great show of concern for Jayne's welfare would come across as false.

Though Jayne's bed had been raised to a sitting position, she was lying on her right side. Lesley tried not to wince at the swelling around her eyes and the bruises near her mouth.

"How are you?" Mo asked.

Jayne peered up at them and cleared her throat. "I feel fine. The medication is doing its job."

"And the physicians are pleased," Carol added. "She should be discharged the day after tomorrow."

"We'll come and get you," Lesley said.

"You don't have to," Jayne replied.

At the same time, Carol said, "That would be great."

They stared at each other. Mo raised her hand. "I vote for coming to get you, so that's three to one."

"That settles it, then," Carol said with a smile. "Oh, and she's agreed to stay with Ronald and me. Just for a little while."

"I don't want her to worry," Jayne said, her tone suggesting to Lesley that she'd rather return to her apartment.

"Will they replace your tooth before you leave?" Mo asked. A physician had informed them of the lost tooth while detailing Jayne's injuries after her surgery.

"No, I have to come back next week." Jayne held her hand in front of her face. "When all this has calmed down."

Lesley shifted her weight. "Did Carol tell you they caught the two men who attacked you? They've already been executed." If Jayne's attackers had thought they were acting in the interest of the Way, they'd been sorely mistaken. Violating the Way was never an acceptable course of action.

Jayne nodded. "Carol told me."

They lapsed into a silence that quickly grew awkward. "Well, I guess we'll get going," Lesley said, not seeing any reason to remain just to engage in forced conversation. They'd put in their few minutes so no one would talk—at least not about their failure to visit their Chosen. "We'll drop in again tomorrow."

"Thank you for coming," Jayne said. "And thank you for last night . . . for saving me."

Mo coloured slightly. "I think you need to thank the physicians for that."

"You helped, too. And you stopped the attack."

"You don't have to thank us for upholding the Way," Lesley said.

Jayne met Lesley's eyes. "I think I do," she said quietly, then looked away, leaving Lesley wondering what she meant. Jayne couldn't be implying they were weak in the Way. She had no reason to insult them and her voice hadn't contained a hint of derision.

"We'll see you tomorrow, then," Mo said after a moment.

Lesley absently murmured a good-bye, her mind still turning over Jayne's remark.

They were halfway down the corridor when Carol called their names and caught up to them. "I hate to do this, but can I ask you for a favour?"

"Sure," Lesley said, curious.

"I'll need to go to Jayne's apartment to get clothes and a few other things. I'd rather not do it alone," she said sheepishly. "Ronald could go with me, but having two military along would be even better."

Any other time, Lesley would have thought Carol paranoid, but not today. "When were you thinking of going?"

"I thought maybe we could go tomorrow. I could leave with you after you've visited Jayne."

"I can't go then," Mo said. "I, uh, have a meeting tomorrow afternoon. We're planning to visit right after lunch and then I'm off." Mo wasn't going to a meeting; she was going to the *Falcon* to pick up her things. Lesley planned to go with her, for moral support. "But Les is free." Mo nudged Lesley's arm. "You should be enough of a deterrent."

"That's true," she said wryly, interpreting Mo's response as permission to change their plans. "I'll go with you."

Carol sighed, looking relieved. "Thanks."

"But are you sure Jayne won't mind me going to her apartment?"

"Of course not. But I'll mention it to her, make sure she knows."

Lesley nodded. "We'll see you tomorrow, then. Oh, and beep us if you need anything else."

"I will."

"Are you sure it's okay?" Lesley asked Mo as they walked to Lesley's aviacraft.

"Yeah. I just want to be in and out, pack my stuff and go. I appreciate that you were willing to come with me, but I can handle it myself." Mo smiled, but Lesley could see the strain around her eyes.

She put her arm around Mo and squeezed her. "It's not your fault Jensen is being unreasonable."

"I know," Mo mumbled. "And there are worse things that can happen. Look at Jayne."

A chill ran up Lesley's spine. She tightened her arm around Mo, suddenly wishing she was going with her to the *Falcon* after all.

KEVIN MOTIONED FOR Cynthia to take a seat, and sank onto the sofa.

"Do you want anything, Cynthia?" Gwen asked. "Tziva, juice, an apple turnover, perhaps? They're fresh."

Cynthia shook her head. "No thanks, Gwen, I'm fine."

"If you're sure," Gwen said, then sat next to Kevin.

"Out with it," Kevin said. "You look as if you're about to explode."

Cynthia sighed and leaned forward. "Has Brock sent our dispatch yet?"

"No, he hasn't. He found out Thompson is on leave, so we'll wait until she's back on duty." Kevin rubbed the back of his neck. "I don't like the delay, it gives Adams more time to influence them. But we don't have much choice. Glad to see you're concerned, though. You didn't seem too enthusiastic about the whole thing at the meeting."

"Yes, well, I'm asking because I'm wondering if we should send it," Cynthia said, grimacing.

"Of course we should send it. Why wouldn't we?"

"The poor girl was attacked last night."

Kevin's eyes bulged. "The poor girl? The poor girl? If the imbeciles who attacked her hadn't bungled it, we wouldn't have to send a letter."

Cynthia and Gwen gasped.

"Well, it's true," he said, unrepentant.

"You normally wouldn't dream of saying such a thing," Cynthia said. "How could you even think of condoning murder?"

"Stop standing up for her!" he roared. Gwen placed her hand on his arm, but he shook it off. "Do you remember how you were after the Incident, Cynthia? You *wanted* the children executed. It was all you thought about twenty-four hours a day. You even neglected Paul. He was probably starting to wonder if you'd remember his name at your Joining Ceremony."

"You'd be surprised what thirteen years and a good counsellor can do for you," Cynthia said tartly. "As for Paul, do you know how difficult it was for him? We barely knew each other when he was thrown into the middle of a family crisis. Perhaps that's why I'm not very enthusiastic about adding to the problems Thompson and Middleton already have."

"What problems? They prepare a case to execute and they're done."

Cynthia gaped at him. "Do you honestly think it's that simple? The children . . . they weren't the ones who committed the crime. If we start executing children for the crimes of their parents, where do we stop? Should we execute the parents of criminals? The siblings? Should we have been executed along with Brenda?"

Kevin shot to his feet. "Don't you dare put us on the same level as the Adamses!" he shouted. "Do you know why it's called the Adams Incident and not the Hill Incident or the Stewart Incident? Because they were the criminals! They instigated the whole thing! They were the ones who—"

"Kevin!" Gwen's voice cracked. She glared at him as she rose and strode to the door. The sight of the tiny, wide-eyed figure peering into the living room made him wince. He forced a smile. "It's all right, Alex," Gwen said. "Papa didn't mean to shout. He won't do it again." She flashed Kevin a pointed look. "Let's get you back to bed."

When their footsteps had faded, Kevin turned to Cynthia and lowered his voice. "Peter Adams killed her. Why should that . . . that monster have children walking around? He took advantage of an innocent twenty-year-old. Brenda had her whole life ahead of her until that criminal decided the Tradition wasn't good enough for him."

"He was executed."

"So what? It was over in a second. That's not punishment."

"So you want to punish his daughter, too?" Cynthia shook her head. "Back then, I agreed with you. But we were wrapped up in our grief and convinced that Brenda was a victim."

"She *was* a victim!"

"No, she wasn't."

Kevin balled his hands into fists and raised his arms above his head. "Why, Cynthia? Why did it happen?" He dropped his arms to his sides. "I used to ride with her on the train sometimes, keep her company on her way to those so-called art lessons. I was her big brother. I was supposed to protect her, not deliver her into the arms of a depraved predator." His face twisted in anguish. "I rode with her that day, waved good-bye, said I'd see her later. I can still see her smiling and waving at me, and all that time . . . she . . ." His voice choked off; he turned away.

"She was an adult. She knew what she was doing," Cynthia said softly.

Kevin felt her hand on his back. "He was forty-five years old, Joined, with children. She was twenty. Twenty! Practically a child. It was him. He made her do it."

"It wasn't rape. Interior investigated that possibility, remember?"

"The investigators forced Brenda to cover for him."

"On the contrary, I think they were hoping it was rape. It would have saved her life and meant that only three committed Chosen Violations, not four. Why would they make an innocent Rymellan cover for someone they had mounds of evidence to condemn? Why would they make a Rymellan cover for anyone? It doesn't make sense."

He whirled to face her. "So it was all Brenda's fault?"

"No! But she certainly wasn't a victim."

Kevin stared at her in disbelief. The years since the Incident must have addled her brain.

"It's time to put it behind us, Kevin," she said quietly. "I thought we had, until this triad came up."

"This isn't just about us. It's about saving the Way."

Cynthia rolled her eyes. "You don't really believe that, do you?"

"It wasn't just Peter. Look at his Chosen. They were both at it. And she's their flaming daughter!"

"Who hasn't done anything wrong. Those involved in the Incident are dead. They're all dead."

"Not all the Adamses are dead," he growled.

"Neither are all the Stewarts and Hills."

For a split second he wanted to hit her, and almost did. Horrified, he moved away and shoved his hands into his pockets.

"Are you all right?" Cynthia asked.

No. He'd almost hit her. Amazing, how just thinking about the Adamses could corrupt someone.

"Let it go. You don't want to go the same way as Papa. We both know his anger—his obsession for revenge—killed him."

"Which is exactly why I won't let it go. I won't let an Adams destroy more families."

"What about Gwen and the children?" Cynthia pointed toward the doorway. "Do you think she's happy about this? You don't see the concern in her eyes?"

"She's concerned about the triad and what Adams might do."

"No, she's concerned about you. As for the triad, the only reason I wish it didn't exist is because it's dragged all this up again. Drop it, Kevin. Forget the letter. Talk to your counsellor."

No. He'd suffered, his family had suffered, and he wouldn't rest until Peter Adams' family had suffered.

AN IMAGE OF Jayne lying on the path, bleeding, flashed through Lesley's mind as she and Carol approached the location of the attack. "It happened here." Lesley stopped and pointed, though the path looked pristine. The cleaning crew had done an admirable job.

Carol shook her head. "She was almost home. I wanted her to stay with us longer, but she wouldn't hear of it. She expected the usual talk and nothing more. I couldn't shake the feeling that something worse might happen." She left the "and I was right" unsaid.

Two military stood near the entrance to Jayne's apartment building. Lesley had noticed the increased military presence the moment she'd stepped off her craft. "Access to this building is restricted to those who reside here," a sub-lieutenant said when Lesley and Carol reached the entrance.

"Though I suppose you're an exception," the sub-lieutenant's partner said, apparently recognizing Lesley. His gaze shifted to Carol. "But who are you?"

"I'm Carol White. Jayne Adams' cousin."

"We're here to collect some of her things. She'll be staying elsewhere for the next while," Lesley said.

He nodded. "Probably wise. You'll need the code. You'll have to beep Commander Ramsey for it."

"There's an alarm on her door," the sub-lieutenant added.

"I see."

"Attacks, alarms—utter madness," Carol muttered as Lesley beeped Ramsey for the code.

Lesley followed Carol to Jayne's apartment and disarmed the alarm. After a moment's hesitation, she followed Carol over the threshold. During her brief visit with Jayne, Lesley had made a point of mentioning that she'd accompany Carol to the apartment. Jayne's muted reaction had left Lesley wondering if Carol had persuaded her to go along with the idea against her wishes. She felt as if she were an intruder.

The tidiness of the apartment's living room was the first thing that struck her, followed by the two bookcases stuffed with books.

"I'll nip into the bedroom and pack some clothes," Carol said as she disappeared through a doorway.

Curious, Lesley crossed to the bookcases and scanned the book titles. Among the usual histories and dramatizations found on every Rymellan's shelves sat several art technique books; Jayne must like art. A couple of framed sketches hung on the room's walls. Lesley moved closer to one and examined it. A pencil sketch of a lone tree; simple but haunting. She looked for the artist's name in the corners, but it was unsigned. She moved to the other wall to study a sunset rendered in coloured pencils. It transported her back to when she and Mo used to watch the sun go down at the lake, something they hadn't done since they'd reunited. They'd have to go soon, somehow make time for each other in all the fuss.

"Do you like it?" Carol asked.

Lesley turned around. "Yes, I do. It reminds me of the sunsets over our lake."

"Your lake?"

"On the estate." She turned back to the drawing. Again, the artist's name was absent. "Is it the same artist as that one?" She pointed to the tree sketch. They were similar in style.

Carol nodded. "The same artist did all of them."

Lesley could only see the two. There must be others hanging elsewhere in the apartment.

"Though that's the only one in colour. Coloured pencils are dear, so she doesn't trade for them very often."

"Jayne did these?" Lesley said, finally connecting the books with the sketches.

"Uh-huh. Painting is actually her strong point, but she can't afford the supplies and stubbornly refuses to let me chip in for them."

"Why hasn't she mentioned it?" Wouldn't Jayne be eager to tell them about her artistic talent?

"She hasn't exactly received a lot of encouragement," Carol said wryly. "In fact, most people have been downright cruel with their . . ." she lifted her hands and wiggled her fingers in air quotes ". . . critiques."

A few days ago that would have surprised Lesley, but the last forty-eight hours had been an eye-opener.

"So I think she's worried about how you and Mo might react, especially with a certain article hanging over her head."

Lesley stared at her. "She actually thinks we'd exercise the article because we don't like her sketches?"

Carol shrugged. "Considering that most people would like her executed for no reason at all, you can hardly blame her. And it's not just that. Her work is important to her. I think you can appreciate how demoralizing and humiliating it would be to have not one, but two Chosens putting it down."

Even if she'd hated Jayne's sketches and considered her a talentless hack, Lesley would never put them down, and she was sure that Mo wouldn't either. But Jayne didn't know them, and they didn't know her. Just as she and Mo needed to make time for each other, they needed to spend time with Jayne, somehow block out the commotion swirling around the triad and focus on each other. "I like the two sketches I've seen, but since she's sensitive about her art, I'll wait for her to initiate a conversation about it." She'd suggest to Mo that she do the same.

Carol shifted her weight. "Since we're on the subject, let's get one thing out in the open right now. Jayne's papa was an artist. He painted. He taught her the basics, and then some. When she wasn't at the Indoctrination Academy, she spent most of her free time in his studio." Her face and voice hardened. "This information will probably go into the yes column when you and Mo are figuring out whether to kill her, but better you hear it from me than from someone else."

"We're not trying to figure out whether to kill her!" Lesley exclaimed, her anger overriding diplomacy.

Again Carol shrugged. "Not at the moment, but it's early days. I doubt the upset around the triad will continue at the same fevered pitch it's at now, but it'll never go away completely. Neither will the Adams taint."

"We understand that." Or at least they were starting to.

"She's my cousin," Carol said, looking slightly contrite. "I care about her."

Lesley wanted to say they wouldn't exercise the article, but she couldn't—not yet. The best she could promise was that they wouldn't exercise it on a whim, which was hardly comforting. "What about her brother?" she asked, choosing to pick up on the cousin part. "She didn't invite him to supper with us and neither of you have mentioned him visiting her at the infirmary."

Carol grimaced. "Yeah, her brother," she said slowly. "They're not close. Okay, they're not speaking to each other. If you want to know more, you'll have to talk to her—though if I were you, I'd wait until she says something. But you could be waiting a while. As far as she's concerned, he doesn't exist." She pointed over her shoulder. "Anyway, I'll just grab a few things from the bathroom and kitchen, then we can be on our way. Oh, and welcome to the family!" she chirped. "What's left of it, anyway," she muttered as she turned away.

MO SET HER violin down in the corner of her bedroom, next to the rest of her belongings. Les dropped a bag to the floor. They stood back and surveyed the clutter. "That's it. My life for the past four years." Mo put her hands on her hips and sighed. "I don't know why I feel depressed about it. I was planning to bring everything here before Jensen grounded me anyway. I guess it's because I've been told I'm never going back."

Les put her arm around Mo's shoulders. "Never is a long time. I still think we'll end up on a ship at some point."

"Yeah, *we*," Mo said, brightening. "Thanks for helping me carry all this junk here. I was tempted to land the craft right outside the house, but with my luck, a patrol would have chosen that moment to pass by."

"Are you sure you should be saying this to an Interior officer?" Les asked.

Mo looked at her and noted Les's small smile. "I'm still getting used to you being in Interior. I know it's been almost two years, but for me, it's still new."

"I wouldn't have been able to strike you." Les lifted an eyebrow. "But I would have told you to move the craft."

"Can you strike me for ignoring you?" Mo ducked out from under Les's arm and flopped onto the bed. She rolled onto her back and laced her fingers behind her head. "You haven't said anything about Jayne's apartment."

"You didn't seem in the mood to talk."

Mo leaned up on one elbow. "I want to hear about it."

Les sat next to her. "I stayed in the living room while Carol collected what she wanted. I mainly looked at her books." That figured. "She's neater than you are."

Well, give her a flaming medal.

"Oh, but I found out something interesting. She's an artist."

She looked up at Les in surprise. "Who, Jayne?"

Les nodded. "A few of her sketches were hanging around the apartment. Apparently she draws all the time, usually has a sketchbook with her wherever she goes."

"She hasn't had one when we've seen her."

"Carol said she's shy about it."

"Kind of like you and your flute."

"No," Les said. "I got the impression that Jayne might not think she's any good. Apparently others have put down her drawings."

"Is she any good?"

Les was silent for a moment. "One person's masterpiece is another person's eyesore. I liked the two I saw, but I'm not an expert."

"You'd think she would have at least mentioned it." The perfect time would have been when Adelaide was badgering Jayne about her vocation.

"We've barely spent any time with her. That's why I told Carol we'd spend Wednesday with her." Les touched Mo's arm. "I hope you don't mind."

"The whole day?" Mo said slowly.

"Until Carol comes home."

"We'll be taking her to Carol's tomorrow."

"I said we wouldn't stay long. And it will help Carol if we go over there on Wednesday. She needs to get back to the Learning Academy."

Before her notification meeting, Mo hadn't given a second's thought to how the Incident had affected the relatives of those involved. Now that she'd had a taste of the Adams taint herself, she was surprised that Carol's vocation involved working with children. "I'm amazed that Carol's allowed to teach."

"I was too, so I asked her about it. She's not allowed to teach classes with students under twelve years old."

"They could have told her she couldn't teach at all."

"They tried. She was accepted to college before the Incident. They were going to revoke her acceptance, but she protested, and several of her instructors backed her up. The age restriction was a compromise."

So Carol had fought back. Good for her. "That was pretty brave of her, especially right after the Incident."

"Carol doesn't strike me as the sort of person who backs down easily." Les shook her head. "See? We know more about Carol than we do about Jayne. We've spent more time with her, too."

Mo's comm unit beeped. She glanced at its display. "It's Ross," she murmured, sitting up. Hopefully Ross wasn't beeping to ban her from the pilot training complex. "Middleton."

"Am I getting you at a bad time?" Ross asked

"No."

"I was wondering if you'd like to have lunch, perhaps the day after tomorrow? We can meet in the residence dining room."

Mo hesitated. Lunch with Ross would get her out of that day with

Jayne, or at least part of it. But that would mean leaving Les with Jayne. Alone. "Uh, sure, but I can't make it Wednesday. How about Thursday?"

"Mmm, doesn't work for me. Friday?"

"Okay."

"Say, 12:30?"

"Sure."

"I'll see you then. And I am looking forward to seeing you. Ross out."

Mo took her time sliding the comm unit into its holder. She'd never thought that Ross looking forward to seeing her would choke her up. She felt Les's eyes on her.

"Doesn't sound like she's upset about the triad," Les said.

"Even if she was, she couldn't do anything to me, as far as my career goes. She doesn't oversee domestic patrols." *Oh no.* She turned to Les. "Larson does. Remember him? He's in with Morton."

Les shrugged. "We can't worry about what everyone else will do. It's out of our control."

It felt like their entire lives were out of their control.

"I've been thinking about what we do control," Les said, crossing her legs. "We control how we respond to the pressure. We control how we present ourselves. When we're out with Jayne, we have to treat her as our Chosen. We have to be absolutely impeccable in public."

"I know that."

"And I still think we need to signal where we stand on the triad right now. So I thought that perhaps we should arrange to go to the Dance Hall. With Jayne."

"The Dance Hall?" Mo snorted. "Remember I said I'd let you know if you were starting to show signs of insanity? Well, it's happening."

"Mo, people need to see us out. Otherwise they'll think we're hiding, or aren't accepting her as our Chosen."

"We haven't been to the Dance Hall together for almost two years. Our notification party doesn't count."

"Before we separated, we went every time we were on leave, and usually more than once," Les reminded her.

Yeah, just the two of them. Now it would always be the three of them. This reminded Mo of the days when she and Les wanted to be alone, but were stuck babysitting Andrew and Nathan.

"We'll have to go sometime."

Mo looked at her. "Maybe I want to enjoy the illusion that we're Chosens—just the two of us—for a little while longer." For the rest of their lives, if only that were possible. Even if they ended up exercising CT134, they'd never be just each other's Chosen again. Alive or dead, Jayne would always be with them. Mo let herself fall back onto the bed and blew out some air. "You're not dancing with her," she said, accepting one inevitable eventuality and fighting another.

Les sighed. "I can't ignore her. Neither can you. We've danced with other women before. It's never been a problem."

"This is different."

"Why?"

Mary's words came back to her: *But this Adams woman, she's not just anybody. She's Lesley's Chosen. The Chosen Council says they're meant for each other.* "It just is." Mo folded her arms. "Why do we have to go so soon? Why can't we wait?"

"We won't be going tomorrow," Les said. "She still needs time to recuperate. But I think we should go soon. Not only for appearance's sake, but because the only way we're going to figure out if this triad has a chance of surviving is if we start living like one."

"What?" Mo shrieked.

"Publicly!" Les rubbed her forehead. "We have two years to figure this out. The sooner we start acting as a triad, the sooner any problems will surface and we can get some idea of whether this arrangement we've all agreed to will actually work."

Mo pressed her lips together. She hated it when Les made sense and it meant she'd have to agree to something that frightened her. "I'm dancing with her first."

"Okay."

"And if the band is playing a song I like, you're dancing with me, not her."

Les groaned. "You like most songs."

"Okay, so it could take a while." Weeks, maybe months.

Les gave Mo a withering look. "Come on. It's only a dance."

Even though Mo knew she'd have to relent, she took her time responding.

"Mo!"

"Okay, okay. I'll tell you when you can dance with her."

"And don't stare at us the whole time. I don't want to feel two holes burning into my back."

"Well, that's just it," Mo said. "Before, when you were dancing with someone, I could too. Now I can't."

"So talk to someone or get something to drink." Les brightened. "I know, let's invite the family along. Karen's eager to meet Jayne. Neil and Barbara will probably go, if we ask them."

Oh, great, then she'd have everyone staring at her in sympathy when Les danced with Jayne. But on the other hand, having others along for support the first time they stepped out with Jayne could make everything else easier. "Maybe they should meet Jayne before we go to the Dance Hall, but yeah, let's invite them. Strength in numbers and all that." She wagged her finger at Les. "But don't you dare invite Jayne to the lake. Because if you do, I won't forgive you for a long, long time." If ever. "The lake is on private property. We don't have to put on a show there."

"I would never suggest that." Les grabbed Mo's finger and kissed it. "Talking about the lake, I was thinking earlier that we haven't been since we reunited."

"When have we had the flaming time?" Mo said. "First it was preparing for the notifications, and now it's recovering from them." Which would probably take the rest of their lives.

Les chuckled. "Let's go tonight."

"Let's," she said, though sadness overshadowed the pleasure she usually felt about the lake. It would always be like this from now on: snatched time with Les, and a handful of places they could call their own. Not what she'd imagined when she'd let herself picture their lives as Chosens. But she'd take it. Not being Les's Chosen would have been worse—something she suspected she'd say to herself a lot in the coming weeks and months.

"Before I forget, Carol told me something else about Jayne's art," Les said.

"What?"

"Jayne's . . . papa was an artist. Apparently she learned a lot from him."

Mo's skin crawled. "Let's hope art is the only family tradition she carries on."

They stared at each other. Les broke the silence. "Do you want help unpacking your stuff?"

"Sure," Mo said, trying not to sound too enthusiastic. Les helping usually meant Les did most of the work. She sprang off the bed. "Um, why don't you get started, and I'll go down and get us a couple of juices?"

Les nodded, already unzipping a bag.

JAYNE SHIFTED POSITION on the sofa to prevent a cushion from digging into a sore spot. "I would have been fine on my own," she said to Carol.

"Maybe, but I'll feel better if you're not alone." Carol carried her satchel over to the pile of essays that sat on the end table she'd moved within Jayne's reach. The top essay's cover page had a large red *F* and *Article 347!* scrawled across it. "Plus, the three of you should spend some time together without having annoying relatives and murderous animals around." She stuffed the essays into her satchel and dropped it to the floor, then frowned at her comm unit. "They should be here any minute. I was about to say I hope they didn't miss the train, but they don't take the train, do they?" She looked up at Jayne.

"What time will you be back?"

"About two-thirty. It's my early day today."

Around six excruciating hours of awkward conversation, then.

The knock at the front door drowned out Jayne's sigh. She listened to Carol greet Lesley and Mo, then told herself to relax as Carol led them into the living room.

"Make yourselves at home," Carol told them. "Eat anything, drink anything, comm station is over there in the corner if you want to use it." She put her hand on her hip. "Now, she's not supposed to move around much. Her sketchbook is over there. Jayne, ask them for it when you want it. You know you will at some point."

Jayne inwardly cringed. Wasn't it time for the annoying relative to leave?

"Anyway, I've got to go," Carol said, as if reading Jayne's mind. She grabbed her satchel. "Beep me if you need anything, though my comm unit is off when I'm teaching."

"We'll be fine," Jayne said tersely. Carol sounded as if she were giving instructions to babysitters.

"Do you want one of us to fly you to the Learning Academy?" Mo asked.

"No, no, it's only a ten minute train ride away." Carol smiled. "I'll see you all later."

The front door thumped shut. Without Carol, the living room was suddenly quiet, and the silence quickly grew awkward. "I wonder if 0.543 seconds is a new time-to-awkwardness record," Mo said, to Jayne's delight. The remark instantly sapped all awkwardness from the room.

"Why don't I go make tziva?" Lesley glanced around.

Jayne pointed toward the kitchen. "Through there."

"Thank you." She disappeared through the archway.

Mo sat in one of the chairs across from the sofa. "You're looking better. Are you feeling better, too?"

"I'm a little stiff, but yes, I'm feeling much better." Jayne's tongue roamed toward the gap for the hundredth time. "I'll get my new tooth on Monday."

Mo peered at her. "You don't really notice it."

Jayne nodded. Fortunately she still had her two front teeth and the ones closest to them.

"Les!" Mo shouted, startling Jayne.

Lesley appeared in the archway. "What?"

"You didn't change the counselling appointment to Monday, did you?"

"No. Carol said you had an appointment for your tooth then," Lesley said to Jayne. "Did she mention that I'd contacted the counsellor and postponed our appointment?"

"No, she must have forgotten."

"Carol said you'd be free on Wednesday, so I changed it to then. The appointment's at 2:00."

Maybe Carol should go to the flaming appointment!

"I'll be back on duty on Thursday, and you'll be active on supply soon," Lesley said to Mo. "It'll be tough finding a good time to see this counsellor."

Mo snorted. "I don't even know why we have to go. What's she expecting us to say?"

Lesley shrugged. "Let me get back to the tziva." She turned back to the kitchen.

Jayne searched for something to say, fearing another awkward silence. "What does active on supply mean?" she asked.

"Oh, right. Sorry." Mo leaned back in the chair. "I'm a fighter pilot. I've been away on tours for the last, um, four years, but I've dropped from the next tour. Not because of the triad. I dropped before I knew about it. Les and I have to figure out where our careers are going."

"You mean you've been away in space?" Jayne asked, surprised. What about Lesley?

Mo nodded. "On a ship called the *Falcon*. Since I won't be going on tour anytime soon, I've joined the supply list. I'll be flying out of a space station, filling in when someone's on holiday or ill. Not all pilots go on tours. We spent the first two and a half years after graduation flying what's called domestic."

"You mean you and Lesley?" She couldn't see Mo meaning anyone else.

"Yeah. Les used to be a fighter pilot—well, she still is. She was flying supply until they told her—" Mo's face froze. "I'll let her tell you. It has nothing to do with the triad."

Jayne couldn't tell if Mo was lying and wouldn't call her on it, even if she could. "So Lesley was in Defence at one point?"

"Yeah. She transferred into Interior when she was twenty-five."

They'd put their relationship on hold around that time. Were they forced apart, or had Lesley voluntarily transferred? Jayne wouldn't dare ask.

"Before then, she was on the *Falcon* with me."

"Do you know where a tray is?" Lesley asked from the archway. "No, forget that. Mo, come help me."

"I guess I'm the tray," Mo murmured as she passed Jayne.

The tziva couldn't be ready yet. Jayne strained to listen to the voices in the kitchen, wondering if Lesley had summoned Mo so she could talk to her privately, but she couldn't make out a word. She took the opportunity to check the time on her comm unit, which she'd tucked underneath one of the sofa's cushions. Only another five hours and fifty minutes to go, which would probably feel like five days.

And Carol was wrong. Lesley may have seen a couple of sketches, but that didn't mean Jayne could sketch in front of them. And since Lesley was unfailingly polite, her reaction to the sketches wasn't surprising. Jayne didn't mind. Politeness may be dishonest, but it was easier to bear than outright ridicule.

She started to roll onto her back, winced, and quickly returned to her former position. While she wasn't as sore as yesterday, she still found lying on her back uncomfortable. Fortunately she preferred sleeping on her side.

Since Lesley and Mo didn't seem about to return, she retrieved her comm unit again and checked the morning announcements. One headline immediately jumped out at her: *Cmdr. L. Finney and Lt. Cmdr. L. Thompson to receive the Medal of the Protector at an upcoming awards ceremony.* She requested the full article.

The Preeminent Ruler will award Commander L. Finney and Lieutenant Commander L. Thompson the Medal of the Protector for their participation in the capture and execution of Anthony Burke Owen. Government Hall will play host to this magnificent occasion. Senior members of the military and government will be in attendance, along with a number of Rymellan luminaries. Counsellor C. Abrams will receive the Commendation of the Way at the same ceremony, for her role in protecting the Way. The date, time, and guest list will be announced as soon as they are available.

She read the announcement again. Lesley had to know about the medal, at least. Jayne quickly dismissed the notion that Lesley hadn't mentioned it because Owen had committed a Chosen Violation. More likely, she hadn't had an opportunity to bring it up since their notifications. Between the badgering relatives and everyone clamouring for Jayne's execution, it was hard to get a word in edgewise.

If the triad survived, Jayne assumed she'd be invited. Perhaps they hadn't announced the guest list because they first needed to know whether Lesley would arrive at the ceremony with one Chosen or two. In fact, the timing of the announcement was curious. Maybe it was intended to remind Rymellans of Lesley's dedication and strength in the Way. Or maybe she was reading too much into it.

How ironic would that be, having an Adams on hand to watch the Preeminent Ruler award a medal related to a Chosen Violation—and to the Chosen of an Adams! Jayne could almost laugh about it, if she wasn't recuperating from being beaten and stabbed nearly to death. Hopefully those upset with her presence would limit their displeasure to whispers and dirty looks. She chuckled to herself. Assuming she made it to the ceremony.

Lesley and Mo's voices grew louder. Jayne quickly turned off the comm unit and shoved it under the cushion.

"I'll put this here," Mo said, setting a mug down where Carol's essays had been. Lesley looked around. Apparently deciding against squeezing herself onto the other end of the sofa, she handed Mo her mug and fetched a chair from the kitchen. Jayne couldn't blame her; she preferred it that way. When she stretched her legs, she wouldn't accidentally kick Lesley.

"At this point, the counsellor will probably want to know that we're talking and making an effort to see each other," Lesley said, picking up the earlier conversation. "It would be good if we could tell her we're planning to go out together. Mo and I enjoy dancing, so we thought perhaps we should go to the Dance Hall when you're feeling better."

The Dance Hall! Jayne reached for her tziva, even though it would be too hot to drink. Would Lesley and Mo expect her to dance with them, or would an appearance inside the hall be enough? Because she didn't know how to dance.

It wasn't that she'd never been interested in dancing; she would have loved to go to the dances at the Learning Academy. But when she was fourteen, her uncle had sat her down and suggested that it would be best if she waited for someone to invite her to dances and parties, rather than making the first move. They'd both known that nobody would ever invite her out and that she'd never dream of asking anyone on a date. But it would have allowed him to say that he'd advised her against it, had she screwed up the courage to approach anyone and caused offence. He needn't have worried.

The closest she'd come to the Dance Hall was listening to Carol talk about it. Carol had invited her to go on several occasions, but Jayne had always declined. She would have ended up sitting alone all night unless Carol made a point to sit with her, and that would hardly have been fun for Carol.

"We thought we'd go to C3's Dance Hall," Lesley said.

"C3-10's Dance Hall, to be more specific," Mo added. "That's the closest one to us."

Lesley nodded. "It's where we'll go when we're settled, so we figure people might as well get used to seeing us there."

So the past few days hadn't completely shattered their optimism and naivety. "Just let me know when you'd like to go," Jayne said, knowing she had no choice but to agree.

"Invite Carol and Ronald. We're inviting our siblings," Mo said.

With Carol and Ronald along, maybe it wouldn't be so bad.

"And a friend of mine has invited us all to supper," Lesley said.

Mo snorted. "She's more than a friend."

Jayne perked up her ears. Mo couldn't possibly mean . . .

"She's my commanding officer," Lesley said. "And my mentor. And C3's commander."

"And a descendent of the last triad," Mo added. Jayne detected a hint of derision in Mo's voice and looked at her, but Mo chose that moment to sip her tziva.

"Her name's Laura Finney," Lesley said.

Finney? She'd executed Owen and was getting a medal for it. Who would they expect Jayne to eat with next, the commander who'd executed her parents? Were all their friends in the military? Jayne heaved a mental sigh. Her life had suddenly become a minefield. She didn't have anything against Finney per se, but she was starting to feel surrounded by orange cloaks. Their lives were absorbing hers—not that she'd had much of one to begin with.

"Is there any day you wouldn't be able to make it in the next couple of weeks?" Lesley asked.

She'd have to check with her sketchbook. "No, any day is okay."

"Make it the same day we're seeing the counsellor," Mo said. "That'll really make it a day to look forward to."

Now Jayne was certain that either Mo didn't like Finney, or had some type of problem with her. Lesley frowned and shot Mo a look, but didn't say anything. "Do you play cards, Jayne?" Mo asked. "We should do something, or the time will drag."

She found Mo's honesty refreshing. Fortunately she often played cards with Carol and Ronald. "I think there's a deck in the kitchen drawer, the one on the right."

Lesley stood. "I'll bring you a chair too," she said to Mo.

They were soon huddled around the end table. Mo picked up the deck of cards. "I played a lot of cards on the *Falcon*," she murmured as she deftly shuffled the deck. Jayne prepared to lose.

MO SLOWED HER pace as she approached the Military Academy faculty residence, then bolstered herself and pushed open the door. The pilot training complex was a twenty minute walk away. Those involved with the training program usually ate in the mess hall or grabbed a snack from the complex's canteen. She'd rarely recognized her fellow diners when she'd stayed at the residence while on leave, and suspected today would be the same. Wait—would Ann still be here? No, she would have returned to 72 by now. And Mo hadn't heard from her since the triad announcement. Had it frightened Ann away, or was she too busy cracking triad jokes to anyone who'd listen?

When Mo entered the dining room, Ross waved at her. She made her way to the table and nodded. "I hope I'm not late," she said, noticing the jug of tziva. She was sure she was on time.

"No, no." Ross motioned for Mo to sit. "I was early. Help yourself."

Mo flipped over the mug at her place setting and filled it with tziva. She glanced around as she took a sip, but nobody was staring at her. Nobody knew her, so she wasn't surprised. It wasn't as if she had a *Triad Member* sign stuck to her back.

"I'm glad you came," Ross said. "Baker told me about Jensen."

"Yeah, I guess I'll be seeing a lot more of 72 than I thought." She stared down at her mug. "Though to be honest, even if Jensen hadn't grounded me, it probably would have been a while before I went on tour again." If ever. "Even if it was just me and Les, she's in Interior now and moving up the ranks."

"I hope she's still moving up the ranks," Ross murmured. "Has she had any trouble?"

Mo shook her head. "But she's been off duty since the announcement. She goes back next week."

Ross smiled sympathetically. "You were probably expecting to spend a relaxing two weeks together."

"Yeah, we were." Mo was unable to keep the bitterness out of her voice. Their excitement and joy at the realization they were Chosens felt as if it had happened years ago, not last week. She was starting to think of her life in terms of pre-triad and post-triad, it had changed that much.

Ross cleared her throat. "I hope you won't think badly of me when I say that Jensen's decision might be advantageous to me."

"Why?" Mo asked, but satisfying her curiosity had to wait while the server took their lunch orders. "Why?" she asked again when he'd moved away from the table.

"Well, I just happen to have an open position in the faculty—"

Mo raised her hand and shook her head. "I am not standing in front of a classroom."

Ross's brows shot up, then she leaned over the table, laughing. "For practicums," she gasped. "I wouldn't expect you to teach a class."

Mo sipped her tziva and tried not to look peeved. The thought of her teaching a class wasn't *that* funny. "You mean a practicum supervisor?" she asked, once Ross had calmed down.

"Yes. You'd work out of 72. Remember the first time you flew an actual fighter?"

It was an experience she'd never forget. She'd felt as if she were flying a sim, until it had suddenly hit her that she was actually in a fighter in that hostile environment known as space. If anything went wrong, she couldn't just whip off her helmet, leave the simulator, and try again later. Flying hundreds of simulations hadn't prepared her for that humbling and terrifying few seconds after reality kicked in. Those who quickly pulled themselves together, as she had, usually graduated from the program. Those who didn't usually wanted out anyway.

"I can see you do remember," Ross said, amused. "The instructors who accompany students on their first few flights are highly experienced for a reason."

"You mean you want me in the instructor's seat for Fighter Practicum 1-A?"

Ross nodded.

"I have controls back there, right? I can take over, if necessary?" No flaming way was she sitting in a fighter with a completely green pilot if she couldn't control the craft. Despite the recent turn her life had taken, she wasn't suicidal.

Ross nodded again, a smile spreading across her face. "You were a new pilot once."

"Yeah, but I knew what I was doing." Though she'd spoken the truth, she realized she sounded arrogant. "Sort of."

"We can work around your supply assignments. If you only accept assignments when given a certain amount of notice, we'll know when you're available."

"I'll think about it."

"You have friends in the program, Mo. It could be a good place for you right now."

Friends? Since when had she needed friends? Okay, dumb question, but she was still getting used to the idea that some would no longer judge her based on her abilities.

The server arrived with their lunches. "When do you need an answer?" Mo asked, unfolding her napkin.

Ross scratched her head. "The next round starts in a couple of weeks. Can you tell me by Monday?"

Mo nodded. She'd talk it over with Les, then decide.

"With that out of the way, maybe you'll fill me in about how you are. I heard about what happened to your other Chosen. Jayne, right?"

"Yeah."

By the time they'd finished eating, Ross knew everything Mo wished to share, and had persuaded her to fly a sim. "Don't worry, everyone will be fine," Ross said, apparently sensing Mo's apprehension.

Nobody pointed as they strode through the lobby of the pilot training complex; in fact, several nodded to her. The equipment room sounded awfully crowded. "Are you sure we'll get a simulator?" she asked Ross.

Suddenly she was surrounded by applause. It took her a moment to realize that the room was filled with familiar faces and that every-one was clapping for *her*. "You really want me to take that instructor's position, don't you?" Mo said, to much laughter. A lump formed in her throat as she surveyed those assembled and returned nods and smiles.

 RYMELLAN 2

"We wanted you to know that this is still one of your homes away from home. And yes, we'd be delighted if you'd accept the position."

"But we're not trying to pressure you," said one of Mo's former practicum instructors. Those around Mo chuckled.

She squared her shoulders. "Well, the commander and I came here to fly a sim, and we're going to fly the most difficult one at the highest setting." From the corner of her eye Mo glimpsed Ross turning to her. "You're all welcome to watch this tour pilot in action. Maybe you'll learn something." She grinned at the catcalls and boos that echoed around the room. "Let's suit up."

An hour later, she left the complex, a strut in her step and her spirits soaring. Why bother with counsellors when she could just fly a sim? Her comm unit beeped twice. She glanced at its display and rolled her eyes. Fitting that Ann would send her a dispatch now.

Mo, when are you coming up here? I want to hear all about what it's like to be in a triad. Are you sure there's enough of you to go around?

Mo shook her head.

Anyway, I thought I'd better warn you that Leeds is on 72. Remember her?

Lieutenant Leeds, the one who'd wanted Les?

She came in on a shuttle yesterday, from 65. I asked around and apparently she's here to stay. You won't believe this—she's flying patrols. You might want to check who you'll be flying with before you accept an assignment.

I was going to beep you, but I figured you'd be busy, what with two Chosens and assaults and all that. Later.

Flaming great! Wait until Les heard about Leeds. Mo could avoid 72, but she'd looked forward to flying with pilots she'd served with right after graduation, those who'd decided not to go on tour. She'd also have to turn down Ross's offer. But—why should she stay away because of Leeds? Leeds should be the one to stay away. If she had any decency, she'd apply for a transfer to another space station as soon as she found out that Mo would be flying out of 72.

Mo rammed the unit into its holder, then wanted to scream when it beeped. Shock ran through her when she read the name *J. Adams*. Maybe someday, seeing *Adams* on the display wouldn't faze her. Probably around the time Jayne's name changed to Thompson. Was there a simulator free? She already needed another round of counselling.

"Yes, Jayne," she said, her irritation fading as curiosity took over.

"I need to talk to you about the Dance Hall."

"Okay."

Silence, then, "I can't dance."

So Jayne might stomp all over Les's toes? What a shame. "Don't worry about it. Not everyone is a great dancer."

"No, I don't know any dances. I don't know the steps."

"Oh."

"I've never been to the Dance Hall."

Mo's surprise quickly passed. This *was* Jayne. But wouldn't Carol have invited her at some point? "You've never been? Never, ever?"

"No. I thought I'd better tell you before we go. I don't want to embarrass you and Lesley. So . . . can one of you teach me to dance?"

Memories of clumsily dancing around a field with Papa passed through Mo's mind. He and Mama had taught her to dance when she was about thirteen, so she'd be ready for the dances at the Learning Academy when she left the Indoctrination Academy at fourteen. Les had learned around the same time. They'd tried dancing with each other, had giggled as they'd lurched to the music in each other's arms. Of course, they hadn't liked each other then the same way they did now. Or had they?

"You're the only ones who can teach me," Jayne said, bringing Mo back to the present. "If you don't want to do it, do you think Lesley will?"

No! "I'll teach you. Les wouldn't want to be bothered with something like this."

"It's a good thing I didn't beep her, then," Jayne said sombrely. "I wouldn't want to annoy her."

"Yeah, you did the right thing, beeping me. You should probably always do that. If you want to talk to Les about something, or ask her to do something, it's probably best to run it by me first, so I can tell you how to approach it. Les can be uptight about things." Well, she could . . . sometimes. Okay, that disapproving voice in her head could just be quiet now. Mo was only protecting her relationship. Even Jayne had said the triad hinged on their relationship. "I don't want you to get on her bad side. That would make things more difficult."

"No, I agree. And thank you. I appreciate the advice."

"We all want the triad to work," Mo said feebly.

They arranged a time for their first dance lesson, with Mo assuring Jayne that if they had to delay the Dance Hall until she was ready, it wouldn't be a problem.

On the way to her aviacraft, Mo tuned out the voice that still nagged at her. She would do anything to keep Les, except execute Jayne for no reason. She might have a harder time looking at herself in the mirror, but if Les fell for Jayne, she'd feel a lot worse.

LESLEY LOWERED HER flute when the front door thumped shut. She'd promised to help Papa prepare supper. After cleaning her flute and putting it away, she headed downstairs.

"Was that your flute I heard?" Papa asked when she entered the kitchen.

She should have shut the window. "Yes, it was." While separated from Mo, she'd forced herself to play a couple times a week, but hadn't written a single note of music—until today. Reuniting with Mo had reawakened that part of her, despite the triad. "Nothing dire happened at the Military Academy," she said, wanting to change the subject away from her flute. "Commander Ross offered Mo a position."

"Really?" Mama said from the doorway. "A teaching position?"

"A practicum supervisor." As Leeds had been. Lesley had thought that perhaps she and Jayne would eventually go with Mo to 72, whenever she was off duty and Mo was on. Now she wasn't sure.

"She should take it," Mama declared. "She has to find something else now. I doubt Admiral Jensen will change her mind. Even if she does, you're moving up and Mo isn't. Your career has to come first."

Lesley bit her tongue and started to peel the bowl of potatoes Papa set in front of her. It was futile to try explaining to Mama that because Mo wasn't striving for admiral didn't mean she had no career goals.

"Oh, did you hear anything more about the medal ceremony?" Mama asked.

"As a matter of fact, I did." Lesley kept her eyes on the knife she was working over the potato so she wouldn't cut herself. "They sent me the proposed guest list and asked if there was anyone missing."

"Is *she* on it?"

"Yes, she's on it."

Mama grunted. "Did they say when it is?"

"No."

"We're on it, I hope."

"Yes, you're on it."

"I wonder if we'll be sitting with the Preeminent Ruler."

She stifled a chuckle. "They didn't send a seating plan. I'd imagine they want to finalize the guest list first." And if anyone would be sitting with the Preeminent Ruler, it would likely be herself, Laura, Counsellor Abrams, and their Chosens. Mama would be green with envy, especially since an Adams would be put on the same level as the guests of honour.

Lesley wasn't really looking forward to the ceremony. Jayne's presence would likely make it a tense affair, and she'd have to worry about two Chosens. Normally she'd have no trouble working a room, but this time she'd have to introduce Jayne to everyone. And Mo. What a bittersweet event—the first official function at which she'd introduce Mo as her Chosen, but in the same breath, introduce Jayne. The organizers of the event were probably having fits. Everyone would want to be seated near the guests of honour—would want to meet them and offer their congratulations—but nobody would want to rub elbows with an Adams.

She wished Mo could have had more time in the spotlight as her only Chosen—ideally, their entire lives. No matter what happened, Lesley had to make sure that Mo knew she was special to her. The Chosen Council had selected two Chosens, but her heart had selected only one and had never wanted anyone else.

"I received the cases from the archives today," Papa said as he whipped the peeled potatoes away from her and handed her a head of lettuce. "Chop."

"What cases?" she asked, confused.

"The ones presented under CT134."

The lettuce could wait. "Did you look at them?"

"Not yet."

"We did peek at one on the train," Mama admitted. "It was shorter than I'd expected."

Papa turned to Lesley. "And we're not the only ones interested in them.

When I thanked the clerk for sending them so promptly, he said it would have taken longer if he hadn't already retrieved them for someone else."

"I'm sure we're not the only advocates curious about them, though our curiosity isn't idle." Mama popped a piece of raw carrot into her mouth and crunched on it. "Why don't we read the cases together, after supper?"

Lesley bit back an enthusiastic yes. "Will Jason be here?" Reviewing the cases with him would be a waste of time. He'd twist every point into an argument to support executing Jayne, stifling any chance at an objective discussion. Mama, at least, seemed open to alternative viewpoints, as long as they were presented well.

"He said he was meeting a friend."

Jason seemed to be out a lot lately, probably afraid of running into Jayne. "I'd like to review the cases with you," Lesley said.

"Good," Papa murmured.

"Perhaps you should invite Mo to join us," Mama said. "She should understand the reasons presented for execution."

Lesley turned back to the lettuce so Mama wouldn't see her smile. The prospect of reviewing cases for hours would turn Mo's face a sickly shade of green. "I think she's busy tonight. I'll summarize the cases for her."

"Make sure you do," Mama said. "Anyway, I'm going to read announcements. Shout when supper's ready."

"AND THAT'S THE end of case number eight." Mama leaned back in her chair and sipped some water. "I'm glad most of them were short, or my throat would be sore." She'd volunteered to sit in front of the comm station and read the cases aloud.

"I'm starting to see a pattern here," Papa said.

Lesley was too. "Except for that one case when the executed Chosen actually violated three articles."

Mama nodded. "That one was doomed from the start." She pursed her lips. "If not for CT134, most of these triads would have Joined."

"You mean its existence contributes to the breakdown of triads?" Lesley said, trying not to sound too surprised that Mama agreed with her.

"Hastens the breakdown," Mama corrected. "What seems to happen is that the Principal and one of the other Chosens fall in love, or at least start down that path. And that unnerves the third Chosen, who then starts to act out."

"Or the third Chosen panics . . ."

"And starts to act out," Mama said again.

"Because of CT134 hanging over his or her head," Papa finished. "If CT134 hadn't existed, these triads might have survived."

"But probably wouldn't have," Lesley said. "CT134 exists because most triads weren't successful. But they don't seem to be any more successful with it, so what's the point?"

Mama turned to her. "The point is that one Chosen is executed sooner, before the Joining. No Chosen Violations. No actual capital violations."

"You're saying CT134 was added so the history books can say that triads no longer result in Chosen Violations?" Lesley asked.

"The two remaining Chosens also have a chance at happiness." Papa said.

"That was true before CT134. As Mama said, CT134 hastens the breakdown. Before it existed, triads still broke down, just not so soon. So more often than not, triads were eventually reduced to two Chosens."

Papa nodded. "But it could take years for one of the Chosens to be executed. Imagine how it must have affected the two remaining Chosens. It couldn't have been easy, dealing with the execution of someone they'd lived with for years, and those years had probably been fraught with conflict. Why drag it out for so long? Why not give two of the Chosens a chance at a stable and peaceful life early on? You've read the history. It sounds like a triad is a constant struggle that eventually leads to . . ." His face reddened.

"We're in a different situation," Lesley quickly said.

Mama's brows shot up. "Are you?"

"Yes. Mo and I were in love before the triad. We've already talked with Jayne and come to an arrangement, so she has no reason to worry." Not because of their relationship, anyway. "And you're starting to sound like you think we should exercise the article," she said to Papa.

His brow furrowed. "No. But I can see why some, including the Chosen Council, would consider the addition of the article a success. The Joining is reduced to two before things get out of hand."

"But there's always a chance for the triad to succeed as long as the three Chosens are alive," Lesley said. "Why take away that chance based on what might happen?"

"These cases were presented based on what was happening, not on what might happen," Mama reminded her.

"Yes, but with the exception of that one case, nobody had committed a violation. It hadn't reached that point. Perhaps it never would have."

Mama shook her head. "No. Again, back to the history before CT134. CT134 doesn't create problems that wouldn't have happened without it. It brings problems to light sooner. You said as much to Papa. If the executed Chosen hadn't acted out because of CT134, he or she would have acted out for another reason. CT134 revealed the triad's instability before it Joined."

"You're right," Lesley murmured, though executing a Rymellan who hadn't committed a violation didn't sit well with her. "I can't help but think that it would be better to let the triad take its natural course, rather than pre-empt it based on conjecture."

"More than conjecture," Papa said. "Remember, they knew the history when these cases were presented. Letting triads take their natural course hadn't worked. Those in triads committed Chosen Violations or assaulted each other. You'd rather have that?"

"No, of course I wouldn't." Lesley rubbed her forehead. "These cases are interesting, but I think I have to focus on my triad." *My triad.* She still couldn't believe she belonged to one.

The front door slammed shut. Lesley tensed when Jason strode into the study. "What are you all looking at?" he asked.

"Cases related to CT134," Mama said.

His face lit up. "Does that mean—"

"No, it doesn't," Lesley snapped. "We were just curious, that's all."

He tutted. "No need to get short. At least you're willing to look at the cases. That's an improvement."

"I wouldn't get your hopes up." Lesley pushed back her chair and stood. "The cases are interesting, but our situation is unique."

"Unique?" Jason snorted. "That's one word for it. Those triads didn't have an Adams in them. You know for sure it's only a matter of time."

"No, I don't. I know I'm in a triad with someone whose parents committed Chosen Violations. That's all I know."

He started to laugh, but trailed off when she remained stone-faced. He glanced at Mama and Papa, then looked back at her. "You're not serious! What will it take to convince you? Will she have to commit a Chosen Violation before you see sense? How will you be a commander when you can't come to a decision in such an obvious case?"

"It's not that I can't come to a decision, it's that I won't come to the decision you want in the timeframe you want!" Lesley wanted to leave the room, but he was blocking her path to the door.

Jason's face tightened. "I want what any commander would do."

She shook her head. "No commander would send Jayne to an execution site because of her family history, or at least the ones I know wouldn't." They'd never execute based on what someone might do. They'd only execute based on what someone had done: committed either a capital violation, or a series of violations within a short period of time. Both would clearly indicate that a Rymellan had fallen.

Commanders dealt with facts. Lesley had read enough cases and spoken with enough commanders to know they erred on the side of caution when deciding whether to send a Rymellan to an execution site. If they weren't sure, they held off. If they were, they didn't hesitate. If that weren't true, some commander would have found an excuse to execute Jayne long before now. The point was moot, anyway. When it came to CT134, an overseer would decide whether to execute, not a commander.

"You have no clue what you're talking about," Jason said, rolling his eyes.

"You're right. What do I know? I'm just a trained Interior officer." And that was the difference between her and everyone else in the room. They were advocates who dealt with the theoretical. She was a military officer; she dealt with actuality, the reason she'd chosen the Military Academy over Advocacy College. When Laura had proposed that Lesley write opinions for the military, she'd denied it would be advocacy, and she'd been right. Lesley approached every case from a practical angle. "You don't execute someone based on theory," she said, slicing her hand through the air to emphasize her point. "You execute based on fact."

They glared at each other. Lesley expected Mama or Papa to speak, but they silently watched. "It'll only be a matter of time before you have your fact," Jason said with a sneer. "And if someone were to show that

Adams is a clear threat to the Way, you'd have to listen. You couldn't turn your back on that."

"I wouldn't. But so far, I haven't heard anything that even remotely shows it." Having nothing more to say, she brushed by him, and resisted the temptation to return when murmurs rose in her wake. Let them talk. The fate of the triad wasn't in their hands. It was in hers and Mo's, and yes, Jayne's.

JAYNE FELT AS if she were an intruder in her own apartment. Everything was familiar, yet somehow different. She opened her bedroom door and threw her bag onto the floor.

"You sure you'll be okay?" Carol blew a stray hair off her face. "You could have stayed with us another day or two."

"I'll be fine." She had to return home sometime, and today was as good a day as any, especially since she'd see the counsellor with Lesley and Mo tomorrow. She could tell the counsellor that she'd recovered from the attack, and Lesley and Mo wouldn't think she was afraid to leave Carol's. "You'd better get going, or you'll be late for your first class."

"I'll beep you at lunch," Carol said at the door. "And I'll leave my comm unit on. Beep me if you have to, okay?"

She wished Carol wouldn't worry so much. "You saw the military on the way here. They're still on alert." And probably loving every minute of having to ensure her safety. "Now, go on." She gently pushed Carol out the door and closed it before Carol could protest.

Half an hour later, she zipped up her now empty bag and shoved it into the closet. She'd earned a tziva—it would be nice to sit in her own living room and relax for a bit. She hummed to the music blaring from the comm station as she passed it. According to Carol, the piece was popular with the bands at the Dance Hall, along with several of Jayne's favourites. If Jayne felt brave enough, she'd suggest the music to Mo when they met for her dance lesson. Perhaps she'd make less of a fool of herself if she was familiar with the music. Mo might already have specific pieces in mind, but she probably didn't. Did she even appreciate music? Jayne knew so little about her—about them.

She opened the refrigerator door and groaned at the empty racks. Carol had mentioned taking all the perishables home with her when she'd dropped in that day with Lesley, something Jayne had forgotten until now. Relaxing with tziva would have to wait until she returned from the Trading Centre. But that would mean venturing outside.

Her stomach churned as she buttoned her cloak. Despite the hostility Rymellans directed her way, she'd never felt nervous about going outside. Glares and angry words didn't hurt, or so she'd repeatedly told herself. When she'd dreaded leaving her apartment, it was because she didn't have the energy to face the usual nonsense, not because she was frightened. The possibility that she'd be physically assaulted had never crossed her mind. Those who resented her existence because they considered her a threat to the Way would hardly violate it themselves, or so she'd thought.

Now that two men had crossed the line, would others follow? No, surely the military had made its position on the matter clear by swiftly executing her two attackers. And, as she'd pointed out when trying to ease Carol's mind, the increased military presence Carol had witnessed after the attack was still in evidence. So there was no reason to cower inside her apartment. The only Rymellan who could trap her here was herself.

Determined not to let that happen, Jayne slung an empty knapsack over her shoulder, tucked her sketchbook under her arm, and took a deep breath as she left her apartment. The Trading Centre was only a five minute walk away. She walked briskly, kept her head down, tried not to be paranoid, and gripped the edge of her sketchbook whenever her courage wavered. Nobody harassed her along the way, but she could see animosity in some of the faces she glimpsed, perhaps friends of the two executed men.

The clerk at the Trading Centre didn't smile and engage her in small talk, but that wasn't new. She was soon on her way back to her apartment, feeling a little more confident and looking forward to that tziva.

"So you're still with us," a voice rang out. Jayne inwardly groaned. Not today. She hadn't run into the lieutenant since the execution procession. "I wonder how the physicians felt when they patched you up, knowing that it won't be long until you die at an execution site anyway?" The lieutenant fell into step with her. "Must have rankled. I'm surprised none of them slipped when you were on the operating table."

She kept her mouth shut and continued walking.

"So the Adamses take down two more Rymellans. Cameron and Nicholas were good men."

"You think those who violate Article 235 are good?" Jayne asked, seething at the unfairness of it. Why was everything backward when she was involved? She didn't violate articles, but she was bad, a threat to the Way. When an article was violated and she was the wronged Rymellan, those who'd violated the article were good.

"When I heard that Thompson and Middleton saved you, I thought they were crazy, until I figured out why they did it," the lieutenant said, ignoring Jayne's question.

Her curiosity got the better of her. "Why do you think they did it?"

The lieutenant snickered. "Because you deserve to die at an execution site. It wouldn't have been as much fun if you'd died just anywhere. We still would have partied, but it wouldn't have been the same." She grinned. "Yep, I'd imagine your two Chosens have quite the celebration planned, once they know the executioner's stick has done its work."

Jayne bit back a laugh, probably not the effect the lieutenant had hoped for. If Lesley and Mo ended up exercising CT134, they wouldn't be so callous about it. Jayne didn't know them well, but she doubted a celebration would be on their agenda for that day. They seemed to be treating the triad seriously, or at least they came across as wanting to give their arrangement a genuine chance to work. To them, exercising CT134 would mean they'd failed. And dare she hope that executing her when she hadn't violated any articles would preclude a celebration, as well? Her impression of them just didn't jibe with the lieutenant's, which wasn't surprising, considering the lieutenant had never met them.

"I heard that Thompson's got a pool going at headquarters. Everyone's guessing which day they'll exercise CT134."

The lieutenant sounded even more pathetic. Did she honestly believe that Jayne never talked to them and knew nothing about what was going on in their lives? Lesley was still off duty, and wouldn't run such a pool, in any event. Jayne felt like saying, "Why don't you beep her and put me down for next Friday?" but the lieutenant would probably strike her for some imaginary violation.

"I figure another two weeks." The lieutenant smirked. "I'll be there. I want to watch."

They'd reached her apartment building. "Thank you for the escort," Jayne said, then felt a stab of satisfaction at the confusion in the lieutenant's eyes. She ducked into the building and relaxed when the lieutenant didn't follow her. It must be tough for the woman, having to keep her harassment in check because of all the extra military around. Poor thing.

That encounter had gone much better than the last one. Hard to believe the execution procession had taken place less than three weeks ago, but so much had happened since then. Every glimpse of Lesley during the procession had unsettled Jayne. Now she'd been in the same room with Lesley, eaten and played cards with two military, and felt comfortable. They could still hurt her, but they weren't like the lieutenant. Jayne had learned that not all military were the same. Hopefully Lesley and Mo would realize that not all Adamses were, either.

LESLEY STOPPED AT reception on her way back from lunch to collect the items in her correspondence slot. She'd already handled most of her dispatches, now it was time to tackle any paper that had piled up while she was off duty. "Here you are, Lieutenant Commander," the clerk said, handing her about fifteen envelopes.

She thanked him and continued on to her office, feeling less self-conscious than she had that morning, when she'd entered headquarters for the first time since her notification meeting. Nothing could top the awkwardness at the triad's counselling session the previous afternoon, though. Lesley wasn't sure who'd felt more uncomfortable: the counsellor, or the three counselees.

Fortunately Mo had quickly realized that her two Chosens weren't going to be much help and had gamely turned what should have been thirty second answers into five and ten minute ones. Counsellor Berry had heard in great detail about how Mo would teach Jayne to dance and had seemed pleased that Mo was willing to help. They'd agreed to set another appointment for soon after their night at the Dance Hall, promising they'd go within the next two weeks.

Lesley wasn't looking forward to their next session. Mo had made it clear that she wouldn't do all the talking and that she still thought the whole counselling thing was a waste of time. Lesley agreed with Mo's latter sentiment, but the Chosen Council wanted to monitor them and probably hoped the sessions would prevent problems from arising, or at least help to quell them if they did. Even though the triad had told Berry about their arrangement and weren't experiencing any difficulties at the moment, their sessions weren't likely to end anytime soon, if ever. It would be nice if the Chosen Council could follow them in a less awkward manner.

At least her return to duty had been uneventful so far, but she'd spent most of her time in her office. Those she'd passed in the halls had greeted her civilly, and Laura had made a point of sticking around the office more than she usually did. She'd also eaten lunch with Lesley in the cafeteria and wasn't the only one who'd shown her support. Commander Blair and a few others had stuck their heads around Lesley's office door to say hello, and some had stopped to chat at lunch. Nobody had gone so far as to congratulate her, but Lesley appreciated the effort. If only Admiral Jensen could have reacted in the same manner, or done nothing at all. At least Ross and her colleagues at the Military Academy had stepped in with their support. Mo had accepted Ross's offer—a wise decision.

Lesley sat down at her office desk to shuffle through the dispatches. One envelope caught her eye—it lacked the sender's information. She tossed the others aside, ripped it open with her thumb, and drew out a single sheet of folded paper.

Lieutenant Commander Thompson,

We are writing to offer our support in what must be a difficult time for you. We were shocked to learn that you, strong in the Way and an example that all should follow, are Chosen to an Adams. We feel equally bad for Lieutenant Commander Middleton. Nobody deserves to be linked to the Adams name, least of all, you two.

We are aware of Article CT134 and of the right it bestows upon you and Lieutenant Commander Middleton. We praise the Chosen Council for including it in the Chosen Tradition. The article must be exercised when the Way is threatened, as it is with your situation. We assure you that all Rymellans would support your decision to exercise the article. In fact, we urge you to exercise the article before Jayne Adams follows in her parents' footsteps and tarnishes the Tradition further.

We also remind you that her parents were not executed alone. Two other Rymellans met their end at an execution site; two Rymellans who had been respectable until the Adamses influenced their judgement. Don't let the same thing happen to you and Lieutenant Commander Middleton. Exercise the article before it's too late to save yourselves and the Way. Your service to the Way has been exemplary. You have always defended the Way when it was threatened. Don't fail to protect it this time.

In closing, disobedience means death. Death to those who commit a Chosen Violation. Death to those who disobey. Death to those who violate the Way.

Yours in the Way,

A group of concerned Rymellans

Lesley stared at the letter in disbelief. Who did these Rymellans think they were, suggesting that she and Mo might commit a Chosen Violation? How insulting, implying they were that weak in the Way, especially in a letter that declared them strong in the Way! And did this group honestly believe that she wouldn't protect the Way? Jayne wouldn't be reproducing. The Adams line was over. Finished! Lesley didn't need anyone dictating her priorities and telling her how to go about protecting the Way as if she didn't know.

Why did this group even think she'd want advice from a bunch of strangers? The last thing she needed was more Rymellans meddling in her life. She'd already heard enough from some in her and Mo's families, and was fed up with everyone insisting that a decision to exercise CT134 was easy and obvious. It wasn't. Everyone kept saying Jayne was a threat to the Way, but their only support for that view was pointing out that her parents had committed Chosen Violations. Depraved and shocking? Yes. But her parents had fallen, not Jayne. It would take a much more compelling argument for Lesley to consider exercising CT134, or Jayne herself would have to show signs of falling from the Way.

She held the letter over the mouth of the recycling chute, but snatched it back at the last second and grabbed the envelope from her desk. Minutes later, she tapped on Laura's open office door and marched inside.

"What's the matter?" Laura asked, looking up.

"This." She handed Laura the letter and folded her arms.

Laura's expression grew dubious as she progressed through the letter. She looked at Lesley. "Where did it come from?"

"It was in my correspondence slot. And there's no sender information on the envelope." She waved it under Laura's nose.

Laura frowned. "Nothing in it's a violation, but a military member must be involved. Do you mind if I keep it? I think I'll open a case file, just so we have a record of it."

"Go ahead." Lesley sighed. "The last thing I need is some group pressuring me to exercise CT134."

Laura dropped the letter onto her desk. "It might not be a group. For all we know, it's one person. And now that they feel they've done their duty to the Way, that'll probably be it. So don't worry about it. It's nothing." She tapped her fingertips together. "Though I don't like that it came through our correspondence system."

Lesley wished it hadn't arrived at all. What next, messages to her and Mo on the monitors? "I think I'll keep this to myself. Mo and Jayne don't need to know."

"Don't mention it when you come for supper, you mean? I wouldn't." Laura held out her hand.

"What?"

"The envelope."

Lesley gave it to her.

"I'm looking forward to hosting you all next week," Laura said. "I want to meet Jayne, and it will be nice to exchange more than a few words with Mo."

"We're looking forward to it too," Lesley said, hoping her smile reached her eyes. Mo certainly wouldn't agree with that sentiment, and who knew how Jayne felt about it. "Anyway, I should get back to my office. I have more dispatches to read. Hopefully there won't be any more like that one."

"I'm sure there won't be. And forget about this one. I doubt this group will bother you again."

Lesley hoped Laura was right.

MO PRESSED HER lips together and pulled Jayne to the left. Jayne groaned. "I'm sorry. Why do I step on your foot every time we get to that step?"

"You'll get it," Mo said, fervently hoping Jayne would. Her right foot was probably as flat as a pancake by now. Jayne didn't just step on her foot, she came down on it hard. "You're doing good for your first time." And Jayne was, despite the one step giving her—both of them—trouble. "Do you want to take a break?" At least an hour must have passed since they'd awkwardly positioned themselves and tentatively danced the few steps Mo had demonstrated with an imaginary partner. If anyone had passed by, they would have wondered what she was doing.

"Sure." Jayne let go of Mo. She shook her head when Mo picked up her flask of water and pointed to Jayne's. "So how big is the dance floor at the Dance Hall?"

Mo swung up her comm unit to turn off the music, then surveyed the field as she sipped her water. They'd quickly decided that Jayne's living room wasn't large enough for dance lessons. At Mo's suggestion, they'd flown to the Middleton estate and traipsed to a field that was hidden from the house, though a military patrol could wander through at any time. "It's smaller than the field. When we've been dancing, we've always remained within the area of a typical dance floor." She turned to Jayne. "I think I must have done that unconsciously."

Jayne smiled, then squinted past her.

Mo followed her gaze. "She found us!" She dropped her flask and ran to Les.

"You aren't dancing," Les said after they'd hugged. "I expected to see you whirling around the field."

"We're taking a break." Mo glanced over her shoulder. Jayne had sat down, apparently deciding to wait for them to return to her, rather than intrude.

Les looked toward Jayne. "Maybe I should have a dance with her."

"You know what? She's tired, and I'm hungry. I was just thinking that I'd like to eat soon."

"Okay," Les said, to Mo's relief. "Your papa and Nathan are home. I told them we'll be making supper."

"Andrew wasn't there?"

"No."

Andrew was hardly around lately. It couldn't be a girlfriend. He usually wasn't tight-lipped when he was seeing someone.

"How's the dancing coming along?" Les asked.

"She's picking it up pretty quickly," Mo said. "Another hour or two and she'll be ready. We're only practicing basic steps, though."

"She'll learn as she goes along."

"I know, but when we're at the Dance Hall, we'll have to carefully choose our dances with her. It could turn out there aren't two opportunities the whole night."

Les gave her a pointed look. "She doesn't have to be perfect. Stop trying to prevent me from dancing with her. I'll have to dance with her sometime."

Mo made a mental note to be more subtle next time. "I just don't want to put her into an embarrassing situation," she said, despite knowing she wasn't fooling Les. "Anyway, let's go eat." She cupped her hand to one side of her mouth and shouted, "Jayne, we're going to have supper now. Can you bring my flask?"

Jayne rose, clutching the flasks' straps with one hand and picking up her sketchbook with the other. Since Mo had never seen Jayne actually open the sketchbook, today or any day, she was starting to wonder if it was filled with blank pages. Maybe Jayne just needed something to hang onto while away from home.

When Jayne reached them, she handed Mo her flask. "Thanks," Mo murmured. Jayne mumbled a hello to Les, who returned her greeting. They started to walk to the house.

"Mo said the dancing is going well," Les said, taking Mo's hand.

"I doubt her right foot would agree," Jayne said dryly, making Mo smile. She hated to admit it, but she sort of liked Jayne. Jayne was quiet and accommodating, and easy to hang out with. When she opened her mouth, something interesting usually came out. And if her last name wasn't Adams, nobody would want them to execute her because there was no indication that she was weak in the Way. Not a single sign.

Mo would rather not be in a triad, but wishing she wasn't in one would be pointless. Wishing Jayne would go away would be pointless too. There was only one way to get rid of her, and Mo would never agree to it. She'd eaten with Jayne, played cards with her, and now danced with her. Jayne wasn't some anonymous person to Mo, as she was to all the airheads calling for her execution. Mo was uncomfortable with Les having another Chosen and would do everything she could to make sure Jayne stuck to their arrangement. What she wouldn't do was kill Jayne to keep Les to herself. She knew in her gut that doing so would kill all three of them.

Fortunately Les felt the same way and had stood up to those in their families who'd wanted a swift execution. Mo would have to get used to having a third person hovering in her peripheral vision whenever she and Les were out together. But that was better than losing all respect for the person who stared back at her in the mirror and the one who sometimes slept next to her at night.

LESLEY YAWNED AS she shrugged off her cloak and hung it. It was only 19:30, but a full day of meetings always wore her out, especially when the last meeting of the day ran more than an hour over schedule. She'd grabbed a bite to eat at the cafeteria before heading home, and looked forward to a quiet evening with a book, though Mo had said she might drop in.

"Lesley!" someone yelled as she climbed the stairs.

The shout had come from up the hallway. She backtracked in time to glimpse Jason going back into the study. He wasn't alone. Her parents peered up at her when she stepped inside. The atmosphere felt tense; she suspected that heated words had been exchanged, but between whom and about what? "Where've you been?" Jason snapped.

"On duty. I beeped Mama." As a courtesy. She *was* twenty-seven.

"You said your meeting would run a bit late. It's almost 8:00."

"I ate supper in the cafeteria. What's wrong?"

Her parents exchanged glances. Jason opened his satchel, pulled out a black binder, and handed it to her. She opened it and read the top page.

Case for the Execution of Jayne Adams under Article CT134
Prepared by Advocate Christopher Phillips
File: CT1455-B

Blood pounded in her ears. She read it again, then closed the binder. "What is this?" She kept her voice steady, concealing her anger.

"A case that shows Adams is a threat to the Way," Jason said smugly.

She turned to her parents. "Did you know about this?"

They shook their heads. "We found out when Jason gave it to us a couple of hours ago," Mama said.

Lesley noticed the open binder on Papa's desk and the closed one on Mama's.

"Mary and I commissioned the case," Jason said, perching himself on the edge of Mama's desk.

"Don't tell me you've dragged Mo into this, too," Lesley exclaimed.

"Mo needs to read it, just as you do. Mary gave it to her a few hours ago."

Then why hadn't Mo beeped her about it? "You shouldn't have done this behind our backs."

"What were we supposed to do?" he said, his tone reasonable. "You and Mo refused to listen to us, so we thought that if an advocate laid it all out for you in a logical and rational manner, you might come to your senses. Adams threatens the triad, and because of that, she threatens the Way. Everyone else can see that. You need to see it too, before you Join and it's too late."

Lesley looked at her parents. "I assume you've read it?"

"We have," Papa said.

Mama tapped the binder in front of her. "It argues that the Chosen Council wouldn't have accounted for the Incident when assessing Jayne."

"How could it?" Jason said. "Who would ever have thought that both Chosens in a Joining would fall? It's unthinkable. Nobody's sick enough to even imagine it."

"Let me finish," Mama said, frowning. "Phillips asserts that the Incident invalidates Jayne's personality tests, that an event of such magnitude would have severely affected her. It would have changed her, perhaps damaged her in some way."

"So now she's a victim? And so we execute her?" Lesley wanted to toss the binder over her shoulder in disgust.

Jason threw up his hands. "Don't you get it, Lesley? She's not your Chosen. She might have been before the Incident, but she isn't now."

She'd never tell him that she'd suspected all along that Jayne wasn't her Chosen, though not for the reason Phillips had put forward.

"The case includes supporting material that backs up Phillips's assertion," Papa said. "You should read it."

So now it would be three against one, and they had a case to wave in her face. "I'll read it." She couldn't ignore it. "But I'm not happy about you going behind our backs," she said to Jason. "We said we wanted time. Why couldn't you respect that?"

"Because the longer you take to make a decision, the more likely you are to Join with her. And once that Chosen ring is on your finger, there's no way out. You have to exercise the article soon, before it's too late."

For a moment, she wondered if he was behind the letter she'd received from that concerned group. She wouldn't put it past him to stoop that low. "I guess I'd better start reading it, then." Not for his benefit, but because she wouldn't sleep until she'd read the case. "I'll read it in my room."

She left the study and headed upstairs. The moment her bedroom door was shut, she tossed the binder onto her desk and punched Mo's code into her comm station. "Why didn't you beep me when Mary gave you the case?"

"Because I was afraid I'd say a few things about your brother I'd regret," Mo said. "I figured I better calm down first. I'm still waiting."

"Don't go easy on him on my account." Lesley pulled the chair from underneath the desk and sat down. "Is Mary still there?"

"No. She dumped this on me and left. Have you looked at it yet?"

"I just got it."

"Les, her whole life is in there. I flipped through it and saw a report from the Learning Academy, from when she was six years old! This is completely unfair."

Lesley nodded, even though Mo couldn't see her. "I told Jason they shouldn't have gone behind our backs."

"Well, that too, but I'm talking about how we have all this information about her. And now what? We pick over her life." Mo sighed. "I don't feel good about this. It really isn't fair at all."

Lesley agreed, but refusing to read the case would be irresponsible. "We have to read it."

"Yeah, I know we have to flaming read it!" She could visualize Mo's tight face. "Why don't I come over?" Mo said.

"I think it would be better for us to read the case separately, make up our own minds about it." And she wanted to pore over the case in much more detail than Mo would. If she judged it lacking, it would be her against three advocates. "I'll come over tomorrow, as soon as I'm off duty. We can discuss it then."

"I don't know if I'll have finished it by then."

"You have the rest of tonight and all day tomorrow to read it. I don't know about you, but I want to read it and deal with it before we see Jayne again." Silence. "Mo?"

"Yeah, okay," she said quietly.

"You all right?"

"No, I'm not. This stinks. But I'll hold my nose."

For a moment, she reconsidered Mo's offer to come over, but rejected it again. "I'm going to start reading, then. I only have tonight." She hesitated, then said, "I love you."

"I love you too." Mo paused. "I won't blame Jayne for hating us if she finds out about this. I don't know how I'll look her in the eye next time I see her. I'll know way more about her than I should."

"I don't like this, either."

"I know, but you'll be able to shut everything out and read the case like an advocate. I'll just get angrier. But I know I have to read it. I want my say."

"Mo, your assessment of this case matters more to me than anyone else's." Not only would Mo's emotional reading of the case balance Lesley's logical reading of it, but they had to agree on CT134. If they disagreed on such a fundamental issue, the triad would be in trouble, and not because of Jayne. "I'll beep you when I leave headquarters."

They said good-bye and disconnected. Lesley stared at the black binder. She opened it and read the title page again, then rubbed her forehead. When she flipped to the next page, there'd be no going back. If she read something she wished she hadn't, it would be too late. Lesley read cases all the time, many of them in folders like this one and with similar title pages. This was the first one that made her hands clammy.

Yesterday Hall had told her that she'd been accepted into the commander training program and would enter it next month. Laura always said she'd do anything to protect the Way and didn't shy away from decisions to execute. Lesley was confident that she wouldn't either, but hoped the first person she condemned to die wouldn't be someone the Chosen Council had entrusted to her. She braced herself and turned the page.

MO SCRUTINIZED PAGE sixty-four of the case, considering every angle. When satisfied, she released the folded page with a snap of her wrist. It cleared the bed, then nosedived to the floor. She groaned. Page forty-two had flown the best, making it across the room and skimming along the window before gliding gracefully onto her desk. Time to try a new design. She picked up her comm unit and selected *Paper Flyer Design #23.* Ooh, this one looked intricate, and probably wouldn't fly very far. Given the rhetoric weighing down every page, she was surprised any had managed to clear the bed at all.

If she had to read the same point again, written slightly differently, she'd throw up. Advocates must be paid by the word. Okay, so the Incident may have affected Jayne. How many years had this Advocate Phillips spent at college to come up with that brilliant conclusion? With a sigh, Mo removed page sixty-five from the binder and glanced at it. Oh yeah, the military report about Jayne's level three violation, filed by one—she searched for the name—Lieutenant C. Bradley. According to the "report," Jayne had provoked Bradley, called her names. Come on.

Mo's indignation grew as she folded the paper according to the design's instructions. Jayne was the sort who said "excuse me" when someone stepped on *her* foot. Most of all, she wasn't stupid. If she'd called Bradley the names listed in the report, they probably would have struck her with a level five and executed her. She'd never dare provoke military—ever.

Phillips's whole case was dumb. Mo would never agree to use it as a basis to execute Jayne, but would Les? If Les agreed with the case, Mo would have to stand up not only to Mary and Matthew, but to the Thompsons, including Les. Her against all those advocates and an Interior officer? She wouldn't stand a chance. But would Les stand with them? She was definitely a Thompson, but she wasn't an advocate. She'd defied her parents' wishes regarding her career, and Mo was sure she'd stand against her family regarding the case, too. Les would agree that it was more an overblown theory than anything, otherwise Mo didn't know her as well as she thought she did.

The paper flyer was ready. Mo released it, and wasn't surprised when it hit the bed about two feet away from her. Nope, too intricate.

"Did you at least read the case?"

She twisted toward the door. Les was leaning against the door frame, her arms folded. "You're here already?" Mo blurted.

"I said I was almost at the estate. I guess you've been so absorbed in the case, time flew by."

"I did read it first," Mo said sheepishly. Fortunately Les didn't look upset. "Did you finish it?"

Les nodded.

"What do you think?" Dreading what Les might say next, Mo braced herself, hoping they weren't about to argue.

Les unfolded her arms but didn't move from the doorway. "Well, Phillips's argument is compelling, and he's probably right. It's possible that Jayne is no longer the best match for both of us, which would mean the triad shouldn't exist."

Mo swallowed.

"And because it's possible that Jayne isn't really our Chosen anymore, we could run into problems."

Her heart sank. "Yeah, but we have an arrangement. What problems . . ." Mo trailed off when Les raised her hand.

"I agree that all the possibilities he raises are real possibilities. But I don't agree with his conclusion. I can't execute someone based on possibilities. It's possible the Incident affected her, but not in ways that invalidate the Chosen Council's data." Les's eyes narrowed. "It's possible that she changed in such a way that she's now a better match for you than I am."

Mo's mouth dropped open. "What?"

"It's possible." Les finally walked into the room and sat on the bed. "See? I can do it too. Draw any conclusion I want based on his argument. Let's say he's right and the Incident invalidated Jayne's data. That doesn't mean Jayne's the odd one out in the triad now. It could be you or me."

Mo's shoulders sagged as the tension drained from her. "I hate advocates. Well, the ones I'm not related to." And one to whom she was. Flaming Jason! Les's parents would probably support him. Les and Karen were the only sane ones in that family.

"What do you think?" Les asked.

"I think if she commits a capital violation, she goes to an execution site, like every other Rymellan. And I feel guilty for invading her life. Did you read her final report from the Learning Academy? Where is it?" She hopped off the bed, went to the pile of wrecked flyers near the window, and found page fifty-one. "Listen to this." She unfolded the flyer and smoothed the paper. "'Jayne refused to mix with the other students. She rarely said a word to anyone, and never interacted with her peers or participated in group activities. She spent all her free periods by herself, filling her sketchbook. It's no wonder the other students didn't respect her. She didn't respect them.'" Mo shook her head. "And listen to this, written by her art instructor. 'I try to be positive about my students' work, but I can't, in good conscience, offer false praise to a student who displays such a shocking lack of talent. I don't want to encourage Jayne's delusion. Jayne, if you'd spent as much time preparing for your classes as you did churning out drawings nobody will ever want to see, perhaps you would have passed one of your subjects.'

"Can you believe that?" Tears sprang to Mo's eyes. "Even if it's true, did that instructor have to be so cruel?" She remembered how much Ann's taunts had hurt her; she'd almost given up on her dream to become a fighter pilot because she'd started to believe them. Those who said words were only words and couldn't hurt were rarely the ones on the receiving end. The instructor's words angered her. She couldn't imagine how Jayne had felt when she'd read them.

"It's not true," Les said, so loud that Mo jumped. Then she realized that Les was next to her, and leaned into her when she felt Les's arm around her shoulders. "I'm not an art instructor, but the drawings I saw looked good to me. I think I can tell when someone can't draw at all."

Mo tossed the report on the floor. "I wish she'd show us some of her work. I know you said we should wait for her to do it, but I don't think she'll take that step, not for a long time." Mo certainly wouldn't, not after an instructor had told her she was deluded. "I might bring it up at some point." Les didn't protest.

"So it sounds like we agree about the case," she said, looking up at Les.

"We do." Les paused. "It's a dangerous case."

"What do you mean?"

"It could be true. If we'd been leaning toward execution, this would definitely have pushed us over the edge. And if we'd already decided on execution and this was the case prepared for us, she'd be dead by now. We would have drawn the conclusion we wanted, and the overseers would probably have been happy to go along with us. Jayne probably doesn't realize it, but she's lucky she ended up in a triad with an Interior officer." She squeezed Mo. "And a Defence officer who puts more stock in what she knows than what she's told."

Mo grinned. "I end up there eventually," she said, thinking again about how she'd almost believed Ann's nonsense. "You know what surprised me about the case? It sort of says the Chosen Council made a mistake."

"No, it doesn't. The Chosen Council is constantly refining its methods based on past results. The case states it couldn't have accounted for an event like the Incident, since nothing like that had ever happened before. Frankly, I'm not sure it ever can, though it will probably try." She lifted her arm from Mo's shoulders and reached for her comm unit. "I'll beep Jason, let him know what we've decided."

"No!"

Les turned to her in confusion.

"All that'll do is start another round of badgering. Let's string them along for a while, tell them we're thinking and researching or something."

"We'll have to tell them sometime."

"Yeah, but not today." Mo decided to ask what had been on her mind since Mary handed her the case. "What about Jayne? Do we tell her about the case?"

"I think we should. Our families know. Someone could inadvertently mention it to her."

"Or do it deliberately."

Les nodded. "This might be difficult, but we have to stand with her, even against our families. I'm glad we've come to an arrangement, because that's the only way I can see the triad working." She hesitated, then continued. "And I already doubted she was our Chosen before reading the case. But when we're in public, she's our Chosen and our arrangement doesn't exist."

"You mean we don't mention the arrangement, right?"

Les chuckled. "Yes."

"Maybe we should just Join. That'll put an end to CT134 once and for all. Then we could relax and get to know each other instead of strategizing."

"That might not be a bad idea," Les said, startling Mo. "But even after we Join, we'll still have to present a united front in public. We'll be able to stop worrying that the slightest crack in the triad's public facade will have everyone screaming for Jayne's execution, though."

And start a family. The prospect of Joining sooner rather than later excited and frightened Mo. After her notification meeting, Joining had gone right out of her mind. Now . . . She met Les's eyes. "Did we just decide that we're not going to exercise CT134? I mean, we've been telling everyone we want to give it time, but I think we just decided we don't need more time."

"Did we?" Les cocked her head. "Or have we known all along? Those first few days after our notification meetings, when we were reeling so badly we hardly knew what we were doing? Inside, we both knew exactly what you said earlier—that we'd never send a Rymellan who hasn't committed a capital violation to an execution site."

As soon as Les said it, Mo knew it was true. "And if we have problems with our arrangement?"

"Then we work together to solve them. Why should Jayne automatically go to an execution site because we're having problems? Is that how we'd solve any problems?"

No, they could do better than that, and would. "Then we're really going to Join," Mo breathed. "We're really going to be a triad."

"We won't Join tomorrow, but yes. Unless Jayne sends herself to an execution site, we'll be a triad." Les took Mo's face in her hands. "I don't know what's going to happen. I suspect our lives will be a little more interesting than we'd expected, and I can't promise you we'll never regret this decision. But I can promise you this: I'll always love you, Mo Middleton. Nothing will ever change that."

Warmth flooded through Mo; she couldn't breathe. At that moment, she believed they could face anything, as long as they were together. Tears threatened a second time, but this time they were happy ones. Did she wish it would only be her and Les in the Joining Chamber? Oh, yeah. But after reading the case and understanding even further what Jayne had endured—still endured—Mo couldn't resent her for ending up in a triad with them. In a way, she was glad. They wouldn't be Chosens to her like they were to each other, but they'd respect her. Jayne deserved at least that. She slipped her arms around Les's neck and pulled her close. "I love you, too," she murmured. "And I know this sounds crazy, but I want to celebrate. Let's go out for supper."

"If we go out—"

"I know." They didn't have to go with her, but they should. Mo let go of Les and picked up her comm unit from the bed. She punched in a code. "Jayne?" she said as soon as they were connected.

"Yes?"

"Have you eaten yet?"

"No, I haven't."

"Great!" Mo smiled at Les and reached for her hand. "Les and I would like to take you out for supper."

SHIELDS DOWN

·····

JAYNE DRAINED HER TZIVA AND SET her mug on the kitchen table. "Would you like another cup?" she asked her two guests.

Lesley glanced at Mo. "No, thank you. I'm on duty tomorrow, so we should get going."

"Thank you for supper," Jayne said, still hardly believing they'd beeped her out of the blue and invited her to go out and eat with them. Spontaneous social invitations only happened to other people.

"We enjoyed it," Mo said, but she sounded sombre and her shoulders were stiff. Just minutes ago, as they'd enjoyed the nightcap Jayne had offered, she'd been smiling.

Lesley fingered the black binder lying on the table in front of her. When she'd brought it with her to the apartment, Jayne had assumed it was an important Interior document she didn't want to leave out of her sight. But now she realized that if her assumption was correct, Lesley would also have taken it into the eatery.

"We have something to tell you," Lesley said.

Jayne swallowed. "Okay."

Lesley was silent for a moment before she said, "My brother and Mo's sister engaged an advocate to prepare a case under CT134."

"We didn't know." Mo's voice was unusually loud. "We only found out when they shoved it at us."

"But we had to read it," Lesley said quietly. "We thought it only fair that you should read it too, if you want to." She pushed the folder toward Jayne.

It was fortunate that Jayne had put her mug down, because her hands were shaking. Half of her wanted to read it, while the other half wanted to rip it into little pieces to feed into the recycling chute. Fear gripped her. She sat on her hands and tried to calm herself. If they intended to present the case, they wouldn't have taken her out for supper. Either that, or she'd completely misjudged them. No, she wasn't that bad at reading people. They'd have to be the coldest, most sadistic Rymellans on the planet to suggest that she read a case they were going to present.

"We're obviously not going to present it," Lesley said, as if reading Jayne's mind. "We think we should Join."

"You think we should Join?" Jayne repeated, wanting to be sure she'd heard correctly.

"Yes," Lesley said firmly.

Mo nodded her agreement.

So after reading the case, they'd decided to waive CT134 and Join. "Why?" She kicked herself; that had come out wrong. "I agree we should Join, for obvious reasons. But why have you reached that conclusion?" Not long ago, Lesley had said they'd see how it went.

"We sort of always knew." Mo looked more relaxed now. "But I guess we needed some time to let everything sink in."

Jayne knew Mo didn't mean just the triad.

"Reading the case forced us to clarify our thoughts about CT134," Lesley said.

Mo snorted. "Yeah, I bet Jason and Mary will be really happy when they find out their case helped us decide to Join."

"You haven't told them?" Jayne asked, feeling a little bewildered that CT134 was off the table, just like that. But she wasn't surprised. Based on how they'd treated her over the past month, she would have been shocked if they'd turned around and exercised the article. Still, she hadn't expected them to consciously reach a firm decision so soon.

"We figured we'd string them along for a while, let them think we're considering the case."

Jayne wasn't sure that was the best course of action, but despite Lesley and Mo's decision, she didn't feel brave enough to speak up. They weren't interested in her opinion anyway.

"And we honestly didn't know about the case," Lesley said. "We wish Jason and Mary hadn't gone behind our backs."

When Jayne had visited the Thompson estate, Adelaide's attitude had made it clear that not everyone in the Thompson family was comfortable with her. She'd wondered how others in the Thompson and Middleton families viewed her, and now she knew. They were more than uncomfortable with her; they wanted her dead. She hadn't met Jason, or Mo's sister, so her name alone had condemned her. Did their other siblings feel the same way?

Jayne would soon find out. Lesley's sister had invited everyone to supper the night they'd go to the Dance Hall. Jayne wouldn't expect Jason and Mary to be at the table. But what could she do to smooth things over? She didn't mind trying to compromise and accommodate, but not when it meant going to an execution site. Lesley and Mo would have to deal with their families on their own. She'd gladly support them, but those who loathed her would only resent her involvement.

"Do you want to read the case?" Lesley asked, breaking into Jayne's thoughts.

"Yes, I do." Forget about tearing it up; she wanted to know how it had helped them make up their minds about CT134.

Lesley pushed back her chair and stood. "We can discuss it after you've read it, if you like." She didn't sound too enthusiastic about the idea. The whole conversation had taken an awkward turn, marring the otherwise relaxed and pleasant evening.

Bursting with curiosity, Jayne couldn't help another glance at the black binder as she rose, but it would have to wait until she'd seen her guests out.

"So Mo will pick you up on Friday about five," Lesley said as she slipped into her cloak. "I'm going to Laura's straight from headquarters."

"We'll be having supper together a few times this week," Mo said. "Finney's and Karen's, and maybe after our dance lesson, too."

Jayne nodded. She wasn't looking forward to the supper at Commander Finney's, though. Not only did the thought of dining with a commander intimidate her, but there was tension between Lesley and Mo when it came to Finney, as Mo called her, or Laura, as Lesley called her. Well, she was calling her Commander Finney, unless told to do otherwise. "Carol wants to invite you to supper. She said she'll talk to us about it at the Dance Hall." And she was eating supper at Carol and Ronald's tomorrow. She'd never been so busy in her life!

Mo smiled. "That will be nice."

As soon as they were gone, Jayne returned to the kitchen and flipped open the binder.

Case for the Execution of Jayne Adams under Article CT134
Prepared by Advocate Christopher Phillips
File: CT1455-B

Wow, right there in black and white. She was almost afraid to let the binder out of her sight, in case someone saw it and had her dragged to an execution site without confirming that the case had been presented and accepted. Completely irrational, since that would mean an intruder had entered her apartment. But who wouldn't feel jittery when faced with a document created for the sole purpose of swaying an overseer to execute her? Jayne left it on the table while she poured herself a glass of water, but took it into the bathroom and bedroom as she prepared for bed. She fluffed up her pillow and settled in for some interesting bedtime reading.

KEVIN LED CYNTHIA into the living room and offered her something to drink.

"No, I'm not staying long," Cynthia said, sinking into a chair. "I only dropped in because when I spoke to Gwen this afternoon, she didn't sound herself."

"She's not here."

"I know. She told me she'd be visiting Mama without you. Why didn't you go with her and the children?"

"Because I didn't feel like it!" He dropped onto the sofa and folded his arms.

Cynthia frowned. "That's not like you, Kevin."

"What, I can't have a quiet night in by myself?"

"What's going on? I know something's wrong. Gwen didn't say anything, but I could tell she's worried."

"Nothing's wrong!" Except that his Chosen should be more supportive of him. "Gwen wasn't around during the Incident. She doesn't understand."

"What doesn't she understand?" When he didn't answer, Cynthia leaned forward. "What have you done, Kevin?"

"Nothing," he mumbled.

"What have you done?"

Kevin could tell from her tone that she wouldn't leave without an answer. He shrugged. "A few of us wrote another letter to Thompson."

"What?"

He winced at her shrill voice. "She must have received our first one, but nothing's happened. So we thought we'd better send her another one."

Cynthia sat back, looking exasperated. "What were you expecting? That she'd receive our letter and instantly exercise the article because we told her to?"

"She and Middleton would have engaged an advocate right after their notifications. I don't understand what's taking so long."

Cynthia stared at him. "You don't know if they've engaged an advocate."

"If they haven't, then it's even more critical that we continue to remind them of their duty. We have to counter Adams' influence on them."

"Kevin . . ." She paused, seemingly at a loss for words. "Who did this with you? Why didn't you invite me?"

He snorted. "You have to ask?"

"Do you understand what you're doing? You're sending letters to an Interior officer, dictating what she should do in her personal life. It would be bad no matter who you were sending them to, but an Interior officer?" Cynthia shook her head. "You have to stop," she said firmly.

He thrust his chin out. "I'll stop when Adams' execution is announced."

"And what happens if it isn't? What will you do then?"

"It will be. Thompson's receiving the Medal of the Protector."

After a moment Cynthia said, "So?"

"She won't let Adams live."

"She will if she doesn't see Adams as a threat."

That wasn't possible. Everyone knew Adams was a threat to the

Way. Cynthia must know it as well, so he couldn't understand why she wouldn't stand with him against Adams.

"If you keep sending Thompson letters, you'll be harassing her. You do realize that?"

"I don't have a choice, Cynthia."

"Yes, you do! Listen to me. You have Gwen and Alexander. Benjamin, Sheila, Patricia. You've got to let this go. For them."

Was she completely stupid? "I'm doing this for them."

"No, you're not! You're doing it for revenge. Not for the Way, no matter what you say." She rose and put her hands on her hips. "So no more letters, Kevin. There's nothing more you can do." When he didn't speak, her face softened. "I've already lost a sister. I don't want to lose a brother, too. Two brothers, if Tom's still involved in this madness. You have to accept that it's out of your hands. Thompson's strong in the Way. Trust her."

Kevin sighed. "I'd like to, but I can't. Adams is in her life now. So it's up to Rymellans to help Thompson, to keep reminding her of what the Way demands. As I said, I don't have a choice."

Cynthia opened her mouth, then clamped it shut and whirled to march from the living room. The front door slammed shut.

For a second, he considered taking Cynthia's advice. He hadn't slept a full night since learning of the triad, and he couldn't concentrate when he was reading cases. Gwen's distress wasn't lost on him either, but as he'd said to Cynthia, Gwen hadn't been around when the Incident had destroyed the Stewart family. Otherwise she'd understand why he was determined to never let an Adams threaten his or anyone else's family again. Cynthia should understand too, but she was weak. She disappointed him.

He pushed himself up from the sofa and returned to what he'd been doing before Cynthia arrived. The glass of water next to the comm station was still cold. He sipped it, then refreshed the day's announcements and searched for one about Adams' execution. It wasn't there. No matter. In five minutes, he'd refresh the announcements again.

SITTING IN THE back garden of the White home, Jayne crossed her legs and tried to focus on Carol's voice. But her mind insisted on wandering back to the case prepared by Lesley's brother and Mo's sister. How could she face Lesley and Mo, after her life had been laid bare? They knew about the bogus level three strike, that horrible final report from the Learning Academy, everything!

". . . over there," Carol said.

"Mmm," Jayne responded absently.

She'd felt two feet tall by the time she'd finished reading Phillips's material. If the case had revealed details about the Incident, that would have more than compensated for everything else it contained. But those details were apparently as inaccessible to Phillips as they were to her, so it had included only a single paragraph about the Incident that stated the basic facts: Joan and Peter Adams had been executed for Chosen Violations, along with two unnamed Rymellans. Jayne already knew that! But what exactly had happened?

Carol gripped Jayne's arm. "You're not listening to a word I'm saying! I just said I saw a pink and purple cow over there."

Jayne shook herself. "Sorry. I keep thinking about the case." She hesitated, then said what bothered her most about Phillips's argument. "It could be true."

"What, that you're so different now that you're not their Chosen?" Carol shook her head. "You were twelve, not three. And frankly, you don't seem much different to me. Quieter and too hard on yourself, but still you."

Jayne sighed. "Even if that's true, it doesn't matter. I've never been their Chosen anyway." She felt compelled to tell them that. Would it be fair, letting them Join with her when she knew they weren't Chosens, especially when Lesley and Mo were probably each other's Chosen and loved each other?

"What if you are? Have you considered that possibility?"

She wasn't. "It doesn't matter whether I am or not, I'd handle things exactly the same way I am now, and so would they. As you said, I'm still me." Still their daughter.

"Did they say when they'd like to Join?"

"No."

Carol gazed into the distance. "One step at a time, I guess." Her eyes focused on Jayne. "It must be a relief. I know it is for me, but to be honest, I would have been surprised if they'd exercised the article."

Jayne too, but she felt depressed, not relieved. The three of them would be trapped in a sham Joining, but what could she do? Telling Lesley and Mo about her suspicions could get her executed. She wasn't willing to sacrifice herself, so that meant living a lie. Though they'd be doing that even if she were their Chosen, representing themselves as a triad in public when they were a couple and a . . . what? A friend?

She could see them being friends, and for the first time in a long time, didn't feel so alone. She wouldn't have to face this latest twist in her life by herself.

When it came to the effects of the Incident she'd always had Carol, but Carol had supported her without experiencing it to the extent Jayne did. It would be odd, being with two people who understood what it was like to be in a triad because they were going through it themselves. They'd face everyone and all the petty-mindedness together. They'd succeed or fail together, too.

"I can see you want to think about it, not talk about it," Carol said, her forehead creased in sympathy. "Let's talk about something else."

There was only one other thing on her mind—for now. She'd worry about the Dance Hall after she was over the more imminent hurdle. "That supper with Commander Finney is on Friday."

"Oh, right," Carol said. "Frankly, I think it's good that c3's commander will not only meet you, but actually talk to you."

Tell that to the butterflies in her stomach that took flight every time Jayne thought about meeting Finney.

"Though I suppose it would be better if you were to meet the new commander. I remember you saying Finney will be a commodore soon."

"Next week, I think. But Lesley said she'll oversee c3 for a while longer." Jayne blew out some air. "Finney's important to Lesley, so I don't want to say anything stupid. And Mo doesn't like her, but I don't know why." She did wonder if it had anything to do with Lesley's sudden career change. But then, wouldn't Lesley resent Finney too?

Carol was smiling at her.

"What?"

"It's nice to listen to you worry about mundane things like meeting your Chosens' friends, rather than about being dragged to an execution site. We all went through this when we were first getting to know our Chosens. You sound like everyone else."

"I do?"

Carol nodded. "We only had to worry about one Chosen, though." She patted Jayne's arm. "You'll do fine."

"I suppose it can't be any worse than that supper at the Thompsons'." What could Finney do to her that Adelaide hadn't already? Except execute her.

MO CHECKED THE navigation panel, then turned to Jayne, who hadn't said much since boarding the craft. "You nervous about meeting Finney?"

"A little." Jayne's grip tightened around the sketchbook on her lap. "What's she like?"

She's a cold-hearted, arrogant Interior officer who ripped us apart, then didn't feel a shred of guilt when we turned out to be Chosens. "I don't know her that well."

"Oh. I got the impression that she and Lesley are close, so I figured you probably knew her too."

No, to Finney, Mo had always been the inconvenient blemish on Les's life that threatened to stall her career advancement—until their Papers had arrived. Now they were supposed to dine together and chat over tziva as if they were old friends. "I've only spoken to her a few times. She's Les's friend, not mine." For Les's sake, she'd tolerate Finney and try to make conversation.

"Do you like her?"

Mo had heard the same irritation in her voice that Jayne must have heard, so there was no point lying. "I did when I first met her. And I was happy when she started to mentor Les. But then she sort of took over Les's life." Mo flashed back to her twenty-fifth birthday, when Les had announced her transfer to Interior and insisted that they couldn't communicate with each other while Mo was on tour—because of Finney. "When we were twenty-five, she forced us to break off contact with each other. I only found out about Les's transfer a few weeks before it happened, and at the same time, I'm told that our relationship will come to an abrupt end, to the point that I'm not even allowed to send Les a dispatch to see how she's doing."

"That must have been rough," Jayne said.

"Yeah. But you want to hear the worst part?" Now that she'd started, Mo couldn't stop. "Finney was at our notification party, and she didn't say one word about forcing us apart. No apology, nothing."

Jayne was silent for a moment. "Well, she was doing her duty," she finally said. "She was probably worried that you might have problems breaking up when your Papers came."

"Okay, but once she knew we were Chosens, don't you think she could have said something like, 'Oh, if I'd known, I would have let you send a dispatch to each other once a flaming month'? Of course Les didn't expect an apology, because as far as she's concerned, Finney's perfect." Mo clamped her mouth shut. She shouldn't have said that last part, but it felt good to finally get it off her chest. Finney was the culprit, though, not Les. "And now Finney's a descendant of a triad too. I should be happy about that, because it means Les has a strong ally in Interior and we'll have a commodore supporting us, but it means we're stuck with her."

Jayne chuckled. "I don't know if that's good or bad."

"It's good." Rationally, Mo knew that. "But every time I hear her name, I can't help but remember that she wouldn't even let us send a flaming dispatch."

"Would it bother you as much if she hadn't been Lesley's mentor and friend, if she'd just been C3's commander and neither of you personally knew her? Would you expect an apology then?"

Finney hadn't been Les's friend when she'd split them up. At that point, she'd still been Finney, not Laura. Mo turned back to the navigation panel to give herself time to think. She'd never looked at the situation the way Jayne suggested. She hated to admit it, but it wouldn't have bothered her so much. Sure, she would have hated the commander who'd separated them, but she wouldn't have expected that commander to show up on her doorstep with an apology after the triad was announced.

But who cared? Finney *was* Les's friend and mentor. And so should have let them remain together after they turned twenty-five? Les had said Finney was more lenient with them because she knew them, that otherwise she probably would have split them up earlier. Was Mo being unreasonable in expecting an apology, or at least some acknowledgment of how she and Les had suffered? Did Finney owe them that, or was Mo expecting special treatment because of Les and Finney's friendship? "I don't know," she mumbled, not wanting to admit to Jayne that her question had raised others that might threaten Mo's long-held view of the situation. "I'll be going to 72 in a couple of days," she said brightly.

"For a supply assignment, or to fly with a student?" Jayne asked.

"A practicum," Mo said, relieved that Jayne had gone along with the change of subject. "I'll be flying with ten students."

"What exactly will you do?"

By the time Mo had finished explaining her role and describing her first few flights in space, it was time to land the craft in the holding area nearest to Finney's home.

"Will you be upset with me if I like her?" Jayne asked as they walked to the house.

"No. I'm not going to tell you who to like. I mean, she's okay. I just wish things could have happened differently." She knocked on the front door. Jayne shoved her hands into her pockets; she'd left her sketchbook on the craft.

A teenage boy with Finney's hair and eyes opened the door and shouted over his shoulder, "Mama, it's them." He faced them. "Oh, sorry. Come in."

Finney and Les were there to greet them in the hallway. Mo wanted to roll her eyes when she saw they were both in uniform. It figured, that Finney would wear her flaming uniform! No—she had to stop putting her down. Finney could have changed, but that would have left Les, who'd just come off duty, the only one formally dressed. Mo and Les had dined umpteen times with friends while in uniform; this was no different.

"Take their cloaks, Ben," Finney said.

Les stepped forward and gestured toward Jayne. "This is Jayne."

Finney nodded. "Pleased to meet you, Jayne."

"And you," Jayne said, nodding in return.

"You know Mo," Les said.

"Not as much as I'd like to," Finney said with a smile. "Call me Laura. Both of you."

Mo forced herself to return the smile. "Pleased to meet you, Laura."

Her smile widened when Les lifted her eyebrows. Well, why fight it? As she'd said to Jayne, they were stuck with Finn—Laura, so she had to let go of her grudge. But for Les's sake, not because Laura hadn't been in the wrong! And not because of anything Jayne had said, either!

"DO YOU NEED help?" Lesley asked as she wandered into the Finney kitchen to return a glass.

Laura shook her head. "Ben and Megan will take care of the dishes." She added the glass to the other dirty dishes and turned to Lesley. "Everyone seemed to get along over supper. Ben was hanging on Mo's every word. He's mentioned Interior, but I won't be surprised if he suddenly wants to be a fighter pilot."

To Lesley's surprise, Mo had been nothing but pleasant and sociable from the moment she'd greeted Laura. She needn't have spent most of the afternoon worrying that Mo would sit slumped at the supper table with a black cloud almost visible over her head.

"You're right—Jayne's quiet, but I get the impression she doesn't miss much." Laura leaned against the counter. "You were quiet during supper, too. Anything wrong?"

She folded her arms. "That letter." Another one from the group of concerned Rymellans, essentially reiterating what the first had said. "I know, I know, I shouldn't let it bother me, but it does. What will happen when the Chosen Council announces our Joining date?"

"If you want me to find out who's sending them through our internal system, I can. From there, we can find out who else is involved, if there are more."

"No." At least not yet. "They're not violating any articles. It's just irritating."

"It's borderline harassment," Laura said. "It's also cowardly to send these letters anonymously. If they believe in what they're saying, they should put their names behind it."

She'd rather not know who they were, or how many they were. Right now, she could imagine two or three Rymellans huddled around a table and dismiss them. "If I get another one, then perhaps we should investigate, to head off trouble when they find out Mo and I have no intention of exercising CT134."

Laura nodded. "Just say the word, and I'll deal with it." She pushed away from the counter. "Shall we go see what story Mo is telling?"

"Before we do, I just want to say thank you."

Laura's brow furrowed. "For what?"

"Having us for supper. Treating us like you would any other Chosens who'd recently been notified."

"If you'd told me a few months ago I'd have a triad and an Adams at my supper table, I would have suggested you see your physician," Laura said wryly. "But I guess I'm not fazed because of my ancestry. As far as Jayne goes, she's your Chosen, and Mo's. That says a lot."

Not if it wasn't true.

"I'm glad you decided to come with me," Lesley said as she swung open the Thompsons' front door. "I thought maybe you'd want to sleep at home, since I have to be up tomorrow."

Mo shrugged. "I should get up too. I thought maybe I'd go to the Military Academy, see if I can fly a sim or two."

"You're not afraid of making a mistake during the practicums? The students probably wouldn't realize it, even if you do."

"No, but I haven't flown an actual fighter in over a month. It feels strange. I—"

Jason came barrelling up the hallway. "Oh, I see you're back from your cozy little supper!" His nostrils flared. "She's not with you? I'm sure you could squeeze her into your bed."

Mo gaped at him. "What's your flaming problem?"

"I don't like being treated like a fool."

"What are you talking about?" Lesley asked. She looked past him to Mama, who was carefully navigating the stairs as she tied the belt on her housecoat.

Jason ignored her shifting gaze. "You, telling me you're thinking about the case when you've already made up your mind. If you planned to present it, you wouldn't be introducing her around. As soon as Mama told me you were all at Commander Finney's, I knew."

"We were invited to supper before you gave us the case."

"You could have said no, but you didn't!" Jason shouted.

"Shh!" Mama's eyes blazed. "Keep your voice down. Papa's sleeping."

"We're seeing a counsellor," Mo said, sounding surprisingly calm. "We're supposed to be getting to know each other."

Jason's attention shifted to her. "Why?"

"Because she's our Chosen?"

"Not according to that case! But you probably didn't read it." He sniffed. "You wouldn't have understood it anyway."

Mo's hands went to her hips. "I read it and flaming-well understood it! You want my assessment? It's a bunch of meaningless hot air!"

"Who cares what you think?" Jason snapped.

"That's enough!" Lesley shouted. "What's wrong with you?"

"What's wrong with *you*?" he yelled, stepping toward her. He was so close she could smell his breath. "You have a case that will do away with the triad and let you and Mo go on with your lives. I don't understand you."

"No, you obviously don't," Lesley said, wanting to step back, if only there were room. The stairs creaked and Mama groaned—they'd awakened Papa. "So I'll make myself clear for you. We're not presenting your case. We're not presenting any case. We've decided the triad will Join." Perhaps Mo would be upset with her for announcing their decision, but Lesley drew the line at Jason insulting her.

Jason's hands clenched. "Get out!" he yelled, his face bright red.

"What?"

"*Get. Out!*" The confused silence that followed aggravated him further. "You're a disgrace to this family! I'm not living under the same roof with you!"

"Then you go, Jason," Mama said quietly.

Everyone turned to her.

"I'd prefer that neither of you go, but if you can't live under the same roof with her, you go."

To Lesley's relief, Jason moved away from her. He swallowed. "But Mama . . ."

"I can stay somewhere else for a few days," Lesley said, leaving unspoken the "until he's calmed down." He'd still be upset about their decision, but perhaps he could bear to live under the same roof when he wasn't in such an emotional state.

"There's plenty of room next door," Mo said, catching Lesley's eye, then dropping her voice so that only Lesley, and perhaps Jason, heard, "and a more pleasant atmosphere."

Mama shook her head. "Lesley belongs here."

Jason flung a forefinger toward Lesley. "You're supporting *her*? She's supporting an Adams."

"She's supporting her Chosen. You have to accept their decision."

"But—"

Mama silenced him by slicing her hand through the air. "The Way says they can decide whether to execute or Join. They've decided to Join. You have no choice but to accept and respect their decision."

"How can I respect a decision when it means welcoming an Adams into the family?" Jason looked to Papa. "Do you agree with this madness?"

"It's not madness!" Mama snapped. "It's the Way."

"And they should protect the Way by removing a threat to it," Jason said. "Don't you see that?"

"Jason, if we thought she was a threat, we'd exercise the article," Lesley said, wishing she didn't feel the need to appease him.

"She's an Adams!"

"That doesn't make her a threat by default." Lesley sighed. "Why don't you meet her? Then you'll see that she's a Rymellan, like everyone else."

"Really? I hadn't heard she has new parents." He pressed his lips together. "I can see I won't get through to you, so there's no point talking. I'm going to bed. Tomorrow I'll look for somewhere else to live."

Mama and Papa parted as he brushed past them and bounded up the stairs. Papa patted Mama's shoulder and murmured, "I'll go talk to him." Mama nodded, her face grim.

"Mama, I don't mind staying at Mo's for a bit," Lesley said when Papa had gone.

"No. He's in the wrong, not you."

"But this is his home."

"And yours. If you go, he'll feel vindicated, and he shouldn't. He's the one who's not following the spirit of the Way. Don't worry about him, Lesley. He's being childish."

She wasn't worried about him; his churlish behaviour irritated her, and she wouldn't forget the insult he'd hurled at Mo. But at the same time, she hadn't expected her and Mo's decision to drive him from his home—or Mama's support, especially against him. "I thought you'd be upset when we told you about our decision."

"I expected it," Mama stated.

"You did?" Mo said.

"Phillips's case is weak. It only sounds strong to those who want CT134 exercised."

"And you don't?" Mo asked, beating Lesley by a nanosecond.

Mama shrugged. "I've tried to keep an open mind."

"We didn't just reject the case, we've decided to Join," Lesley said.

"Again, I'm not surprised, and it is your decision. I wish it was someone other than Jayne, but it isn't, so we have to accept it. She's beneath us, but if we were to execute everyone who was beneath us, there wouldn't be many left."

Lesley couldn't decide whether Mo's face was taut because she was biting back a retort or trying not to burst into laughter.

"And we're Thompsons, or at least you will be soon," Mama said to Mo. "If your decision is to Join, then that's our decision. That's another reason Jason has to go, if anyone does. We have to make our position clear." She wagged her finger. "After this, no one will ever dare say the Thompsons put themselves before the Way." She turned and climbed the stairs.

"For a moment there, I thought I'd entered some sort of altered reality," Mo said when Mama was out of earshot. "Then she started to sound like your mama again." She grinned at Lesley. "But she's on our side!"

"I wish there weren't sides," Lesley said. "As much as I'm annoyed with Jason right now, I didn't want to see it come to this."

"I'll believe he's leaving when I see it. Though I have to admit, I wouldn't mind not seeing him for a while."

Considering how he'd treated Mo, Lesley wouldn't mind, either.

MO'S STOMACH GRUMBLED as she slung her knapsack over her shoulder and sidled into the shuttle's aisle. Not wanting to make breakfast at home, she'd opted to arrive on 72 early so she could eat in one of its canteens. A quick glance at her comm unit told her she had around an hour before her first practicum, plenty of time to find her quarters for the night, dump her bag, and grab a bite. She exited the shuttle and strode up the ramp that led to the waiting area.

"Mo!" Ann rushed over to her.

"What are you doing here? How'd you know I'd be on this shuttle?"

"I didn't," Ann said, falling into step with her. "But you said your first practicum is at 10:00, so it was either this or the next one." She glanced around. "You didn't bring her with you?"

"Who, Jayne? Is that why you're here, to see her?" Mo shook her head. "I wouldn't bring her with me." Not for her first set of practicums, anyway. She slowed to call up the dispatch with the location of her quarters on her comm unit.

Ann chortled. "So she's down there with Lesley for the next couple of days."

Mo slid her comm unit back into its holder. "I'll be surprised if they beep each other," she said, not in the least concerned. "Oh, listen—I'm sorry I didn't get in touch, last time you were down."

"I figured you were preoccupied." Ann elbowed her in the ribs. "Two Chosens! I suppose if you have to Join, that's the way to do it."

"One would have been fine," Mo muttered. Two minutes with Ann and she was already exasperated.

"So how's your family?" Ann asked as they boarded the elevator that would take them to Deck 5.

Mo eyed her suspiciously. Ann had never cared about her family before. "If you mean how are they taking the triad, okay, I guess. Matthew and Mary were upset about it. Mary even prepared a case for us."

"You mean to execute her?"

"Yeah, but we're not going to."

"You mean you'll Join?"

"Yeah. Mary's okay with it. I think preparing the case got it out of her system. She figures she did her bit and that's it. But Les's brother moved out. He's staying with a friend."

Ann gasped. "He moved out of the house? I wish I wasn't stuck up here. This is better than the theatre!"

Mo grinned. "Not when you're living it." They stepped off the elevator and turned left. "We're all going to the Dance Hall in a couple of days."

Ann groaned. "Why couldn't you have made it for when I was off shift?" she said, exactly the response Mo had hoped for.

"You'll meet her eventually." Mo pressed the button to open the door and stepped into the pristine room that would be hers for the next thirty-six hours or so.

"So how are your brothers?" Ann asked as Mo dropped her knapsack to the floor.

Mo gave Ann a quizzical look. "They're fine."

"I'm just being polite. I met them all at your notification party."

Being polite? That wasn't Ann. "I want to go to the canteen, I haven't eaten breakfast. You flying soon, or do you have time to come with me?"

"I'm coming with you," Ann quickly said, her eyes shining. "I'm not flying until 13:00. I want to hear everything, from the time you were notified."

She'd hear what Mo wanted to tell her. Mo led the way out of the room and they set off for the canteen on Deck 7.

"So you're a practicum instructor now." Ann snorted. "If the students could look behind them, they'd wonder where you were. They'd think they were all alone and panic."

"They'll see me get into the craft and hear me speaking to them," Mo said, wondering why she bothered responding to Ann's little barbs. Though Ann was slipping. Normally she would have told at least five short jokes by now.

"Oh, I found out more about Leeds," Ann said. "She's still a lieutenant. You outrank her!"

Yet another reason for Leeds to resent her. Mo wasn't surprised that Leeds' conduct at the Military Academy had stalled her career. But despite Leeds deserving the consequences of her actions, Mo couldn't gloat, not when the triad had affected her own career. "I hope I don't run into her."

"She's flying nights, so you probably won't."

Even so, Mo would keep an eye out for her. And flying nights? Leeds' career really had taken a nosedive.

When they reached the canteen, Mo ordered a cheese and tomato omelette with toast. "You're not having anything?" she said to Ann.

"I already had breakfast."

"So how's your family?" Mo asked. Ann's shrug drew Mo's eyes away from the cook's preparation of her omelette. Did Ann not know, not care, or both? It definitely meant she didn't want to talk about it. Mo returned her gaze to the cook. "You seeing anyone?"

"No!"

Ann's tone caught Mo's attention. "You sure?"

"I'm not seeing anyone, okay? I don't have time."

Mo narrowed her eyes. "Did you just break up with someone?" If so, it would have been a short relationship, considering Ann had been single at their notification party. Then again, Ann didn't really have relationships; she had one-night flings.

"No, I didn't. Why the sudden interest in who I'm seeing?"

"I'm just making conversation. You've never been testy about it before."

Ann exhaled loudly. "Okay, I didn't mean to jump all over you. I'm not seeing anyone, and I haven't broken up with anyone, either."

Though she suspected that Ann was touchy because she'd recently been dumped, Mo let the subject drop. "You want to have a late supper with me? My last practicum finishes at 19:00 and then I'll be at a loose end."

"Sure. Maybe we can go to my quarters afterward and play cards."

Mo shook her head. "Let's play in one of the recreation rooms."

"I don't want to play with anyone else. We won't be able to talk."

"That's not why I'm suggesting it. I've been notified, remember?"

Ann snorted. "And you think someone will report us because we're in my quarters alone? Everyone knows I'm diff-oriented." She frowned. "Though I suppose you can't be too cautious, with you becoming an Adams."

"I'm becoming a Thompson!" But she'd be Joined to an Adams, and that would mean constant scrutiny by airheads eager to put two and two together to get five. "But you're right, I can't be too careful." Ironically, her association with an Adams meant she'd be held to a higher standard.

"YOU'RE READY," MO announced. She glanced at her comm unit. "We still have a half-hour until Les shows up. Do you want to wait for her here? It's such a nice day."

"Are you sure I'm ready?" Jayne asked anxiously.

"Yeah. I mean, there's more to learn, but you know all the basic steps."

"And you're sure I need to dance with you and Lesley?"

"It won't look good if Les and I only dance with each other." What would Counsellor flaming Berry say? "You'll do okay," she said, trying to calm Jayne's obvious fear. "You won't be alone on the dance floor."

Jayne swallowed, then bent to reach for her sketchbook—and stopped.

"No, if you want to draw, go ahead," Mo said casually. She'd bitten her tongue at Jayne's apartment, pretended she hadn't noticed the sketches on the walls. Maybe Jayne would show her one today! "We have time to sit for a while. I wouldn't mind reviewing my notes about the practicum sessions I just did." She should have polished her impressions while still on 72, but it had been easier to hang out with Ann and the other pilots. Flying was much more fun than paperwork, even when she wasn't at the controls. "I'll sit over here." She settled on the ground and pulled out her comm unit. From the corner of her eye, she saw Jayne sit down and flip open her sketchbook.

Mo chuckled when she read over her notes about the first student. Oh yeah, him. The report given to the student at the end of the practicum would include her impressions, so *The idiot can't navigate and shoot at the same time* wouldn't do. *The student was unable to do two things simultaneously.* No, that wasn't specific enough. When the drone had come into range and she'd ordered him to fire, the craft had suddenly pitched forward and taken on a mind of its own. He'd panicked; she'd sighed into her helmet and calmly engaged auto-navigation, surprised he hadn't accidentally activated the big green *AUTO-NAVIGATION* area on his panel himself as he'd flailed around. *The student lost control of navigation when firing the craft's weapon.* Better. She tapped it in.

Fortunately his later attempts at navigating and firing had been smoother, so she'd put his initial attempt down to that first-time-in-space panic. *He recovered quickly and was able to eliminate drones 2 through 10 while manually controlling the craft.* And he was probably in the simulator right now, flying every single sim on manual control.

After updating her notes for the next three students, she was already bored. She eyed Jayne, who was intently focused on whatever she was sketching. Giving in to her curiosity, Mo moved closer and tried to peek, but Jayne sensed her and quickly closed her sketchbook. Mo wouldn't be thwarted that easily. "Can I have a look? I've already seen some of your sketches."

Jayne's brow furrowed. "When?"

"In your apartment."

"Oh."

"I won't laugh. I'm just curious. You'll have to show me sometime. I'm going to be around for a while."

"That's true." Jayne's smile looked forced. "All right, then." She flipped open her sketchbook and rested it on her lap. "I've been working on leaves, trying to capture the detail in them."

Mo noticed the leaf clipped to the page. Her eyes moved to the drawing underneath it. Yep, it looked like a leaf. Some people could probably talk at length about the sketch and all its nuances, but all she saw, and would ever see, was a leaf, plain and simple. She never would have expected her Chosen—one of them—to be an artist. "It's coming along well," she said, wanting to offer praise. "I mean, I don't know much about drawing, but I wouldn't look at this and think it's terrible."

Jayne flipped the sketchbook shut. "So you think it's terrible?"

"No!"

"Then why say it's not terrible?"

"Because it's not terrible."

"It's okay, Mo. You don't have to like my drawings."

But she could tell Jayne was hurt. Trying to counter the spiteful things others had said about Jayne's drawings had backfired. "No, I like it. There's nothing wrong with it. But Carol told Les that people have put down your drawings. And . . . I read your final report from the Learning Academy." When Jayne's face flushed she quickly added, "I was just try-ing to be encouraging, because I don't agree with what your instructor wrote. Honestly, your drawing isn't terrible. Can I see it again?"

Jayne didn't look at her. "I don't know."

Mo wanted to kick herself. Why did she have to be so impatient? She should have listened to Les and waited until Jayne offered to show her drawings. But would she ever have taken that step? "Jayne, I screwed up, okay? I shouldn't have pushed you into showing me your sketch. And honestly, if it was awful, I wouldn't have said the 'not terrible' bit. I would have said it looks good and left it at that. Now that I've seen a few of your drawings, I think that instructor was even more of an airhead."

Her assurances weren't smoothing over the damage she'd caused. Jayne's face was still tight, and she wasn't opening her sketchbook. Congratulations, Mo flaming Middleton! She needed to learn more about building confidence in others, because her approach with Jayne had resulted in the opposite effect. "I'm sorry. I guess I'll be the last person you'll ever want to share your work with."

"You were thinking about my feelings, I guess," Jayne said. "Most don't." But her sketchbook remained closed.

"You do know your art instructor was incredibly rude because of who you are, right? I can't draw even a tenth as well as you, but my art instructor was polite on my final report. He wouldn't have dared write what yours wrote, even though I can barely draw to save my life." If he had, her parents would have complained to the Learning Academy. Who had been Jayne's guardian and why hadn't they taken offence? Mo didn't feel comfortable asking; it hit too close to the Incident.

"You don't like to draw?" Jayne asked.

"It's not that I don't like it—I doodle like everyone else. I'm just not talented in that area. I always preferred music class." She smiled. "Maybe I should play my violin for you, so you can tell me it's not terrible."

"You play the violin?"

Mo nodded.

"I'd like to hear you play."

"Really?" Mo grinned. "I'll have to think about what piece to play for you."

Jayne moved her sketchbook off her lap so she could stretch her legs. "Lesley doesn't play anything, does she?"

Mo hesitated. Les did, but only for her. But unless Les intended to keep her flute a secret for the rest of her life, Jayne would have to at least know she played. "The flute."

Jayne's eyes widened. "Lesley plays the flute?"

"Yeah. But she doesn't like performing for people. She hates it. I've belonged to the military orchestra and to a quartet, but Les always refused to join anything like that. When she was taking lessons, she played for her instructor and me. Now it's just me." Though she hadn't played for Mo since they'd reunited. Next time they were at the Thompsons and nobody else was home, Mo would ask her to play, even if it meant fetching her violin. "She writes music too."

"That's interesting," Jayne said, sounding almost skeptical. She picked up her sketchbook and rested it on her lap again. "Should I at least ask her if she'll play for me? I don't want her to think I'm not interested."

For a moment Mo considered saying yes, imagining the look of horror on Les's face. But that would be mean, and Les wasn't stupid. Subtlety, remember? Plus she didn't want to set Les and Jayne against each other, because that would spell trouble for the triad. She wanted them to be friendly, but not too friendly. "If I were you, I'd wait until she tells you she plays the flute, because that'll mean she's ready for you to know. Otherwise you'll probably embarrass her."

"You sure?"

"Positive. She doesn't even play for her parents."

"Okay." Jayne looked down at her lap. "Do you still want to see my sketch?"

"Yeah!"

Jayne flipped open her sketchbook, but to the first page, not to the page with the leaf clipped to it. "I don't know if we have time, but I figured we might as well start at the beginning."

"We have time," Mo said without looking at her comm unit. She leaned closer to Jayne, peered at the drawing of another leaf, and kept her mouth shut.

LESLEY HUNG HER cloak beside her office door and sat down behind her desk. It had been a while since she'd been out on patrol, but she'd been asked to fill in for a vacationing Interior officer. Her days usually consisted of writing opinions and perhaps investigating tips for Laura. When she'd first transferred to Interior, she would have expected that writing so many opinions would bore her. But Commander Blair, impressed with her work, had slowly requested more and more of her time. To Lesley's surprise, she enjoyed reading cases and considering whether it would be practical for Interior to enforce an amendment.

Tonight was the supper at Karen's, followed by the Dance Hall, so she didn't want to leave the office too late. She pulled up an incomplete dispatch to Blair and finished typing it. While she was reviewing it one last time, her comm station beeped. "Thompson."

"Sub-lieutenant Weber at Reception, Lieutenant Commander. There's a Cynthia Stewart here to see you."

She didn't recognize the name. "Can you send me her file identifier?"

"Yes."

Lesley scanned Stewart's file. Stewart lived in F4. What was she doing at B2 headquarters, asking for Lesley? "Did she say why she wants to see me?"

"Just a moment." Thirty seconds later, Weber reactivated the connection. "She says it has something to do with a group of concerned Rymellans and that you'll know what she means."

Lesley rolled back her chair, both astonished and curious. "I'll be right there." Would this woman pressure her in person, right here in headquarters? She'd have to be insane.

Weber pointed when Lesley strode into the lobby and approached the reception desk. "Over there."

Lesley moved over to the woman waiting in one of the chairs. "Cynthia Stewart?"

Clutching a satchel on her lap, Stewart looked up. "Yes."

"I'm Lieutenant Commander Thompson. Would you follow me, please." Lesley led her to an interview room off Reception and invited her to sit in one of the chairs arranged around a table. Stewart took a seat and rested her satchel against the chair. She crossed her legs, uncrossed them, then crossed them again. Lesley sat across from her.

"Do you know why I'm here?" Stewart blurted before Lesley had a chance to speak.

"The sub-lieutenant mentioned the group of concerned Rymellans, so I assume you're here about the letters I've received."

Stewart's head bobbed, but she remained silent.

"Did you send the letters?" Lesley prompted.

She shook her head, but said, "Well, I was there when they decided to send the first one."

They. So it was more than one.

"But I didn't feel comfortable with it. And—and now I'm worried that he won't stop and will keep harassing you and cross the line. That's why I decided to come and see you."

Lesley clasped her hands on top of the table and tried to look reassuring. "Why don't you start at the beginning?"

Stewart nodded, then jumped when her satchel fell on its side with a thud. She stared at Lesley in horror.

"It's okay," Lesley said, forcing a smile. "Just start at the beginning."

"Okay." Stewart sighed. "It started thirteen years ago," she said, intriguing Lesley. "Does my name mean anything to you? The name Stewart?"

Lesley shook her head. "No."

Stewart gaped. "You don't know?"

"Know what?" Lesley said carefully.

"My sister, Brenda, was one of the four executed during the Adams Incident." Lesley hid her surprise with difficulty as Stewart continued. "We tried to have the children—the Adams children—executed, but we failed. So when the triad was announced and Kevin found out about CT134 . . ."

"You thought you'd have a second chance. Is Kevin the one you're concerned about?"

"He's my brother, and yes, I'm concerned about him. He sent you the second letter. I don't know who else was involved. I wasn't comfortable sending the first, and he knew that. So he stopped involving me."

"Is he in the military?"

Stewart's brow furrowed. "No."

"Then who's using our internal system to send the letters?"

"Lieutenant Brock," Stewart said.

Lesley mentally filed away the name. "So you're concerned that your brother will send me more letters and—"

"I'm sure of it! He keeps checking the announcements for news that you've exercised the article. I'm afraid of what he'll do if you don't."

And since they weren't going to, they had a problem.

"I thought, okay, we'll send you our opinion and then we've done what we can do." Stewart frowned. "To be honest, I would rather have just ignored the whole thing, but when Kevin invited me to the meeting I didn't think I could say no. But I thought once we sent the letter, that would be it. When I found out he'd sent you another one, I couldn't believe it. And his Chosen is worried about him, because he's obsessed with it. Obsessed!" She drew a deep breath and exhaled loudly. "I didn't know what to do. I've agonized over this for days, and even now, I feel like I'm betraying him. But I don't want to see him in trouble."

"You did the right thing," Lesley said, though she found it interesting that Stewart had sought her out in person, rather than going to her local military outpost. Perhaps she'd wanted to see with her own eyes that Lesley wasn't a monster, or perhaps she'd hoped to keep the matter private. The latter wouldn't be possible—the letters were now an Interior case.

"What are you going to do?" Stewart asked.

"We'll talk to Kevin."

Her hands went to her face. "Argamon," she breathed. "Can you keep me out of it? He won't understand that I did it for his own good. He's already angry with me for not fully supporting him."

"I'll try," Lesley said, meaning it. Not only was she familiar with how it felt to sound the alarm for someone's own good, but this Kevin would need his family's support, including his sister's. Lesley didn't want to turn him against her, especially since Stewart's "betrayal" was motivated by love.

"I'm sorry. About the letter," Stewart said, tentatively meeting Lesley's eyes.

"It's all right. You were only offering an opinion," she said, despite how the letter had angered her. She could forgive one letter, and now that she understood the motivation and history behind it, she was glad she hadn't taken its advice. This group didn't want to protect the Way, it wanted vengeance. Lesley slid her comm unit from its holder. "I'd like to ask you a few more questions." Stewart nodded.

After gathering specifics, Kevin's full name and sector of residence among them, Lesley rose and said, "Thank you. I have all I need for now, but we may contact you again."

Stewart followed her lead and picked up her satchel. "Do you know when you'll talk to him?"

"Soon." She could see Stewart's internal conflict all over her face. "You did the right thing," Lesley said again. "Thank you for bringing this to our attention." Stewart nodded, but looked miserable.

Lesley escorted her back into the lobby and said good-bye. The moment Stewart disappeared through the double doors, Lesley headed to Laura's office.

APPREHENSIVE, JAYNE STARED out the window as Mo landed her craft in the holding area near the Dance Hall. Every seat was occupied, and the others—Karen, William, Neil, and Barbara—were following in Lesley's craft.

The supper at Karen's had been more relaxed and pleasant than the one with Lesley's parents. Mo had seemed surprised, and a little nervous, when Mary and Matthew arrived, but she needn't have worried. They'd treated Jayne coolly, but not impolitely. Jayne appreciated that they were making the effort for Mo. Lesley's brother had been the only missing sibling, and nobody had mentioned him.

She followed everyone off the craft. "They were right behind us, so they should be here any minute," Mo said as eyes rose to scan the sky. Soon afterward, Lesley's craft came into view.

Jayne had always wanted to go to the Dance Hall, but now that she was here, she wouldn't mind if she never stepped a foot inside it. Not only did the thought of dancing in front of others intimidate her, but everyone would know Lesley and Mo and sympathize with them. *Poor Lesley and Mo. If they want a night out, they have to drag Adams along.* She agreed with the sentiment so she couldn't fault anyone for thinking it, but that didn't mean she wouldn't mind everyone whispering about her all night.

"Shall we?" Lesley said when she and the others joined them.

Jayne fell into step with Carol and Ronald, grateful for their presence and everyone else's. Inviting them all along had been a great idea. Maybe if she slinked inside with the others, nobody would notice her. No; she, Carol, and Ronald were the only strangers, and once Carol danced with Ronald, it wouldn't take a genius to figure out who the Adams was.

They'd deliberately arrived an hour after the Hall opened so they wouldn't have to wait in line. Lesley led the way through the entrance and apparently paid for everyone, since Jayne and the others were waved through without having to present their comm units. Jayne's nervousness grew along with the volume of the music and voices as they headed down a corridor to what a sign at the entrance proclaimed was the public ballroom. When Lesley pulled open the door, Jayne's heart beat so fast, she felt slightly dizzy.

They entered a huge, dimly lit room replete with tables, refreshments, and too many Rymellans. Jayne lowered her eyes and allowed Lesley's back to guide her. "There are a couple of free tables over there," someone—Matthew?—said. "We can push them together."

She glanced around when they reached the tables, but everything appeared distorted, a blur of people and colour and lights. Chosens naturally sat together, so she ended up between Carol and Mo, with Lesley at Mo's right.

"So this is the great Dance Hall," Mo said to Jayne. "Not much, is it?"

Maybe she'd agree with Mo in a few years, but not tonight.

LESLEY GAVE UP on remembering what everyone wanted to drink and pulled out her comm unit, feeling like a server. She recorded the "orders" she'd already collected and moved on to Nathan.

"I'll go with you to get the drinks," Carol said when Lesley reached her. "You won't be able to carry them all on your own."

They joined the end of the queue for the refreshment table. A minute later, someone behind Lesley loudly cleared his throat. She looked over her shoulder. Douglas Trent, a long-time C3 resident, caught her eye. "I'm surprised to see you here, Lesley."

"Why?"

His eyes flicked to Carol, then back to Lesley. "I'm surprised you and Mo are in the mood for a night out."

"Oh." Lesley faced forward again, hoping to dissuade him from saying more. It didn't work.

"Will you be coming here often?"

This time she turned around. "Yes."

He grunted. "That's unfortunate. I'd like to think my Chosen and I can enjoy a night out without being reminded of certain . . ." his nostrils flared ". . . events."

Now Carol turned around. Trent's eyes bored into her. "We're not used to people like you in C3," he said.

"People like me?"

"Your parents were a disgrace!"

Carol's mouth tightened. "My pa—"

"I suppose I can't fault you for being here, with your Chosens. But mind your behaviour! At least you'll always be in the company of an Interior officer. Or you should be!" He stomped off, apparently deciding he'd rather pass on a drink than stand in line behind an Adams.

Lesley and Carol faced forward again, in time to see the couple in front of them hastily turn as well. "Well, I've been told," Carol said, appearing more amused than irritated. "I wonder what he'll do when I dance with Ronald? Call for the military?" She glanced at one of the on-duty officers surveying the hall.

Lesley chuckled over Trent's case of mistaken identity. "He'll realize his mistake when Mo and Jayne dance together."

"Yes, but Ronald and I might dance before then. If he makes a fool of himself by kicking up a fuss, it'll serve him right."

But that would only result in more hard feelings, something Lesley would prefer to avoid. "Perhaps you should wait until Mo and Jayne dance, then. You can go on the dance floor with them, for support."

"I will, for Jayne's sake," Carol said after a moment. "She'd hate for the military to come swooping in."

The line shuffled forward. "I hope you don't mind me asking, but do you ever have to deal with the same sort of hostility that Jayne does?" Lesley asked. "I know you were almost denied entry to college, but what about to your face?"

"A little, right after the Incident, but my parents worked really hard to distance themselves from the Adams side of the family." She frowned. "Unfortunately, that included Jayne and Robert."

"I thought Jayne lived with you after the Incident." Something Carol had mentioned, not Jayne.

"She did, but my parents weren't happy about it. As soon as she left the Learning Academy, they arranged for her apartment and that was it." Carol's voice changed in imitation of someone Lesley didn't know. "Ooh, we have to think about Tracy and Terry. They'll want to date soon.

Nobody will want them while they're living with an Adams. They're already teased about it."

"Tracy and Terry are your siblings?"

Carol nodded. "Yes, and they were at the age when they couldn't see past their own noses. So my parents found Jayne another place to live, in another sector. They said there wasn't anything available in our sector, but I never believed them."

"She's never mentioned her other cousins," Lesley said. "You seem to be the only one who cares."

"I shared a room with her. Oh, I hated it at first. I was seventeen, and not due to start college for months. The last thing I wanted was a twelve-year-old invading my room, but it's difficult to resent someone who's just lost her parents and has everyone petitioning for her execution." Carol shifted her weight. "I love my mama, but she's Jayne and Robert's aunt, whether she likes it or not, so *please*. You don't turn your back on family, especially when they don't deserve it." She shook her head. "Anyway, sharing a room with Jayne—"

To Lesley's disappointment, they reached the head of the line and had to stop talking. Minutes later, they carefully maneuvered back to the others, each carrying a tray of drinks.

Mo rose from her chair the moment Lesley set her tray down on the table. She grabbed Lesley's hand. "Let's dance." Lesley had no choice but to follow her onto the dance floor.

"You won't believe what happened while we were in line." She encircled Mo's waist with her right arm and grasped Mo's right hand. They fell into step with the music.

"What?" Mo said.

"Douglas Trent thought Carol was Jayne and let her know what he felt about her presence here." She felt Mo's chuckle.

"Just ignore him. We've been coming here for years."

"It's not us he cares about." When they swung toward the edge of the dance floor, Lesley glanced at their table. Jayne was talking to Karen.

"I think I'll ask Jayne to dance right after we're finished," Mo said. "That'll get the tongues wagging." She sounded like she relished the idea. "You know, I tried not to imagine this."

"What? People upset because we're out with Jayne?"

"No, us. Here, after our notification meetings." Mo looked up at her. "Sometimes I still can't believe we're Chosens. It would be better if we weren't in a triad, but what's most important is that we're Chosens."

Lesley smiled, leaning in to caress Mo's back. "I'd rather be in a triad with you than not have you at all. But if I had the choice, I'd rather have only you."

Mo rested her head against Lesley's shoulder. "Keep saying that and we'll be just fine," she murmured.

JAYNE WATCHED THE couples spin around the dance floor, mesmerized by their rhythmic movements and the kaleidoscope of colours. One couple in particular interested her: Lesley and Mo. They looked so relaxed, and held each other close. When she danced with Mo, everyone would see that she was merely an acquaintance to her or, at best, a friend. If she danced with Mo. Now that she was here, the prospect of dancing in front of all these people made her want to run into the bathroom and throw up. Would it matter if she didn't dance with Mo? She was here. Wasn't that enough?

The band received a smattering of applause when it finished playing. Lesley and Mo left the dance floor and reached Jayne as the band launched into its next tune. Mo held out her hand. "Jayne, would you like to dance?"

No! Absolutely not! "What about Lesley?" she asked, stalling for time.

"I want to sit down," Lesley said.

"And I don't." Mo beckoned to Jayne. "So come on. The only other person I can dance with is you. Are you going to make me stand here with my hand out? You don't want to waste all your hard work, do you?"

Her stomach in knots, Jayne accepted Mo's hand and forced herself to stand. Now would be a good time for the roof to collapse. No, a small fire would be enough to distract everyone without hurting anyone. Or if she was lucky, someone would trip her on the way to the dance floor, hoping to make a fool of her. She couldn't dance with a broken ankle, right? Too late. They'd reached the dance floor.

She gulped when she felt Mo's arm around her shoulders. "Just pretend we're out in the field," Mo said as she took Jayne's hand. Easier said than done! On the Middleton estate, gawkers hadn't surrounded them.

Out of the corner of her eye, Jayne noticed couples leaving the dance floor—quite a number of them. "Look at me," Mo said. "On three."

She forced her eyes to Mo's face. On the third beat, they stepped. And stepped again.

Mo nodded. "Keep looking at me."

A couple brushed past them, coming onto the floor. Carol and Ronald, she saw, when Mo swung her around. And Mo's brother and his Chosen were dancing, too.

Mo's hand tapped Jayne's back. "Focus."

She did, trying to fool herself into thinking that she and Mo were dancing in a field, alone.

LESLEY SIPPED HER juice, watching Mo and Jayne dance. Karen pulled out the chair next to her and sat down. "I wish William hadn't chosen this moment to go to the bathroom," she said.

"There are enough couples on the floor," Lesley said, though not as many as usual.

"So how does it feel?"

"How does what feel?"

Karen nodded toward the dance floor. "Seeing them dance?"

"I've seen Mo dance with other women plenty of times."

"But not with her Chosen."

"And mine." On paper. She looked at Karen. "I know that sounds weird."

"It's definitely the first time I've sat with someone while they watch their Chosen dance with someone else. But I guess I'll be doing that all the time now." Karen sipped her drink. "I'm glad watching them doesn't bother you."

"If Mo wasn't my Chosen, I wouldn't be here right now. In fact, I couldn't be here. But she is, so I can dance with her if I want. Jayne can't do anything I can't do."

Karen touched Lesley's arm. "I'm glad it worked out for you."

Lesley raised her eyebrows. "I wouldn't exactly say it worked out."

"You have Mo."

"That's what I keep telling myself."

Karen glanced at the dance floor. "I'm surprised you didn't dance with Jayne first, given that you're the Principal."

Lesley shrugged. "Mo wanted the first dance," she said, keeping Jayne's dance lessons to herself and hoping Mo wouldn't mind too much when it was her turn to dance with Jayne.

THE BAND SEGUED into its next piece. "Do you want to keep dancing?" Mo asked Jayne.

"What about Lesley?"

"She's busy talking to Karen." Or at least she had been the last time Mo had looked in her direction. They performed a half turn, and she leaned slightly to the left to avoid Jayne's left foot. While practising with her, she'd learned the hard way to compensate. Now she did it without thinking, and realized with a start that Jayne felt familiar. It felt perfectly natural to be swinging around the dance floor with her. The result of all the time they'd spent preparing for this evening, no doubt.

Mo had never felt completely comfortable before when she danced with someone other than Les, but then, she'd rarely danced with the same person as often as she'd danced with Jayne. And Jayne was around the same height as Les. That probably explained it; not many women were as tall as Les and Jayne.

A tricky move was coming up. "Don't forget: step, step, then quick-step twice," she reminded Jayne, then focused on the music.

AS JAYNE FOLLOWED Mo off the dance floor, she wanted to pump her fist into the air. She'd done it! And as far as she could tell, she hadn't made a fool of herself. When they reached the table, she picked up her drink and drained it in one go.

Lesley and Karen broke off their conversation. "Tired?" Lesley said to Mo.

"No, I just figured it was your turn to dance with Jayne."

What? Jayne had hoped that dancing with Mo would be enough to satisfy whoever cared.

"Are you sure?" Lesley asked.

Mo nodded and murmured something Jayne didn't catch. "You don't have to dance with me if you don't want to," Jayne said, fervently hoping that would be the end of it. "I've danced with Mo."

"Yes, but I don't want people to think I don't want to dance with you,"
Lesley said. "We should have one dance, at least."

Would this nightmare ever end? *Breathe!* "Okay." A minute later, she
faced Lesley on the dance floor.

"I'm slightly taller than you, so I guess I'll lead," Lesley said.

"Mo always leads," Jayne blurted.

"That works out, then."

They awkwardly assumed position and fell into step with the music.
Jayne winced when she stepped on Lesley's foot. "Sorry," she mumbled,
then mumbled it again seconds later. "I'm used to dancing with someone shorter."

Lesley's mouth twitched. "So am I."

Of course she was—what a stupid thing to say! Jayne couldn't believe
it when she stepped on Lesley's foot yet again. What was the matter with
her? She'd suddenly developed two clumsy feet. Sure, she'd stepped on
Mo's foot, but not every five seconds. It didn't help that Lesley's hand
burned a hole in her back, or that she was acutely aware of the warmth
of Lesley's other hand in hers and of the softness of Lesley's neck, or
that the room was much too warm. Dancing with Mo was so much
easier; she felt comfortable and could concentrate, maybe because she
looked over Mo's head.

Argamon! She'd stepped on Lesley's foot again. "I'm sorry. I'm not
usually this bad. When I first started dancing with Mo, I kept stepping
on her right foot, but I've improved and I think Mo's learned how to
avoid my foot—" *Shut up!* "—and so I don't step on her foot as often
anymore, but maybe that's because Mo knows how to get out of the way,
not because I've improved." She felt as if she were gasping for air and
wondered if Lesley noticed.

"We're just not used to dancing with each other," Lesley said. "We'll
get better, just like you and Mo have."

Lesley's gaze unnerved her. She looked down—at Lesley's breasts!
Blood rushed to her face and she quickly raised her head. Fortunately
Lesley was looking past her, probably searching for Mo. Jayne didn't
mind. She took a deep breath, then winced again when she felt Lesley's
foot under hers.

MO LANDED HER aviacraft next to Les's, wishing she hadn't agreed to go to the Thompsons' after flying everyone home. She hopped off her craft and immediately spotted Les, who was sitting on her bike, reading something on her comm unit. "How long have you been here?"

Les slid her comm unit into its holder. "Not too long, actually. I had a quick tziva at Karen's after I dropped off everyone else. Oh, I forgot your bike isn't here." Les dismounted and rested her bike against her aviacraft.

As they walked to the house, Mo tried not to think about Les and Jayne dancing together, but her mind seemed determined to torture her. They'd made such a striking couple, both tall and slim. Jayne didn't have to look up to gaze at Les, and Les didn't have to bend down so Jayne could loop her arm around her neck. Positioning themselves must be so natural and effortless. Now how would they feel when they danced with a pipsqueak?

"Jayne didn't mention the case, and I figured it wasn't the right time to bring it up," Les said. "Perhaps we can ask her about it after our next counselling session."

Mo grunted.

"She did okay on the dance floor. She's definitely more used to dancing with you than she is with me, though."

"Why do you say that?"

Les hesitated. "She kept stepping on my feet."

Ha!

"She'll get used to me."

"Yeah." *Unfortunately.*

"Considering it was her first time out at the Dance Hall and she seemed pretty nervous about it, she did well."

"Yeah."

After a long silence, Les said, "It must be tough, entering a room full of people you know won't appreciate your presence. Jayne's a strong person."

Jayne, Jayne, flaming Jayne! Could they please talk about one of the other fifty-five billion possible topics of conversation?

"At least tonight, everyone kept their thoughts to themselves. Except Douglas Trent." Les chuckled. "And he accosted Carol. Sure, there were hostile looks and some people avoided the dance floor when we were on it, but otherwise it went okay. They don't see a triad every day. They'll get used to us."

"They weren't upset because a triad was at the Dance Hall," Mo snapped. "They were upset because Jayne was there. If we were in a triad with anyone other than Jayne, we wouldn't be getting half the flak we're getting."

"It's not Jayne's fault."

"It doesn't matter if it's Jayne's fault or not, I'm just stating a fact."

"She can't change who she is."

Mo blew out some air. "I know."

Les looked at her. "What are you upset about?"

"Nothing."

"Mo."

What would she say, that she didn't like Les dancing with Jayne? What was the point? Les couldn't avoid dancing with her. "Nothing. I'm just tired." Les's eyes remained on her. "We should have left earlier. We didn't take into account that we had to fly everyone home."

Les squeezed her. "I'll try to be quiet when I get up tomorrow. You can sleep in."

To Mo's relief, Les looked away. She shouldn't mind Les dancing with Jayne—Les dancing with others had never bothered her. But those others hadn't been Les's Chosen. *This Adams woman, she's not just anybody. She's Lesley's Chosen. The Chosen Council says they're meant for each other.* Yeah, Mary had probably laughed herself silly when Les and Jayne had gone onto the dance floor. *I'd rather be in a triad with you than not have you at all. But if I had the choice, I'd rather have only you.* No, Mo had to remember that Les loved her. On top of that, they had an arrangement with Jayne, and Mo would do everything she could to prevent Jayne from breaking it.

Jayne better not betray her. Because if she did, Mo would make sure she regretted it for the rest of her flaming life.

KEVIN SIPPED THE tziva at his elbow and tried to focus on reading the case on his comm station. As far as he knew, none of his colleagues had noticed how distracted he was at work, but that would quickly change if he missed a deadline. Maybe an incentive would help. Once he'd finished reading this section and was sure he'd understood the argument it presented, he'd take a break and check the daily announcements. With that in mind, he forced himself to slowly read the next sentence.

His comm station beeped. Argamon! "Yes, Daniel," he said to his clerk through clenched teeth.

"There's an Interior officer here. She'd like to see you."

An Interior officer? "Bring her in." He leaned back in his chair, determined to look casual. Why would an Interior officer want to see him? All his current cases were unremarkable, and the military rarely offered its opinion in person.

Someone rapped at the door. "Come in," Kevin called.

Daniel swung the door open. "Lieutenant Commander Sheldon," he announced. A middle-aged woman strode into the office, her thick, long hair almost obscuring the insignia on the front of her cloak.

Daniel hovered, his eyes shining with curiosity. "Thank you," Kevin said to him. After a disappointed Daniel had left, Kevin gestured toward the guest chair. "Please, sit down." He forced a smile. "How can I help you?"

Sheldon opened her data collector. "We're interviewing the relatives of those executed during the Adams Incident."

A shiver of surprise ran up his spine, but he managed to keep his face blank. "Why?"

"We know many Rymellans have been discussing Article CT134 in relation to the Thompson triad, and we thought it would be prudent to see how those close to the Incident are bearing up. It's only a formality."

"Still, it's very upsetting. What will my colleagues think?"

Sheldon shrugged. "Probably that I'm here regarding a case. Now, what do you think about the triad?"

It was his turn to shrug. "It's nothing to do with me, is it?"

"Seeing an Adams featured prominently in announcements hasn't bothered you? Everyone's talking about her, too."

"It's a bit upsetting," he admitted. A smidgen of truth wouldn't hurt; it might seem strange if he were taking it in stride. "Reading that an Adams will Join brought back things I'd rather forget. I'm sure most Rymellans feel the same way. But my family managed to put the Incident behind it."

"After the Incident, your family petitioned to have Robert and Jayne Adams executed."

He swallowed and clasped his hands on his desk. "That's right."

"You must have been upset when your petition was denied. Do you still want to see them executed?"

More than anything. Hopefully Thompson and Middleton would come to their senses. "Yes, we were upset, but we accepted the decision of the overseers, even though we felt it was short-sighted. One of the reasons I aspired to my current position was to make sure that, should another family face what we did, it won't be turned down when it petitions for appropriate punishment." He met her eyes. "That's how I dealt with it, Lieutenant Commander."

Sheldon grunted. "Does 'a group of concerned Rymellans' mean anything to you?"

He sucked in his breath, his mind racing. Sheldon knew about the letters! It had never occurred to him that Thompson would show them to anyone other than Middleton. Withholding information from the military was a capital violation. Gwen's face flashed across his mind, along with the children's and Mama's. Mama had already borne enough pain for two lifetimes. Another execution in the family would kill her.

"Answer the question, please," Sheldon said.

He hunched his shoulders and focused on a pen lying on his desk. "I . . . it might."

"It might," Sheldon repeated. "Does it, or doesn't it?"

Trapped. Kevin swiftly quelled his panic. To come out of this with his reputation intact, he had to keep his mind clear. He picked up the pen and stared at it while rotating it in his fingers. "It does."

"Are you a member of this group?

He briefly closed his eyes and nodded.

Sheldon hooked her data collector to her belt. "Let's continue this conversation at a military outpost. If you would come with me, please."

His fingers trembled as he buttoned his cloak. How embarrassing, being led from his office by an Interior officer! Daniel's eyes would probably fall out of his head when they passed his desk. But Sheldon did Kevin a favour. "One of my superiors has asked to speak to an overseer in person about an upcoming case," Sheldon said to Daniel, loud enough that those nearby could hear. "I hope this won't inconvenience you."

"Oh, not at all," Daniel said. "I can reschedule any appointments."

"Thank you."

Kevin felt everyone's eyes on his back as he followed Sheldon to the stairs.

Twenty minutes later, his eyes widened when she led him into a military outpost room already occupied by Cynthia and Tom, seated next to each other at a square table. Without a word, Sheldon left them, closing the door behind her.

Tom leaped to his feet and pointed at Kevin. "You egged us on! I knew we shouldn't have done it. I knew it!"

"Well, we did," Kevin said mildly, too anxious to get worked up over Tom's temper tantrum. "It's too late to change your mind now and plead innocence." He pulled out the chair next to Tom and sat.

"You said we couldn't get into trouble for offering our opinion about CT134. You said lots of Rymellans would be offering their opinions. So why aren't they here? Why isn't everyone who was at the meeting here? Where's Brock? Why are we here for sending one letter?"

"One letter?" Cynthia said. "You don't know about the second one?"

Tom turned to her. "What second one? Don't tell me you sent another one."

"I didn't." She jutted her chin toward Kevin. "He did."

"Are you out of your mind?" Tom's voice rose. "Why did you send another letter?" His hands went to his head. "I can't believe I allowed myself to get mixed up in this. We should have left well enough alone."

"And let Adams Join with two military members and bring down the Way?" Kevin said. "If every Rymellan were as fickle as you, the Way would have fallen centuries ago!"

Tom's eyes bulged. "Don't you dare question my dedication to the Way. You—"

"Quiet, both of you!" Panic tinged Cynthia's voice. "Someone could walk through that door at any minute. Do you want them to see you at each other's throats? For all we know, they're watching us right now."

Tom stared at Kevin, then shook his head and sank into his

chair. Kevin scowled and looked straight ahead, already sick of the condemnation in his siblings' eyes.

The air grew heavier as the minutes ticked by. Was the room hot, or was it just him? He stood to unbutton his cloak and throw it over the back of his chair, then wiped his hands on his pants. "I wish someone would come," he said as he sat back down, more to himself than anyone. A horrible thought struck him. What if Thompson was coming? He'd have to look her in the eye, discuss what he'd written in the letters.

Suddenly he felt small and petty. Seeing the Adams name again, seeing that Peter Adams' children were prospering, had irritated old wounds, ones he'd thought had healed, or at least scarred over, long ago. Perhaps Cynthia was right and they'd allowed the emotion of the moment to override good judgment. He pulled a handkerchief from his pocket and patted his brow.

They all jumped when the door swung open. A woman strode in. Kevin had to reach back to his Indoctrination Academy days to recognize the insignia on her cloak. A commodore—you didn't see one of those every day. They had more power than commanders! Kevin was sure he'd seen her before, but couldn't remember where.

The commodore stopped on the other side of the table and surveyed them. Kevin tried to hold her gaze, but when her cold eyes rested on him, he couldn't help looking away. She unbuttoned her cloak, then splayed her hands on the tabletop to lean toward them. "I'm Commodore Finney. I currently oversee Sector C3, Lieutenant Commanders Thompson and Middleton's sector of residence."

Finney! Now Kevin placed her: at the head of the execution procession for the last Rymellan who'd committed a Chosen Violation. Beside him, Tom sounded as if he was hyperventilating. Kevin swallowed. They were letters, only letters! He couldn't think of an article that would see them executed for sending letters. The worst they could be guilty of was harassment, and that wasn't a capital crime.

"So, you've been sending unwelcome letters to Lieutenant Commander Thompson," Finney said. "Have you done anything else I should be aware of?"

Cynthia and Tom glanced at him, either because they regarded him as their leader or because they weren't sure he'd stopped at two letters.

"No," he murmured. His siblings followed suit.

"Nothing else?"

"No," they all repeated.

"Then let's discuss the letters."

Tom cleared his throat. "Excuse me, Commodore. I'd like to point out that I wasn't involved with the second letter."

"Neither was I," Cynthia said quickly.

"I see." Finney began to pace the length of the table. "So you're responsible for the second letter," she said to Kevin. "Along with Lieutenant Brock."

Her words shocked him to his core. Had Brock betrayed him? Maybe Brock had turned the second letter over to his superior instead of sending it to Thompson.

"I know you weren't the only ones involved with writing the first letter," Finney said. "But I understand that you instigated it. Specifically you, Kevin Stewart." She stopped pacing; her eyes bored into him. "Have you met Lieutenant Commanders Thompson and Middleton?"

Kevin shifted in his seat. "No."

"You don't know them?"

"No," he repeated.

"Did you follow the recent Owen case on the monitors?"

He nodded.

"Have you seen the announcement that Lieutenant Commander Thompson will receive the Medal of the Protector?"

He nodded again, feeling smaller by the minute.

Finney scowled. "So you're aware of Lieutenant Commander Thompson's reputation, but for some reason, you thought you needed to tell her how to uphold the Way."

Brenda's reputation had been stellar until she'd met Peter Adams. Why didn't Finney recognize the danger Thompson and Middleton were in?

Finney raised a finger. "Do you think she appreciates receiving advice from strangers about how to conduct her personal life?" She stepped back and glared at them. "Given your family history, I would have thought you'd want to avoid any hint of trouble. And you, Kevin Stewart, are an overseer. I don't often have conversations like this with overseers."

"Junior overseer," he said lamely, despite being one of the youngest overseers in service—no small achievement.

"Keep this up, and you won't be making senior!"

"He won't be sending any more letters," Cynthia said, making him feel like a child.

"No, he won't. As it stands now, you haven't committed a violation." Finney's voice hardened. "But if Lieutenant Commander Thompson receives another letter from you, or you communicate your views about Article CT134 to her in any other way, I'll strike you under Article 265 and send you to the Indoctrination Academy for a refresher. The same goes if you contact Lieutenant Commander Middleton or Jayne Adams."

"Article 265!" he blurted in shock. "That would be heavy-handed. If we were anyone else, we'd be struck under 267." When Tom and Cynthia stared at him in horror, he shrank back into his chair. Had he lost his mind, arguing with a commodore in a flaming military outpost?

Goosebumps rose on his arms when Finney's eyes settled on him. He felt as if death itself had touched him. To his surprise, her mouth turned up at the corners. "So if I understand you correctly, you don't think it's acceptable for me to treat you differently because your name is Stewart. I shouldn't prejudge you—correct?"

He nodded.

"Then stop prejudging Jayne Adams based solely on her name."

"But that's different. Her parents committed Chosen Violations."

"And yet, she's not here. You are. Your behaviour has come to the attention of Interior, not hers. I'd stop worrying about her and start worrying about yourself."

"She's right, Kevin," Cynthia said softly. Tom grunted in agreement.

"You don't want a level four strike on your record, do you?" Finney said. "You've had your say, so you've done all you can. It's time to let it drop, understand?"

He didn't have much choice, not if he wanted to see his children grow up. "Yes," he mumbled.

"Good. I've spoken to all your counsellors, so they're aware of the situation. I expect you to discuss your concerns about Jayne Adams and anything related to the triad with them, not with Lieutenant Commander Thompson. One of my colleagues will prepare a schedule of appointments with your counsellors and dispatch them to you. I'll be monitoring your progress. I'll also be keeping my eye on you, and so will your sector commanders." Her eyes narrowed. "I don't want to see the three of you again. Next time, I won't be so forgiving. Lieutenant Commander Sheldon will be by shortly to escort you out." Finney strode from the room.

"I don't want Gwen knowing about this," Kevin said quietly. "If anyone asks, I was here to consult on a case."

Tom rubbed his temples. "I don't care what you say. I just want to forget the whole thing."

Cynthia nodded vehemently. "Yes, Kevin. You heard what she said. No more letters. You—we've—had our say. Look how seriously they took the two you sent. You can't send any more."

"I wonder if Brock is in trouble," Tom murmured.

"Who cares about Brock?" Kevin muttered. Peter Adams had won—nothing else mattered. Yes, yes, he'd done his part to try to end the Adams threat, but that would be small comfort when the next Adams Incident happened. At least this time, his family wouldn't be destroyed. So let Thompson and Middleton Join with Adams. Why should he care? When the Chosen Violations occurred—and they would—he'd be secure in the knowledge that he'd tried, but they'd refused to listen to him.

The only mistake he'd made was to stick his neck out for two Rymellans who were obviously determined to ruin their lives. For his trouble, he could have received a major strike on his record, or worse. Gwen and the children's faces swam across his consciousness. No, he'd no longer put his family and its reputation in jeopardy. The Way would deal with Jayne Adams and anyone foolish enough to trust her, just as it had dealt with her worthless parents.

Sheldon arrived and escorted them to the exit. As soon as Kevin was alone, he beeped his counsellor.

MO FOLLOWED LES and Jayne from Counsellor Berry's office, waiting until she was sure Berry couldn't hear before she exploded. "Okay, I am sick and tired of doing all the talking. My throat's sore!" She cleared her throat to drive home her point. "Berry must wonder if you two ever talk when we're alone. She probably feels sorry for me, having two mutes as

Chosens. Well, she knows you're not mute, because she's seen you on the monitors," she said to Les.

"We're not that bad," Les said calmly.

"Yes you are! I mean, come on. You could have said lots about the Dance Hall. When she asked if anyone gave us any trouble, you just sat there. You could have mentioned Douglas Trent."

"Who's Douglas Trent?" Jayne asked.

"He wasn't a problem," Les said. "He said his piece, then left us alone."

Mo slapped her thighs. "It doesn't matter! Talking about him would have taken up five or ten minutes."

"Who's Douglas Trent?" Jayne asked again.

"Just some idiot who thought Carol was you," Mo said, not wanting to get sidetracked. "Look, you know I believe in counselling—when there's an actual problem. That's not why we're seeing Berry."

Les slid open her aviacraft's door. "Right now we're seeing Berry to prevent problems from arising."

"Yeah?" Mo retorted as she climbed inside. "Well, if you two don't start pulling your weight at these appointments, there will be a problem arising."

Jayne chuckled.

"What?" Mo barked at her.

Jayne settled into her habitual seat behind Mo before she said, "I was just thinking that the first problem we might talk about with Berry is a problem that came about because we're seeing her."

"Yeah, and I'll probably be the one who spends the entire hour talking about it." Mo laughed as the absurdity hit her.

Les's hand hovered over the navigation panel. "So what are we doing now?"

Mo checked the time. "It's a little early for supper. Maybe—" Her comm unit beeped. "Middleton."

"Archer," said a deep voice. "Sorry for the short notice, but can you fly a couple of shifts, starting tomorrow? One of the pilots has to attend a farewell ceremony."

"What time?"

"One shift tomorrow at 16:00, then a second one Wednesday at 12:00."

She glanced at Les, then said, "Yeah, sure."

"Thanks, Mo. I'll book quarters for you."

"Oh—uh, I was going to be on 72 on Thursday and Friday anyway, so I'll want to stay Wednesday night, too. Can you make sure I get the same quarters for all three nights?"

"No problem. See you tomorrow, then." Archer disconnected.

"So you'll be gone for four days," Les said.

"Not quite. I'll be around tomorrow morning and back by supper on Friday. So around three days, if you add the time up." Which would mean Les and Jayne would have three days alone. Oh, they wouldn't see each other. She'd be surprised if they beeped each other.

Les's hand was still over the navigation panel. "Where to?"

"Do you want to eat supper at my place? It'll probably just be Papa." Nathan was spending a lot of time at his college studying for exams, and Andrew never seemed to be around. "We can hang out there until we're ready to eat."

Les looked over her shoulder.

"Sure," Jayne said.

Mo reached over and punched in the coordinates for the Middleton estate. The craft lifted off.

"Oh, I received instructions about the medal ceremony," Les said, unperturbed.

"Instructions?" Mo said.

"You'll probably receive them eventually. I think I got them because I have a role that evening. You'll probably get a watered down version."

"Anything we should know?" Jayne asked.

Mo detected a hint of nervousness in Jayne's voice, but didn't want to embarrass her by turning around. "I wonder when they'll send out the invitations."

"I don't know," Les said. "And no, there isn't anything special you need to know, except that it's a formal ceremony."

"Oh," Jayne said. "Formal dress, then."

"Yes."

Mo wondered if Jayne had anything to wear. The outfit she'd worn at her notification meeting would work.

"I'm expected to give a speech," Les said sheepishly.

Mo looked at her. "Seriously?"

She nodded. "I guess I can start working on it while you're on 72. I've already received the guidelines."

Good. Between her duties and writing the speech, Les wouldn't have time to see Jayne. Not that Mo had been worried about it. Nope. Not really.

LESLEY LOOKED UP from her monitor when someone tapped at her open office door. Laura walked in. "You won't believe this," she said.

"What?"

"I had another look at the medal ceremony guest list, figuring it might be, uh, another source of inspiration for my speech."

Lesley stifled a grin. Public speaking didn't intimidate Laura, but she'd made it clear that since they wanted her to give a speech that met strict guidelines, they should have written it for her.

"Kevin Stewart is on it!"

"He is?"

"Yes. The name didn't mean anything to me when I first looked over the list."

Nor to Lesley. Everyone knew about the Adamses. The other two involved in the Incident had always been shadowy, unnamed figures, until the day Cynthia Stewart had unmasked one of them. "I wonder how he'll react when he receives the invitation."

"I'm wondering if I should raise a concern and have him removed from the list."

"He must be on it because he's an overseer," Lesley murmured.

"Agreed, but not every overseer is invited. You know how we're usually issued a block of invitations to these sorts of events that we rotate around to different officers? I bet they do it the same way."

And it had been Stewart's turn to attend. "Someone had to submit his name. If you have him replaced with another overseer, his superiors and colleagues will probably find out and wonder. It could affect his career. I'm not sure he deserves that for sending me two letters."

Laura's hand went to her hip. "So you'd rather put him in the same room with Jayne, at a ceremony filled with members of the military and government, and the Preeminent Ruler?"

Lesley imagined shouts erupting in the middle of the ceremony, or worse. "I admit, the thought's a little scary. But if he causes trouble in that environment, he's already fallen. Perhaps this sounds terrible, but I'd rather he commit a violation in a room filled with military and witnesses, than on a path Jayne is strolling along."

"Point taken."

"And seeing Jayne might help him. Right now she's some monster he's built up in his mind." Lesley knew from experience that seeing an imagined foe could make all the difference.

"All right, I won't ask to have him removed. But I'll have a few words with him when I spot him, let him know I'm watching him."

"And I'll mention it to Jayne. I don't want her to be unprepared, in case he approaches her." Unfortunately, that meant she'd have to tell Jayne and Mo about the letters, to explain how she knew about Stewart's connection to the Incident and why his presence at the ceremony could be a problem. Lesley wasn't looking forward to the conversation; it would be the first time she'd explicitly discuss the Incident with Jayne. The prospect made her squirm.

As Laura drew breath to reply, Lesley's comm station beeped. "We'll talk later," Laura mouthed. There wasn't much left to say anyway.

Lesley frowned at the name on the display. "Thompson. Yes, Counsellor Berry?"

After initial pleasantries, Berry said, "I'd like to see you, Lesley. Do you have ten or fifteen minutes to drop in later today?"

"Well, I do, but Mo's up on 72 for the next few days, and I'm not sure if Jayne is available."

"That's fine. I'd like to see you alone."

"Oh." Why? "All right. Um, would 5:15 this evening be okay?"

"Sure. It won't take long. I'll see you then."

Lesley glanced at the time. Over three hours to wonder what Berry wanted. She mentally reviewed their last session, but couldn't think of anything she'd said that would warrant time alone with Berry, especially since Mo had been right and she hadn't said much at all. Perhaps Berry wanted to discuss why she didn't say more, but that would apply to Jayne, too. Had Berry also arranged to see Jayne alone? Lesley didn't want to ask, in case Berry hadn't.

Three long hours later, she was settling into one of the comfortable chairs in Berry's consultation room. She declined tziva and tried not to look anxious. "Thank you for coming," Berry said. "I know it's early days, but I've noticed something during our sessions, and I thought it prudent to bring it up now."

"I see." Lesley crossed her legs. Her new position immediately felt uncomfortable, but if she moved again, she'd look nervous.

"I'm glad you, Mo, and Jayne are making the effort to see each other," Berry said. "I'm very pleased about the Dance Hall. But I've noticed that Mo spends time alone with Jayne, but you don't. Can you tell me why?"

She hadn't realized Berry was keeping track! "What about Jayne? Are you calling her in, too?"

"I think we both know it's highly unlikely that Jayne will beep you and ask to see you alone. You'll have to be the one to take that initiative, and I'm wondering why you haven't."

Mo was right. This whole counselling thing was a waste of time. "Mo's not on duty all the time, like I am. And Jayne's more comfortable with Mo."

"Maybe because she sees Mo more often."

"No, because I'm an Interior officer."

Berry was silent for a moment. "If that's true, then that's all the more reason for you to spend some time alone together. If you won't let her get to know you, she'll never see past your uniform."

Not able to bear the discomfort any longer, Lesley uncrossed her legs. Doing so made her realize how taut her body was. She tried to relax. "Why can't we just let things happen naturally, instead of forcing them?"

"Why would you have to force yourself to see Jayne alone?"

Was that all counsellors could do? Ask questions?

"Lesley?" Berry prompted when Lesley didn't reply.

"Look, I don't have anything against seeing Jayne alone. It's just never occurred to me."

"So you won't have any problem beeping her tonight and setting up a time to see her alone? It doesn't have to be an all-day affair. Start with an hour. Meet her for lunch." Berry's mouth turned up at the corners. "It will give you and Jayne something to talk about at our next session."

Mo would love that, sitting there listening to her and Jayne talk about their lunch date! *Mo.* Lesley had never given any thought to seeing

Jayne alone because Mo always volunteered to do it. She hadn't minded going along with her, especially since she understood why Mo was so quick to step in. Did Berry realize the trouble seeing Jayne alone could cause? "Mo won't like it if I see Jayne alone," she stated, hoping that would be the end of the matter.

Berry curtly shook her head. "If that's going to be a problem, then we should surface it early, so we can deal with it. Avoiding the issue won't make it go away. It will only make it worse."

"I know. I guess I hoped . . ." Well, she wasn't sure what she'd hoped. She couldn't avoid seeing Jayne alone forever. They'd eventually live together. If Mo couldn't handle them being alone by then . . .

"Mo has to accept that she can't always be around when you're with Jayne," Berry said, her eyes on Lesley's face. "Do you mind when Mo's alone with Jayne?"

"No." But she trusted Mo. Why couldn't Mo trust her after all these years? She'd never given Mo any reason to doubt her. "I'll beep Jayne," she said, wanting to end the conversation.

"Just see her for an hour, for lunch," Berry suggested again. "If there's a problem, we'll deal with it together."

Easy for Berry to say—she wouldn't be there when Mo exploded. All Berry could do was help pick up the pieces. Lesley forced a smile. "All right." She stood, signalling that the conversation was now closed and not caring whether Berry agreed. But despite her eagerness to leave the room, she paused at the door. Now there were two conversations she wasn't looking forward to, and she wouldn't mind Berry's advice on how to approach the second, less personal one. "While I'm here, can I ask your advice about another matter?"

"Of course." Berry gestured to the chair, but Lesley remained near the door.

"Mo and I have never discussed the Incident with Jayne. I have to talk to her about something related to it. It's possible I'll tell her a detail she doesn't know. I don't know, because I don't know what she knows." Lesley chuckled nervously. "Do you have any advice on how to approach it?"

Berry leaned back in her chair and pursed her lips. "Be straightforward, and don't worry if you feel uncomfortable. The Incident is an uncomfortable subject, and talking to someone so closely connected to it will compound the discomfort. I think having a conversation about it will be beneficial."

"Why?"

"Because Jayne needs to know she can talk to you about it. You can't pretend the Incident didn't happen, or deny her connection to it."

"We don't. But I can't see Jayne wanting to talk to us about it."

"Maybe not now, but I suspect you'll all want to talk about it eventually."

Berry could be right. At the Dance Hall, Lesley had been disappointed when her conversation with Carol was interrupted. She couldn't help being curious about what had happened to Jayne after the Incident and how she felt about it. What about her parents? Did Jayne miss them? Love them? Hate them? How did it feel, being the daughter of two people who'd fallen from the Way in such a spectacular fashion? Was the rift with her brother related to the Incident? If Jayne's parents had died any other way, would Lesley be as hesitant to ask her these questions? Then again, Jayne had never asked Mo how her mama had died. That was another uncomfortable conversation in their future, one Jayne was probably waiting for Mo to initiate.

Lesley shifted her weight. "At least I won't be alone. Mo will be with me. I'll tell her about it first."

"No," Berry stated flatly. "You said you might be telling Jayne something about the Incident she doesn't know. She should hear it first, not Mo." She raised her hand when Lesley opened her mouth to speak. "I know you're more comfortable talking to Mo, but put yourself in Jayne's shoes. How would you feel if Mo always told Jayne about things that concern you before she told you?"

Lesley didn't have to think too hard to know it would bother her. But to explain how she knew about Stewart's connection to the Incident and why his presence at the medal ceremony would be worrisome, she had to tell Jayne about the letters she'd received. Mo would not react well to Jayne hearing about the letters first, especially if she was already upset because they were spending time alone.

"If having Mo there will make the conversation that much more comfortable for you, then tell Mo with Jayne, not before her," Berry said.

Lesley nodded, accepting Berry's advice. "I'm sorry. I've taken up more of your time than I should have."

Berry smiled. "No, that's all right. And the fact that some issues are arising is encouraging. I'd be worried if that wasn't the case."

When Lesley reached her aviacraft, she sat in the pilot's seat and pondered whether to beep Mo and tell her about the conversation with Berry. She decided against it. Mo would only stew about it on 72 and return itching for a fight.

Jayne would probably be available for lunch while Mo was still on 72. Wouldn't it be better to see her and then tell Mo about it in person, after the fact? Mo couldn't worry about something that had already taken place without affecting their relationship. She wouldn't have time to build the lunch into something it wasn't and couldn't torture herself when Lesley and Jayne were at lunch, brooding about what they were discussing and how long they were lingering over their meal. When Lesley told Mo about the lunch, she could tell her exactly what they'd discussed, where they'd eaten, and how much time they'd spent together. Mo couldn't twist reality, no matter how hard she tried.

She beeped Jayne and patiently waited for her to respond, knowing from experience that a half-minute wait wasn't unusual.

"Yes," Jayne finally said.

"I just saw Counsellor Berry. She's concerned that you and I aren't spending time alone together, so I told her we'd have lunch." She thought she heard Jayne chuckle. "Are you available Thursday?"

"Yes." Jayne paused. "What does Mo think?"

Lesley hesitated. "She won't be back from 72 until Friday. I'll mention it to her when she gets back," she said casually.

"You sure you shouldn't tell her before we go?"

"Why?" Lesley said, bristling. "We're only having lunch because Berry's forcing us to. Mo won't care. Why make a big deal of it, when it's nothing?"

Silence.

"I'll tell her next time I see her. Don't you tell her."

"I won't," Jayne said.

"Why don't I pick you up at your apartment at noon?" Lesley said.

"Sure."

"I'll see you Thursday at noon, then. Good-bye." She disconnected without waiting for a reply, then felt churlish. The lunch wasn't Jayne's fault. Not only that, Jayne had no idea of the upset one innocent lunch might cause, didn't know that telling Mo in advance would only lead to Mo blowing it out of proportion and spending the rest of her time on 72 worrying.

Lesley grudgingly admitted that Berry was right. If they didn't tackle this issue now, it would only get worse. She punched in the coordinates for the Thompson estate and tried to relax while the auto-navigation system flew her home. But one possible disaster kept nagging at her: Mo finding out about the lunch before Lesley had a chance to tell her. She considered beeping Mo again, but after weighing Mo definitely brooding about the lunch against Mo possibly finding out about it, she stuck to her original decision. The odds that Mo would find out about the lunch were slim. To reduce them further, Lesley whipped off a quick dispatch to her, asking if she'd fly directly from the shuttle base to B2 headquarters upon her return, so they could have supper together, just the two of them.

She winced when Mo's enthusiastic "yes" arrived five minutes later.

MO SPOTTED A familiar figure coming toward her as she stepped off the elevator on Deck 7. "Ann!"

Ann wiggled her fingers. "Hey! Anyone accidentally eject today?"

Mo grinned. "I wasn't doing practicums. Those are tomorrow. Most students have already been out at least once now, anyway." She nodded down the corridor toward the canteen. "I'm just going to pick up a snack. Want to come? And Derek said everyone's meeting for cards at 20:30."

"I don't feel like playing cards."

"You want to hang out and do something else, then? I played last night." And she'd probably play tomorrow night, too.

"I don't know."

"Come on. Want to fly a sim?"

Ann's eyes lit up, but she shook her head. "I can't. I, uh—I'm going down to the planet. So I can't go to the canteen with you, either."

"I thought you weren't going off shift until next week."

"I'm not."

Strange. "Is your mama okay?"

Ann shrugged. "I don't know."

Then why—Ann had been conspicuously absent from cards last night, too. Mo hadn't thought anything of it at the time, but now . . . She noticed the dark half-circles under Ann's eyes. "Did you go down last night, too? Aren't you flying the morning shift this week?"

"Who are you, my mama? See you tomorrow." Ann brushed by Mo.

Mo turned around and watched her stride away. Ann must be exhausted, going down for evenings. She'd have to either return to 72 very late, or rise early so she could make it back in time for her shift. The only reason Mo might do that was to see Les. *Oh!* "Ann!"

Almost at the elevator, Ann turned around.

Mo tried not to smile as she closed the distance between them. "Who is he?"

"Who?" Ann said, but her red cheeks gave her away.

"I can't believe it. You're running yourself ragged going down to the planet to see some guy?"

"What if I am?" Ann snapped.

"No, I'm happy for you. You must really like him." For Ann, spending the night with someone and remembering his name the next day was a relationship. Mo had always understood why she was a Solitary.

"He's just a bit of fun," Ann said, but Mo wasn't fooled. Could Ann possibly be in love? Mo smiled at her.

"Stop looking at me like that!" Ann said, frowning. "I told you, it's just a bit of fun."

Uh-huh.

"Maybe you should come down with me. Who knows what Lesley and Jayne are getting up to?"

Mo opened her mouth to reply, then realized as Ann pressed the button to summon the elevator that she was just trying to change the subject. "What's his name?" Mo said instead. "Where'd you meet him?" The elevator door swooshed open. Ann stepped inside. "What's his name?" Mo asked again from the corridor. She pressed her thumb against the button that would hold the elevator.

Ann folded her arms. "Come on, let the elevator go. You're not only holding me up, there could be other people waiting for it."

"Tell me his name and I'll let you go," Mo said, grinning.

Ann leaned from the elevator and pushed Mo away. "I don't think so," she said, then waved at Mo as the elevator door shut. Mo lunged for the *Open* button, but she was too late. Oh well. Feeling a bit foolish, she glanced around the corridor. Fortunately, it was deserted. She straightened her shirt and set off for the canteen.

So, Ann had a boyfriend, and it could be serious. Was he in the military? How long had it been going on? Ann hadn't rushed down to the planet the last time Mo was on 72.

Her comm unit beeped twice. She opened the dispatch from Ann and read a single word: *Andrew*. So why couldn't Ann have just told her that? Was she really that shy about her relationship that she had to answer questions via dispatch? Since Ann was so reluctant to divulge details, Mo would have to drag them out of her. Nah, she wouldn't. After tonight, she'd only be on 72 for one more evening and would probably play cards again. By the time she had the chance to have an extended private conversation with Ann, the relationship would probably be long over. If Mo mentioned the name Andrew, Ann would say, "Who?" just as she always did and be back to hanging around with Mo whenever she could, taking every opportunity to suggest that Les and Jayne were having fun while Mo was on 72.

When Ann had tried to divert the conversation to them, Mo had been pleased, for once. She wanted to tell Ann that Les missed her so much, she'd suggested that Mo fly right to headquarters so they could have supper when she arrived back on Rymel. Mo might finally see Les's office! Nope, she wasn't concerned about Les and Jayne at all. She had that situation completely under control.

JAYNE PULLED OUT the chair across from Lesley and hoped that lunch would be less awkward than the time they'd already spent together. Except for a brief conversation about where to eat, they'd barely said a word in the fifteen minutes it had taken to walk here, and the silence hadn't been comfortable. Now they'd be staring at each other.

A server came over and filled their glasses with water. Jayne wondered if he knew who she was. He probably recognized Lesley. "I only have about an hour," Lesley said when he left.

Message received. Lesley would probably rush them out of the eatery while she was still chewing her last mouthful of food. She'd clearly rather be anywhere else than here. Jayne wondered if it was her, Mo, or both of them, and felt uncomfortable seeing Lesley behind Mo's back. Why hadn't Lesley told Mo? As she'd said, this was nothing, and she was right—so why the secrecy? Then again, Mo wouldn't think anything of it; why would she? Telling her would be giving the lunch a significance it didn't have. Mentioning it as an afterthought when Mo returned was all it deserved.

Jayne briefly met Lesley's eyes and tried to come up with something to say. Would Berry ask them what they'd talked about? She wouldn't be too impressed when they told her they'd eaten in silence.

When Lesley picked up the menu the server had left in front of her, Jayne eagerly followed suit. She wouldn't mind spending the entire lunch hidden behind a menu, and suspected Lesley wouldn't, either. But they soon had to surrender their shields to the server, who took their orders and left them alone again. They sat in silence, looking everywhere but at each other.

Lesley eventually rested her elbows on the table and leaned forward. "I doubt Berry will let us get away with seeing each other alone only once." Jayne could hear the sigh in her voice. "I thought today would be a good time to tell you about my next assignment. I've been accepted into the commander training program. I'll be starting it in a few weeks."

"Congratulations," Jayne said, genuinely pleased. Apparently the triad and having an Adams as a Chosen hadn't derailed Lesley's career, or Mo's. "How long is the program?"

"Six months."

"And then you'll be assigned to a sector?"

"I'm not sure. Not all commanders oversee sectors." Lesley hesitated, then continued. "I spend most of my time writing opinions for overseers. I don't know if that will still be my primary focus, or if Admiral Hall will want me to take a more active role in the enforcement side of things."

"Which would you prefer?" When Lesley leaned back and didn't answer, Jayne opened her mouth to apologize. What was she thinking, asking personal questions like that? Lesley had only brought up her future promotion for something to say. But then the server was at their table with their meals, and Jayne realized Lesley had spotted him on his way over. Willing to let the subject gracefully drop, she unfolded her napkin.

"I'd prefer to write opinions," Lesley said, surprising her.

"It sounds like advocacy." She looked up from her plate when Lesley chuckled.

"I thought the same thing when Laura first suggested it to me, but it's not."

"How is it different?"

Lesley rested her fork on her plate. "Well, advocacy is more theoretical. When my parents work on a case . . ."

The sun streaming through the nearby window accentuated the blueness of Lesley's eyes. Jayne had already noticed they were blue, but not how striking they were, especially framed as they were by her pale skin and blonde hair. When Jayne had first told Carol and Ronald the identity of the other two triad members, Carol had implied that Lesley might be on the monitors because of her looks. Maybe she was right.

". . . military is more interested in whether it's practical to uphold . . ."

But only right in the sense that how one appeared on the monitors was one factor among many in choosing an announcer. Jayne would strenuously protest the notion that Lesley's beauty was the only reason she was on the monitors. There was no denying she *was* beautiful, but there was also a lot going on behind those . . . uh, deep blue eyes. Lesley was also—she'd stopped talking! And Jayne was staring at her!

Lesley shook her head and picked up her fork. "Sorry, I didn't mean to bore you by going on like that."

"You weren't boring me." *But please don't ask me about what you just said!*

"I guess it's important to me that people know the difference between what I do and what an advocate does."

"Why?" Jayne asked, hoping Lesley would restate the difference for her.

Lesley shrugged. "I wanted to be an advocate once." She quickly looked down at her plate, telling Jayne not to expect further explanation.

Argamon! She'd have to somehow ask Mo, hopefully before seeing Berry. She imagined Berry asking her to explain the difference between Lesley's role and an advocate's, then told herself not to be silly and gulped down some water.

They ate in silence for a while. Lesley glanced around. "There aren't many people here for this time of day."

"It's more crowded when the Learning Academy lets out," Jayne said. Not that she made a habit of eating here. Soon after moving into her apartment, she'd quickly learned where and when crowds of students congregated, and always avoided them when out.

"Do you mind if I ask what you thought about Phillips's case, since it's safe to talk?" Lesley asked, then quickly added, "But if you don't want to talk about it, just say."

Jayne's hand tightened around her knife as the irritation and humiliation she'd felt while reading the case rose within her again. She wouldn't mind getting a few things off her chest about Phillips's little masterpiece, but she'd have to be careful and polite. "I don't mind discussing it," she said, handing Lesley the opportunity to guide the conversation.

"We weren't happy when we found out Jason and Mary had gone behind our backs. And we felt it unfair that we . . ." Lesley trailed off. Unsure if Lesley wanted to finish chewing her food or if she was thinking, Jayne waited. "It wasn't fair that we were handed so much personal information about you."

Blood rushed to Jayne's face. No, it flaming wasn't! But the damage was done and it wasn't their fault, so she couldn't be angry with them.

"Mo said that maybe we should give you our Learning and Indoctrination Academy records."

For a split second, Jayne almost considered that a good idea, and imagined herself lounging on her sofa with tziva, sifting through their records and laughing at the humiliating comments on their reports. But there were two problems with that scenario: first, there wouldn't be any humiliating comments, and second, she wouldn't laugh if there were. To their credit, it sounded as if they hadn't laughed, either. "I wasn't happy to see my records laid bare as part of the case," she said. "But you and Mo didn't ask for them, so I don't expect you to return the favour." There, she'd sounded reasonable, but if the knife in her hand hadn't been metal, it would have snapped in half.

"I guess Phillips included them to demonstrate that you've changed," Lesley said, "but I think he misinterpreted."

"Really?" How would Lesley know, or Phillips, for that matter? They hadn't known her before the Incident. Did they think reports and observations could tell them who she was?

Lesley laid her knife and fork on her empty plate. "I don't think you changed. I think the way everyone treated you changed, and so your interactions with them changed. You didn't change on the inside, but you seem quieter since the, uh—" She floundered.

Jayne instantly rescued her—or was she rescuing herself? She wasn't ready for this conversation, either. "Carol says I haven't changed, and I don't think I have either, not fundamentally." But despite being the same person she'd been before the Incident, she still didn't believe she was Lesley and Mo's Chosen.

Telling them that would be pointless. She doubted they'd exercise the article, but she could be wrong. Joining with a Chosen they didn't want was one thing; Joining with someone who wasn't their Chosen would be another, and perhaps ask too much of them. Still, her suspicion gnawed at her, and she suspected the desire to tell them would only grow over time, as her trust in them deepened. Could she honestly carry this secret into the Joining Chamber? She'd always wonder what they would have done if they'd known, and feel guilty every time they struggled to honour her as their Chosen.

She pushed her dilemma aside and decided to raise her main objection to the case, which wasn't personal. "I don't think Article CT134 should be in the Tradition," she said, feeling comfortable questioning the article's existence because it was still open to amendments. Plus, Lesley would have read the historical treatise on triads from Watkins, and probably more. She knew the Chosen Council's handling of triads wasn't cast in stone. "And I'm not saying that because of my situation, though I'll understand if you don't believe me," she said wryly.

Lesley pushed her plate aside and leaned her elbows on the table again. "Why don't you think it belongs in the Tradition?" she said, her eyes bright with interest.

Suddenly embarrassed, Jayne cleared her throat and hoped she'd sound coherent. "Well, it puts all the blame onto one Chosen. If a triad is failing, isn't that the fault of all three Chosens? Why should only one Chosen be punished?"

"I don't think the Chosen Council sees it as a form of punishment."

No? Tell that to the executed Chosen.

"I think it's more about removing the weakest link that will probably, eventually, drag down the entire triad," Lesley continued.

"But that's my point," Jayne said, stabbing her finger on the table. "Aren't the other two also weak? If they were strong, wouldn't they try to work with the other Chosen to overcome their problems? Exercising CT134 is giving up. It's taking the easy way out. How is executing your Chosen honouring your Chosen?"

Lesley drew breath to respond, but the server chose that moment to clear away their plates and ask whether they wanted dessert and tziva. Jayne expected Lesley to decline and use the interruption to end their conversation, but Lesley said, "I wouldn't mind a piece of cake with tziva. What about you?"

"Don't you have somewhere to be?" Jayne asked, offering Lesley a graceful way to end their lunch. At least forty-five minutes must have passed by now.

Lesley dismissed Jayne's concern with a wave of her hand. "I still have time."

Jayne looked out the window to hide her surprise. Lesley not being pressed for time didn't shock her; Lesley's willingness to continue the conversation did.

"I've had similar thoughts about CT134," Lesley said when the server moved away.

Hoping her expression was now neutral, Jayne turned back to her.

"But I'd like to hear more about what you think, before I tell you my thoughts. What if the two Chosens can't work with the third Chosen, because that Chosen is being unreasonable or isn't willing to work something out?"

"How did it get to that point in the first place? It seems to me there must have been warning signs well before CT134 was exercised."

Lesley nodded. "I'm not sure I mentioned this, but my parents and I read some of the cases presented under CT134."

"Oh."

"We were just curious," Lesley said quickly.

"I wouldn't mind reading them."

Lesley's eyebrows rose. "Really?"

I can be curious too! she almost blurted. "They're part of our history. Triads, I mean."

Lesley smiled. "I'll dispatch them to you. Most of them are similar, so let me tell you about one of them. Because you're right, there were warning signs."

Jayne listened intently as Lesley described what she remembered about one of the cases, and was slightly annoyed when the server interrupted them with their tziva and dessert. Sometime later, she nodded absently when the server collected her plate and held the tziva jug over her empty mug. "So you can see the similarities between those three cases," Lesley was saying.

"What about the rest?"

"In one case, the executed Chosen did commit violations. What happened was . . ."

When the server returned yet again and asked if they'd like a fresh jug, Lesley glanced at her comm unit and frowned. "No, thank you. We have to get going." She looked sheepishly at Jayne. "It's almost 3:30."

What? They'd been talking that long? The students would start arriving soon. In a daze, she followed Lesley from the eatery. She couldn't remember when time had last passed so quickly when she wasn't sketching.

"I'm sorry if I talked your ear off," Lesley said.

"No, I enjoyed the conversation." And she felt guiltier about not voicing her suspicion that they weren't a real triad. She agonized over that as they walked in companionable silence, bouncing between locking away her suspicion until she died and telling Lesley now, while she had the chance. One thing was certain: she had to say something before they Joined, or never say anything at all. To her mind, bringing it up after they'd Joined would serve no purpose other than to mock them.

"I'll dispatch the cases to you. We can discuss them next time we see each other alone for Berry."

"Sure," Jayne said, looking forward to it, and knowing in her gut that she might be about to ruin their surprisingly enjoyable afternoon. If Lesley and Mo had been treating her terribly, perhaps she wouldn't feel so compelled to tell them that Phillips was probably right and she wasn't their Chosen, that in fact she never had been. But despite her unwelcome presence in their lives that would forever deny them the life they'd wanted, they were doing their best to include her; they weren't taking the easy way out. They deserved to know. She had to stop hiding behind the excuse that she couldn't tell them because they might execute her. They wouldn't. They'd know it wasn't her fault, though it would give them another reason to resent her. Still, she had to get it off her chest.

Jayne had a good look around to ensure nobody was nearby, then plunged in. "Lesley, I want to tell you something, but before I do, I want you to know that I believe in the Chosen Tradition." *I'm not like my parents.* "I respect the Chosen Council." When Lesley stopped walking, she did too, and faced her. "I don't think we're Chosens. I think this triad was deliberately created. I don't know if they did it so you'd execute me, or if they didn't trust me to be on my own as a Solitary, but I'm sorry you two ended up with me." She couldn't deny that she was also grateful. "I know it sounds shocking," she said, though if Lesley was shocked, she was hiding it well, "but I couldn't let you Join with me without saying anything."

Lesley arched an eyebrow. "So now we can execute you?"

The amusement in Lesley's eyes surprised her. "No!" she said firmly.

"I'm glad you're getting to know us." Lesley motioned for Jayne to continue walking and fell into step with her. "I don't believe we're Chosens, either."

Jayne was glad they weren't still sitting across a table from each other.

"Don't misunderstand me. I believe in the integrity of the Chosen Council, but I find it curious that out of all the women on Rymel, we ended up in a triad with you. So I've suspected all along that you're not our Chosen. But I can understand why someone thought putting you into a triad with us would protect the Way. There are extraordinary circumstances involved."

Lesley had suspected all along? "Does Mo think the same?"

Lesley took her time answering. "We talked about it after our notification meetings. She's not entirely comfortable with the idea. She said we should assume the triad's authentic, and she's right in the sense that we have to behave as if it is. The Chosen Council says we're Chosens, and so we are." She was silent for a moment. "At least we know our arrangement should work. If we really were Chosens, things could get complicated, I guess. But we aren't. So we don't have to worry about any inconvenient . . . feelings."

"No," Jayne said faintly.

"But that doesn't mean Mo and I won't honour you as our Chosen."

Her throat tightened. "I know. Thank you for being so honest."

Lesley shrugged. "I want you to understand why Mo and I insisted on our arrangement. It's not because we're weak in the Way."

They'd reached the point where Lesley's aviacraft was in one direction and Jayne's apartment in the other. Unsure of what Lesley wanted to do, Jayne slowed her pace.

"I'll walk you to your apartment," Lesley said.

"No, you don't have to do that. I'll be fine."

Lesley looked at her. "You sure?"

"Yes. Really, I'll be fine. I haven't had any problems since the attack." And she suddenly wanted to be alone.

Once again, they stopped walking and faced each other. "It's good that we cleared the air about the triad and our suspicions," Lesley said, "but from now on, we're Chosens. We never had that other conversation."

Jayne nodded. "Thank you for lunch. I enjoyed it."

"More than you expected?"

She nodded again, then her mouth dropped open in horror. "I mean—"

Lesley held up her hand. "It wasn't as bad as I expected, either. And Mo will be happy too—we might actually say something at our next session. Anyway, I should go." She turned away, then turned back. "Oh, Mo's birthday is coming up. We should talk about it."

"Okay." Jayne returned Lesley's wave and watched her walk away, wondering why she felt so deflated. She *had* enjoyed the lunch, and the conversation afterward. Maybe she missed having her sketchbook under her arm. She'd left it behind, more self-conscious about it with Lesley than with Mo. Next time she'd take it with her. Why care what Lesley thought? They weren't Chosens. They had an arrangement. Short of violating the Way, Lesley wouldn't care how Jayne conducted herself.

She shoved her hands into her cloak pockets and trudged toward her apartment. After telling Lesley about her suspicion, she'd expected to feel relieved, not depressed.

I don't believe we're Chosens, either. . . So we don't have to worry about any inconvenient . . . feelings. Lesley was right. Ironically, the triad had a better chance of survival because she wasn't their Chosen. And Jayne would have a better life than she'd expected, one she wouldn't have dared dream about. Two Chosens who respected her. Freedom to sketch. A respectable family name. A quiet home on a private estate, sheltered much of the time from the hostility she'd experienced since the Incident. She should be delirious.

But she wasn't.

At least we know our arrangement should work . . . we don't have to worry about any inconvenient . . . feelings.

She was disappointed.

SHATTERED DELUSIONS

. . . . .

M O PUSHED OPEN THE DOUBLE DOORS to B2 headquarters and pulled out her comm unit instead of bothering reception for directions to Les's office. "I'm here," she said when Les responded. "Do you want to guide me?"

"No, I'll come and get you."

Mo chuckled. "Oh, I get my own personal escort."

"I'll be there in a minute." The connection went dead.

She stared at her comm unit. Okay, it hadn't been the most brilliant thing to say, but wasn't Les pleased to hear from her? They hadn't seen each other for a few days.

While she waited, she watched Interior officers bustling through the lobby, many clutching documents in their hands or tucked under their arms. How could Les stand working behind a desk for most of the day, reading dreary cases and writing opinions? Mo would rather sit in a cramped cockpit, barely able to move. Cases were an insomnia aid—except for Phillips's case. She'd stayed wide awake while reading that one.

Mo smiled as Les strode toward her. "So I finally get to see—" she infused her voice with mock awe "—the office." Les's mouth didn't even twitch. Mo fell into step with her, but didn't try to engage her in conversation. Hopefully Les would loosen up over supper.

"This is more spacious than I expected," she said of the office Les ushered her into; she wandered around the desk, glanced at the images sitting on it, and frowned.

"We need to talk about that," Les said from behind her. "If I display one of you, I'll have to display one of Jayne."

Mo inwardly sighed. "You better put out images of us, because everyone else does. Do we even have an image of Jayne?" She turned in time to see Les shake her head. "Maybe we should have one taken of both of us. No, all three of us."

"I don't want to stare at myself all day," Les said sourly.

Mo wouldn't mind staring at her all day. "I don't stay in quarters long enough to put images out, but I wouldn't mind a more recent one of you on my comm unit."

"We'll talk about images next time we see Jayne," Les said, sounding almost irritated.

"Are you okay?" Mo asked, reaching for her.

"I'm fine," Les murmured, but her hug felt indifferent, as if she were going through the motions.

Mo pulled back and searched Les's face. Her concern deepened when Les let her go and walked over to shut her office door. Mo had expected them to leave for supper.

"I want to talk to you for a minute," Les said, moving to one of the guest chairs.

"Okay," Mo agreed, hoping to find out what was bothering her. She sank into the other guest chair, then looked on in dismay as Les walked behind her desk and sat down. "What's going on? Am I in trouble?" She smiled, determined to lighten the mood.

"Berry beeped me while you were on 72. She was concerned because I wasn't spending any time alone with Jayne."

Counsellor flaming Berry! "You're busy! You don't have time to see Jayne."

"Well, I did see her."

"What?"

"I saw her. We had lunch together yesterday, but only because Berry wanted us to."

They had lunch together yesterday.

"We had to see each other alone at some point."

Mo squeezed the arms of the chair. "Why are you only telling me now? Oh, apart from the fact that I can't react here. You couldn't have told me when we got to my aviacraft? Or better yet, before you had flaming lunch with her?"

Les leaned forward and rested her elbows on her desk. "I thought of telling you, but I didn't want you to worry about it."

Mo sat abruptly back. "Should I be worried?"

"No!"

She folded her arms and stared at Les.

"We only went because Berry insisted. I thought it would be good to get it out of the way, so I could tell you all about it when you got back."

"So tell."

Les shrugged. "We went to an eatery near Jayne's apartment. We had lunch, talked for a bit, and left. That's it."

"What did you talk about?"

"Some of the cases that were presented about CT134, mainly."

Ha! Les had probably bored Jayne to tears.

"She asked to read them, so I dispatched them to her."

Flaming Jayne! "She was probably being polite. How long were you together?" When Les hesitated, Mo knew she wouldn't like the answer.

"A few hours."

"A few hours?" Mo blurted. "You said lunch!"

"We talked over tziva and dessert. She seemed interested in the cases, and you know how I like discussing that sort of thing. I would have stayed that long with anyone."

But it hadn't been anyone. It had been Jayne.

"Now we'll have something to say at our next counselling session," Les finished.

"Like that's supposed to make up for it."

Les's face tightened. "Make up for what? We didn't do anything wrong."

"You went behind my back. What am I supposed to think?"

"That I was afraid of how you'd react because of how you've reacted in the past?"

"This is different. Jayne's not just anyone, she's your Chosen," Mo said, echoing Mary's stupid comment that always ran through her mind at moments like this.

"Jayne respects our relationship."

When Les rolled back her chair and rose to come to her, Mo stubbornly kept her arms folded. It would take more than a hug to appease her!

Les sighed. "Jayne suggested that I tell you about the lunch right away. I'm the one who decided to wait. I told her not to tell you."

So Jayne had thought of her, but had gone along with Les. Mo brought her right hand up to her mouth so she could chew her thumbnail, but kept her other arm across her stomach. Rationally she'd known nothing had happened the moment Les opened her mouth about the lunch. But the part of her she couldn't control—the part convinced that Les would be taken away from her—refused to relent. It had taunted her for years, except for that glorious three-day respite when they'd known they were Chosens but not about the triad.

"I can't avoid seeing her," Les said. "Not only will Berry expect it, but we'll eventually live together."

Mo studied her thumbnail. "I know, but I don't like it. And I know that's too bad because I'll have to get used to it, but I don't like it."

Les frowned down at her. "Maybe Counsellor Berry can help."

"How? What can she do? Tell me what I already know? I know I'll have to learn to live with it." But she didn't know how.

"I wish you'd trust me."

Mo looked up at her. "I do trust you." It had always been about everyone else, and now it was about Jayne. But wasn't that a good thing? Jayne wouldn't dare throw herself at Les. If their arrangement didn't stop her, her lack of confidence would. But Mo would still fret, especially if Les and Jayne were seeing each other behind her back. She wagged her finger at Les. "I don't like being kept in the dark. From now on, tell me when you'll see Jayne *before* you see her."

Les drew breath.

"Tell me, Les. It might drive me crazy, but the alternative is me wondering what you two are doing the entire time I'm on 72." And Ann's constant insinuations wouldn't help. "So tell me, okay?"

"I will. In fact, I'll tell you before I set anything up with Jayne, so you'll know before she does."

"Good." That was exactly the way it should be. Mo stretched, finally ready to forgive.

"I panicked," Les said sheepishly. "I didn't appreciate Berry calling me to task. Unfortunately she'll do it again if I don't see Jayne by myself every once in a while." Her brow puckered.

"Counsellor flaming Berry," Mo muttered as she stood. "I told you these counselling sessions are a waste of time." She reached for her. This time, Les's hug was warm. Mo leaned into her and closed her eyes. She'd probably hyperventilated for nothing, but she'd be more diligent, make sure Les did tell her every time she saw Jayne—in advance.

"Do you want to go eat?" Les said.

Mo nodded. Now that she'd calmed down, she felt foolish. What had she repeatedly told herself? That if they had to be in a triad, they were lucky it was with Jayne. Any other woman would have demanded that they widen their relationship to include her. Berry had pushed Les and Jayne together, not Jayne, who'd apparently wanted Mo to know about the lunch. So Mo could stop worrying. Jayne had firmly stated that she wanted two friends—nothing more—and Mo believed her. She had to.

KEVIN STARED AT the screen in disbelief, his mouth dry. Why him? Normally he'd jump at the opportunity to rub elbows with government members and senior overseers, but not when he'd be in the same room with *her*.

"It's the social event of the year. We have to go," Gwen said softly, her hand on his shoulder. She leaned over him to peer at the screen. "Look who's on the list. Senior Overseer Crane. Senior Overseer Brooks. Four admirals. The Preeminent Ruler! I wonder who'll be at our table."

She was trying to look on the bright side, but he couldn't see one. The only names on the guest list that mattered were Lieutenant Commander Thompson, Lieutenant Commander Middleton, Commodore Finney, and *her*. He patted his forehead with a handkerchief.

"This is your big chance," Gwen continued. "You want the senior overseers to be familiar with you. You never know when a senior position will open up."

"We probably won't be sitting with them. And it's not as if we were specifically invited, is it?" he said desperately. "They always allocate seats for overseers at events like this. I don't know why we were selected.

Probably my name had risen to the top of the list." Or it was someone's idea of a sick joke. "Nobody will notice if we don't attend."

"What?" Gwen shrieked. "You're not seriously thinking of turning it down! Nobody else will. Rymellans will cancel their holidays for this. Kevin, you can't!"

No, he probably couldn't. What possible explanation would he give? Gwen was right; everyone would be falling over themselves to accept the invitation. He sighed and stared miserably at the screen.

Gwen patted his shoulder. "Look, I know she'll be there and it will be awkward for you, but you won't have to talk to her or anything. You know how these things are. We'll be sitting at a table way in the back, with all the dignitaries and the guests of honour up front. You probably won't even see her."

Yes, he would! Unbelievably, she was Chosen to one of the guests of honour. He couldn't avoid seeing her. But Gwen was only trying to help, he reminded himself. "It says dancing to follow."

"So we'll find a safe corner to sit in and nip onto the dance floor when she's not on it. She has two Chosens to keep her busy. Focus on the overseers. You won't even know she's there."

She wasn't the only guest he'd want to avoid. He'd have to watch Thompson receive her medal and perhaps listen to her speak. Would she sense his presence, know the one who'd sent her the letters sat in the same room? What if she walked by him, looked directly at him? Would his guilt be apparent?

"This could mean so much for you, for your career," Gwen said.

"I won't be promoted because I showed up at an awards ceremony," he retorted.

"But if we don't go, you'll never be promoted," Gwen shot back. "Imagine the talk when it gets around. You've always wondered if your connection to the Incident would ultimately hold you back. Don't give them a reason. Attend with your head held high."

Head held low, more like. He wished he could tell Gwen that seeing *her* wasn't the only reason he didn't want to attend. She knew he'd sent a letter or two to Thompson, but not that he'd been reprimanded for doing so, and by one of the guests of honour. He'd spend the entire night worrying about bumping into the wrong person. What if he bumped into *her*? Could he control himself, mumble, "Excuse me," and move on? Or would he lash out and tell her she should be dead with her name on the Wall of Offenders, not eating finger foods and dancing?

If he didn't want to stall his career, he'd have to trust himself. He reached up, held Gwen's fingers for support, and sent the confirmation that they would attend.

Gwen kissed his cheek. "Thank you."

He nodded, despite the sinking feeling in his chest.

"Wait until everyone hears about this. Even the children will be impressed. And we have to go to the Trading Centre. You have to look smart." She clapped her hands together. "Oh, but you know what would be perfect for you to wear? That pair of shoes your mama gave you—the ones you never wear because they clash with your cloak." She walked toward the hall. "Then again, we don't want to limit our options by a pair of shoes, do we? I'll have a look at them, decide what to do. This is so exciting!"

When Kevin could no longer hear her footsteps as she walked down the hallway, he beeped his counsellor.

JAYNE TUCKED HER sketchbook under her arm and followed Lesley and Mo from Counsellor Berry's office. In the corridor, she skirted around Lesley to walk next to Mo.

"Okay, you both did a little better today," Mo said.

Lesley nodded. "We had the lunch to talk about."

"Yeah," Mo said tersely.

Was Mo upset about the lunch? When she'd picked Jayne up, she hadn't behaved any differently.

They walked in silence to the aviacrafts. When they reached them, Lesley said, "Before I go back to the office, I want to talk to the two of you about something."

Mo gave her a long look. "Okay."

"Do you want to come into my aviacraft for a minute?"

In response, Mo slid the door open and climbed in. "Go ahead," Lesley said to Jayne, then boarded after her. Mo had already plunked into the passenger seat and swivelled toward the pilot's seat. Jayne sat in the seat behind hers.

"It's about the awards ceremony," Lesley said as she slid into her seat. She held up her hands. "Let me start from the beginning. Not long after our notifications, I received a letter at the office. It was signed by 'A group of concerned Rymellans.'" She turned to Jayne. "It advised us—Mo and I—to exercise CT134."

Lesley needn't have looked apologetic. Jayne was used to it and it wasn't Lesley's fault.

"To make a long story short, I received another one, and then we found out who was behind them. His—"

"Why didn't you tell me—us—about the letters?" Mo asked, her face tight.

Lesley looked at her. "Because I ignored them. There wasn't any reason for you to know."

"Is there anything else you haven't told us?"

"No." Lesley waited a moment before continuing. "A Rymellan named Kevin Stewart was behind the whole thing." She looked at Jayne again.

The longer Lesley's eyes bored into her, the more uncomfortable Jayne felt. She didn't know whether to stare back or look away. When unwelcome feelings stirred within her, she quickly turned to Mo, whose attention was, fortunately, on Lesley.

"Do you recognize the name?" Lesley asked.

"No," Jayne said, forcing her gaze back to Lesley so she wouldn't be rude.

"His sister was executed during the Incident."

Lesley couldn't have flabbergasted Jayne more if she'd tried. Now they were both looking at her.

"You didn't know," Lesley stated. Not a leap, considering how shocked Jayne must look.

"No," Jayne managed to murmur. His sister . . . She swallowed. "What was her name?"

"Brenda Stewart," Lesley said without hesitating, deepening Jayne's respect for her.

Brenda Stewart. So she'd been the woman Papa had thrown his life away for? What had been so special about Brenda Stewart that had led him to destroy his family and turn his two children into outcasts? And why had Mama committed the same violation? "What else do you know about the Incident?" she asked Lesley.

"Nothing, beyond what everyone knows."

"You don't know the name of the fourth person?"

"No."

"Neither do I," she said, to forestall the question. In fact, she didn't know any more than Lesley and Mo did. That day was a blur, one that had started with no warning of the horror to come. One minute she was in her bedroom working on some homework; the next she was sitting next to Robert in an aviacraft, trembling and disoriented. She had a vague memory of military bursting in and hurrying her downstairs, but that wasn't what haunted her about that day. It was Mama's piercing wails as Jayne stumbled down the stairs. She could hear them as clearly as she could on that day. She fought the urge to clap her hands over her ears.

There hadn't been an opportunity to say good-bye. Later, when she'd understood what had happened, she'd thought it best that her last memory of Mama was in the dining room, helping her to clear the table after lunch. Papa's chair had been empty, even though the studio was only a five minute walk away. Jayne had noticed that he was spending more time at his studio than usual. To her disappointment, he was also less interested in painting with his daughter. Always an excuse, a reason why he needed to be alone. Perhaps if she'd been older, she would have suspected something was wrong, but she was a naive twelve-year-old who thought her papa was perfect.

The military had flown her and Robert to their aunt's house, where a multitude of relatives were gathered inside. Everyone's emotional state only deepened Jayne's confusion. Hushed voices, tears, nobody wanting to answer her questions . . . some seemed angry with her, tersely shooing her away; others teared up every time they looked at her. She thought maybe someone had died, though there hadn't been such a fuss when one of her great-aunts had passed away, and why wouldn't Mama and Papa be with her? Why had the military rushed her and Robert out of the house and flown them here?

She found a pencil and a few pieces of paper in one of her cousins' bedrooms, wandered into the back garden, and sat sketching, waiting for Mama and Papa to come and take her home. Eventually her uncle found her and told her what she still struggled to comprehend: Mama and Papa had fallen from the Way. They wouldn't be coming for her. Life as she knew it was over.

Jayne had thought the pain would eventually stop and that Rymellans would hate her parents, but not her. She'd been badly mistaken. She was still tainted thirteen years later and probably would be for the rest of her life. Worse, her uncle hadn't been able to answer the one question she'd asked herself over and over: Why? Why would they throw away their lives like that? Why hadn't they cared about her? About Robert? Why? What had been so special about Brenda Stewart?

"Do you know anything about Brenda Stewart?" she asked Lesley. Given how much her voice wavered, Jayne wasn't surprised when Lesley hesitated.

"Only what Laura told me, which isn't much. But are you sure you want to know?" Lesley said softly.

Yes! No! If she didn't know, she'd wonder. "Yes." She kept her eyes on Lesley. Everything else faded away.

"She was taking art lessons from your papa." Lesley grimaced. "She was twenty."

Twenty? Twenty! He'd committed a Chosen Violation with a flaming twenty-year-old? Jayne tossed her sketchbook onto the next seat, shot up, and slid the aviacraft door open. "I—I need some air." Without a backward glance, she marched away from the aviacraft, her hands clenched. Twenty? Flaming twenty? Had he just not been able to control himself, then? He'd thrown away his family for a twenty-year-old?

When she tried to reconcile the parents who'd raised her with the monsters everyone else saw, she sometimes entertained the notion that it hadn't been their fault. That they'd been naive, deceived, somehow drawn into a situation they hadn't understood until it was too late. Sure, she was probably lying to herself, but sometimes she needed that lie. But twenty? He couldn't possibly be blameless. If anything, he'd taken advantage of her. He'd been old enough to be her papa. What had Mama done? Fallen into bed with someone young enough to be her son?

Now Jayne understood why he hadn't wanted her at the studio. She felt sick to her stomach. She'd loved afternoons in the studio, mixing paints and bringing the vision in her head to life, while he sat next to her, offering encouragement, gently pointing out her mistakes, and showing her new techniques. She'd so looked forward to those afternoons as the end of her Level Three neared, but he'd always been busy. The one time she'd gone to the studio without asking, he'd shouted at her, pushed her outside, and told her never to show up unannounced again. Had *she* been there, hiding in the supply room? For the first time, Jayne was glad the military had burned his studio to the ground. She wished she'd never stepped foot into it after returning home from her Level Three. Even now, she wanted to take a shower.

But he'd never offered private lessons, and if he had, he wouldn't have offered them to diff-oriented females—that would only have invited scrutiny from the military. So Stewart must have been in one of his adult classes. Was that how they'd met? Or had they met somewhere else and she'd taken lessons to give her a reason to be in the studio? Had she hung around when classes were over? Had they locked the door, pulled down the blinds—ugh, she didn't want to think about it. Had Mama suspected, or had she been too preoccupied with her lover to notice?

Jayne put her hands on her hips, took a deep breath, and stared at the ground. Wishing she'd had different parents wouldn't help. She was the daughter of two monsters. What did that say about her?

When she heard approaching footsteps, she dropped her arms to her sides and turned around. "You okay?" Mo asked, then frowned. "That's probably a dumb question."

"No, it's not," she said, surprised that Mo had come to see how she was, considering the sordid detail Lesley had revealed. They really were trying hard to honour her as their Chosen. "But I'm fine. Let's go back to the craft." Not in the mood to talk, she hoped Mo would silently comply and breathed a sigh of relief when she did.

When Jayne re-entered the craft, Lesley briefly met her eyes, then looked away, but not before Jayne read the sympathy in them. It was better than hate, but she felt embarrassed and humiliated. "Do you know anything else about Brenda Stewart?" she asked briskly as Mo settled back into her seat.

Lesley shook her head. "Would you want to know, if I did?"

"Yes," she said firmly. "I'd rather know than not know." No

matter how much it hurt. "If you ever find out anything more about the Incident, please tell me."

"You really don't know anything more than we do?" Mo asked.

"No. I was twelve when it happened. I guess everybody wanted to protect me." By the time she'd plucked up the courage to ask her aunt and uncle, they hadn't wanted to talk about it and had advised her to leave it in the past. Carol had received the same advice when she'd asked her parents on Jayne's behalf, and didn't know any more than Jayne did. When Jayne was twenty-one and had somehow found the nerve to march into the local archives and ask to see any public records related to the Adams Incident, she'd learned that there weren't any. Maybe Robert could tell her more, but she'd die before she asked him. "You mentioned Kevin Stewart."

Lesley accepted the change of subject, perhaps as eager to move along as Jayne was. "Yes. After the Incident, there were petitions . . ." She trailed off.

"Yes, there were," Jayne snapped, not angry with Lesley, but with those who'd wanted her dead. "I'm sorry. Memories," she said curtly. "Was he behind one of the petitions?"

Lesley nodded. "And he instigated the letters to me."

"So why are you telling us this now?" Mo asked. "It sounds like you found out who he is and told him to stop."

"We did. But he's an overseer."

An overseer? Great.

"And he'll be at the awards ceremony."

Mo's mouth dropped open. "Are you flaming serious? I thought they sent you the guest list."

"They did. Laura and I discussed whether we should request his removal, but we decided against it. It would probably affect his career."

Jayne's mind raced. She'd be in the same room with the brother of the woman Papa had chosen over his family. And this Stewart woman had chosen Papa over her relatives. Could Jayne blame this Kevin Stewart for wanting her dead? She didn't agree with him, but she understood his pain, probably better than anyone else.

"You might run into each other—or worse, he might approach you," Lesley said to Jayne. "So I thought I'd better warn you."

"Or maybe you should have taken him off the guest list," Mo said.

Jayne shook her head. "No. I don't want anyone's career ruined over me." Especially when her papa had taken advantage of his sister. "If he approaches me, he approaches me. I can't see him making a scene." Or at least she hoped he wouldn't. "How old is he?" Since he was an overseer, he must be older than they were.

Lesley thought for a second. "Late thirties."

Then he was an adult during the Incident. He probably knew details she didn't. She'd be standing in the same room with someone who might be able to answer long-held questions, but she couldn't speak to him, would have to resist the temptation to beg him for answers.

"We'll stick close," Mo said. "Or rather, I'll stick close. You'll have to work the room," she said to Lesley.

"I'll want to introduce you to everyone. Both of you," Lesley quickly amended.

Everyone would love meeting an Adams. Yet another reason to dread the evening. "I'll probably wear the same outfit I wore at my notification meeting," Jayne said, hoping her shame wasn't evident in her voice.

"That's fine," Lesley said.

"We'll be wearing the same uniforms," Mo added.

Yes, but they didn't have a choice, and they might have something to say about her attire when she was still wearing the same outfit in five years. "True," she mumbled. When Mo met her eyes, she blinked back the tears that suddenly welled and quickly looked away. Argamon!

"Is that everything?" Mo asked Lesley as Jayne lowered her head and surreptitiously dabbed at the corners of her eyes. "Or are there other things going on related to the triad that we should know about?"

"I didn't tell you about the letters because there wasn't any reason to. And yes, that's everything." When neither of them spoke, Lesley said, "Well, I should get back to the office."

Jayne almost asked if she could read the letters, then stopped herself. Why bother? They wouldn't contain anything new.

Lesley touched Jayne's arm. "I'm sorry I shocked you."

"It's okay. I'd rather be shocked and know than not know," Jayne said. When Lesley lifted her hand, the absence of her touch was palpable.

"We'll see you later." Mo leaned toward Lesley and kissed her. "We'll probably be home, but beep us before you leave, in case we decide to go for a walk or something."

"Okay." Lesley glanced at Jayne. "See you later."

"See you later," Jayne replied, then followed Mo off the craft. She groaned as it lifted off. "There goes my sketchbook."

Mo reached for her comm unit. "I'll beep her, tell her to come back."

She gently grasped Mo's arm. "No, it's okay. I can do without it for a few hours."

"You sure?"

She nodded. "I'm sure."

MO LOWERED HER violin and held her breath. When Jayne clapped enthusiastically from the edge of the sofa, Mo raised her bow with a flourish and bowed. "So, not terrible, then?" she said when she straightened.

Jayne smiled. "No, not terrible at all."

Mo's performance had accomplished what she'd hoped—it had brightened the mood brought on by the conversation in Les's aviacraft. Jayne had hardly said two words on the way to the Middleton residence. Mo couldn't blame her; she'd want to hide in her room herself, if she'd heard that her papa had committed a Chosen Violation with a twenty-year-old. Of course, Papa would never do such a thing. He wouldn't even think it. But Jayne's papa had done it. For a second, Mo glimpsed the guilt and shame that burdened Jayne on his behalf. She was pleased that her playing had managed to lighten it, if only for a minute or two.

Wanting to see more of Jayne's smile, Mo launched into a light ditty, dancing around as she played. Jayne's smile broadened, transforming her face. *She should smile like that more often.* She looked so relaxed and happy that Mo couldn't help but smile, too. "Okay, I'm done," she said as Jayne clapped again. She'd entered "showing off" territory and didn't want to overdo it.

"I didn't recognize that last one," Jayne said.

"That's because Les wrote it."

Jayne's brows shot up. "What?"

"Not what you were expecting, I bet. You were probably expecting something like this." One more wouldn't hurt. She poised her bow over the strings, then marched around the coffee table, playing a military tune devoid of energy and creativity. The one time she'd played it during a concert, she could have sworn she heard snores from the audience. Unfortunately the boring tunes were never short; they went on and on and on, and this one was no exception. When she rounded the coffee table and approached Jayne for the sixth time, she lifted her bow. "Okay, that's enough of that." She dropped onto the sofa next to Jayne and rested her violin on her lap.

"You played it well," Jayne said.

"Don't bother. No matter how well that one's played, it saps all the energy from the universe."

Jayne chuckled.

"Not that I'm implying Les does that!" Mo added. The quickest way to sap all the energy from her universe would be to remove Les from it. "But you probably thought she writes music like that."

"I hadn't really thought about it."

Good. The less Jayne thought about Les, the better. Mo leaned forward and placed her violin and bow in the case lying open on the coffee table.

"I hope you'll play for me again," Jayne said.

"Oh, I definitely will." Unlike Les, Mo needed little encouragement to play for others. "I'm trying to decide whether or not to apply for the military orchestra." Though if she was accepted, it would mean spending the occasional night or two away, in addition to the time she already spent on 72. How many intimate lunches between Les and Jayne would that translate into? "It mainly plays at the military academies."

"Will you have time?"

"Yeah." In fact, she had too much free time on her hands right now, and might have even more when her round of practicums finished next month. Ross had been dropping hints about Mo taking on the practicum for Basic Maneuvers 1-B, and Mo had been leaning toward agreeing—until Les had told her about the lunch with Jayne. She knew she couldn't turn down assignments she'd otherwise enjoy because of Les and Jayne, but that wouldn't stop her from worrying about them while she was stuck on 72.

Joining the local military orchestra might not be so bad, since it practised at the C6 Military Academy and played at academies in sectors

A through D. It would play with orchestras in far-flung sectors a couple of times a year, but that would be it, and she could probably persuade Les, and maybe Jayne, to go with her.

Despair suddenly flooded her—it would be impossible to keep the two of them apart, no matter how hard she tried! She had to trust them. Why couldn't she trust them?

"I could go to all your concerts," Jayne said. "I'd look forward to them. If you wanted me there."

She sounded as if she meant it. Mo smiled weakly. "It would be nice to have a friendly face in the audience." She forced herself to meet Jayne's eyes. She couldn't see her as an enemy, or the triad was doomed. Time for a change of subject. "Um, I hope you don't mind me bringing this up, but I want to talk about the awards ceremony."

"Why would I mind?" Jayne asked, her brow furrowing.

"Well, I couldn't help but notice that you're . . . concerned about what you'll wear."

Jayne's face flushed.

"Wearing the same outfit would be perfectly fine," Mo said quickly, "but if you want to wear something else, we could go to the Trading Centre and . . . uh . . ."

"No." Jayne looked at her lap. "I don't have the credits, Mo."

"I meant I'll—"

"I know what you meant. I don't—I wouldn't be comfortable with it, okay?"

"If I wasn't in the military, I'd get myself a new outfit."

Jayne rose and crossed to the window. "So you think I should wear something else," she said, her back to Mo.

"No!" Why did she always say the wrong thing when having a sensitive conversation with Jayne? "I meant that instead of spending the credits on me, I'll spend them on you."

"But you *are* in the military, so you don't have to spend any credits."

"But I'd like to," Mo said. Jayne stared out the window, her shoulders stiff. The silence grew heavier, but Mo didn't regret raising the subject. She wanted Jayne to feel comfortable at the awards ceremony. "When we Join, we'll link our accounts. You'll lose your allotment. So I don't understand—"

Jayne whirled. "Why are you bringing this up now, today, after what Lesley just told me? Don't you think I have enough on my mind already? Why do we have to talk about this now?" Her eyes widened. "I'm sorry. I shouldn't have said that," she said, her voice barely a whisper.

"Why not? It's what you're thinking."

Jayne covered her mouth. For a moment, Mo thought she might throw up.

"Look, I know it's not the best time, but the awards ceremony isn't that far off. And, I don't know, I guess I thought if I bought you a new outfit, it would be one less thing for you to worry about."

To Mo's surprise, Jayne returned to the sofa, sat next to her, and clenched her trembling hands in her lap. For a split second, Mo almost reached over and covered them. She stopped herself, remembering who she was with. Reflex. Just reflex.

"I know we'll join our accounts," Jayne said quietly. "And I know you're only trying to help." She swallowed. "But it's embarrassing."

"All Chosens join accounts."

"And all Chosens contribute to the joint account."

"Jayne, I didn't earn 99 percent of the credits in my account." In fact, 99.99 percent would be more accurate. "My parents gave them to me on my eighteenth birthday. The same goes for Les."

"It doesn't matter," Jayne said tersely. "They're still your and Lesley's credits."

"What are you going to do when your allotment is cut off?"

Jayne was silent for a moment. "I don't know."

Was she planning to starve? Mo tried not to get frustrated, especially since she'd probably feel the same way in Jayne's shoes. It would take time, and probably a few more conversations, before Jayne would feel even halfway comfortable with the idea of their joint account. For now, Mo would focus on achieving the smaller victory. "There will be a lot of Rymellans at the awards ceremony. Important Rymellans. And you've probably already figured this out, but every speech will be about Chosen Violations."

Jayne nodded.

"So . . . I don't know, if you'll feel better in a new outfit, let me buy you a new outfit."

"It won't really bother me," Jayne said, but Mo could tell she was fibbing. "Most of the people who'll be there weren't at my notification meeting. Just you and Lesley and your parents."

"Les and I won't care that you're in the same outfit." But Adelaide might.

"You will when I'm in the same outfit the next time, and the next time."

Hopefully Jayne would be less stubborn about their credits by then. "Given Les's future, there will be a lot more ceremonies and receptions to attend." Mo smiled when Jayne sighed. "I feel the same way."

Jayne looked at her. "You do?"

Mo shrugged. "About these official functions? Yeah. The best part will be the food." But she wouldn't allow Jayne to sidetrack her. "Adelaide might have something to say if you wear the same thing you did at your notification meeting. She's the only one who might care."

"She probably will care," Jayne murmured.

"So let me buy you a new outfit."

"No," Jayne said firmly. "And I don't want to talk about this anymore."

Mo shook her head. "Has anyone ever told you you're stubborn?"

Jayne snorted softly. "Carol."

"Well, Carol's right. You'll have to back down on this when we Join, you know."

"I won't have a choice then. I do now."

"If you change—"

The front door opened. "Hello, stranger," Mo said when Andrew wandered into the living room. "I was wondering if you still lived here."

He grinned. "Been busy. Hi, Jayne."

"Hi," Jayne murmured.

Andrew sniffed the air. "I don't smell supper cooking."

Mo snatched up the cushion next to her and flung it at him. He laughed as he dodged it. "You know where the kitchen is," she said, pointing. "And Les will be here for supper, too." Mo was hoping she'd arrive soon, since Les had said she'd cook the meal.

Andrew picked up the cushion and tossed it to Mo. "Papa's not far behind me, so we'll have quite a few around the table tonight. Oh, when will you be going to 72 next?"

Mo tucked the cushion back in its place. "Why?"

"Just wondering."

"In a couple of days."

"Thursday?"

She nodded. "Why?"

"Just wondering!" When she glared at him, he added, "I thought I might have a few friends over and didn't want to bug you."

Mo narrowed her eyes. He'd never worried about his friends bothering her before. She barked a laugh and nudged Jayne's arm. "Oh, he's bringing over a girlfriend."

"No, I'm not."

"Don't worry, you'll have the house all to yourself. Except for Papa and Nathan. That'll be cozy."

"Nathan will be at his soccer game."

Oh, right.

"And Papa has a meeting that night."

"You already checked?" Mo snickered. "Definitely a girlfriend, then."

Andrew threw her a dirty look and stalked off.

"Maybe he's just having friends over," Jayne said.

"No, then he wouldn't care who's going to be home." Though she didn't understand why he was so worried about her presence. The few times he'd brought a woman home, Mo hadn't given him any trouble. Well, maybe she'd teased him a bit afterward, but he'd always taken it in the spirit intended and brushed it off.

What had they been talking about before Andrew? Oh, yeah. "If you change your mind—about the outfit—just let me know. The offer is always open." She considered adding "no matter what you need," then decided that probably wouldn't be a good idea. "So what do you want to do now?"

Jayne stood. "Maybe we should start supper."

"Yeah, okay." Chopping vegetables wouldn't be so bad when she had someone to talk to. "Do you like to cook?" she asked Jayne as they walked to the kitchen.

Jayne nodded.

Two Chosens who liked to cook. Mo could hardly believe her luck!

TWO DAYS LATER, Lesley finished reading the draft of her speech and leaned back in her office chair. It met the guidelines and sounded all right, but she'd deliver it with Jayne staring at her from the head table. She stood behind every word in the speech, including those that harshly condemned Chosen Violations, but it would be difficult not to feel awkward. Everyone's eyes would be on her when she rose from her seat to go to the stage, the seat next to the daughter of two criminals who'd spat on the Chosen Tradition. To them, that daughter was her Chosen. Would anyone take her seriously when she spoke? Could she sound convincing, knowing what was running through everyone's mind? It was unfortunate that her first speech on the subject with Jayne present would take place at such a grand affair.

How she'd feel on stage wasn't Lesley's only concern. How would Jayne feel? Listening to someone rail against Chosen Violations wouldn't be new, but this time the speaker would be someone with whom she'd spend the rest of her life. And it would probably be a surreal experience for those assembled, to be in the same room with an Adams when Rymellans were being celebrated and rewarded for capturing and executing someone who'd committed a Chosen Violation. Lesley wouldn't be surprised if everyone's attention was on Jayne during the speech, not her.

She couldn't do anything to make the evening more comfortable for everyone, but perhaps she could do something for Jayne. Perhaps it wouldn't be so bad for Jayne if she wasn't hearing the speech for the first time. The more Lesley thought about it, the more she liked the idea of sending Jayne her speech in advance. Why not do it right now, when she still had time to change it? The deadline to send it for approval was still a few days away.

She typed a quick note, attached her speech, and sent the dispatch to Jayne and Mo, so Mo wouldn't feel slighted. Lesley glanced at the time on her comm station. Mo probably wouldn't read it by the deadline, if at all. She'd soon be on her way to the shuttle base and wouldn't be home for a couple of days. Mo loved Lesley dearly, but a dry speech about Chosen Violations couldn't compete with cards and gossip. Jayne was different.

Lesley wasn't surprised when a dispatch arrived as she relaxed in her aviacraft on the way home: *Thank you for sending me your speech. I've read it, and I think it flows really well and the tone is appropriate for the event. If you sent it to me because you're worried about how I might feel—well, you're probably not, but just in case, don't worry about me. I agree with what you'll say. I know everyone in the room would find that hard to believe, but I do. To be honest, listening to your speech will be the easy part. Just being at the event and meeting people will be the hard part.*

Actually, I will mention one thing about your speech. I noticed that you never refer to the Incident. There was one part where I thought maybe you were dancing around it, and it would be clearer if you just said it (I marked where). I don't mean to be critical. Your speech is fine as is. But I thought I'd mention it in case you wanted to just say "the Adams Incident" and didn't because of me.

Lesley found the marked passage and chuckled. She hadn't realized it as she was writing, but now she could see that she *had* danced around it. As written, hers would probably be the first lengthy speech on Chosen Violations since the Incident that didn't explicitly mention it, which might set more tongues wagging than if it did. Kevin Stewart would probably be convinced that Jayne had influenced Lesley's speech. She had, but not in the way he'd suspect.

As Lesley was tapping in her reply, her comm unit beeped. "I wasn't expecting to hear from you so soon," she said to Mo. "Are you beeping me from the shuttle?"

"I'm at home. My shifts were cancelled."

"Don't tell me Jensen had something to do with it."

"No, nothing like that. Apparently the pilot I was going to cover for doesn't have to be down here now. So they don't need me. It would have been nice if they'd beeped me before I was halfway to the shuttle base." Mo paused. "Anyway, do you want to come over tonight?"

"I can't. I thought you'd be on 72, so I said I'd sit with Mama while Papa runs through a case he's presenting tomorrow. I gather he's a bit worried about it." Even though she expected Mo to say no, she said, "You can come listen too, if you want."

"Uh, yeah, you know what I'm going to say, right?"

Lesley chuckled. "Yes. I mean, no."

"Exactly. Oh well, I thought it would be nice if you brought over your flute so we could play together."

"I could come over tomorrow, right after my shift," Lesley suggested.

"Yeah, do that! And beep me later."

After agreeing to do so, Lesley returned to her dispatch to Jayne: *You're right; it would be clearer to explicitly mention the Incident at the point you marked. I have to admit, it will take some time for me to give speeches about Chosen Violations, or even talk about them, without feeling awkward because you're listening. So it helps to know that you've read the speech and will know what's coming.*

I've been meaning to mention something to you—something she should probably mention in person, but doing it this way was easier—*Laura and I belong to a group that investigates possible Chosen Violations. In fact, Laura leads the group. Investigating tips is one of my main duties, in addition to writing opinions for overseers. I would have told you this when we had lunch, but we got caught up talking about other things.* Well, it had briefly crossed her mind. *I'm sure someone will refer to our group at the awards ceremony. Now you'll know what they're talking about. As far as the ceremony goes, stick with Mo and you'll do fine. I'll be expected to circulate, but I'll stay with you two as much as I can.*

Jayne's reply arrived as Lesley was walking to the Thompson house: *Thank you for telling me. You're getting the medal for the Owen case, so I already knew you participated in investigations regarding Chosen Violations. I wasn't aware of your group, though. I wonder if groups like yours existed before the Incident.*

An interesting question.

I saw you (and Laura) in the execution procession for Owen. I never would have imagined that I'd actually meet you and that we'd exchange a series of dispatches like this.

That made two of them.

MO PONDERED HOW to answer the questions Sheila and David had asked in their dispatches: *Do you miss being on tour? When will you be back?* She sort of missed it. With everything going on, she hadn't had much time to gaze out the windows in 72's observation deck and wish she were on one of the ships about to undock. The real question was whether she'd miss it in time, and she didn't know the answer. So far, flying the odd shift was tiding her over nicely. She also had the practicums. They weren't "real" flying, but they were satisfying in their own way, though she tried not to wonder if the student pilots would go on tour before she did. Even if she and Les somehow figured out how they could all go on tour together, only Jensen could answer the *when* question.

Deciding to defer her replies until morning, Mo glanced at the time on the study's comm station. Les was probably still listening to Alan drone on about his case. Mo was glad she was in this study, rather than the Thompsons'. Not in the mood to do anything in particular, she pulled up the last two Defence bulletins, and was skimming the second one when the front door opened and animated voices filled the hallway. She chortled. Oh yeah, Andrew and his "friends" were here, though from the sounds of it, only one friend was with him—a woman, just as Mo had suspected. Best of all, he didn't know she was home. She hadn't seen him since finding out her shifts on 72 were cancelled. Papa was at a government meeting and Nathan at his weekly soccer game, so Andrew would think he had the house to himself.

Mo sat quietly and listened to their chatter as they hung their cloaks and went into the living room. The woman's voice sounded familiar, but she couldn't place it. She'd give them time to get cozy, then wander in, plant herself in one of the chairs, and pretend she planned to sit there all night. She couldn't wait to see Andrew's face! Payback time for all those nights she and Les had babysat him and Nathan when they'd rather have been alone.

She gave them ten minutes for good measure, then crept down the hallway, trying not to giggle. There wasn't much talking going on, so she wasn't surprised to see Andrew leaning over his girlfriend, engaged in a passionate kiss. Mo put her hands on her hips. "Aren't you going to introduce me to your friend?"

Her words had the desired effect. Andrew jumped and looked over his shoulder, horror written all over his face.

"I hope I'm not interr—" Mo's jaw dropped open when Andrew drew back, revealing his girlfriend's face. "What in the flaming Argamon are you doing here?"

Ann leaped up from the sofa at the same time Andrew stood. They both stared at her.

"What are you doing here?" Mo repeated, not quite believing her eyes.

"What are *you* doing here?" Andrew asked.

"I live here!" Mo looked at Ann. "This is the Andrew you're seeing? My brother? My flaming *brother*?"

"You're supposed to be on 72," Ann said, far from contrite.

"Where I could see you head down to the planet to see my flaming brother?"

Ann's hands went to her hips. "What's wrong with me seeing him?"

"You introduced us," Andrew reminded her.

She'd introduced them? "When?"

"At your notification party. You told me to dance with her."

"I wouldn't have told you to dance with her if I'd known it would lead to this!"

"What's your problem?" Ann snapped.

Andrew took Ann's hand. "We like each other."

Mo wanted to gag. "She doesn't like anyone, Andrew. She's using you."

Ann yanked her hand from Andrew's and marched up to Mo. "Excuse me?"

"Come on, Ann, if he wasn't my brother and you weren't playing some sick game, he'd already be history."

"That's not true!" She turned to Andrew. "See? This is why I said it would be better if she didn't know."

"I bet you did," Mo shouted. "Do yourself a favour, Andrew. Find yourself another girlfriend." She whirled and headed for the front door.

"Where are you going?" Andrew asked, following her.

"Out!" No way was she sleeping here, with Ann and Andrew across the flaming hall.

"Look, Mo, I don't understand what the problem is. She's your friend. Why is it so bad that we're seeing each other?"

Mo turned to tell him that she wasn't sure Ann could truly be a friend and that he'd soon be tossed aside without a second thought. Before she could, he blurted, "I like her." He swallowed. "We have fun together."

The vulnerability in his voice and face stayed her tongue. Unfortunately he'd have to learn about Ann the hard way. "It's weird because she is my friend," she said, forcing out the "friend" part. "It would have been nice if you'd told me. Then it wouldn't have been such a shock."

"I was going to tell you, but Ann thought we should wait until we'd been together longer."

No, Ann had planned to dump him without Mo ever knowing. But Mo's warnings would be wasted on Andrew, who was clearly in the "Ann is perfect" stage of the relationship. She'd just have to be there for him when he rapidly progressed to the "I hate Ann" stage. "I'm going to Les's, so you two can have the house to yourselves. I'll see you tomorrow." Without waiting for a reply, she stepped out the door, quickly mounted her bike, and pedalled away.

Her comm unit beeped twice as she rammed her bike into the rack near the Thompsons' front door. Just in case a superior was trying to contact her, she checked the sender. Ann. Curiosity got the better of her; she paused outside the door and opened the dispatch.

Mo, why did you run off like that? We could have talked. You know, now that you've been notified, you'll have to get those jealous rages under control.

Okay, that was it! Why had she bothered? Without reading the rest, she jabbed the delete key several times, then wanted to drop her comm unit and stomp on it. But she'd have a difficult time explaining what happened when she requested a replacement. "I had a temper tantrum" wouldn't go over well.

She swung open the door and marched to the study, where Alan was standing at his desk, reading from a file in front of him. Les and Adelaide listened attentively from their chairs. Mo leaned against the doorframe. "Excuse me," she said, then loudly repeated it when nobody looked at her.

Les did a double-take. "Mo! I didn't think you were coming."

"Come in and join us," Alan said.

"No. Thanks. I need to speak to Les."

"Is everything all right?" Adelaide asked as Les frowned and rose.

"Fine." Mo led the way up the stairs and didn't speak until Les had shut her bedroom door behind them. "You won't believe what just happened."

"What?" Les said, her face now taut.

"Andrew came home with his latest girlfriend. Guess who? Ann."

"Ann," Les said slowly, shaking her head.

"Hawkins!"

"Ann Hawkins? Lieutenant Ann Hawkins?"

"Yes!"

"Oh."

Les's lack of concern irked Mo. "Ann's dating my flaming brother!"

"I know you've had problems with Ann, but I thought the two of you were friendly."

"Yeah. Sort of. But that doesn't mean I want her dating my brother. Why's she with Andrew? She can't find anyone else to date?" She stiffened when Les stepped toward her, and sank onto the bed. "She'll hurt him."

"So will anyone he dates."

"Not like her! She'll do it deliberately. Everything's a game to her." Mo remembered Ann's harassment during the pilot program evaluation and how Ann had brushed it off later, as if it had been nothing: *Lighten up! No hard feelings, right?*

This was Mo's fault. When Ann left the *Falcon*, Mo could have been rid of her once and for all. But no, she had to answer her dispatches, because she was missing Les and feeling sorry for herself.

Les sat next to her and reached for her hand. "There's nothing you can do."

Mo glared into space. "I can tell her to stay away."

"I wouldn't do that, if I were you."

Mo sighed.

"He's twenty-two, old enough to take care of himself."

"Yeah, and she's flaming twenty-seven!"

Les shrugged. "If he'll turn twenty-three before she turns twenty-eight, that wouldn't be unusual for Chosens."

"But they're not Chosens!" Mo snapped. She took a deep breath. She was angry with Ann, not with Les, and certainly not with Andrew. "He doesn't know what she's like. I'm going to talk to him."

"He won't listen to you. If you try to interfere, all you'll do is push them closer together."

That was the last thing she wanted. She pulled her hand from Les's and flopped back onto the bed with a groan. "I introduced them. I told them to dance together."

Les chuckled. "I remember now."

"It's not funny! Am I the only one who cares about Andrew?"

"No. But there's nothing you can do."

Mo wasn't sure she could stand by and watch Ann set Andrew up for a gigantic fall. Worse, she'd then have to see Ann swaggering around 72 with a perpetual smirk on her face, asking her how Andrew was every five minutes.

"I take it you're staying here tonight," Les said.

"Yeah, I am. And do you mind if I sleep on this side of the bed? I want a clear path to the bathroom, in case I have to throw up."

Amusement flashed across Les's face. "Andrew's never been that serious about dating," she said. "They'll probably hang out for a while, get bored, and move on."

No, they'd hang out for a while, Ann would humiliate him, and she'd move on. In the meantime, Mo would be stuck in the middle, and when things did blow up, she'd have to endure Ann's gloating on 72 and Andrew's pain at home. "I have to do something!" she moaned.

"Mo, you'll only make things worse. Stay out of it. If Ann is playing some game, the worst thing you can do is react. Just ignore it. She'll get bored."

"You're right," Mo mumbled, planning to avoid Ann. If she ran into her on 72, nothing would stop Mo from speaking her mind.

JAYNE RIFLED THROUGH her closet, wondering what she hoped to find. The outfit Carol had bought her was the only formal outfit she owned. It was suitable for the awards ceremony, but Jayne had already worn it. Considering that she'd patched most of her other clothes and usually didn't care what she wore, that shouldn't bother her—and wouldn't, if not for Adelaide, and perhaps Lesley and Mo. They said they didn't care, but had Mo truly offered to buy her another outfit because she wanted her to feel comfortable? Or was she just being diplomatic? Jayne sank onto the bed, pulled out her comm unit, and beeped Carol.

"If they say they don't care, then they probably don't care," Carol said after Jayne had told her why she'd just vainly searched through her closet.

It was the "probably" that worried Jayne. "Mo offered to buy me a new outfit. She said it was so I'd feel comfortable, but I don't know if that's true."

"So what are you worried about, then? You're getting a new outfit."

"I turned her down."

"Why?"

She rose from the bed and paced. "Because it's humiliating."

"It's humiliating that your Chosen wants to buy you a present?"

"That's not what she'd be doing. And it's not just that. I'm going to lose my allotment."

"There's nothing you can do about that," Carol said firmly. "You'll link accounts with them when you Join, anyway."

"I'm sure they'll appreciate my three credits."

"There's nothing you can do." Jayne heard Carol's exasperation. "You'll have enough adjusting to do without creating problems."

"I'm not creating a problem, Carol! It's a real problem for me."

"What, that you'll be dependent on them? Right now, you're dependent on Rymellans you don't know."

Something Jayne tried not to think about.

"Take it one step at a time. Beep Mo. Tell her you'll take her up on her offer. If she wants to do something nice, let her do something nice. You *will* feel more comfortable at the ceremony in a new outfit, right?"

Jayne nodded, then remembered Carol couldn't see her. "Right. But I wish I could take care of myself."

"Apply to college."

"What?"

"Apply to college. Art school."

Jayne sat on the bed again. "I can't."

"Why not?"

"Because I won't get in." As she'd told Carol every time they'd had this conversation over the past few years.

"You won't know until you apply." When Jayne remained silent, Carol said, "So let's say you apply and you're turned down. At least you'll know for sure. You could be accepted."

"Even if I am, nobody will buy anything I create. You know that."

"Do it for you. You'd enjoy art school, and if you were in college, you wouldn't feel so bad that they're supporting you."

"I don't know, Carol." What was the point, when she wouldn't get in? If her name didn't disqualify her, then her portfolio would. Not one art teacher had encouraged her. Nobody, except those who didn't want to offend her—and she could count them on one hand—had ever said a positive word about her drawings. She told herself it was because of who she was, but maybe she just lacked talent and her name was a convenient

RYMELLAN 2

rationalization. When they turned her down, she still wouldn't know if she was deluding herself, so why bother?

"Think about it," Carol said. "You have nothing to lose by applying. And beep Mo about the outfit. You want to, otherwise you wouldn't have beeped me."

Jayne chuckled. "You know me too well."

Carol's voice softened. "Yes, I do. And I think you should apply to art school. And that's the last thing I'll say about it," she added when Jayne drew breath. "For now. Beep Mo. Bye." She disconnected before Jayne had a chance to respond.

Jayne stared at her comm unit for a minute, then punched in Mo's code. Oh good, she wasn't answering. Leaving a message would be easier. "Hi, Mo. It's Jayne. I've decided to take you up on your offer to buy me an outfit for the awards ceremony. It's really generous of you, and I appreciate it very much. Let me know when you're available to go to the Trading Centre. I'm available anytime. Okay, then. Bye." Should she have said thanks again at the end? Or would that have been too much?

Mo beeped her fifteen minutes later. "Sorry, I was in the shower. Yeah, that's great! But I don't have to go to the Trading Centre with you unless you want me to."

"You sure?"

"Just authorize me to transfer credits into your account. I mean, if you want me there, I'll go. But to be honest, I'll probably be bored. I hate trading for clothes."

Jayne could relate. "Maybe I'll take Carol with me, then."

"Yeah, do that."

"I really appreciate it, Mo. Thank you."

"It's nothing. Anyway, I have to go. I promised Nathan I'd fly him to class."

They said good-bye. Jayne would feel more comfortable at the ceremony, but she didn't feel comfortable now. Maybe Carol was right and she should apply to art school. At least while her application was in, she'd feel as if she were trying to do something with her life—or fool herself into thinking she was, since the gesture wouldn't result in anything but a rejection dispatch. And then what? Would she still cling to the belief that she had talent, or would the rejection suck all the joy from drawing? No matter what happened, she'd still be dependent on Lesley and Mo. So maybe applying to art school wasn't such a good idea. It wouldn't solve anything in the end, and might force her to relinquish a long-held delusion, one she wasn't ready to give up.

MO READ THE dispatch from Archer and snapped off her comm unit in disgust. "Great."

Les looked up from her late supper. "What is it?"

"Archer wants me to do a couple of shifts, one Sunday and one Monday." Maybe she could avoid Ann, though Ann would probably seek her out. Mo's icy silence in response to Ann's dispatches hadn't deterred her from sending three or four a day. "You're on duty, I guess?"

"I am on Monday."

There went that idea.

"I'd go with you, if I could," Les said, giving Mo a sympathetic smile.

"I suppose you'll see Jayne on Sunday," Mo said, trying not to sound surly. "Otherwise Berry will wonder."

Les swallowed a mouthful of food and pointed her fork at Mo. "Take Jayne with you."

"What? Are you serious?"

"Why not? Her presence might keep Ann away, and you won't have to worry about us seeing each other. We'll have to see each other at some point, but maybe you'll have calmed down about Ann by then."

Mo doubted it. "Where's Jayne supposed to sleep?"

"You can request two bedrooms. They have to comply. You're notified Chosens, not Joined."

Mo considered Les's suggestion more seriously. Having Jayne along *would* prevent her from sitting in her quarters brooding about Ann, and Les seeing Jayne.

"Jayne has to go sometime," Les said. "This would be the perfect introduction to 72. It's a one-night stay, not four or five nights."

"And you won't mind?"

"No. I trust you."

Mo detected a slight edge in Les's voice and knew it wasn't because Les was worried, but because of the unspoken *Why can't you trust me?* "I wonder how everyone will react to Jayne being on 72."

"You'll have to find out sometime. You could wait until I can go too, but that might be a while. And you sort of need someone to go up with you now."

That was true. She turned on her comm unit again and beeped Jayne. "How would you like to go with me to 72 on Sunday?" she asked after they'd exchanged greetings. "We'd come back on Monday."

"72?" Jayne exclaimed. "Are you sure you want me along?"

"Yeah, I'm sure. It's only for one night. I'll have to fly a couple of shifts, but they're only four hours each. You can stay in our quarters, if you want. But I'll show you a couple of places you might like." The observation deck was high on the list. "You'll have to go sometime, so we thought a one-night stay would be a good way to start."

"So Lesley knows?"

"Yeah. She's right here." Mo held the comm unit out so Les could say hello. "So what do you say?"

"Is Lesley coming too?"

"No, she's on duty on Monday."

Silence, then, "I hope I don't throw up."

Mo smiled. "If you suffer from space sickness, it's better to find out now. Don't worry, it's easy to remedy. So what do you say?"

"Okay, I'll go," Jayne said, sounding mortified. "What time?"

"I'll pick you up around 8:00. In the morning."

"Do I need to bring anything special?"

"No, just pretend you're staying overnight with a friend." Which she was. "Bring your sketchbook. You might find some interesting things to draw."

"Oh, I'll bring it," Jayne said fervently.

An image of a white-knuckled Jayne clinging to her sketchbook flashed through Mo's mind. She stifled a giggle. "I'll see you Sunday morning, then."

As soon as they disconnected, she beeped Archer. "It's Mo. Sure, I'll fly those shifts. Can you book me quarters with two bedrooms? I'm bringing my Chosen."

Archer, who'd been on 72 forever and knew of her and Les's relationship, chuckled. "Had an argument with Lesley?"

"Not that Chosen. My other Chosen."

"Oh," Archer said, suddenly serious. "I see. Um, all right."

"See you Sunday?" Mo said after several seconds of dead air.

"Yes. Archer out."

Mo stared at her comm unit, then looked at Les. "What do you want to bet that he's beeping Larson and whoever else he can think of right now? I won't be surprised if they tell me I can't bring her."

"They can't do that," Les said. "If they don't want her on 72, they'll have to ban you, as well."

"Wouldn't that be great! The closest I'd ever get to a real fighter is the simulators."

Les pushed her plate away. "They won't do it. They'll hold their noses. You're too good to be completely and utterly grounded. Ross would fight it, and so would others."

Still, Mo held onto her comm unit, expecting it to beep at any moment with the news that she'd been removed from the domestic supply list. Only after Les finished dessert did she slide it back into its holder.

JAYNE TRIED NOT to cling to Mo as they left the shuttle and strode into the waiting area. "Grab my arm," Mo said over her shoulder. Surprised, and grateful not to have to fight the urge, Jayne grasped Mo's arm.

The waiting area was busier than Jayne expected and seemed unnaturally quiet, given the number of Rymellans milling around. A few whispers and a cough here and there, but that was it. Was talking against a rule? Blood rushed to her cheeks. They weren't here to see her, were they?

Mo confirmed her fear after they'd passed through the waiting area and entered an elevator. "Can't get away from the gawkers, I guess," she said as she pressed a button labelled D6.

"Maybe you shouldn't have brought me."

"You had to come sometime. Was the shuttle ride okay? You seemed better after we lowered the window shade."

Something about being surrounded by nothingness rattled Jayne. "You must think I'm fragile. You and Lesley zoom around in fighters, but I can't handle a shuttle ride."

"It was your first time. You'll get used to it."

Like she'd get used to the fact that she was now on a space station orbiting around the planet, a space station that could drop from space at any moment and burn up in the atmosphere, incinerating her and everyone else on board in an instant? Her grip tightened around Mo's arm. "Oh, sorry!" she said, letting go.

"I didn't even notice," Mo said with a smile. Then she frowned. The elevator door swooshed open. "It should be to the left." Mo led the way to her quarters, stepped inside, and surveyed the room. "I didn't realize how much larger two-bedroom quarters are. Nobody I hang out with has ever been at the stage of needing two bedrooms. Well, David, a friend of mine—he needed two bedrooms on the *Falcon*, but I don't remember his quarters being that much larger than mine."

Jayne glanced around, struck by the room's sterling appearance. A cleaning crew had obviously visited after the last occupant had left, and the lack of personal belongings, ornaments, and trinkets lent the room a sterile air. She was almost afraid to touch anything.

Mo peered inside both bedrooms. "They're identical, so do you want the left or the right?"

"It doesn't matter."

"Are you a late sleeper?" Mo asked as she shrugged the knapsack off her back and dropped it just inside the door of the room on the left.

"No."

"You hungry? It's a little early for lunch, but I have to fly at 12:00. I'll need to head out at 11:40 or so."

Jayne glanced at her comm unit. They had about an hour. "Let's eat, then."

"Why don't you come with me to the canteen? Then you'll know where it is, in case you want to get a snack while I'm gone."

Jayne wasn't sure she'd have the courage to roam around the space station on her own, but since it sounded as if this stay would be the first of many, somehow she'd force herself out into the corridors. "If I'm up before you tomorrow, I'll get us breakfast." Maybe fewer people would be up and about then.

Mo's face lit up. "That would be great! But I'm flying at 08:00 tomorrow, so I'll be up at 07:00."

Then Jayne would set her alarm for 6:00. She wanted to be useful.

"Anyway, you want to dump your bag?"

Jayne left her knapsack and sketchbook on the bed in her room and accompanied Mo to the canteen, doing her best to commit the route to memory. She was a bit surprised at how few people they passed in the corridors.

"The space station is huge," Mo said when Jayne voiced her thoughts. "And a lot of people are on shift. I'll show you around tonight. I want to take you to one of the observation decks. You can see Rymel!"

Hopefully she wouldn't faint.

They decided to take lunch back to Mo's quarters, where they made fast work of their sandwiches. Jayne tried not to panic when Mo headed for the door. "I'll be back at around 16:20," Mo said, making Jayne mentally subtract twelve to convert from military time. "Oh, send Les a dispatch, let her know we made it here okay. And you don't have to stay in here. Walk around. If you get lost, um . . . beep Les! She can guide you back. Or ask someone. We're in quarters D6-155."

"Okay," Jayne said, intending to stay inside until Mo returned.

"Oh, and look over the emergency instructions near the door. If there's an evacuation, just follow everyone else."

Emergency? Evacuation? Jayne forced herself to think about something else. What did one say to a pilot about to go on patrol? "Be careful."

"I can do this in my sleep," Mo said with a dismissive wave of her hand. "But I will. See you later."

Jayne busied herself with unpacking her few items and slipping them into a drawer, which took all of five minutes. She sent a short dispatch to Lesley, then settled on the sofa to sketch, and forgot where she was. Before she knew it, it was almost 4:00. She wandered over to the small kitchen area she'd noticed. Mo might appreciate a tziva when she returned.

The instant she turned on the portable water boiler, a chime rang. Heart racing, she frantically glanced around. Was it a fire alarm? Maybe she wasn't supposed to use the boiler? But the kitchen was stocked with tziva powder, the boiler had clearly been used, and smoke wasn't pouring from it. When the chime sounded again, she decided to peek into the corridor outside, in case it was some type of drill—or an emergency! Her breath caught in her throat when she opened the door and came face to face with a woman standing outside.

     RYMELLAN 2

The lieutenant coolly eyed her. "So you *did* come with her. Took you long enough to answer the door."

Oh! "Uh . . ."

"I know she's not here, but since she's ignoring my dispatches and would probably close the door in my face, I figured I'd give you a message. Tell her I want to talk to her. Today. She can't ignore me forever." The lieutenant whirled and strode away.

Perplexed, Jayne leaned into the corridor and watched her receding back, then ducked inside when she spotted another officer coming toward her. What was that about? She could hardly wait to ask Mo.

She didn't pounce on her the moment she returned, but waited until Mo had accepted a mug of tziva and dropped into one of the comfortable chairs with a contented sigh. "Thanks," Mo said after a sip. "I could get used to this."

"You had a visitor. A lieutenant."

Mo's face darkened. "What did she want?" she asked wearily.

"How did you know it was a 'she'?"

"Lucky guess. Did she tell you her name?"

"No. She just said she wants to talk to you today. And something like you can't ignore her."

Mo rolled her eyes. "Sure I can."

"Who is she?" Jayne asked, too curious to let Mo be coy.

"Her name's Ann. She's dating Andrew." She barked a laugh. "Dating. Right. More like using."

But how was Mo involved, apart from being Andrew's sister? "How long have they been dating?"

"Oh, I don't know, ten minutes, which is longer than Ann usually stays with a guy."

It sounded as if Mo knew Ann more than just through Andrew. "How long have you known her?"

"We went to the Military Academy together, and we served together until she left the *Falcon* a few tours before I did. We've kept in touch." Mo shook her head and muttered, "Unfortunately."

"You don't like her?"

Mo shrugged. "I don't know. Sometimes she's okay. I've never quite figured her out. But I do know that she doesn't stay in relationships very long, and she doesn't have to date my brother. It'll be a mess when they split up, because she'll forget about him within twenty-four hours, but he'll mope around the house for a month, blaming me for introducing them."

Ah. Jayne filed away that useful bit of information.

Mo stared at her over the rim of her mug. "Was she rude to you?"

Not wanting to upset Mo further, Jayne shook her head. Ann had been more terse than rude, though she hadn't introduced herself. Truth be told, Jayne was glad Ann had said her piece and left, rather than insisting on hanging around.

"Don't let her in here," Mo said, as if reading Jayne's mind. "If she shows up tomorrow, tell her you gave me her message and she has my answer."

"Okay," she said, not thrilled at potentially being caught in the middle. If Mo were to ask for her advice, she'd tell her to talk to Ann and clear the air. But given the stubborn set of Mo's shoulders and mouth, that wasn't likely to happen.

"Anyway, forget about Ann. What did you do while I was on shift?"

Jayne told Mo about her afternoon, but left out her confused reaction to the door chime, and how disappointed she was that Lesley hadn't replied to her dispatch.

MO PUT HER hand on Jayne's arm as they approached the entrance to Observation Deck 2. "There are a ton of windows, so you might feel a little disoriented at first."

"Will there be a lot of people?" Jayne asked.

"No. It's nothing new to us. There might be one or two, but unless a ship is docking or there's a large meteor passing by, it won't be crowded. Oh, and I hear it's a popular spot for dates." Mo wouldn't know. She and Les had sometimes sat in the observation deck, but not on "dates." Then again, they'd held hands; they'd snuggled; they'd enjoyed themselves. But Mo had never seen their evenings here as dates. She didn't consider it a date when they went out for supper or to the Dance Hall, either. Maybe such activities were only dates during the getting-to-know-each-other stage.

She pushed the *Open* button and hoped Jayne wouldn't faint or feel sick. "Not many here," she said as she stepped over the threshold. "Where do you want to sit?" When Jayne didn't reply, Mo turned to her. Jayne was standing absolutely still, her mouth partly open and her eyes glazed. "Jayne? Jayne!"

Jayne's eyes focused on Mo. "Sorry. This is amazing!" She walked to the nearest window and peered out. "I can't believe that's Rymel."

"Yeah, it is," Mo said, pleased that Jayne was enthralled, not green.

"And here we are, up in a space station, just hanging here and orbiting around . . . dependent on life support systems for every single breath we take . . ." Jayne's hand went to her throat.

"Why don't we sit down?" Mo took Jayne's elbow and steered her to the nearest sofa.

Jayne opened her sketchbook the moment they sat. "I wish I had coloured pencils," she murmured.

"Why?" Mo asked, not sure if she was supposed to have heard.

"So I could try sketching . . ." She grimaced, then turned to Mo and swept her arm toward the windows " . . . space. I could use my pencil, but I'd prefer to inject colour."

"There's a Trading Centre here. We can get coloured pencils."

"No. We're already here. Let's enjoy the view."

Mo suspected that Jayne didn't have the credits for coloured pencils, which reminded her that she still had to transfer credits into Jayne's account. When she did, she'd tack on a little extra and send Jayne a dispatch about buying coloured pencils for next time. She pointed. "You see that ship docked over there, near the platform marked 4A-122?"

Jayne nodded.

"It's a medical research ship, like the *Falcon*. Similar model, but the *Falcon* is newer. I think that model—" She broke off when someone stopped directly behind them. Okay, whoever it was had the entire deck to choose from, but they decided to stand behind her and Jayne? Irritated, Mo turned around at the same time that Ann bent over and stuck her head between them.

"Well, isn't this cozy," Ann said with a smirk. "Not very original, though. You couldn't have thought of somewhere else, Mo?"

"What in the flaming Argamon are you doing here?" Mo snapped, leaning away from her; Jayne did the same.

"I know, I know, two's company, three's a crowd. Oh, wait. That doesn't apply to you, does it?"

"Get lost!"

"I wouldn't have to interrupt your intimate evening if you'd answer my flaming dispatches."

"Why, so you can rub in how much you'll hurt my brother when you dump him?"

Ann sniffed. "You'd think you were his mama."

Blood pounded in Mo's ears. "If my mama were alive, she'd send you on your way."

"I doubt it." Ann stepped back. "She wasn't as uptight as you."

If Ann hadn't moved out of reach, Mo would have throttled her. "Come on, Jayne. Let's go." She stood.

"No, wait! Look, I just want to talk to you, okay?" Ann clasped her hands in front of her. "Please?"

Ann's pleading surprised Mo. She hesitated and glanced at Jayne, who was still seated. "Maybe you should talk," Jayne said softly.

Maybe, or Ann would follow her around and badger her. "Make it quick!" She sat back down and let out a loud, exasperated sigh.

"I'm not playing games with your brother," Ann said, dropping onto the sofa next to Mo.

"Come on! Out of all the guys you can date, you're dating Andrew?"

"I'm dating him because he's your brother and that's how I met him."

"You met a lot of guys at our notification party."

"Yeah, but I like *him*." Ann blushed and looked down at her lap.

She wasn't serious, was she? That could be even more of a nightmare. Ann wouldn't quickly get it out of her system and go back to being an annoying friend Mo only saw occasionally. She'd be on the estate, at the Dance Hall, smirking and hanging off Andrew. When Mo went to the bathroom in the middle of the night, she might bump into her. And would the Middletons be stuck with her for events like the Festival of the Way? Ann's own family didn't seem to want her. "You're not serious about relationships. It won't last."

"How do you know?" Ann retorted, her eyes flashing. "You don't know anything about our relationship and how we feel about each other."

As far as Mo was concerned, the less she knew, the better.

"You're so flaming arrogant! You think I'm with Andrew because of you. Everything revolves around you."

"Well, it's a little odd, you ending up with my brother."

Ann's jaw clenched. "I already told you, the whole reason I met him is because he's your brother. You introduced us!"

"I introduced you to him and a ton of other guys who live in c3."

"I don't like those other guys. I like *him*."

They glared at each other.

"You're going in circles," Jayne said; Mo had almost forgotten she was there. "Mo, you can't do anything about it, so there's no point getting upset."

Mo knew Jayne was right; rationally, she'd always known that Ann and Andrew would ignore anything she said and carry on however they wanted. But she was still upset, and would have preferred to hear Jayne's advice privately, so Ann wouldn't feel victorious.

Ann gestured to Jayne. "Now we know who has the brains in the triad."

Jayne frowned. "I don't like to see Mo upset."

"You're in for a rough ride, then. It doesn't take much to get Mo going. Ask Lesley."

"Ann!" Mo's head felt as if it would explode.

"I'm joking!" Ann shook her head. "Can't you just give me and Andrew a chance? You don't have to like it, but can you not fight it?"

Surrendering rankled, but Mo didn't have much choice. Unfortunately Andrew did seem to like Ann—she couldn't imagine why—so being stubborn with her would upset him. "I don't like it, but I'll stay out of your way." She stuck her finger in Ann's face. "But if you intentionally hurt him, I'll make your life a misery. I mean it! When you break up with him, be polite about it."

"Maybe he'll break up with me."

Mo could hope.

"So are you going to talk to me now?"

"I guess so," Mo mumbled.

"I'm going off rotation tomorrow, so you might see me at some point."

Oh wonderful; she looked forward to that!

"Andrew said you—the three of you," Ann glanced at Jayne, "are going out for supper on your birthday. You want to meet for lunch?"

"I'll think about it."

"With Andrew too."

Was there a barf bag around? "Don't push it."

"Bring her." Ann looked at Jayne. "You haven't introduced us, so I don't know her name."

"Give me a break! Ann, this is Jayne, as you flaming-well know. Jayne, Ann. Ann is a pilot, like me." And the bane of her flaming existence.

Ann nodded toward Jayne but her attention remained on Mo. "I'll let you get back to your date." She winked. "See you at home. Bye, Jayne."

Mo seethed as she watched Ann leave the observation deck. Andrew must be crazy. He liked *her*?

"She's pretty rude to you," Jayne said.

"Yeah, well, that's Ann. She's rude to everyone."

"Why do you stay in touch with her?"

Because she'd always suspected that Ann would be devastated if she didn't. For some bizarre reason, Ann had latched onto her and seemed to see her as a friend, maybe her only friend. Most of the time, Mo didn't mind her company. They both loved to fly sims and Ann was fun to hang out with, once she stopped pushing Mo's buttons. This relationship with Andrew, though . . . it would end badly, and her friendship with Ann would suffer as a result. Maybe Ann really did like him, or maybe she didn't care as much about their friendship as Mo thought. "She's usually okay," Mo said, in answer to Jayne's question. "She doesn't mean half of what she says."

Jayne looked dubious, but said, "I hope you didn't mind me jumping in like that."

"No. Well, I wished you'd told me privately, but it was probably better that you told me now, when we could call a truce. It sounds like I'll be seeing her on the estate soon." She sighed.

"It'll run its course."

"I know. I just don't want to see Andrew hurt, that's all." Mo forced a smile. "Anyway, do you think you're brave enough to walk with me to the windows so I can point out a few sights to you? You can hang onto my arm." Her smile became genuine when Jayne nodded. Too keyed up to sit, she leaped to her feet. "Great! Let's start over there."

Jayne gripped her sketchbook with one hand and grabbed Mo's arm with her other. "Don't let me float away."

"You won't," Mo said. "We're perfectly safe. But if you're worried, hold on tight." She didn't mind at all when Jayne did.

LESLEY WAITED UNTIL the server had poured their after-supper tziva before broaching a subject she hoped wouldn't upset Mo. "I thought maybe we should talk about our house— arranging to have it designed and built," she explained when Mo and Jayne looked confused. "I assume we'll want it ready for our Joining Ceremony, or fairly soon afterward."

"We haven't set the date for the Joining Ceremony," Mo pointed out, her voice even and her face relaxed, much to Lesley's relief.

"We should probably talk about that, too."

"Is this a tradition with you?" Mo asked.

"What?"

Mo held her hands apart as if measuring an item. "Bringing up big topics when we're celebrating my birthday." She dropped her hands and narrowed her eyes at Lesley. "Though this is a happier topic than the one you brought up on my twenty-fifth."

Lesley nodded, unperturbed. She could understand if Mo still felt some resentment about that.

"Were you thinking about William?" Mo asked.

"Yes."

Jayne lifted her mug. "Karen's Chosen?"

"He's a construction coordinator," Mo said. "So he'll sit with us and ask us what we want, and then oversee the project."

Lesley sipped her tziva. "The first thing he'll do is hire an architect, so we should discuss what we want. Not tonight, but I want us to start thinking about it."

"How long do you think it will take to build it?" Jayne asked.

"It depends on what we want."

Mo's brow furrowed. "Who had that house built last year? Papa was telling me about it when I was on leave."

"The Scotts?" Lesley asked.

"Yeah. He said it took around four months, from the time they hired the coordinator."

"We'll probably want a larger house. Didn't they give theirs to Catherine when she Joined?"

"Catherine's their youngest daughter," Mo said to Jayne. "And yeah, they did. The house was too big for just them."

"That's why I think we'll need something bigger. We'll be starting a family." Lesley couldn't help but smile at Mo, who smiled back. "We can ask William how long it'll take, once we've given him some idea of what we want."

Mo met Lesley's eyes. "What if it's six or seven months, or longer? I don't think we should wait that long to Join."

"Things have calmed down a bit."

"Les, we can't say for sure that things have calmed down. What about that Kevin Stewart? Who else is out there? We're vulnerable until we Join. I mean, yeah, we can withstand the pressure, but why not get rid of it?"

Mo had a point, though planning a Joining Ceremony would take time, especially since Mama would want a lavish reception, despite the triad and Jayne—perhaps especially because of how things had turned out. She'd want to show that the Thompsons could handle anything thrown at them.

"What are you thinking about?" Mo asked.

Lesley realized she was chuckling. "Nothing." She cleared her throat. "I'd say we have to give Mama at least a month's notice, probably more. And if we Join before the house is ready, you'll both have to live with us. Mama will insist on that because I'm the Principal."

"What about Jason? He can't live with that friend forever."

"I don't know, they seem to be roommates now. And in a few months' time, he'll be in a position to receive Papers."

"Poor woman," Mo muttered. "Though he won't get them right away."

"I did," Jayne said.

"So you did," Mo said with a smile. "Let's hope he's not the Principal, so we're not neighbours."

Lesley suspected he'd live off the estate, no matter what happened.

"Sorry," Mo said half-heartedly. "I know he's your brother . . ."

"I don't want him as a neighbour either." She lifted her tziva and took a sip. "So do you want me to talk to William about coordinating the house for us, and to ask Mama how long she'll need to plan for the Joining Ceremony?"

Mo nodded.

"What about you, Jayne?" Lesley asked when Jayne remained silent.

Jayne took her time answering. "I think you should ask your parents if they'll mind me living with them before you plan anything else."

"They'll agree to it because it's tradition. Even if they hate the idea," she added, for honesty's sake. "Mama, in particular, won't stand for us living elsewhere. It's either their house, or our house." But perhaps Jayne hated the idea, too. "What about you? Would you have a problem living on the estate?"

"I would if they didn't really want me there." Jayne sighed. "But I don't want to prolong the pressure on you two by waiting until the . . . other house is ready."

"Let me talk to them," Lesley said.

"I want to know the truth. If they don't want me there, tell me," Jayne said firmly, and a little more loudly than she usually spoke.

"I will."

They stared at each other, the air heavier than it had been. Mo plunked her mug on the table and straightened her shoulders. "Should we talk about the awards ceremony next week? Jayne, we thought maybe I should pick you up around lunch. We can all get ready at Les's. We don't have to be at Government Hall until 18:00."

Jayne's brow furrowed. "The invitation said 17:00."

"We'll be with one of the guests of honour." Mo waggled her eyebrows at Lesley. "I think they want us to make an entrance when everyone's already there."

Jayne's face flushed. Lesley could relate. A triad, an Adams, Kevin Stewart, and balancing her attention between Mo and Jayne so neither would be offended—she couldn't wait for the evening to be over either.

LESLEY ADJUSTED HER collar, sighed, and adjusted it again. Why did collars on dress uniforms have to feel so uncomfortable? Mo's reflection appeared beside hers in the bedroom mirror. "It looks fine. Relax. It's not like you to stress over something like this."

"It's the first official function we're attending as a triad, and I just happen to be one of the guests of honour. We can't sit in the back and avoid everyone." She turned away from the mirror. "We should try to keep an eye on Jayne."

"Don't worry, I'll stay with her while you're busy making small talk." Mo brushed a thread off Lesley's sleeve. "Point out Kevin Stewart to me, so I'll know who to watch."

"I'll try, but I've only seen an image of him. Laura met him."

"Then I'll ask her to do it."

Lesley slowly exhaled. "It was nice of you to buy Jayne an outfit. If you'd mentioned it earlier, I would have chipped in."

Mo shrugged. "I don't think she's that comfortable with it, so I didn't want to make a big deal about it. We'll have to talk to her at some point, so she doesn't insist on sleeping in the garden because she didn't contribute to the house."

"Perhaps she can contribute in other ways."

"What do you mean?" Mo asked, frowning.

"Perhaps she can take the lead on working with William to design the interior."

"She's an artist, not an interior designer."

"I know. But of the three of us, she'll probably do better on the interior design."

Mo shrugged again. "I suppose that's true."

"Lesley!" Mama bellowed from downstairs. "What are you doing?"

Lesley inwardly sighed and offered Mo her arm. "Shall we?"

Mo slipped her arm into Lesley's and they descended the stairs together. Jayne, Mama, and Papa waited at the bottom. "Finally!" Mama said. "What were you doing up there?"

"We have plenty of time." Papa smiled. "I'm looking forward to your speech."

The pride in his eyes warmed Lesley. She returned his smile. "I'll be glad when it's over." Even though she'd already complimented Jayne on her outfit, she did so again. "You look nice."

"Thank you," Jayne said, her cheeks colouring.

"But you're slouching!" Mama said. "Tonight you're representing the Thompson family. Stand proud. Don't skulk around."

"Let's get our cloaks on and head to the aviacraft," Lesley said, hoping to rescue Jayne from more of Mama's "suggestions." She caught Mo's eye as they reached for their cloaks, and had to press her lips together so she wouldn't chuckle or give any hint that Mama's behaviour amused her. It could be a long night, especially for Jayne.

KEVIN GLANCED UP at the second-floor hall entrance, then at the head table, then at the hall entrance again. Why had he looked at the head table? They couldn't possibly be there. Since he was checking the entrance every two seconds, he'd know the moment they arrived. He pulled a handkerchief from his pocket and patted his brow.

Gwen touched his arm. "Did you see who's seated a few places over? Senior Overseer Brooks! If the couple between us gets up to dance, make your move. Oh, and decline the sauce with the second course. You always dip your sleeve into it, and that won't do, not tonight." She waved at a new arrival. "Belinda! Over here."

The hall filled. Rymellans stood chatting in their dress uniforms, or in expensive clothes they'd probably never wear again. Kevin sucked in his breath when he again scanned the head table. A server was pulling out several chairs! As he searched for the intended occupants, those seated nearest to the north stairway suddenly rose, while those already standing looked up. A smattering of applause grew into a crescendo. Kevin's heart beat so fast, he felt faint. He wanted to sit down, but that would be rude. Instead, he lowered his head and clapped.

"It's not them," Gwen said into his ear.

He forced himself to look. Commodore Finney and a man Kevin presumed was her Chosen stood at the top of the staircase.

"She looks just like she does on the monitors," Gwen said as Finney nodded several times to acknowledge the applause. Kevin already knew that; he'd sat in the same room with her as she'd dressed him down.

An usher stepped forward to greet the Finneys and motioned for them to follow him. Finney and her Chosen started down the steps, revealing the two children and an elderly couple standing behind them.

"That must be her parents, and her son and daughter," Gwen squealed.

"Yes." He rubbed clammy hands together and was about to sink into his chair when someone clapped him on the back.

"Kevin, how are you?" a voice bellowed. "Looks like we're sitting together."

He managed not to groan aloud. It figured they'd be seated at the same table as Frank. He forced a smile as he turned around to nod to him.

"I bet you couldn't believe it when you received the invitation," Frank said, making Kevin wonder what Frank knew about the Stewarts and the Incident. He relaxed when Frank added, "I know I couldn't. I bet everyone's green with envy."

Kevin would have gladly given his invitation to someone else, though that would have disappointed Gwen.

"And how about Thompson? Not only is she getting a medal, but she ends up with two Chosens. Some people have all the luck. Okay, one's an Adams, but still. If I was a Chosen, I wouldn't mind two." He guffawed loudly, drawing the eyes of those nearby.

Kevin wiped his brow again. The last thing he'd wanted was to attract attention, and he had to end up seated with a loudmouth.

"I suppose, being a Chosen, you shouldn't really think about what it would be like to have two, should you?" Frank said, grinning.

"I suppose not."

Frank clapped him on the back again, pushing Kevin forward a step. "What's the matter with you, Kevin? You look like you're at a farewell ceremony. This is the event of the year, my friend. I'd wonder about someone who didn't seem to be enjoying himself, you know what I'm saying?"

Kevin had to get away from him. "Excuse me, Frank. I just saw someone I need to talk to."

"I hope they have better luck with you than I have," Frank said, shaking his head.

Kevin ignored him and caught Gwen's eye as he walked away from the table, hoping she'd understand. He maneuvered to a row of paintings on the east wall of the hall, and gazed at the faces of the former Preeminent Rulers so he wouldn't be staring into space. Too bad he couldn't stand here all night, instead of having to watch Thompson and Finney at the podium. At least he wouldn't have a clear vantage point of the head table during supper, and everyone would face away from him during the speeches. He might be able to stand glimpsing the back of her head every once in a—

"Kevin Stewart," a low voice said behind him. He turned around and froze.

"I saw your name on the guest list and thought I'd come over and personally greet you," Finney said.

He stared at her.

"Smile, Kevin. People are watching us. Being seen having a conversation with one of the guests of honour should raise your profile, especially if you stay out of trouble, which I'm sure you'll do tonight. If you speak to the other guest of honour or her Chosens, be polite."

The last thing he'd do was speak to them! He forced another smile, something he expected to do often throughout the evening. "I have no intention of speaking to them." He stopped himself from saying that he'd rather be anywhere but here; she might interpret it as not supporting the military. They might be standing in Government Hall, but this was a military function, through and through. He'd never seen so many orange cloaks in a cloakroom, and the majority of those in attendance were in dress uniform.

"I considered contacting the organizers to remove your name from the guest list, but I decided to give you the benefit of the doubt. So if you do happen to bump into them, watch yourself. Understood?"

"Yes," he mumbled.

"Good. Enjoy your evening." She walked away, and was quickly drawn into conversation with a group waiting to speak to her.

Kevin swallowed. Enjoy your evening? It was already a flaming disaster! Forget about hovering near the portraits; he'd return to the table and stay there until it was time to leave.

He'd made it halfway back when everyone suddenly rose again. Applause filled the room. Kevin's legs turned to jelly. This time . . . He gripped the back of the nearest chair and looked up at the entrance.

Thompson appeared so calm, standing there with her two Chosens, one at each side. "The one who isn't in uniform must be Adams," he overheard someone say. Yes, the short one must be Middleton. The other one . . . the other one . . . even if she'd also been in dress uniform, he would have known. Argamon, it was Peter Adams all over again! He closed his eyes and placed his hand against his forehead. *Brenda, how could you? How could you have waved and smiled that day, knowing what you were doing? Knowing you were lying to me, to everyone! To your brother, to your family, perhaps even to yourself? What were you expecting? How did you think it would end? Why, Brenda? Why, why, why?*

He was no longer in Government Hall. He was in his twenties, standing on a path near the Adams studio, shielding his eyes as he waved to his sister on a gloriously warm and sunny day. The sister he'd idolized. The sister who'd betrayed them all.

MO WASN'T REALLY paying attention to Les's speech. She'd sat through two practice runs and could probably have delivered the speech herself, in a pinch. After a meal she'd savoured— though if she'd declined the second dessert, maybe her pants wouldn't be cutting off the blood circulation to her legs—it was nice to relax before the dancing and schmoozing began. Papa was seated at one of the government tables. She glanced his way, and almost raised her hand in greeting when he seemed to look at her—then remembered where she was sitting and kept her hand down.

One chair over, Jayne was perched on the edge of her seat with her hands tucked under her legs, completely focused on Les. Mo had to admit that having Jayne on an equal footing with her at events like this rankled. She'd been devoted to Les for thirteen years, and her best friend before then. Jayne hardly knew her. But to everyone here, she and Jayne were Les's Chosens. At every public function and social event, it would be her, Les, and Jayne. Rymellans would always speak of them as a triad; they'd never view her and Les as a couple. It was as if their life before their notifications didn't count. Mo couldn't be angry with Jayne, though. She could resent the situation with every fibre of her being, but she couldn't blame Jayne, who'd been shoved into the triad as much against her will as theirs.

Jayne hadn't been a part of Les's life all these years, but that was why she'd never threaten their relationship. They'd been through too much together, supported each other through thick and thin, shared every milestone in their lives. They even shared a Chosen! Jayne couldn't come between them if she wanted to, and she didn't.

Deafening applause broke out around Mo, who rose to her feet with everyone else, slightly bewildered but quickly gathering that Les had finished her speech. She grinned with pride as Les saluted the Preeminent Ruler and carefully made her way down the steps from the podium. "I'm proud of you," she murmured when Les sat down, then eyed the Medal of the Protector pinned next to Les's other awards. Les smiled and held Mo's hand underneath the table.

The Preeminent Ruler moved to the podium. "And now, my fellow Rymellans, I invite Commodore Laura Finney to come forward."

Laura rose from her place at the other end of the table as Mo let go of Les's hand to clap. The moment the applause died down, Les grabbed Mo's hand again and held it tightly. Mo's eyes suddenly felt moist. Maybe everyone else didn't see a difference between her and Jayne when it came to their places in Les's life, but Les did. Les did.

"ABOVE ALL, WE must always honour our Chosen. Or Chosens," Laura said, nodding in Lesley's direction and earning chuckles from those assembled.

Lesley wanted to slide down in her chair. She'd grown more and more uncomfortable as she'd listened to Laura's speech, her right hand in Mo's and her left resting on her lap. Every time Laura mentioned the Chosen Council, Joinings, anything related to the Chosen Tradition, Lesley felt like a failure. She'd just received the Medal of the Protector for protecting the Chosen Tradition, yet she was blatantly honouring one Chosen and slighting the other. Because, of course, Jayne wasn't really her Chosen—or so Lesley had told herself the moment Watkins had read Jayne's name.

Had someone arranged the triad in a misguided attempt to protect Rymellans from an Adams, or had it been easier to believe that than to accept Jayne? Lesley had said to her parents that if Jayne had been her only Chosen, she'd have had no choice but to accept her, and so that was what she and they must do. But her words to them had been just that—words.

Lesley wanted to stand up, apologize to everyone, and give back the medal. She hadn't accepted Jayne—she hadn't even tried. She'd come up with a flimsy excuse to dismiss her and hold her at arm's length, one that would never cross the minds of most Rymellans. Why had she quickly jumped to the conclusion that the triad wasn't real and never questioned herself about it until now? How could she ever have believed that the triad was a sham without seeing how weak in the Way that belief was? Those looking down their noses at Jayne for being weak in the Way were condemning the wrong triad member.

MO SIPPED HER drink and eyed the plate of bite-sized sandwiches a waiter had placed on their table. She reached for one at the same time Jayne did. Their hands bumped into each other. "Sorry," Jayne said, pulling hers back.

"No, you go ahead. I shouldn't really have one, considering how much I've already eaten." But she would anyway, and lifted one from the plate as soon as Jayne's hand was safely out of the way.

"I'm surprised she doesn't get bored," Jayne said.

"Who?"

"Lesley. Every time she moves to a new group, they have the same conversation."

Mo chewed a mouthful of sandwich before replying, "Yeah, that's why I was relieved when the admiral wanted to talk to her alone." She felt a little guilty over how quickly she'd escaped to the table, especially since Les had seemed subdued when greeting people. Not knowing her, they hadn't noticed, but Mo had. Maybe Les *was* bored and would appreciate a supportive Chosen on her arm, instead of one who took off at the first opportunity. Though Mo hadn't acted alone; Jayne hadn't hesitated when Mo suggested they beat a hasty retreat. Since everyone had acted as if she didn't exist, Mo couldn't blame her.

"I wonder what would have happened if you'd spoken." Mo chuckled, then felt mortified and wished she could take the flip remark back. She never would have said anything like that when she'd first met Jayne! "Sorry."

Jayne smiled. "It's okay. I wondered the same thing. They probably would have ignored me."

Unfortunately Jayne was probably right.

"I might apply for art school."

"Really?" Mo said, surprised by the abrupt change of subject and the words themselves.

"I need to do something. To contribute."

Oh. "Don't feel you have to. We should talk about this. I mean—"

"I'll feel better if I'm at least in school." Jayne reached for another sandwich and popped it into her mouth. "I'll have to put together a portfolio, which will take some time," she said after swallowing. "I'd like to paint—for the portfolio—but I need supplies. I didn't use all the credits you gave me for the outfit—I'll pay you back! It's just that . . . painting is—"

"Jayne, don't worry about it. Applying for art school is a great idea! I'll transfer more credits to your account so you can get whatever supplies you need. No, why don't I just link my account to yours? We'll do that eventually anyway, right?"

Jayne shook her head. "I can't just take your credits whenever I feel like it. I don't want to do that."

But Mo didn't care! Frustrated, she bit her tongue. Maybe Les was right about letting Jayne take the lead regarding the interior design of their future home. She took a deep breath. "Okay, use whatever's left over from the outfit, and if you need more, let me know. Maybe we can negotiate something." Though at the moment, Mo couldn't imagine what. The whole thing was silly—her account was overflowing with credits, most of which she hadn't earned herself. Chosens shared everything, including credits. So why was Jayne being so flaming stubborn? Mo grabbed another sandwich, mainly to shove it into her mouth so she wouldn't say anything she'd regret.

"I will pay you back."

"Pay me back when you've graduated from art school and you've sold some paintings."

Jayne shook her head. "That'll never happen."

Mo wasn't sure if she meant the graduating part or the paintings part.

"I've always wanted to paint a mural. But that would require a lot of supplies." Jayne paused. "And a wall."

Mo struggled to keep a straight face as she put her hand on Jayne's arm. "Supplies aren't a problem. But the wall . . ." She glimpsed Les walking up to a group of military. Les smiled and nodded, but Mo had caught the pensive expression on her face before the false smile masked it. "Do you mind if I go see how Les is doing? You can come with me, if you want."

"No, that's okay. You go. I'll have another sandwich." Jayne reached for one, dislodging Mo's hand from her arm.

"Sorry," Mo mumbled; she'd forgotten it was there.

KEVIN WATCHED MIDDLETON walk away from the head table, resisting the urge to dart after her and warn her about the snake in their midst. The situation was more serious than he'd thought. He'd looked on in horror as Middleton and Adams chatted, Middleton with her hand on Adams' arm. It hadn't taken Adams long to snare Middleton; she clearly had her wrapped around her finger. His eyes bored into Adams' back. *Look at her, sitting there, thinking she belongs. The military present should be escorting her from Government Hall or, better yet, to an execution site!* Instead they were milling around with a threat to the Way right under their noses. "Did you see that?" he murmured to Gwen.

"What?" Gwen said with a sigh.

"Adams and Middleton. They looked very cozy. Adams is doing to her what her papa did to Brenda."

Gwen shook her head. "Kevin, they're Chosens. Will you stop watching them, please? Go talk to the other overseers—do something, don't just sit here." She pointed. "Look, the band is setting up. We'll be able to dance soon."

Dance? How could she think about dancing? Had everyone lost their minds? They were all acting as if Adams wasn't there. But perhaps all wasn't lost. Thompson wasn't paying much attention to her. She'd introduced her around, but since then had seemed content to let Middleton deal with her. Did she want to exercise CT134, but Middleton had already fallen for Adams' false charm? Her speech had been rousing and inspirational; if not for her inaction regarding Adams, he wouldn't doubt her strength in the Way. Perhaps Thompson wasn't fooled and knew exactly what Adams was, but Middleton refused to cooperate with her and exercise the article.

His jaw clenched when a server placed another plate on the head table and Adams reached for whatever it held. *Look at her, sitting there at a place of honour, probably with a smug look on her face.* He shot from his chair, unable to stand it any longer.

"Kevin!" Gwen barked.

He ignored her. Adams was alone. He might not have another chance.

HOPING HER IMPATIENCE didn't show on her face, Lesley listened to an officer whose name she'd already forgotten. Nothing seemed to be registering; tonight was one of those nights where she tried to nod in all the right places and toss in a word here and there. Fortunately this officer seemed to enjoy the sound of her own voice.

When Mo hovered in her peripheral vision, Lesley seized the opportunity to get away. "Would you excuse me a minute? I'd just like a word with my Chosen."

The officer nodded. "Of course. I'll wait right here."

With some effort, Lesley prevented her smile from wilting. She grasped Mo's elbow and walked her to an empty spot. "Thanks for rescuing me."

Mo peered at her. "Are you all right? You look . . . tense."

"I'm fine," she said, her voice tight.

"You sure?"

"Yes. I haven't had a moment to myself, that's all, and I still haven't met half the people here. Admiral Hall says a group of overseers want to meet me, too."

Mo lifted an eyebrow. "I wonder if that will include Kevin Stewart."

Lesley had wondered the same thing, and wasn't looking forward to it. She glanced over at the head table. Jayne was sitting alone, munching on something. Jayne. Her Chosen. Argamon! Lesley rubbed her forehead.

Mo touched Lesley's arm. "Why don't you take a break? Come over and sit with us."

"No!" When Mo frowned, she added, "I have too many people to meet."

"I'll get Jayne and we'll come with you. I'll try to be chatty."

No! "No, I'll only worry about the two of you."

"Les—"

"The dancing will start soon. I'm looking forward to dancing with you."

Mo's face relaxed, but she didn't look pleased. "I hope you have time. I know you'll have to dance with Jayne, but dance with me first."

"I wish I only had to dance with you." Lesley fervently meant it. She dreaded dancing with Jayne; in fact, she'd avoid going anywhere near her, if she could. If Jayne really was her Chosen . . . She had to figure out what that meant for her, for Mo, for all of them, something she couldn't even start to do here, not while she was on display with the Medal of the Protector pinned on her chest. She wanted to rip it off and hide it.

"Are you sure you're all right?" Mo asked.

"I'm fine. Why don't you go back to Jayne so she's not by herself? I'll join you when I can."

Mo hesitated. "Okay. But if you want us with you, come get us, okay? And when the music starts, I'm coming to get you."

"Good. I'll need rescuing again by then." Her smile probably didn't fool Mo, but Mo let it go.

"The band is getting ready, so I'll see you soon." Mo walked away—in the opposite direction from the head table.

"Mo."

Mo turned around.

"What about Jayne?"

"I'm going to the bathroom. She'll be fine until I get back. Nobody wants to talk to her—except us."

Lesley silently corrected her: *Except you.*

JAYNE ROSE WHEN Mo walked away from Lesley. She'd said she didn't mind if Mo went to see Lesley, but she'd expected Mo to return to the table so she wouldn't be alone for long. Argamon, listen to her! She sounded like a cowering child who needed her hand held. Did it matter that everyone always looked away the moment she met their eyes? Who cared that people gawked from a distance? Rymellans had reacted that way most of her life. But usually it wasn't military officers and government members doing the gawking and avoiding.

She was only here because she was Lesley's Chosen—on paper—and when she could at least see Lesley or Mo, she felt safe. But now she was on her own and looked at the floor, wondering what to do. Should she sit back down? Follow Mo? Join Lesley? No, her presence would only make those speaking to Lesley uncomfortable, and the last thing she wanted to do was embarrass Lesley. She'd follow Mo. At least she'd be moving, not sitting by herself.

Eyes downcast, Jayne had only taken a few steps when someone grabbed her arm, startling her. She stopped, turned around, and tried not to look surprised.

"Watch your posture! It's terrible!" Adelaide snapped. "You're representing the Thompson family. You should stand tall and proud, not look like a frightened rabbit."

"I'll try," she mumbled, grateful for Adelaide's company, but also terrified.

Adelaide rolled her eyes. "Do more than try. Is this how you'll stand on the steps of the Chosen House when you Join with my daughter? Because several have mentioned that they'll be outside the Chosen House for your Joining Ceremony. The Joining of a triad is a historic event. I was just thinking about how it'll almost be a public event, when I spotted you slinking around as if you have Argamon strapped to your back. It won't do. You're almost as tall as Lesley. When you're on those steps, I want to see—" Jayne winced when Adelaide's fingers dug into her wrist. "The Preeminent Ruler—she's heading this way!" Excitement strained Adelaide's voice. "Not a word, understand?"

Jayne nodded, knowing she wouldn't dare say anything anyway.

The Preeminent Ruler smiled at Adelaide as she approached. "Adelaide Thompson, I believe."

Adelaide murmured a greeting.

"And you must be Jayne Adams," she added, briefly meeting Jayne's eyes, then refocusing on Adelaide.

Rather than being offended, Jayne quickly forgave her. The Preeminent Ruler could have spoken to Adelaide at any time, but had deliberately chosen this moment. Even those with no political acumen wouldn't be seen talking to an Adams in this crowd without having given it a great deal of thought. Jayne silently thanked her for the show of support—for Lesley. She wasn't under any illusion that the Preeminent Ruler wanted to support an Adams.

"Your daughter is an inspiration to all Rymellans," the Preeminent Ruler said. "I told Admiral Hall how fortunate we are that she pursued a military career."

"Yes," Adelaide said, nodding. "My Chosen and I were absolutely delighted when she told us she planned to sit the entrance exam for the military. 'Lesley,' we said, 'serving in the military is one of the most honourable vocations a Rymellan can choose.' We made sure to nurture and encourage her ambition at every opportunity."

The Preeminent Ruler swept her arm in front of her. "And look where it led. The Medal of the Protector is a great honour, and well-deserved. Rymel is in your debt, and your Chosen's."

Jayne could almost feel Adelaide quivering with pride.

"I SUPPOSE I shouldn't keep you," the talkative officer said to Lesley. "Congratulations again."

"Thank you." Lesley breathed a sigh of relief and quickly moved away before the officer changed her mind. She pretended not to notice another officer beckoning to her and strode to the nearest exit, needing a break and wishing it wouldn't be rude to leave the reception early. A glance at the head table made her wonder where Mo and Jayne were, then she spotted Jayne and Mama talking to the Preeminent Ruler. Any other time, she would have joined them, but could she look the Preeminent Ruler in the eye, with the Medal of the Protector on her chest and the Chosen she'd denied standing next to her?

Seeing Mo approach them clinched the decision for her. Hoping they hadn't seen her, Lesley managed to make it into the lobby without having to accept more congratulations. But even out here, someone waved to her. Once again, she acted as if she hadn't seen the invitation. Perhaps she'd be safe outside.

For an instant, as she pushed open the nearest door, she saw herself bursting from Government Hall and running away from the congratulations, the expectations, the lie. But when could she stop running? She had no choice but to return to the reception, paste that false smile on her face, and play the role she'd been born to play. Before she returned to the lie, though, she wanted a few minutes of honesty. She stood alone outside while those inside celebrated her strength in the Way.

TREMBLING WITH ANGER, Kevin watched as the Preeminent Ruler conversed with Adams, Middleton, and a woman he'd earlier deduced was Thompson's mama. Had everyone gone mad? Didn't anybody care about what had happened to Brenda? Had they forgotten?

"Kevin!" His hands clenched as Gwen pulled on his arm. "You can't keep doing this. Maybe we shouldn't have come."

He yanked his arm away. "You're the one who insisted we accept the invitation," he spat, then regretted his words when she blinked rapidly. He sighed. "She looks so much like him."

"But she's not him."

She was his flaming daughter! Oh, the Preeminent Ruler and Thompson were moving away, leaving Adams alone with Middleton.

"Come back to the table." When he didn't move, Gwen sighed. "What are you planning to do? Shout at her, here, in the middle of the reception? What do you think will happen? You'll be the one in the wrong."

Yes, apparently he would be, because the entire universe had been tipped on its ear! His heart raced—Adams had left Middleton and was walking in his direction!

"Kevin!" a voice cracked from somewhere far away. Feeling as if he were dreaming, he moved toward Adams.

JAYNE SCANNED FOR the bathrooms in the direction Mo had pointed, then froze. Laura had pointed Kevin Stewart out to her and Mo earlier, and there he was, directly in her path and heading her way! Panicking, she whirled, strode into the lobby, and pushed open the nearest door, not knowing where it led. She glanced around in confusion when she stepped outside.

"Adams!"

She turned around. Stewart had followed her outside.

A woman came through the door after him. "Kevin, no!" she cried.

He stopped in front of Jayne and pointed a trembling finger. "You know who I am, don't you?" Barely able to breathe, she opened her mouth to squeak out a reply, but he continued. "You—your family—you—"

"Is there a problem, here?" someone asked from her right. Relief flooded through her; she couldn't believe it! Lesley.

"No, there's no problem," the woman said, grasping Kevin's arm, her Chosen ring clearly visible on her finger. "We were just leaving."

Stewart shook his Chosen's hand away. "I don't know how you can show your face here!"

Jayne swallowed. "I'm here with my Chosens."

His face reddened. "Chosens? What do you know about Chosens?"

Lesley thrust out her hand. "Watch yourself."

"You're an Interior officer," he said indignantly. "You should—"

"Yes, I'm an Interior officer," Lesley said with an edge to her voice, at the same time Stewart's Chosen muttered an apology and tried to pull Stewart away. "I'm also Jayne's Chosen, and we warned you to stay away from her."

Stewart's Chosen stopped tugging at Stewart and stared at him, open-mouthed. Jayne felt for her. She didn't know. He hadn't told her about his meeting with Laura. Did she know about the letters?

He pointed at Jayne and met her eyes. "Your papa—"

Lesley stepped forward. "Go inside, Kevin Stewart, or I'll strike you under Article 267."

Moved by the tears lurking in his Chosen's eyes, and by the shocked recognition of the anguish and bewilderment in his, Jayne touched Lesley's arm. "No. Please let him say what he has to say." She braced herself.

When Lesley stepped back, Stewart took the gesture as permission to proceed. "Your papa killed my sister. She was twenty. Twenty! He took advantage of her. He destroyed our family. Your family should have been destroyed, too." He glared at her, his lips trembling.

Jayne swallowed. "I was only twelve. I didn't do anything wrong."

"They raised you." His lip curled. "Do you honestly believe you're different? That you won't do exactly what they did? You *are* them."

"That's enough!" Lesley barked. "Go. Now. Or I *will* strike you. And I suggest you leave the reception."

"Come on, Kevin," his Chosen said, her face ashen. "I'm sorry." She looked at Jayne. "I'm so sorry."

"Will you stop apologizing?" Kevin shouted.

"I'd go now," Jayne said to his Chosen, who didn't seem to know what to do.

Lesley stepped forward again. "Go!" she shouted. "Or do you want to be hauled out by military in front of your peers and the Preeminent Ruler?"

Either Lesley's words finally got through to him, or his Chosen's wet cheeks brought him to his senses. He threw Jayne one last dirty look, then stomped away. His Chosen chased after him.

Shaking, Jayne covered her mouth and turned away.

"Are you all right?" Lesley asked.

She nodded.

"He shouldn't have spoken to you like that, especially since we'd already warned him. I could have struck him."

"He's not angry with *me*, Lesley. Not really." She'd seen his anguished and confused eyes in the mirror enough times, when she'd wondered how they could have done it and wanted someone to blame. Stewart blamed her papa, and given the circumstances, she couldn't disagree with him. But for the longest time, she'd blamed herself, convinced that there had to be a connection between her arrival home from the Indoctrination Academy and the chaos that ensued a few weeks later.

If she hadn't been home, would it still have happened? Could she have prevented it? Why hadn't she suspected? In hindsight, her parents had seemed tense, almost uncomfortable, during their last visit at the Indoctrination Academy, but what child would jump to the awful conclusion that they were involved with others? She hadn't given the visit much thought, until she'd lain awake at night after the Incident, searching for answers.

She didn't blame herself, not anymore, but ironically, she probably understood how Kevin Stewart felt more than most did. He could say the same about her, if he didn't see her as a monster. "I hope he's seeing a counsellor," she murmured, still not facing Lesley.

"He is. But that doesn't seem to be helping much."

No. She was frightened for him, and for his Chosen. "What are you going to do?"

"We should definitely keep a closer eye on him. I'll let Laura know what happened. Perhaps she'll speak to his counsellor."

"She won't do anything more than that, will she?" When Lesley didn't answer, Jayne turned to her.

Lesley shrugged. "I don't know. But I trust that she'll handle it in the most sensitive manner possible."

Jayne didn't know Laura well, but if Lesley trusted her, so did she.

"Are you sure you're all right?"

"I'm fine." It hadn't been the most pleasant experience, but it could have been worse and fortunately, had taken place outside. "Thank you for stepping in." When Lesley had arrived, she hadn't thought, *Oh no, an Interior officer is here.* She'd been relieved that it was Lesley, and had even asked her to let Stewart speak. And now, gazing at her . . . Jayne focused on the gleaming medal pinned to Lesley's chest. "I—I met the Preeminent Ruler earlier," she said, to fill the silence. "With your mama. She—your mama—she's very proud of you. She said she's glad you're in the military."

"Did she?" Lesley grunted. "Well, I wouldn't believe everything you hear."

Puzzled by Lesley's reaction, Jayne looked up at her face, but Lesley's expression was bland. Jayne quickly shifted her attention back to the medal.

"Would you like to see it?" Lesley asked.

"What?"

"The medal."

Was she that obvious? "I can see it."

"No, I mean really see it." Lesley reached down and ripped it from her jacket in one smooth motion. She held it out to Jayne. "Here."

Jayne gingerly reached for it—the Medal of the Protector. Would it somehow know she was an Adams and burn her when she touched it? Apparently not. The metal felt cool to her fingers when she took it and dropped it into the palm of her other hand, careful not to scratch herself with the pin, which was still open. The Medal of the Protector. In her hand. Here she was, standing outside Government Hall with Lieutenant Commander Lesley Thompson, holding the Medal of the Protector.

Tomorrow, Rymellans would read about the medal presentation and the lavish reception, and wonder what it had been like to be there. A few months ago, she would have been one of them. But while other Rymellans might have aspired to be at such a ceremony one day, her imagination never would have stretched that far. Yet here she was, with one of the guests of honour, and the medal in the palm of her hand.

She moved closer to one of the outdoor lights to examine the silver medal more closely. The insignia of the Rymellan government adorned its front; the inscription *Death to those who commit a Chosen Violation* was underneath the insignia. The reason Lesley had received the medal came rushing back, along with the familiar shame. She cleared her throat, then flipped over the medal and read the inscription on its back: *Lt. Cmdr. Lesley Thompson*, and underneath it, *Interior Division*. "They were probably relieved they didn't have to include 'Adams' in the inscription," she mumbled. Blood rushed to her face when she realized how loudly she'd spoken.

Lesley's mouth turned up at the corners. "I doubt they expected us to Join before the medal ceremony. But if I ever receive another medal, my name will take up much more room."

"I'm sure you'll receive more medals," Jayne said absently, still awed by the one she held in her hand. She couldn't hold onto it forever. "Thank you for letting me look at it."

Lesley took it back and stared at it. "I'd just stick it in my pocket, but everyone expects me to be wearing it." The sigh in her voice surprised Jayne. "It was easier to pull off," Lesley mumbled as she struggled to pin it back onto her jacket.

Jayne hesitated, then reached for the medal. "I—I can do it." When Lesley didn't protest, she carefully guided the pin through the jacket's thick cloth, hoping she wouldn't fumble it and poke the pin through the shirt underneath and into Lesley's skin. "There," she said, patting the medal, then snatching away her hand before she gave in to the urge to reach up and straighten Lesley's collar.

"Thank you."

She gazed into Lesley's eyes. "I was—am—honoured to be here, at the ceremony," she said, knowing Lesley wouldn't care but unable to resist the compulsion to tell her. "The medal . . . it's a great honour . . . I'm proud . . ." Her cheeks were on fire, but she couldn't look away, mesmerized by the clear blue eyes that stared back at her. Time seemed to stop.

Then Lesley's pale skin flushed a deep red and she stepped back. "Uh, we should go back in," she said, motioning toward the door. "Mo's probably wondering where we are."

"Yes, absolutely, we should," Jayne said, feeling mortified and stupid. *I'm proud?* Could she have said anything more embarrassing? She'd obviously embarrassed Lesley, who was already walking away, too polite to run. She mumbled a "thank you" as she walked through the door Lesley held open for her, wishing she could hide for the rest of the evening, or at least from Lesley. She was making a fool of herself! Lesley wasn't even her Chosen, so she shouldn't be feeling this way. How could she have a crush on her? Because this had to be a crush, right?

Jayne had thought that part of her was dead. She'd known she was same-oriented because she'd always fantasized about women, not through actual experience. The odd time she'd caught herself reacting to a woman that way, always from afar, she'd quickly reminded herself that nobody would want to date her, touch her, or be seen with her. Eventually the reminder wasn't needed; a smile from the most attractive woman on the planet wouldn't have affected her. But she was reacting to Lesley, who could be the most attractive—Argamon!

She'd better get over it, and quickly, because nothing could ever happen between them. They had an arrangement, one she intended to keep. Kevin Stewart was wrong! She wasn't them, or remotely like them. When she made a vow, she kept it. Maybe it wasn't Lesley, per se. Since the Incident, not many Rymellans had treated Jayne with respect. Lesley and Mo were kind to her, paid attention to her, didn't figuratively spit in her face. Maybe she'd feel this way about any Rymellan not related to her by blood who treated her as one would any other Rymellan. But then, why wasn't Mo affecting her in the same way?

The band was playing; the music grew louder as she entered the reception hall, acutely aware of Lesley walking next to her. The bathroom could wait for fifteen minutes, plenty of time for Kevin Stewart to leave.

She wanted to groan and hold her head in her hands when Mo waved at them from the head table. Yes, Mo, the one in a relationship with Lesley and someone Jayne would never, ever hurt, because Mo was funny, and kind, and always considered her feelings. And Jayne loved spending time with her, and now that she was getting to know her, would choose to spend time with her, because . . . oh no. No, no, no!

Mo stood when they reached her. "Where have you been? You said you were going to the bathroom," she said to Jayne, then turned to Lesley. "And do you know how many people have asked me where you are? Everyone's looking for you!"

"Sorry. I was outside getting some air when Jayne ran into Kevin Stewart," Lesley said.

Mo's eyes widened. "Are you serious? What happened? Did he say anything?"

Jayne opened her mouth to reply, but Lesley put her arm around Mo's shoulders and squeezed her. "We'll tell you later." She looked at Jayne. "Do you mind if I dance with Mo before I have to make the rounds again? I might not have another chance. And I'm sorry, but I probably won't be able to dance with you. I'll try, but I might not have time."

"Don't worry about it," Jayne said, disappointed.

"Will you be okay on your own?" Mo asked. "Oh, wait, there's Papa." She motioned to Michael. "Can you keep Jayne company while I dance with Les?" she asked him. "And then I'll dance with you," Mo said, smiling at Jayne.

Jayne tried to smile back, but Mo and Lesley were already turning toward the dance floor. Michael pulled out a chair and sat down. His face lit up at the sight of the almost full dessert tray. "We didn't have this selection at our table," he said indignantly, reaching for a piece of chocolate cake.

She sat next to him and tried to make polite conversation, when all she wanted to do was find somewhere private, curl up into a little ball, and die.

"YOU SHOULD DANCE with her," Mo said as they threaded their way to an empty spot on the dance floor.

Lesley stopped and faced her. "I thought you didn't like it when I danced with her."

Mo didn't respond until they'd assumed position and fallen into step with the music. "I don't. But it's all about appearances, right? Isn't that what you keep telling me?"

Yes, when she'd been lying to herself. Now that the delusion had been shattered, dancing with Jayne would be uncomfortable, especially when—no, she must have been mistaken. For a moment outside, she'd thought Jayne was looking at her in the same way Mo did. But she must have imagined it. Admitting that Jayne was truly her Chosen didn't mean that Jayne had those sorts of feelings for her. Lesley had to calm down, get through tonight, then try to get her head around having two Chosens.

"You can't snub her, not here," Mo said.

"You're right. I'll do my best to dance with her." Though she dreaded it. "You go first, though. I really do have to get back to circulating."

"Yeah, you do. People have been looking for you."

Lesley heaved a sigh.

Mo drew back. "Are you okay? You seem . . . I don't know, agitated tonight. Your speech is over, and you've never minded making small talk before."

Normally she wasn't wearing a medal she didn't deserve, and didn't feel dishonest every time she praised the Chosen Tradition. She'd always seen herself as strong in the Way, would never have imagined that she'd stumble and refuse to accept what every other Rymellan embraced. How could she have denied her Chosen?

Mo squeezed Lesley's hand. "Les, you're worrying me."

She shook herself. "Sorry. It's been more overwhelming tonight than I expected." And in a way she hadn't expected.

"Now's your chance to relax, even if it's only for a few minutes. Though nothing says we have to stop dancing when this piece finishes." Mo grinned up at her. "Let's keep dancing until you're ready to face every-one again."

Lesley drew Mo to her, so Mo wouldn't see the tears in her eyes. If she could, she'd never let her go. They'd stay on the dance floor for the rest of their lives, holding and supporting each other as they always had—just the two of them. But that would be another delusion. The one she'd carefully crafted had shattered, and no matter how hard she tried, she couldn't fool herself again. She had two Chosens: Mo and Jayne. The Chosen Tradition demanded more of her than it did of most Rymellans, and if she was truly strong in the Way, she would honour it.

Her grip around Mo's waist tightened. Tonight, everything had changed. She and Mo would face the toughest challenge of their lives: struggling to honour the Way while fighting for the survival of their relationship. Lesley had always seen herself as strong in the Way, but now the Way would test her in a way she never could have imagined. Their survival—hers, Mo's, and Jayne's—would depend on her percep-tion of herself proving true, and not just another shattered delusion.

AUTHOR'S NOTE

.....

Thank you for reading *Rymellan 2: Shattered Lives*. If you enjoyed it, you might like my fantasy novel *The Salbine Sisters*:

She gave up everything to become a Salbine Sister, member of a religious order of powerful female mages. But when Maddy nearly dies while trying to draw forth elemental fire, she learns that Salbine has withdrawn from her the gifts every sister works to master. Feeling trapped in an order to which she no longer has any right to belong and believing herself unworthy of the love of Lillian, one of the most powerful mages in the sisterhood, Maddy begs the abbess to let her travel to another monastery to research her condition. On her journey, Maddy's faith in both herself and Salbine are tested to their limits.

The Salbine Sisters is available at online bookstores (print and eBook).

Until *Rymellan 3*...

~ Sarah Ettritch

www.ingramcontent.com/pod-product-compliance
Lightning Source LLC
Chambersburg PA
CBHW051602100726
47898CB00001B/196